NEW HOPE

A BUR OAK BOOK

RUTH SUCKOW

NEW HOPE

FOREWORD BY

PATRICIA ELLEN MARTIN DALY

UNIVERSITY OF IOWA PRESS Ψ IOWA CITY

University of Iowa Press, Iowa City 52242
Acknowledgments and foreword
copyright © 1998 by the University of Iowa Press
All rights reserved
Printed in the United States of America

Originally published in 1942 by Farrar & Rinehart, Inc.

http://www.uiowa.edu/~uipress

This book is published with the kind assistance of the
Estate of Ferner Nuhn and the University of Iowa
Libraries Special Collections Division.

Printed on acid-free paper

Library of Congress Cataloging-in-Publication Data
Suckow, Ruth, 1892–1960.
    New hope / by Ruth Suckow; foreword by Patricia
    Ellen Martin Daly
        p.   cm.—(A Bur oak book)
    ISBN 0-87745-630-5 (paper)
    I. Title.   II. Series.
  PS3537.U34N48   1998
  813'.52—dc21   97-43862

98 99 00 01 02 P 5 4 3 2 1

TO
THE MEMORY OF
MY MOTHER AND FATHER

CONTENTS

ACKNOWLEDGMENTS

Patricia Ellen Martin Daly

WORKING ON this edition of *New Hope* has been a labor of love for me. In that labor of love, I have been joined by many other people who believe, as I do, that *New Hope* has been too long out of print and Ruth Suckow too little remembered. Without their help, this edition would never have come to be.

First, I wish to thank Barbara Camamo, executor of Ferner Nuhn's estate, for her unflagging support and assistance in clearing copyright issues and granting permission for this critical edition. Robert Stafford, former attorney for Nuhn, was also most helpful in this regard.

I am particularly indebted also to Bob McCown, current president of the Ruth Suckow Memorial Association and curator of the Special Collections Division of the University of Iowa Libraries, where the Suckow papers are housed. I am also grateful to other members of the Ruth Suckow Memorial Association, including past officers George Day, Leedice Kissane, Sr. Sara McAlpin, and Dorothy Grant.

The following scholars read drafts of my introduction and made helpful comments and suggestions: Leedice Kissane; David Wilson, professor emeritus of the University of California at Davis; Langdon Elsbree, professor emeritus of Claremont McKenna College; and Michelle Tartar of Eastern Illinois University. They have my deepest gratitude.

Without the support of Neumann College, where I serve on the faculty, *New Hope* would still be out of print. The college granted me a spring 1997 sabbatical, which enabled me to do the research that has culminated in this book. In addition, the college librarians went out of their way to assist me in securing not only the 1942 reviews of *New Hope* and other relevant articles but also the Suckow books that are currently out of print. I am especially indebted to Donna Kutnick, director of the library, and to Jacquie Roach and Craig Conrad for their help.

Two groups of Quakers also assisted me in this project. Hockessin Friends Meeting of Delaware, my Meeting, funded my trip to California, where I interviewed many people who knew Suckow and Nuhn, and also supported me morally and spiritually in this project. Members of Claremont Friends Meeting extended warm hospitality and assisted me in every possible way in learning more about Suckow and Nuhn, who were among the founders of that Meeting. I am particularly indebted to Aimee Elsbree, librarian of Claremont Friends Meeting, who helped me locate invaluable documents in the well-organized Ruth Suckow Memorial Library there. Thank you all, Friends.

In addition, I am grateful to Phil O'Brien, director of the library at Whittier College, who cleared the way for me to do research in the archives of the Pacific Yearly Meeting at Whittier, where I found much valuable information.

Most important, I also wish to thank Holly Carver of the University of Iowa Press; Mary Russell Curran, who provided meticulous copyediting; and Dave Elder, Nuhn's cousin. Finally, I am deeply grateful to Natalie Ireland, my daughter, for her unceasing support, and to Gene Hillman, my significant other, for his generous assistance and his constant support of this project.

May this critical edition of *New Hope* give us all renewed hope for the future.

AN IOWA GARDEN OF EDEN:
A FOREWORD TO *NEW HOPE*

Patricia Ellen Martin Daly

THE YEAR was 1942. Around the world, darkness and despair prevailed. Poland, Denmark, Norway, Luxembourg, Holland, Belgium,
and France had all fallen to the Nazis. German submarine attacks
and air raids on Great Britain were strangling the British Isles. The
German army was advancing into Russia, gaining strongholds in
areas people thought were impenetrable. The battle for North Africa
had tipped in favor of German and Italian forces. The Japanese had
bombed Pearl Harbor, captured British and American territories in
the South Pacific, and joined forces with the Germans and the Ital-
ians. China had declared war against the Axis powers. In many coun-
tries, hate-filled officials were driving innocent citizens into concentration camps and all too often torturing and killing them. The
world seemed to have gone mad.

In the middle of this maelstrom, a quiet writer from Iowa
named Ruth Suckow published a radiant, joyous novel, a consciously
American fable that admirers hailed as "a kind of gem" and an "Iowa
idyll."

The novel portrays a sunlit two-year period in the life of New
Hope, a brand-new town that took shape in northwestern Iowa in
the last decade of the nineteenth century. It's a town in which everyone cooperates at the start with the goal of "working together for the

future." Beyond the small perimeter of New Hope lies "the rolling immensity of the land," the great, golden, open countryside presented, as it is in some Cather novels, as an almost mystical force. Told largely through the eyes of two children, the story concerns the arrival of a new, exuberant minister and his family, of the growth of the church and the community during his stay, and of the special love that develops between his daughter and the son of the town's banker. Evocatively named characters and places suggest that the author intends the story to radiate symbolic as well as literal meanings.

"They were living in a morning world," says Ruth Suckow of her characters. In stark contrast to the horrors most people were experiencing in 1942, life in New Hope is marked by unusual optimism, trust, communal spirit, democracy, and—above all—light. The people of *New Hope*, particularly the two joyful children who are central characters, are pervaded by "a fresh morning glow" both actual and figurative. New Hope's residents draw sustenance from one another, from the beauty of the Iowa countryside, from the Christian faith nurtured by their two churches, and from faith in the future and democratic principles.

Who was Ruth Suckow and why did she publish *New Hope* at this time? The answers to these questions are as elusive as the answers to What is art? and What makes an artist? It is possible, however, to respond to them in part.

RUTH SUCKOW, THE WRITER

"Ruth who?" When Suckow scholars mention this writer, even to literary experts, the questioning response they receive is almost always accompanied by mystified stares. "Never heard of her" is the usual follow-up. That was definitely not the case during the first part of the twentieth century.

"The most remarkable woman now writing short stories in the Republic," proclaimed H. L. Mencken in his 1926 review, published in the *American Mercury*, of Suckow's first collection of short stories,

Iowa Interiors. With the encouragement of her Iowa City literary mentor, critic and writer John Towner Frederick, Suckow had sent three short stories to Mencken at the *Smart Set* in 1921. Money from the beekeeping operation she was running in the tiny town of Earlville, Iowa, had enabled her to support herself while she wrote them. Responded Mencken in a 1921 letter, "I tell you frankly that they are the very best stories a new author has sent to the *Smart Set* in five years." He and critic George Jean Nathan then praised, encouraged, and helped the twenty-nine-year-old writer as she produced a stream of superbly crafted stories, novels, and novellas over the next ten years.

In a 1922 *Literary Digest* article, Nathan ranked Suckow with Willa Cather, Joseph Hergesheimer, Sherwood Anderson, and Eugene O'Neill as one of "the five distinctly literary appearances in the last ten years" and proclaimed her "the most important short-story writer that America has produced in the last decade." Sinclair Lewis echoed that praise in a 1922 letter to Mencken, saying, "She is extraordinary—reality, high visibility, lucidity, vision, the real stuff." In a previous letter to Lewis, Mencken had introduced her: "I lately unearthed a girl in Iowa, by name Ruth Suckow, who seems . . . to be superb. . . . She follows after you, Dreiser, and to some extent, Anderson, but she is also a genuine original."

Mencken and Nathan were not alone in their praise of this young minister's daughter from Iowa. In *The American Novel: 1789–1939*, Carl Van Doren claimed that "Ruth Suckow came nearer than any other writer has done to representing the whole of American life on farms and in the small towns." To a great degree, the reading public in America apparently agreed with him: Suckow's early novels and novellas, published by Knopf, sold well; her 1934 book, *The Folks*, was designated a Literary Guild selection; and her stories were routinely accepted by such magazines as the *American Mercury*, *Harper's*, *Scribner's*, and the *Century*. "She scarcely encountered a single rejection," says her 1969 biographer, Leedice Kissane. After Suckow was an established writer, editors from the *New Yorker* and other top literary magazines wrote her letters asking her to submit short stories.

Throughout the thirties and forties in particular, she was widely anthologized in prominent short-story collections. Although *New Hope* is more symbolic than her earlier works, it was well received upon its publication in 1942. Suckow was valued not only for her achingly real pictures of Iowa life but also, among other things, for her portrayal of intergenerational conflict, of children, and of girls struggling to widen their options as they tried to mature into women.

In a 1928 article in the *Saturday Review of Literature*, Allan Nevins insisted that Suckow had "one of the best, because one of the truest, of all the literary voices of the Union. . . . Her work will assuredly live."

Nevins was wrong. For reasons that are as mysterious as they are outrageous, most of Ruth Suckow's work was out of print during the fifties and sixties. That changed in 1977 when the Arno Press republished her first novel, *Country People*, and *Iowa Interiors*, with introductions by Elizabeth Hardwick, as part of its "Rediscovered Fiction by American Women" series. In 1988, the University of Iowa Press issued *A Ruth Suckow Omnibus*, which contains some of her best short stories as well as her novella *A Part of the Institution*. Her novel *The Folks* was also reprinted by the University of Iowa Press in 1992.

These reprints, as well as the many volumes of Suckow manuscripts and correspondence now available at the University of Iowa Libraries, testify to a gifted, painstaking writer. They also reveal a remarkable woman.

RUTH SUCKOW, THE PERSON

Born in 1892 in Hawarden, then a brand-new town in northwestern Iowa, Ruth Suckow was always very much her own person. The daughter of a liberal Congregationalist minister and an artistic mother, Ruth was encouraged as a child to be true to herself and to follow her literary bent. In the memoir she published in 1952, she describes herself as a little girl sitting on the floor in her father's study, playing with paper dolls or contemplating *Stoddard's Lectures* as her father worked on his sermons. She also engaged in "the kind of activity that even then I liked best of all others—literary composition—. . . in the scarcely broken stillness."

Her mother, Anna Mary Kluckholn Suckow, waged a slow, losing battle with thyroid disease much of Ruth's young life, so the budding writer was often left to the care of her brilliant, artistic older sister, Emma, her aunt, or her father, the Reverend William J. Suckow. So that he could tend to her while he was making pastoral calls in the countryside, her father constructed a wooden seat that he affixed to the handlebars of his bicycle. As he pedaled over prairie roads, his quietly observant little daughter trained her attention on the life of the countryside and small towns around them—drinking in, according to her memoir, the smell of the "deep brown loessal soil" and the wild roses, the song of the lark, and the "impression of this great open, rolling region on the edge of the West" as one "of breadth and freedom under the immensity of the blue sky." Her fiction—especially *New Hope*—is pervaded by the passionate love of the land that these and other excursions bred. Moreover, in the village and farm homes of her father's parishioners, Ruth soaked up the precise details of their lives that would also make her writing so memorable.

Suckow had many opportunities to observe a wide variety of life. Before she was sixteen, her father had moved the family to five different parsonages, and she spent a part of every summer on her grandparents' farm. In 1910, she enrolled in Grinnell College, but she left three years later to study for two years at the Curry School of Expression in Boston. When her sister, Emma, then a wife and the mother of two children, contracted tuberculosis and Anna Suckow's thyroid disease worsened, Ruth's family moved to Colorado to take care of their health. Ruth joined them in 1915, enrolling in the University of Denver, from which she received bachelor's and master's degrees in English in 1917 and 1918 respectively. Determined to be a writer, she searched for a way to support herself that would give her the greatest amount of time and freedom. Rejecting full-time teaching as too time-consuming, she began to learn the apiary business in

Denver from a Delia Weston in 1919. That same year, her mother
died, and Ruth moved back to Earlville, where her father had accepted a pastorate. Ruth had had her differences with her mother,
but she loved her fiercely and missed her very much.

Ruth was closest to her father, whom she describes in her memoir as "always a person in his own right—an original character."
Largely a self-taught man, Suckow had a keen mind and an open,
tolerant, independent nature, even in his ministry. He had worked as
a timber cutter and as a farmhand in his youth and retained all his life
his "look of a woodsman," characterized by a "firm, alert, simple
bearing" and the "vigorous, deft . . . hands of a man who was both an
intellectual and a craftsman." Determinedly optimistic about the future of the human race, particularly if people would embrace his liberal, caring approach to religion, he spent hours composing clear,
spare, simple, but ringing sermons—models of rhetorical practices
and patterns that his daughter says she absorbed. Despite the expectations of his parishioners that he would bring Ruth and her sister up
to be exemplary minister's daughters, he encouraged them to be upright while pursuing their own paths, even in religion.

On one occasion, and only one, he deviated from this encouragement—during the First World War. To the horror of his younger
daughter, who found such behavior at odds with the New Testament,
he began preaching militaristic sermons and called her "a moral cow-
ard" for her pacifist stance. Ruth was already disillusioned by the
mediocrity and hypocrisy of some church members; this turnabout
by her father constituted an "earthquake shock" that caused her to
break with formal religion for many years. Despite this conflict, her
father continued to support not only her postsecondary education
but also her efforts to set herself up as a writer. In 1919, he gave her
the capital she needed to establish her beekeeping business in
Earlville.

From 1919 until 1929, Ruth Suckow's "Orchard Apiary" in
Earlville was her home base. Petite and slim, she labored long,
strenuous hours at her hives, showing up still energetic, however, at
John Frederick's literary evenings. Recalling one such evening,

Frederick described her thus: "Her clear skin was browned from days out of doors. She was small and cool and comradely. She talked genuinely and generously, and what she said crackled and burned with the fire of a tremendously vigorous intellect, ruthless and fearless, and yet tempered by profound understanding and sympathy."

The honey she harvested enabled her to write part of the time during the summer and most of the time during the winter. A steady stream of short stories and novels flowed from her typewriter, establishing her by 1924 as an acclaimed writer. Winters she migrated to places like Chicago and New York, where she was sought after by many literati.

Tragedy continued to haunt Suckow's life, with the death of Emma's young son in 1920 and of Emma herself in 1923. Nevertheless, Suckow pressed on with her writing. She remained devoted to Emma's daughter the rest of her life, helping her niece in many ways, as she did many other relatives and friends.

Suckow's writing attracted the attention of a noted intellectual, writer, artist, literary critic, and fellow Iowan named Ferner Nuhn, who wrote a favorable review of her work. New York was also a temporary roost for Nuhn, who hailed from Cedar Falls, Iowa. Starting in 1926, according to Dorothy Grant, who knew them both well, he drove the ninety dusty miles from Cedar Falls in his Model-T Ford during the summer months to court the independent beekeeper/ writer. Suckow finally married him in November 1929, beginning an extremely close, mutually supportive partnership that was to last thirty happy years and bear much fruit in literary, intellectual, and spiritual endeavors, including the founding of two Quaker meetings. Contrary to the custom of the time, Suckow used her own name professionally. In her private life, however, she often identified herself as Ruth Suckow Nuhn and sometimes as Mrs. Ferner Nuhn.

Nuhn comes across in his correspondence and in interviews with people who knew him as a kind, brilliant, optimistic, principled man who shared Suckow's independence of spirit, compassion for others, love of literature, and New Testament–based pacifism. In his own work, he tended to focus on analysis, and he wrote, among other things, two books on American culture that were greeted with much respect by serious critics. Comments in Nuhn's handwriting on Suckow's manuscripts indicate that she often turned to him for his opinion on her works in progress. He was always one of her most devoted supporters; after her death in 1960, he founded the Ruth Suckow Memorial Association in Iowa and worked with his second wife, Georgeanna (Ruth's cousin), to assemble Ruth's papers for the University of Iowa Libraries.

For several years following their marriage, Nuhn and Suckow traveled widely, spending some time in artists' colonies. They passed the summer of 1933, for instance, at the MacDowell Colony, along with Padraic Colum, Edwin Arlington Robinson, Thornton Wilder, Willa Cather, and others. The following year, when the Literary Guild designated Suckow's highly acclaimed novel *The Folks* as one of its selections, her fame mushroomed.

During the Spanish Civil War, Suckow read André Malraux's *Man's Hope* and began wrestling with the question of what gives people hope. As people all over the world succumbed to the horrors of the Depression, and, in some cases, to fascism, it was a most pressing question to many writers. Rejecting the violence and hatred she felt Malraux was suggesting as the source of hope, she turned to a rereading of the Bible and gradually rediscovered the central importance of the New Testament to her life. In particular, she was struck by how much, for her, the "Bible took on final significance, as enshrining the life of the greatest character, at the center of radiance." To Suckow, that character was Jesus.

In 1935, Nuhn accepted a job as an information officer with U.S. Secretary of Agriculture Henry Wallace, whom he had known and admired greatly in Iowa. He and Suckow then lived near Washington, D.C., for two years, attending a White House concert at the invitation of the Roosevelts in January 1936 and spending their summers at Robert Frost's farmhouse in South Shaftesbury, Vermont. Suckow's correspondence from this period indicates that Nuhn was working on his study of American culture, *The Wind Blew from the East: A Study in the Orientation of American Culture*, which was eventually published by Harper in 1942. Since both *New Hope* and *The Wind Blew from the East* deal explicitly with the meaning of the American experience, and since Suckow and Nuhn were in the habit of sharing their ideas and writings with each other, they probably engaged in many conversations that mutually enriched these two books.

At the end of 1936, the couple moved back to Cedar Falls, where Suckow continued to write. She also taught part-time at nearby colleges and tended to her father, who was in failing health. According to Clarence Andrews's *A Literary History of Iowa,* Iowa in the thirties was exploding with literary activity by such prize-winning authors as Alice French, Hamlin Garland, Susan Glaspell, Josephine Herbst, and Herbert Quick. Suckow was working on *New Hope* at this time and immersing herself in the life of her beloved homeland.

Suckow's father died in March 1939, and his grief-stricken daughter spent the summer traveling in Scandinavia with her husband. They returned on the day war was declared, an event that disturbed Suckow greatly. As she recounts in her memoir, which focuses primarily on her spiritual development, her father's death prompted her to reread the Bible, particularly in the context of his sermons, and to return slowly to organized Christian religion through membership in the Religious Society of Friends (Quakers). In the years immediately following her father's death, she was also wrestling with *New Hope,* which went through more than one evolution before it finally emerged in its present form. Well received by most critics, *New Hope* was also briefly considered as movie material by Hollywood.

After *New Hope's* publication, Suckow struggled with worsening rheumatoid arthritis and thyroid disease. Despite her health problems, however, she continued to write, as well as to support conscientious objectors by visiting them in Civilian Public Service camps and encouraging them to contribute to a literary anthology she was compiling of their work. Her pacifism brought disapproval from many literati, but according to Dave Elder, Nuhn's cousin, "Ruth was always her own person." Nuhn had also registered as a

conscientious objector, and he supported his fellow objectors by rais-
ing money for them and visiting their camps.

Suckow's increasing problems with arthritis led her and Nuhn
to move in 1947 to Tucson, Arizona, a resort town they disliked for
its superficiality, transient residents, and miserably hot summers.
Soon after they arrived in Tucson, they helped organize the Tucson
Friends Meeting, according to Bob Vogel, who oversaw fieldwork
for the American Friends Service Committee in that region. Correspondence from the period reveals that Suckow and Nuhn were
both deeply involved in the life of their small spiritual community.

When Suckow's arthritis improved, they moved for a final time
to Claremont, California, a small town surrounded by orange groves.
Entranced with the citrus-scented, "Congregational" flavor of
Claremont in the 1950s and the proximity of its growing colleges,
they settled happily into a small house and the life of the town and
then helped organize the Claremont Friends Meeting. After a few
years, however, Suckow's arthritis began to worsen again. Despite
great pain, she continued to write, producing not only *The John
Wood Case* in 1959 but also an unfinished piece called *Some Boundless
Thing* and first drafts of a number of other stories. Pictures of her in
the later fifties show her aging rapidly. She died in her sleep January
23, 1960.

RUTH SUCKOW AND AMERICAN REALISM

As Margaret Stewart Omrcanin has noted in the conclusion to her
book on Ruth Suckow, *New Hope* represents something of a departure from the realistic novel for which Suckow had become famous.
In a letter to Sinclair Lewis, H. L. Mencken said that her novels in
the twenties and thirties reflected, to a great extent, the realism that
Lewis, Sherwood Anderson, Theodore Dreiser, Willa Cather, and
Suckow's fellow Iowan Hamlin Garland had made famous. It was a
realism that insisted that America's ordinary small-townspeople and
farmers were equally appropriate as subjects for literature as were the

"heroic" figures created by James Fenimore Cooper and Herman Melville. It was also a realism that did not hesitate to portray the seamy side of life. In his essay on realism and naturalism in *American Literature to 1900*, Malcolm Bradbury suggests why this shift from romances concerned with "myth and the encounter with nature and the wilderness" to realistic novels focused on society and history occurred:

> Realism . . . became an essential literary means for coming to terms with the new American history—the hard facts and dark lessons of the Civil War, the new social and industrial processes, the exploration of the spreading mass of American society and American geography as the nation enlarged, the rising conflicts of an age of massive urbanization and immigration, the new democratic skepticism. . . . It became the natural voice of a generation of writers who had not grown up under Boston tutelage, but came from the farmlands and the cities and wrote in a familiar vernacular. (321)

"It was not one tendency but many," declare Bradbury and Ruland in *From Puritanism to Postmodernism*, "ranging from local-color regionalism, that extension of the geographical and empirical reach of American literature that Howells firmly supported, to wider-ranging novels of social process or political corruption" (205). Like Anderson, Cather, and Sinclair Lewis, Suckow was often identified as a local-color regionalist. It was a label she persistently repudiated, insisting that her works conveyed universal themes and did not just focus on portraying the country's midwestern region.

In addition, although she is often lumped with Anderson, Lewis, and Dreiser, she is much less critical of midwestern "commonfolk" than they are. Her works suggest a far greater compassion for the trials and tribulations of farmers and their counterparts in small towns, as well as a greater love of, and belief in, the power of nature. Suckow's approach to realism may be closer to Willa Cather's, a possibility that deserves further exploration. In fact, some of Suckow's female protagonists seem to fit the description Bradbury and Ruland give of Cather's female pioneers: "[H]er energetic, resourceful heroines express a vitalism she celebrated in books that evoke a prairie aristocracy pursuing an idealistic and spiritual life in a harshly material world" (247). A number of the prominent women in *New Hope* evoke this kind of "prairie aristocracy."

While *New Hope* still reflects, to a great extent, the realism for which Suckow had become known, it is a different, more upbeat realism. Omrcanin notes that prior to the 1940s, "the deeply felt emotions which recur most frequently in her characters are loneliness and isolation, nostalgic yearnings and the sadness that comes with the realization of lost security" (183). Before *New Hope*, this critic maintains, "all of the novels end on a note of defeat, uncertainty, frustration, and doubt resulting from the weakening of old values and the failure to establish satisfactory new ones in a changing society" (88). Set for the most part in towns and on farms in Iowa, they portray the pain and ugliness of rural life along with its rewards, with the greatest attention paid to the grimmer aspects of life. According to Omrcanin, *New Hope* "was the first of her works to express positive, clear-cut affirmations that had only been intimated previously," a change which she feels is "partially explained by the religious development she recounts in her memoir" (184).

How is this change evident in *New Hope*? Suckow does not completely abandon her characteristically realistic approach. As Kissane notes, "Her Iowa scenes are clearer, more down-to-earth in this work than in any of the others" and "Clarence and Delight are simply two completely real and engaging youngsters" (123–25). Indeed, her characters' flaws and foibles are as evident as their virtues, and the bare, primitive town has a kind of austerity too. Evil makes its appearance in the form of an ex-convict janitor who betrays the congregation's trust and steals from the collection, and it is reflected as well in the church members' narrow-mindedness about other religions. However, as Sr. Sara McAlpin notes in her dissertation, "*New Hope* is permeated with a brilliant light consistently affirming its pervasive positive values of endurance, adjustment and fulfillment" (460).

Why did Suckow write her most luminous novel in the darkest of times, when she was also coping with her grief over her father's death and the early years of World War II? She described her intention in a March 1942 radio interview with John T. Frederick: "In this particular novel, I went back to an early day and tried to make that early day live in the book as it was . . . I think we can regard past time in two ways, either as a past or as a beginning. That is, we can look back to mourn for what's gone and never will come again, or we can look back to get an understanding of our origins and so draw knowledge and faith for the future."

In portraying the "morning world" of the unusually happy, cooperative community of New Hope, Suckow was symbolically drawing on not only a familiar emblem of the "origins" of American democracy but also her own origins. Greater understanding of both in the late thirties gave her, despite the hardships she had experienced, "knowledge and faith for the future"—gifts she wanted to give her readers.

"More like Hawarden than any other town" is how Suckow described the town of New Hope in a 1942 letter to her lifelong friend Caroline Woodhams. In the author's memoir, published as part of *Some Others and Myself* ten years later, she discusses her hometown:

> My birthplace was a small town on the western border of Iowa. It was a new town, had been in existence not much more than ten years when my father, mother and older sister moved there. . . . The atmosphere was of youth and freshness. . . . The town—with its frame houses and box elder trees, its Dry Run cutting the town in two and its muddy western river some distance away, with its great rolling countryside that gave a feeling of openness and loftiness—lay as if in morning light. Everything seemed to be just starting up, just beginning. . . . I count it my great good fortune that I was thus able, in early childhood, to have an actual share . . . in that central experience of American life—the experience of a fresh beginning. (175–76)

In this same section of her memoir, Suckow quotes her father's description of Hawarden from his autobiography:

> The church was young, and had worn no ruts, developed no hampering traditions. The people were amenable to any reasonable leadership and ready to give enthusiastic cooperation; . . . it was more like one big family. (176)

Almost identical qualities mark the town of New Hope. Moreover, New Hope's minister, the Reverend William Greenwood, greatly resembles the portrait of Suckow's father contained in her memoir. There, she describes her father as a caring, broad-minded, self-educated man with "keenly set, far-seeing, blue-gray eyes," a man who spoke in a "forceful voice, with its singularly clear resonance," and moved with a step that was "exceptionally springing, eager, and full of vitality." Greenwood is described in almost the same terms in *New Hope*.

People provided with love and security in their early years usually develop a deep level of trust, confidence, and optimism that carries them through the most awful of tragedies; but in the late 1800s, happy early childhoods were rare. Even rarer for females were childhoods in which a girl was surrounded not only by the love of a supportive mother and father but also by a caring, concerned community. In her memoir, Suckow describes her life in Hawarden as a "golden period," a "beginning in joy and confidence, not in fear," a beginning that had "almost the quality of a legend." *Some Others and Myself* also gives us a moving picture of a visit Suckow paid to Hawarden as a guest speaker during the Second World War, probably during the early forties, when she was trying to finalize *New Hope*. The visit made her realize that the "legend had a real basis," that growing up in Hawarden had prepared her to leave "ready to go on." Despite the bits of darkness that had spotted her early childhood and the terrible darkness currently imposed by the war, the outcome of her visit was renewed hope: "I began to understand the meaning of the great prologue to the Gospel According to John: that, 'The light shines in the darkness, and the darkness has not overcome it.'"

One of the gifts of *New Hope* is that, whatever our childhoods were like, reading the novel allows us to experience, vicariously, a "beginning in joy and confidence." It also immerses us in a sense of light, which emerged from the strength, joy, and optimism Suckow derived from a nurturing father and mother, from a happy childhood in a secure, loving family and community, and from her rediscovery of the centrality of Christianity to her life. That light—which her experience of darkness could not overcome—sustained her as she grieved for her father and endured the long years of the war. Because of her willingness to keep working at *New Hope* in the late thirties and forties, we too are "ready to go on" when we finish reading it.

Correspondence concerning *New Hope*, principally with John Farrar, the book's publisher, and his assistant, reveals that Suckow reworked the novel several times. A June 1939 letter from Farrar's assistant indicates that Farrar expected it by 1941. On February 20, 1941, Suckow wrote him as follows: "What I have done this winter, is to take the material of the second part, and compress it into a final chapter instead. . . . I believe this . . . brings out better a certain poetic quality of past and present mingled."

"Hope springs eternal, so can Suckow be far behind?" begins a somewhat frantic reply from Farrar dated February 24, 1941. Apparently, he had begun work on the jacket copy and other aspects of production and was eager to have the finished product in his hands. Nuhn began handling production details around this time, reviewing the jacket copy and advising Farrar on June 2 that Suckow was revising the last eighty pages. On June 24 he informed Farrar that she was "expanding it some as she rewrites" and that the "80 pages will be around 150 pages."

On July 22, Nuhn regretfully informed an undoubtedly desperate Farrar that the "second and final part" of *New Hope* "just hasn't 'jelled' right so far." The "jelling" apparently occurred soon after that, and the finished manuscript was on its way to Farrar and Rinehart in New York. Carbons of the manuscript drafts in the University of Iowa Libraries reveal that several items were excised. Also dropped was a long sequel, written in a far more realistic vein—indeed, sounding a great deal more like *The Folks* in style, tone, and subject matter. In this sequel, Clarence Miller returns to New Hope, sophisticated and perhaps even a bit jaded as a result of experiencing some of life's grimmer realities. In excising these parts of her story, Suckow was clearly deciding to veer away from the unflinching "portraits of the unpleasant" for which she was famous and venture into the realm of romantic myth and legend. Commenting later on *New Hope*, Suckow maintained, however, that the novel was realistic in its own way. "The fortunate example," she said in her 1942 radio conversation with John T. Frederick, "is just as real as the unfortunate example." She elaborated as follows: "You know we used to be at a phase in our reading when we wouldn't accept the unfortunate as real, because we said it was too dark or pessimistic or not normal. Now we tend to be in another phase when a fortunate example can't be real. It may be beautiful, but for that very reason, it can't be real. And that is just as lopsided. The fact is that reality lies in the truth of an example, whatever it is."

CRITICAL VIEWS OF *NEW HOPE*

When *New Hope* was published, many critics shared Suckow's perception of her novel's special brand of realism. "The darker side of small town life has in recent years had abundant attention," declared Lee E. Cannon in a review in the *Christian Century*. Cannon praised the fact that "Miss Suckow shows us the brighter side of Main Street," thereby creating "a novel the realism of which leaves no bad taste." "She somehow makes dull and hackneyed people worth knowing and listening to, monotonous cornland worth looking at . . . all this without prettifying and romanticizing," extolled Richard Cordell in the *Saturday Review of Literature*, adding that the novel's "cheerfulness and warmth are achieved inoffensively and honestly."

The *New Yorker* reviewer seemed to agree with Cordell, claiming that "Miss Suckow creates a snug, neighborly little world, in which fried chicken and hot biscuits go nicely with the milk of human kindness. A happy epitaph to a safe and simple period of our history." Writing in the *Atlantic Monthly*, R. M. Gay pointed out that the plot of *New Hope* "is the sort of story that might easily have been just sweet or inane"; instead it "is amusing, charming and heartening," and Gay attributed this achievement to Suckow's close knowledge of her material as well as to her art. So did Cordell. Rose Feld, in a review in the *New York Herald Tribune*, also cited Suckow's art: "Her characters emerge with clarity against a period background excellently drawn; her writing, except in rare lapses, has the structure of good craftsmanship."

Most critics found a great deal to praise in *New Hope*. Many, however, found faults. Chief among these was what Cordell called the "need for a more resolute narrative." Other critics echoed *New York Times* reviewer Edith Walton's assessment: "Though her book is at times slow-moving and, I think, over-roseate, it does cast somehow a kind of drowsy golden spell and at its best has a quality of enchantment." And while Robert Littell of the *Yale Review* found *New Hope* "like its own setting . . . somewhat flat," he declared that "there is a warmth and wholesomeness here for which one should be grateful on cold and bitter days."

Subsequent literary critics have generally agreed with the majority of *New Hope*'s first reviewers about its merits but have differed in their assessment of the genre to which this novel belongs as well as in their interpretation of its symbolism. Indeed, because of its unique blend of the realistic and the romantic, as well as its rich veins of symbolism, *New Hope* has sparked greater differences among critics than other Suckow works. Kissane, for example, believes that the novel is distinguished by the "quality of youth recaptured" and that "the author of *New Hope* is revealing, through the thin veil of allegory, what life becomes for a little boy when Delight is part of it." "There are unquestionably elements of Utopia in *New Hope*," she says. She also finds qualities of myth and legend that "have a perpetual freshness about them, breathing of early times when the world was young." Her judgment is conclusive: "It is a parable, surely, though probably not primarily intended to suggest a return to 'the good old days' of our country. Its meaning would seem to be far more universal—the innocent freshness of an uncorrupted time that allowed the liberation of the spirit through imagination."

According to Margaret Omrcanin, who discusses *New Hope* in her book *Ruth Suckow: A Critical Study of Her Fiction*, "The town itself is the protagonist." In Omrcanin's view, the novel portrays "a quasi-utopian society with enduring values of communal fellowship," and "a community where the values of the folks are still the realities," thus communicating Suckow's "belief in change, progress and a forward-looking quality as essential characteristics of American life." Omrcanin also believes that the novel "has the quality of a legend" and that it symbolizes, "in the origin and life of this community," the "central experience of American life, the fresh beginning." "The personal idealism explicit in *New Hope*," she maintains, "is the system of values to which her characters cling in every novel and in which she herself seems to have faith and confidence."

In her article "Ruth Suckow's *New Hope*: A Symbolic Parable," Mary Jean DeMarr agrees that the novel "dramatizes life in an apparently idyllic community." DeMarr maintains that "it is equally true that almost from the beginning we are shown that this utopian period is but a brief phase, unable to endure and carrying the seeds of its own withering." As in *The Great Gatsby*, the American dream portrayed in *New Hope* ends "in lies and disillusionment." Just as the preexisting Canaan was "foredoomed to failure," so is *New Hope*; this is shown in the actions of the thieving janitor, in Clarence's killing of the muskrat, and in "Mr. Greenwood's call to a bigger and better church on the west coast, a move which is to permanently separate Clarence and his Delight."

As quoted by Clarence Andrews, Martin Mohr views *New Hope* as a "nostalgic idealization of a simple happy time before the outside world intruded on the complacency of . . . Iowa." Andrews says that Mohr considered the novel "deficient in having no story line . . . and in the inconsequential quality of many of its events." As noted earlier, many of the critics who first reviewed *New Hope* pointed to these same problems.

I also believe the novel has its flaws, particularly in its occasional narrative drag and in the lack of full characterization of all but the children and Greenwood. However, it seems to me that when viewed as the poetic chronicle of a realistic but symbolic legend of a town that actually existed, *New Hope* can be forgiven its faults. In my view, the richness of its meaning stems not only from the reality of Hawarden at the turn of the century but also from the two symbolic veins Suckow seems to be tapping in this novel. The first cluster of symbols, which plays just beneath the surface of the narrative, concerns the contrast between Old and New Testament thought; the second relates to the Adamic myth, as recently described by female critics.

In her novel, Suckow created a predecessor town for New Hope, naming it Canaan and describing it as a "desolate landscape" ruined by a cyclone and peopled by a few almost lifeless individuals. She thus clearly associated the promised land of the Old Testament with ruin. In contrast, *New Hope* seems to symbolize the New Testament values that Greenwood espouses so deliberately in his first sermon on John's text, "Light is come into the world":

> This was what Mr. Greenwood would stand for in his preaching: for the New Testament, its brightness of hope, its promise of new life, its creative spirit, turning away from the dark historic involutions of the old books . . . the doctrine, not of power and might and darkness, but of goodwill, of love, of communal, not tribal effort, and of light, more light.

Despite their human flaws and failings, the people of New Hope, for the most part, do try to live this doctrine of goodwill and of communal effort; it is a major source of the light that fills the novel.

Many scholars of American literature agree that a central, shaping myth of American culture is the Adamic myth, or the myth of America as a New World Garden of Eden. This myth of the new Eden and the American new Adam was first delineated by R. W. B.

Lewis, who noted the persistent belief by Americans that the settlement of the New World represented "a divinely granted second chance for the human race, after the first chance had been so disastrously fumbled in the darkening Old World" (5). This formulation of the myth was widely embraced by literary scholars such as David Noble and Leo Marx, as well as by American historians. Lewis says Cooper's Natty Bumppo is the quintessential Adamic hero, a "self-reliant young man . . . whose characteristic pose . . . was the solitary stance in the presence of Nature and God" (91). Up until 1975, most scholars focused on the many literary representations of the Adamic myth created by male authors and conforming to this image of a heroic, self-reliant, isolated lover of a foreboding wilderness.

In her first book, *The Lay of the Land: Metaphor as Experience and History in American Life and Letters*, feminist scholar Annette Kolodny documents in extensive detail the hold this male version of the Adamic myth has had on the public imagination in American history. "Eden, Paradise, the Golden Age, the idyllic garden," she says, "were subsumed in an image of an America promising material ease without labor or hardship, as opposed to the grinding poverty of previous European existence; a frank, free affectional life in which all might share in a primal and noncompetitive fraternity" (6). In her second chapter, Kolodny demonstrates that the image of America as a paradisial garden in which the human race could make a fresh start dominates the tracts, letters, journals, histories, and other accounts written by men from the sixteenth to the eighteenth centuries. She proceeds to suggest that the widespread imaging of the American land as both virgin and mother led to psychological conflict and destructive attitudes toward nature as well as toward women.

In a 1981 article entitled "Melodramas of Beset Manhood: How Theories of American Fiction Exclude Women Authors," Nina Baym expands upon many of the ideas Kolodny presented in 1975. Baym believes that the dominant theories of American literary criticism promote a larger myth of "essential Americanness" that has the following characteristics:

The myth narrates a confrontation of the American individual, the pure American self divorced from specific social circumstances, with the promise offered by the idea of America. This promise is the deeply romantic one that in this new land, untrammeled by history and social accident, a person will be able to achieve complete self-definition. Behind this promise is the assurance that individuals come before society, that they exist in some meaningful sense prior to, and apart from, societies in which they happen to find themselves. The myth also holds that as something artificial and secondary to human nature, society exerts an unmitigatedly destructive pressure on individuality. To depict it at any length would be a waste of artistic time, and there is only one way to relate it to the individual—as an adversary. (10–11)

Because the "entrammeling society and the promising landscape" are painted "in unmistakably feminine terms," this myth has "melodramatic, misogynist implications," according to Baym (12).

Kolodny's second book, *The Land Before Her: Fantasy and Experience of the American Frontiers, 1630–1860*, is believed by many scholars to be as important to our understanding of American culture as the pivotal works of Lewis and others. In this study, Kolodny vigorously argues that, particularly in the prairie states, female authors had painted a very different, equally important picture of America as a New World Garden of Eden. In their works, the Adamic hero shared Eden with Eve, and Eden was not a wilderness but a highly interdependent prairie community surrounded by a gently beautiful countryside and peopled by settlers who cared for and supported each other.

In contrast, male writers used imagery portraying the new paradise as a virgin ripe for conquest and exploitation and, often simultaneously, as a broad-breasted mother generously welcoming all as her sons. "The American husbandman," Kolodny says in the first chapter of *The Land Before Her*, "was cast as both son and lover in a primal paradise where the maternal and the erotic were to be harmoniously intermingled." What actually occurred was "a fierce, rapid, viciously competitive struggle between greedy fortune-seekers hell bent on a destructive industrialization which devastated the land." As this industrialization ruined paradise, Americans simply "displaced the garden westward." The "tensions inherent in the recurrent pursuit of the fantasy" drove American men to create the "saving myth" of the "isolate woodland son," whose "figure suggests at least the possibility of harmonious intimacy between the human and the natural." Daniel Boone, Davy Crockett, Kit Carson, and Natty Bumppo are all incarnations of this Adamic "woodland hero."

Initially, according to Kolodny, EuroAmerican women were "dispossessed of paradise" because of this sexualized myth and because "Eve could only be redundant" in the "idealized wilderness garden." Influenced by their theological frameworks and their preferences for cultivated landscapes, Puritan female settlers perceived the densely forested New World as a "howling wilderness." But in the nineteenth century, Kolodny says, American women began "to proclaim themselves the rightful New World Eve" by "redefining the meaning of the garden and, with that, radically reshaping the wilderness Adam as well."

Having for so long been barred from the fantasy garden, American women were also, at first, wary of paradisial projections onto the vast new landscape around them. Their imaginative play, instead, focused on the spaces that were truly and unequivocally of their own making. Then with the movement of the frontier beyond the forested Ohio valley and out onto the open, parklike prairies of the middle- and southwest, women's public and private documents alike began to claim the new terrain as their own . . . a paradise in which the garden and the home were one. (5–6)

Kolodny continues:

For roughly thirty years, then—from about 1830 through 1860— women's public writings about the west purposefully and self-consciously rejected (or refined) male fantasies, replacing them with figures from the female imagination. . . . And, in their promotional writings, as in their domestic novels set in the west, women writers stripped the American Adam of his hunting shirt and moccasins, fetching him out of the forest and into the town. (9)

This female Edenic myth was articulated by such authors as Margaret Fuller and Caroline Soule. Its promise died, Kolodny believes, with the Civil War and with the western settlement of the late 1860s. When it flourished, however, it offered "the enticing image of a flowered prairie paradise, generously supporting an extended human family, at the center of which stood a reunited Adam and Eve" (9).

NEW HOPE AS AN EDENIC TALE

Was the promise of the female Edenic myth dead by 1870? Myths that so powerfully shape cultures die hard; they tend to live on in the imaginations of a culture's writers. As I pointed out in the introduction to the paperback edition of my book, *Envisioning the New Adam: Empathic Portraits of Men by American Women Writers*, I believe the dream of America's Edenic possibilities, tempered by some realism, is voiced in works by nineteenth- and twentieth-century American women writers. Ruth Suckow's *New Hope* seems squarely in that tradition.

Clarence Miller and Delight Greenwood, the children from whose point of view the novel is told, are an innocent, loving couple who seem to embody all the original qualities of Adam and Eve before they succumbed to temptation. Indeed, the name "Delight Greenwood" suggests the joy that arises from harmony with the newly planted Tree of Life. In her biography of Suckow, Kissane acknowledges that "the children themselves dwell in a sort of Eden." Kolodny herself seems to be describing Suckow's novel when she delineates the characteristics of the female Edenic myth in *The Land Before Her*. Could there be a more "enticing image of a flowered prairie paradise, generously supporting an extended human family, at the center of which stood a reunited Adam and Eve" than we find in *New Hope*? Its characters, like the Hawarden townspeople Suckow's father describes in his memoir, function as "an extended human family."

Egalitarian relationships between men and women in *New Hope*, however, are not confined to children. In their marriage, the Greenwoods enjoy a mutually supportive partnership. Mrs. Greenwood, for example, has a great deal of say in her husband's decision to "accept the call" to a new pastorate in the West, and he helps her with domestic chores, particularly the packing and unpacking involved with moves. Moreover, although Greenwood and the other men in the novel find the boundless, great countryside alluring, they remain committed to building up the life of the town rather than exploring or conquering the wilderness.

Ruth Suckow's *New Hope*, therefore, seems to sit solidly in the neglected tradition of female creators of the Adamic myth, which Kolodny has described so well. It is a tradition that has, I believe, many congruences with Quaker values and with the Quaker conception of the Garden of Eden. This view of the myth was articulated by George Fox and Margaret Fell, the two principal founders of the Religious Society of Friends.

The Quakers had a far less misogynistic and far more optimistic interpretation of the Adam and Eve story than did the Puritans. In her groundbreaking 1666 pamphlet, "Women's Speaking Justified, Proved and Allowed of by Scriptures" (see Wallace, 65), Margaret Fell declared that in the first creation God made no distinction between men and women. She asserted further that God intended equality to be even more the case in the new creation established by Jesus, whom Fell and other Quakers routinely referred to as the second Adam. The second Adam served as a model for males and females alike and called both men and women to embrace the communal, caring egalitarian life of men and women depicted in the Acts of the Apostles.

In his book *The Religious Philosophy of Quakerism*, Howard Brinton outlines George Fox's argument that those people who unite themselves with Christ, the second Adam, can rise to a higher state than that of the first Adam and live happy lives. In contrast to Puritan pessimism about fallen man, then, the Quakers brought to the New World a theological basis for optimism: a belief that people could rise up into the Edenic state of the second Adam and work on perfection for themselves and their societies.

This optimism underlies not only the social reforms Quakers instigated concerning the rights of women, slaves, prisoners, mental patients, and others, but also, I believe, the hope voiced by women writers influenced by Quaker values. Suckow seems to belong to that tradition of optimistic American women writers I pointed to in *Envisioning the New Adam*. Also in that tradition, according to Jane Atteridge Rose, is Rebecca Harding Davis, whose last scene in *Life in the Iron Mills* depicts a serene, loving Quaker women taking Hugh Wolfe's devastated widow away to be healed in a peaceful, rural Quaker community. Says Rose: "This last scene . . . asserts a reformative plan implicit in much of Davis' fiction, in which society is restructured on feminine principles: sentimental theology, spiritual integrity and agrarian familial communities" (21). Is not the same plan and the same congruence with Quaker values and the Quaker conception of the Edenic myth echoed in *New Hope*? Is this not, then, another influence on *New Hope*, which was written when Suckow was, according to Dorothy Grant, beginning to hold small Quaker meetings for worship in her home with Ferner Nuhn and a few others? The relationship between *New Hope* and the overlooked Quaker contribution to the Adamic myth needs to be further explored, as do the connections between this novel and recent scholarship by Georgi-Findlay and others on neglected feminist contributions by women to myths central to the American experience, such as the myths of the West and the frontier.

Finally, *New Hope* manifests other feminist influences. Carol Gilligan believes women embrace an "ideal of care" that involves "taking care of the world by sustaining the web of connection so that no one is left alone" (62). According to Gilligan, it is that ethic which prompts women to value interdependence over independence (167). Indeed, this predilection for interdependence and disparagement of solipsism seems evident in the theories of Baym and Kolodny. Moreover, as discussed by Josephine Donovan in *Feminist Theory: The Intellectual Traditions of American Feminism*, most contemporary feminists are moving toward a championing of interdependence among all living things (208). As a kind of paean to interdependence and to the ideal of "sustaining the web of connection," then, *New Hope* is a novel that celebrates feminist values.

According to Elaine Showalter in *Sister's Choice: Tradition and Change in American Women's Writing*, during the twenties and thirties the mostly male leaders of academia and the literary establishment called for a poetry that was "intellectual, impersonal, experimental and concrete" (109) and, in novels, favored an "impersonal account of the struggle between workers and bosses" (118). Women who wanted to write "in the tradition of feminist writers like Olive Schreiner" and make "a place for the lyric, the personal, the myth, and the fantastic" were not taken seriously and became part of what Showalter calls "the other lost generation" (117). Although *New Hope* and its author did succumb to the fate of this "other lost generation," Suckow did not bend to prevailing literary mores and turned to the lyrical and the mythic to produce her tale of her "flowered prairie paradise."

Readers of Suckow's works, and of *New Hope* in particular, may find themselves plagued by questions: Why is so little known about such a good writer? And why are so many of her works out of print? These are troubling questions that do not yield easy answers. As I have noted, Nina Baym suggests that many American women writers have been devalued because their visions and approaches to literature do not fit prevailing theories of literary criticism. Elaine Showalter believes that women writers of Suckow's generation were increasingly marginalized in their time because their subjects, aesthetic techniques, narrative strategies, and/or their linguistic, syntactical, and thematic conventions were at odds with prevailing literary modes that were set by patriarchal men (125). Surely the increasing popularity after World War II of literature that focused on urban life also explains Suckow's eclipse. Suckow's deep modesty, reported by so many people I interviewed, undoubtedly also accounts for the degree to which she has been forgotten. There are, I'm sure, many other factors.

"No book is ever lost," says Showalter, "as long as there are new generations of readers to enjoy it, new generations of writers to be stimulated by it, new generations of critics to reveal its fuller meanings" (126). With the publication of this edition by the University of Iowa Press, *New Hope* joins the growing tradition of "rediscovered" works by early twentieth century women writers. As Showalter says of that tradition, "We must not let it become lost again." Whether or not we agree with Showalter's point of view, let us say the same thing of Ruth Suckow's *New Hope*: "We must not let it become lost again."

WORKS CITED

Andrews, Clarence A. *A Literary History of Iowa.* Iowa City: University of Iowa Press, 1972.

Baym, Nina. "Melodramas of Beset Manhood: How Theories of American Fiction Exclude Women Authors." In *Feminism and American Literary History: Essays.* New Brunswick, N.J.: Rutgers University Press, 1992. First published in *American Quarterly* 33 (1981): 123–39.

Bradbury, Malcolm. "'Years of the Modern': The Rise of Realism and Naturalism." In *American Literature to 1900*, Penguin History of Literature, vol. 8. Edited by Marcus Cunliffe. New York: Penguin Books, 1993.

Bradbury, Malcolm, and Richard Ruland. *From Puritanism to Postmodernism: A History of American Literature.* New York: Penguin Books, 1992.

Brinton, Howard. *The Religious Philosophy of Quakerism.* Wallingford, Pa.: Pendle Hill Publications, 1972.

Cannon, Lee E. "Pleasant Portraits." Review of *New Hope*, by Ruth Suckow. *Christian Century*, 2 Sept. 1942, 1055.

Cordell, Richard A. "Suckow." Review of *New Hope*, by Ruth Suckow. *Saturday Review of Literature*, 28 Feb. 1942, 8.

Daly, Patricia Ellen Martin, ed. *Envisioning the New Adam: Empathic Portraits of Men by American Women Writers.* Vol. 149, Contributions in Women's Studies. Westport, Conn.: Praeger Publishers, 1997.

DeMarr, Mary Jean. "Ruth Suckow's *New Hope*: A Symbolic Parable." *MidAmerica* 15 (1988): 48–58.

Donovan, Josephine. *Feminist Theory: The Intellectual Traditions of American Feminism.* 2d ed. New York: Frederick Ungar, 1992.

Feld, Rose. "A Childhood Idyll Out in Iowa." Review of *New Hope*, by Ruth Suckow. *New York Herald Tribune*, 22 Feb. 1942, 3.

Forgue, Guy J., ed. *Letters of H. L. Mencken.* New York: Knopf, 1961.

Frederick, John T. "Literary Evening, Iowa Style." *The Borzoi.* New York: Alfred A. Knopf, 1925.

Gay, R. M. "*New Hope*." Review of *New Hope*, by Ruth Suckow. *Atlantic*, May 1942, 200.

Georgi-Findlay, Brigitte. *The Frontiers of Women's Writing: Women's Narratives and the Rhetoric of Westward Expansion.* Tucson: University of Arizona Press, 1996.

Gilligan, Carol. *In a Different Voice: Psychological Theory and Women's Development.* Cambridge, Mass.: Harvard University Press, 1982.

Kissane, Leedice. *Ruth Suckow.* New York: Twayne Publishers, 1969.

Kolodny, Annette. *The Land Before Her: Fantasy and Experience of the American Frontiers, 1630–1860.* Chapel Hill: University of North Carolina Press, 1984.

——. *The Lay of the Land: Metaphor as Experience and History in American Life and Letters.* Chapel Hill: University of North Carolina Press, 1984.

Lewis, R. W. B. *The American Adam: Innocence, Tragedy, and Tradition in the Nineteenth Century.* Chicago: University of Chicago Press, 1955.

Littell, Robert. "Outstanding Novels." Review of *New Hope*, by Ruth Suckow. *Yale Review* (Summer 1942): x.

McAlpin, Sara, BVM. "Enlightening the Commonplace: The Work of Sarah Orne Jewett, Willa Cather, and Ruth Suckow." Ph.D. diss., University of Pennsylvania, 1971.

Mencken, H. L. "The Library." Review of *Iowa Interiors*, by Ruth Suckow. *American Mercury* 9 (1926): 383.

Nathan, George Jean. "America's Literary Stars." *Literary Digest* 74 (1922): 44.

Nevins, Allan. "A Painter of Iowa." *Saturday Review of Literature*, 10 Mar. 1928, 666.

Omrcanin, Margaret Stewart. *Ruth Suckow: A Critical Study of Her Fiction.* Philadelphia: Dorrance, 1972.

Rose, Jane Atteridge. *Rebecca Harding Davis.* New York: Twayne Publishers, 1993.

Showalter, Elaine. *Sister's Choice: Tradition and Change in American Women's Writing.* New York: Oxford University Press, 1994.

Suckow, Ruth. "Mid-West Regional Fiction." Radio conversation with John T. Frederick. "Of Men and Books." *Northwestern University on the Air* 1 (7 Mar. 1942).

———. *Some Others and Myself.* New York: Rinehart & Co., 1952.

Van Doren, Carl. *The American Novel: 1789–1939.* Rev. ed. New York: Macmillan, 1940.

Wallace, Terry S., ed. *A Sincere and Constant Love: An Introduction to the Work of Margaret Fell.* Richmond, Ind.: Friends United Press, 1992.

Walton, Edith H. "An Iowa Idyll." Review of *New Hope*, by Ruth Suckow. *New York Times*, 27 Feb. 1942, 6–7.

NEW HOPE

CHAPTER I

Arrival

THAT LONG-AGO midsummer morning shone hot and clear.

It was the morning when the new minister and his family were to arrive in New Hope. They had planned to come now, in July, so that they could get settled in the parsonage before school opened and before all the activities that had come to a lull in the summer months started up again with the beginning of fall.

The minister had been in New Hope before, when he had come to preach as a candidate. But this would be the first appearance for the other members of the family: his wife and little daughter.

The newcomers were to stay with the Dave Millers until their household goods arrived. The Daves had ample room in their new house and liked to entertain company. But they were all nervous as well as proud at the idea of having the minister's family in their house. The girls had been up since five o'clock that morning; Mrs. Dave since long before that. But mama always did think she had to get up in the dark as if she were still the hired girl on the farm! The girls sputtered about it. They and their father tried to reform her, but none of them got very far.

The kitchen, that whole morning, was in commotion. The girls flew around trying to get everything done at once and talking at the same time. Edie kept saying she was crazy to see what kind of wife the minister had.

"If she's anything like Hannah Barbour I won't attend church."

"She won't be. You don't suppose Mr. Greenwood would marry an old vinegar bottle like that!"

There was only a short while left before the train would be due. Edie looked up at the clock and got all excited. She went to the back door and yelled:

"Papa! My heavens, haven't you started yet?"

"Now, Edie, you go back and tend to your knitting. I'll be down to that train in plenty of time."

Edie slammed the screen door. She knew only too well her family's reputation for being late wherever they went —while the Ira Millers could always be counted on to arrive half an hour too soon! Things like that nearly drove Edie wild.

But it was no use trying to get her father started until the very last minute. Then he'd act as if the world was on fire! He paid no attention now to Edie's fuming but went out to the barn to get old Mollie. She came along without any fuss. There was a muffled, maternal gentleness in the hollow sound of her hoofs on the wooden floor, as though to counteract the clumsy threatening noise she couldn't help making. Old Mollie was well known throughout the town and countryside. Dave Miller would have enjoyed owning a good fast horse. But he had to have a gentle nag on account of his wife. He couldn't have got Bertha to go anywhere otherwise. It was hard enough to pry her loose from the house in any event.

"Well, Mollie, want to step right along now!"

Out in the yard, Mollie obeyed the orders to "Whoa— stand still," shuddering her coat from the bothering of the flies, and trying with one eye to get a view of her own hindquarters. She'd heard the rig being hauled out earlier, to get the hose turned on it, and had known she was in for a trip. The two-seated carriage stood shining with cleanliness, the leather seats and top already dry and hot from the sun. The grass smelled fresh where water from the hose had soaked into it.

Mrs. Dave came out to the back porch.

"You're nearly hitched up a'ready! Where's Clarence?"

"Clarence? He was around here when I was washing the buggy. What do you want him for?"

"He wants to go along down to the depot."

"Let him go then."

"Ja, but he's not ready."

"Well, I can't take him if he isn't ready."

The girls had come out too by this time. Clarence had begged them to get him ready right after breakfast, and nobody would stop and take the time. Afterwards, they were all so busy they forgot about it.

"He'll have a fit, papa," Bess protested warmly. "He thinks he's going. He's been counting on it all week."

"Papa can't take him if he isn't here," Edie said.

"No, let him stay around if he expects me to take him."

"But, papa, *lis*-ten!"

"Call him then. Go call him!"

A shout went up. It was heard all over the neighborhood. "Clarence! Clay-rrrence!" Bess ran out to the barn to look. Edie sputtered. He didn't need to go. This might teach him to be around when he was wanted. He'd make papa late for the train *after* all. Bess said, "Oh, Edie, dry up," coming back from a fruitless search of the barn. "Irene," she complained, "I think you might help." Irene shrugged her shoulders. Bertha waited uneasily, afraid her biscuits might be burning, but not wanting to go indoors again until Clarence was found.

At the very last moment Clarence came running, scared to death.

A hustle ensued. Edie was still unreconciled to that kid's being allowed to go along, until even Irene was tired of it, and wanted to know what on earth *she* cared.

"I care about having this family on time for once!"

"Buddle-liddle-liddle," Irene retorted lightly.

Bess wouldn't listen to Edie's scolding. She took Clarence over to the sink to get him scrubbed. Irene was sent flying upstairs to find him a clean blouse. "You'll be ready," Bess kept telling him. Clarence stood breathing hard, with his shoulders hunched, and his eyes tight shut to keep out soapsuds. He drew his breath through his teeth while Bess pulled the metal kitchen comb through his hair. Edie was saying, "*I* wouldn't do that for him!" Bess got down on her knees, and tried to force the buttons of his brand-clean blouse through the buttonholes. Edie always got things starched like boards when she did up the clothes! They heard Edie yank open the oven door all prepared to see the biscuits ruined. Bess and Irene exchanged funny glances over Clarence's head—but he saw them—at Edie's "Hmp!" of disappointment at finding the biscuits all right.

But now their father was shouting outside. Clarence began to whimper and jiggle. He was afraid of getting left behind. Finally he bolted and ran and climbed into the carriage. The girls went running out after him. He looked down at them in scared triumph.

Edie came out in a great state of indignation. "Papa, that kid hasn't even got his shoes buttoned up!"

"He'll have to fasten 'em on the way."

"He *can't*," Edie cried in a voice of tragedy. "He can't fasten shoes while the buggy's going. Not the way you drive."

"Then they'll have to go unfastened!" Dave roared. He'd suddenly had enough of all this nonsense. He slapped the reins. Mollie gave a startled bolt forward.

"Mister, the butter—we need some butter!" Bertha cried in feeble panic.

He didn't hear. He always got away before the women-folks put in their final orders. Dawdle until the last instant, was a common accusation, as if time lasted forever, and then "*Gid*-dap!" without another second to wait. The buggy bumped along out onto the road in a cloud of summer dust.

The whole way to the station, Clarence kept listening for the train to whistle; and when they reached the depot, and nothing was in sight, he suffered a dreadful minute of thinking the train might have been there and gone. They drew up beside the platform and his father leaned out and squinted up the track.

"Well, she's not in sight yet. Those women are always in a stew. Guess I'll go into the depot and inquire."

Clarence climbed out hastily. He was shaky from scare and from the jouncing he'd got. His father always drove lickety-split when mama wasn't in the buggy. That was a joke all over town—the way Dave Miller drove. He always started up as if he had to get to a fire, and then in a few minutes the old nag took her own gentle pace.

"Didn't you get those shoes fastened?"

"I couldn't!"

"You sit right down here on the edge of this platform," his father ordered, "and button up those shoes while I go to inquire. Get right after it now."

Clarence sat down close to the buggy so the men around the baggage room wouldn't see what he was doing. He was in a fever again—this time, because the train might

arrive before he could finish and the little girl would see
him with his shoes unfastened.

He was at it when his father came back. "Still working on those shoes? Aren't you a big enough boy to get
them fixed? Here let's see. Well, maybe they are kind of
hard for a little fellow. Come on, now, no need to get
worked up about it. Don't whine, or I won't help you."
Clarence stopped his nervous whimpering.

He asked after a moment, "Isn't it here yet, papa?"

"What, the train? Well, can't you see it isn't here?
Quarter of an hour late."

Clarence drew breath again. Now he sat contentedly,
letting his leg in its black-ribbed stocking be drawn over
onto his father's knee, for the last hard black buttons to be
squeezed through their buttonholes.

"There, I guess I got you fixed. You ought to learn
to do these things yourself, you're big enough. The girls
baby you too much."

Clarence shut his ears to that. He scrambled up, rubbed
his knees together to get off the dust. His father went over
and began talking to the men outside the baggage room.
Clarence hung around for a while, then wandered off by
himself.

"Don't you disappear again!" his father shouted after
him.

"I won't."

He stopped at the open door of the waiting room, but
there were too many people inside. He wanted to be alone
now, for he was full of restless, happy, uneasy imaginings.

He went daringly to the very end of the platform. That
seemed a long way from the depot. It was out in the country almost. Rough vacant lots stretched on both sides of
the track, grown up to weeds with harsh stems and rank
green leaves. The town was away off beyond, not in sight,
nothing but the livery stable. Some people thought the

town had made a mistake building up so far from the depot: folks going through on the train might think there was nothing here. But others, Clarence's father among them, said it gave more room for growth. You didn't want tracks cutting right through town the way they did in so many places. If papa said that, that was the way it was.

The great high azure had not a cloud: a midland sky in the middle of the morning. The straight, dazzling rails led into a shimmer of distance. Clarence stared up the tracks until his eyes hurt and he had to close them. To Horton forty miles away, the biggest town in this part of the state, was the farthest he'd ever been—and there only about twice. It didn't seem as if he could even imagine any place farther. The cities on the depot sign—Chicago, New Orleans—were nothing but names. He couldn't really believe they were bigger than Horton.

Clarence was in a state of restless ecstasy. That was why, when he was helping (or imagined he was helping) to get the carriage washed, he'd suddenly had to turn and scamper off. When he came to the alley he'd stopped, breathing fast, and gone softly along until he'd reached the patch of sunflowers on the other side of the barn. He'd sneaked in among them and sat hidden on the rough warm ground, in the bitter smell from the big harsh stalks, with the great, open, burning blossoms far above him. He had thought about the little girl coming. The minister had told Clarence, when he was here before, "I have a little girl just about your very size." When Bess had asked what the little girl was like, Mr. Greenwood had answered, "She has long fair hair that hangs below her waist." Her long hair, the sunflowers, the hot summer morning . . . he'd put his forehead against the ground and shut his eyes. Then after a long while he had heard the folks shouting "Clarence!"

Now he felt on the edge of that same ecstasy, but he couldn't be lost in it, he was alert, expectant. He could feel

again that joyful, bashful expectancy when the minister
had said to him, "You two will be great playmates." It
seemed as if the little girl was someone entirely special—
coming from away, bringing strangeness with her—and yet
as if he knew her and somehow belonged with her. Ever
since, he had gone about with the thought of her, whispering her name to himself sometimes, "Delight" . . . and
his favorite haunts, the haymow and the storeroom in the
barn, the sunflower patch, the pasture, had seemed to be
lighted with a magical shimmer, almost like the quivering
glitter above the hot steel rails. Clarence thought now, if
only he had his pony, and could have come galloping up
to the depot! He saw himself in a hat with white plumes,
like the lodge members when they marched. Nobody knew
about his excitement, what it was, or what it meant. Only
Bess had guessed something about it when he'd leaned up
against her and given her a silent hug. If Edie, he thought—
if that mean old Edie—had kept him from coming to the
depot—

Off in the distance the whistle sounded. Clarence went
scampering back to his father.

Now the train came, it was here. The engine thundered by with its great grinding wheels. Clarence braced
himself to withstand the loud excitement, the hot blasts
of steam. Then, when the engine had got past him, he suddenly felt brave and elated. But when the passengers started
getting off the train he went and stood behind his father
in bashful fear.

The company were the last ones out. Just when it began to look as if they might not have come, Clarence saw
Mr. Greenwood's face heated and eager under the summer
straw hat. He handed down two valises which the brakeman took and set on the platform. A lady followed him.
Clarence had just a glimpse of her, anxiously flushed and

smiling. Then came the little girl. Clarence couldn't look. He was so bashful that his eyes wouldn't focus. All he saw was the blur of blue dress as the brakeman swung her down to the platform. But he heard his father's hearty voice: "So here you all are! Welcome!"

The other people on the platform were watching. The morning air was bright with the sense of arrival. There was a feeling of newness all about, exhilarating, hopeful; it seemed to carry the scent of fresh-cut boards across the weedy roughness of the vacant lots.

Clarence heard his father again: "And so this is our little girl!" Dave boosted her high up in the air and then swung her down. She liked it.

Her wide-brimmed sailor hat had got pushed back and was hanging by the elastic. Clarence saw her long braids and her little slippers. She was looking around with bright eyes. Those eyes were oddly set, giving her an air of eagerness. Her voice suddenly sounded out, with a peculiar clarity, seeming almost to create a silence for itself to be heard.

"Is this New Hope?"

There was laughter from all over the platform. But she didn't mind. If Clarence had found that folks were all looking at him, he would have wanted to sink through the platform.

Dave Miller said proudly, "This is New Hope. You're here!"

The very thing that Clarence had been hoping would happen, and trying to hide away from, did happen. Mr. Greenwood caught sight of him.

"Hello, Clarence, hello! So you came down to meet us too?"

"Oh yes," Clarence's father had to answer for him, "he had to come along. Come out here and show yourself."

Clarence felt the eyes of the company all upon him. He felt sick, he was so excited and abashed. Turning away his face he managed to put out a limp hand, which Mr. Greenwood shook heartily.

"Look here, Delight," Mr. Greenwood said. "You wondered who would play with you. I told you there was a little boy just about your size."

Clarence stood in burning distress. All he could think of now was his fear of having to shake hands with the little girl in front of everybody. Wild with excitement and chagrin, he broke away and went running across the platform.

"Hey, wait, hold on a bit!" his father shouted after him.

Clarence wouldn't listen. He climbed up into the front seat of the carriage. His father was taking the company to the baggage room to inquire about the trunks. Clarence began to feel quieted and ashamed. Old Mollie switched her tail and looked around at him mildly. She seemed almost to be comforting him. The leather cushion was burning hot. The weedy vacant lots lay in teeming stillness. The train waited, chugging.

Then it started up again. Clarence turned his head. He couldn't bear to miss out on seeing the train leave. His father and the company were coming toward the carriage now. He stared quickly down the road again.

"Here, sonny," his father said, "you better get out and let the company have first choice."

But the company wouldn't listen to that. There would be plenty of room for them in the back seat. Mrs. Greenwood was afraid the valises would crowd the carriage. But Dave said, no, all kinds of room. Clarence was used to squeezing in anywhere. There were three girls ahead of him, so he'd had to learn to find a place where he could! The valises were stacked in front. Clarence mustn't put his feet on them, and so he had to sit with his legs twisted to the side and his feet almost out of the buggy. Anyway, he'd got his shoes fastened! Old Mollie stood patiently turning her head and trying to stare past her blinders, still switching at the pesky flies.

"All right back there, folks?"

"All right."

"*Gid*-dap. Now, Mollie, get a move on you."

Mollie gave her sudden bolt forward. Mrs. Greenwood gasped and took hold of the buggy rail. The carriage went jolting down the hard dusty road bordered with tall weeds that gave the air a bitter, fresh rankness. There were no trees near the depot. The frame building stood bare in the midst of empty lots. Beyond it was the water tank. Clarence didn't need to say anything now, he could just hold on. His hand felt hot, wet, and dirty, grasping the iron rail. He wouldn't look around, but he could feel the interested stare of the little girl's bright eyes. People who had come in on the train were trudging, lugging their valises, down the long, hot, dusty path that cut through the vacant lot. All of them were looking after the Miller rig. Clarence felt the proud importance of having met the new family.

"You mustn't judge our town by the entrance," his father warned, turning around. "Town all lies over this way."

They were coming to Main Street. The red sandstone and frame, mostly frame, store buildings faced across a broad width of dusty road.

"Our building over there," Dave said, pointing with his whip. "We won't go past it now, we'll take the short cut. This afternoon, if you folks feel like it, we can drive around and see the town."

They turned off Main, and the carriage went bouncing over the first little wooden bridge and up the steep short hill. Heavy rigs weren't allowed to cross here. Some folks wouldn't cross this bridge with any kind of team or buggy. But the company didn't know that. Clarence's father considered it all nonsense; because he liked to take the short cut, mama said. Clarence hung on in his accustomed state of joyous fear.

They reached their own street up on the hill: wide and burning under the summer sun. The rows of scrubby, hastily grown box elders cast scant shadows. From all the houses came the smell of dinner. The Miller house stood newly painted and ample, with a shine of plate-glass window and glitter of lightning rods. Folks still spoke of it as "Dave's new house," although the Millers had been living there for five years. Clarence had been born in that small gray-painted house, away down the hill, on the other side of town; but he couldn't remember ever having lived there. This place was home. The lawn was wider on the corner side. The new birch sapling that they had got from the Horton nursery looked fine. Clarence could see his mother, timidly ready to welcome the company, holding open the screen door and making a little shoo at the flies.

Dave announced proudly, "Well, folks, here we are!"

Clarence scrambled out first. His legs felt cramped and queer from trying to avoid the valises. He was sweaty, and his fresh white blouse, with its wide ruffled collar, was already crumpled. It had stuck to the back of the seat. Clarence waited, standing a little way off, while the company got out. The hot noon air smelled of fried chicken and new biscuits. The petunias along the side of the house stared in bright fresh colors. The birch leaves were a tender green. The company went up the shiny boardwalk that was raised above the grass. Clarence saw how long the little girl's braids were. She walked with a confident swing of her short full skirts. His face got hot to the tips of his ears. They all went into the dimness of the front hall from which came sounds confused of welcome and laughter.

Clarence scampered as fast as he could go it around the side of the house and into the steamy, good-smelling

kitchen. He ran blindly up to Bess, hugged her, and hid his
face against her.

"Have they come?" the girls asked eagerly.

He nodded.

The company were taken up to the front spare room
which the girls had got ready for them the day before; but
they soon came down again, washed and brushed, and
waited in the parlor for the summons to dinner. Bertha
wanted to be out in the kitchen but Dave wouldn't allow it.
"The girls are seeing to things," he told her. "Now you just
let them. Your place is in here with the company." Her face
was flushed from the heat of the stove which she had hastily
left, urged on by the girls, when they'd heard the carriage.
She had just barely got her apron off in time. A wisp of hair
was sticking out of her topknot. The girls hadn't noticed
that. She sat on the edge of her chair in the parlor, distracted
by the sounds from the other part of the house. But the
warmth and expansive heartiness of Dave Miller's hospitality
made the company feel at home.

There was a flutter going on in the kitchen, along with
the usual skirmish.

"Look at that kid. That spot! It's from that old buggy."

"Oh, Edie, shut up."

"I don't care, he can't go in and eat dinner like that."

"Well, who's got time to change it now?"

"Well, I have, if nobody else has."

But Clarence wouldn't let Edie do anything for him.
Bess had to hustle upstairs and find him a fresh blouse. With
a ruffled collar! He wasn't going to wear any old plain collar. "Yes, I'll get you one with a ruffled collar. Now you can
button it up yourself and come on down."

The girls were putting things on the table. They set on
the great platter of fried chicken, the mashed potatoes with
their golden pool of butter, the sweet corn, the dark red

beets. Edie whispered furiously, "Don't put on those biscuits! They'll all get cold. We'll pass those after they sit down."

Irene was the one sent to call the folks to dinner. She took off her apron—Edie and Bess were going to keep theirs on. Bess's apron was pink-flowered organdie with pink baby ribbon run through the insertion; Edie's was just a nice, starched, white apron with embroidered scallops at the bottom. Irene stopped to fix her pompadour at the glass above the sink. She settled her stiffly starched belt with her thumbs and forefingers, smoothed down her skirts around the hips with her palms; turned one way and then the other. Edie was groaning, but she knew she couldn't hurry Irene. Irene had to be satisfied that she looked just so. She went out of the turmoil of the kitchen to stand, immaculate and apparently cool, her smooth cheeks faintly rose-flushed, at the parlor door.

Her father introduced her proudly. "Mrs. Greenwood, this is our youngest girl, Irene. Well," he asked, "have you girls got a little dinner for us? These folks here are just about to starve."

"Dinner's ready," Irene said with gracious politeness.

The moment Irene appeared, Bertha had hurried out to take her place in the kitchen. Nothing could keep her out of there any longer. Dave had to marshal the company into the dining room.

The windows were open, but the noon heat itself made denser the good dinner smells: chicken, sweet corn, biscuits, coffee. Bess and Edie stood smiling in the doorway. Their father introduced them with joking comments, but it was easy to see his pride.

Clarence was there too, but hanging back out of sight. His mother gave him an anxious push and whispered, "Go on." His face hot, his mouth open a little, he edged into the dining room.

Dave stood at the head of the table, important, jovial, expansive. Dave Miller had the reputation of making a wonderful host—while Ira, people said, could put a damper on any gathering.

"Well, mama," he asked, "do you want me to seat the folks?"

Bertha had the places already fixed, but she stood back, ready to motion anxiously if Dave make any mistakes. The minister was to sit at the other end of the table. Bertha wouldn't take that place; she wanted the chair nearest the kitchen. She hadn't wanted to sit down with the rest, but Dave had issued a flat command. His brother Ira's wife always sat down with company, and he wasn't going to have *his* wife stand up and serve. She put Clarence beside her and said Mrs. Greenwood would want the little girl next to *her*. The children's seats were too low, and Bess ran into the front room for some books. She brought Delight the big dictionary; but Clarence had to sit perched on a pile of sheet music—the Miller household didn't run to books. He was blushing and shy on his perch. Unless he sat still, all that music would slide out from under him.

Dave said in a solemn voice, "Reverend, will you ask the blessing upon our meal?"

The minister rose. Silence came over the group. Heads were bowed—although Edie kept a sharp eye on the food to see whether it was cooling. Clarence felt awed. The minister's lean, vigorous hands were spread open above the table. His wife's downcast face was flushed and her eyes had grown moist with pride. The delicate line of her mouth was unsteady. The minister's voice sounded clear and firm.

"Our Father, we give heartfelt thanks that we can meet at this hospitable table and share with each other the food so abundantly provided in this spot, which we believe to be favored among all the places on earth where mankind has taken up his dwelling. May it be the first gathering of many, as happy as this one today. And may we show our thanks by working together with our best strength to further Thy work and intentions in this new community to which we have come through fortunate circumstances."

The clear sincerity of the voice rang out above the laden table. The words came with peculiar directness. They carried special meaning to the people who heard them. At the end, when Mr. Greenwood said firmly:

"Amen."

Dave Miller echoed loudly and devoutly—alarming his wife, and astonishing the girls and Clarence—

"Ay-men!"

The dinner went off so well that even Edie was satisfied.

"Well, they wouldn't have got a better *meal* at Aunt Belle's, anyway," she said afterwards. "Or at Mrs. Vance's either."

Bertha Miller was amazed to see the minister enjoy his meal. A person who wrote and preached sermons, she supposed, must have a delicate appetite. Food was for those who worked. But there was nothing "delicate" about those extraordinarily clear blue eyes, the keen, ruddy face, the springing step, the vigorous handclasp, the thick hair rising in a crest from a boyish cowlick. Mrs. Greenwood was actually the frail one. But that Bertha took for granted. It was part of her feminine code, long ago ground into the marrow of her being, that female creatures looked out for themselves; if anything ailed them (and something nearly always did, because of the mysterious workings of hidden organs) they belittled and concealed the ailment, and maybe doctored themselves in darkest secrecy. Except among themselves, they must never let on. Today, however, Mrs. Greenwood left the table in a flush of elated well-being.

Dave was ready to take the company at once for a

drive to see the town. But Bertha managed anxiously to put a stop to that. The company had been traveling since early morning; he must let them get a little rest. The minister maybe would like some sleep.

"I? No, I don't need any sleep," Mr. Greenwood said. He would read—that was the best rest he could have. But he thought Alice and Delight ought to lie down for a little while. He didn't want Alice to get too tired.

Dave said the womenfolks could go upstairs and make themselves comfortable, "and you'll have the parlor to yourself, Reverend. Clarence," he ordered, "you clear out now."

The girls anxiously brought Mr. Greenwood what reading matter they could scare up. He didn't notice what they were about, until Bess spoke to him diffidently.

"I don't know whether you'll find anything here, Reverend Greenwood. We don't have so awfully much. I guess our family aren't readers."

"What's that?" he demanded. "Oh, I've got something of my own right here. You girls just go on and forget about me. *I* don't need any waiting on," he told her.

He pulled out of his pocket the small edition of Aristotle that his friend Judge Lewis had given him before he left Ballard. He had not had the advantage of reading these things in college—one year in a small denominational school, and a few terms of Teacher's Institute, were all he'd been able to get in the way of formal education. But he was trying to catch up as he went along. Although, to him, nothing equaled or came near the New Testament, yet a glitter of cold pure light surrounded "the classics" in his imagination. The warmth and shiny newness, the homeliness of the Miller household, with good smells of dinner still in the hot, dry, prairie air, made this coldness more remote and intellectually exhilarating. He had the gift of detaching himself from surroundings. The Miller girls were awed when they peeked into the front room and saw, outlined against the plate-glass windowlight, Mr. Greenwood's keen, absorbed, totally un-self-conscious profile.

"What's he reading, Bess?"

Bess whispered, "I don't know. Something he brought along."

There was an exciting session in the kitchen. The girls discussed the company while they were washing dishes. Their mother had been ordered not to help; but by various pretexts—that she must put away the food, and then that she must clean up the stove before whatever had been spilled on it got hardened—she managed to keep busy in the kitchen for as long as the girls were there.

Bess said he was even nicer than they'd thought he was when he'd preached here—the minister, she meant. There was something—she felt that she couldn't express it, but she knew what it was just the same: different from anybody else she'd ever known.

But *she* was nice, too. Even nicer than they'd imagined! It was going to be wonderful to have a minister's wife like this, sweet and pretty and young, after all those years of Miss Hannah Barbour poking her nose into the young peoples' concerns!

The girls chattered, although in lowered voices, as Bess washed, Irene wiped, and Edie flew around putting the dishes away—she didn't trust the others to do that, declared that after Bess or Irene got through nobody could find anything for a week.

"Do it yourself then. We don't object."

Edie was in high spirits, however. She said *now* the Methodists were going to have a run for their money!

"They've always thought they could crow over us. Well, they won't be able to do it any longer. Our minister's wife has theirs beat a mile. I don't care what anyone says."

"She has trouble with her digestion. She asked me for some hot water before she went upstairs."

"Oh, mama!" Irene said. "If that isn't *you*."

They talked about the little girl. Bess thought she was perfectly dear. Not exactly pretty—her features weren't exactly pretty—but there was something so *unusual* about her. Edie agreed with enthusiasm, but Irene was a trifle cool. Her sisters had often observed, Irene was critical of the looks of all other feminine beings, even six year olds, mentally holding up their charms against her own immaculate prettiness. She had a distaste for anything odd. And there was something, not exactly odd but, as Bess said, unusual about this child—the way her eyes were set, that look of eagerness, the color that came and went in her cheeks, her wonderful hair.

Bertha chimed in with Irene. "I should think that hair would take all her strength."

"Why, mama, her hair is lovely!"

"Ja," Bertha sighed, "but it's so long."

She thought the little girl might be spoiled—the only one.

"Mama thinks all only children are spoiled, because Merrill is."

"*He* isn't an only child. What's the matter with you?"

"Well, he's an only son," Irene said. "That's worse."

"So's Clarence an only son."

"Yes, but he hasn't got Aunt Belle for a mother."

"No, I don't," Bertha protested belatedly. She always protested any accusations in regard to her feelings toward "the other family"—but weakly, knowing in her heart they were true.

Clarence had been listening eagerly. Edie kept telling him impatiently not to get in the way. But the girls were used to his hanging around. At night, if the girls were talking, he would come into their bedroom, barefooted, in his skimpy nightshirt, plaintively demanding, "Girls, what are you talking about?" Bess was such a softy, she would always let him stay.

He listened to them now, with a queer sensation of some wonderful happiness swelling bigger and bigger. Something new had come into the life of the place—a brighter element. All at once he felt that he had to be by himself, just as this morning, when he had run and hidden among the sunflowers. Although he had scarcely been able to look at the little girl all through dinner, he knew now what she was like. His mind flashed with bright images. He had never cared about any little girl before. He had always said that he was going to marry Bess.

He ran out into the yard, and kicked at the brown-painted tile in which petunias were planted. The little girl was here, in their own house. Her sailor hat was hanging by the elastic from their hall tree. He was the first one in Sunday School to get to know her. The heat of the air, the colors of the petunias, the white paint of the house—all suddenly hurt with brightness.

He took refuge in the barn, pressing his face against the rough board wall, listening to old Mollie crunching oats in her stall.

Clarence was afraid the grown folks would forget about the drive; either that, or there wouldn't be room for him in the buggy. But it all turned out exactly right. The company came downstairs refreshed and ready. The carriage had plenty of room. Mr. Greenwood was to sit in front and hold Delight on his lap. Then Clarence could sit between the two ladies. Clarence blushed, but only because Mrs. Greenwood was company. He was still innocently accustomed to being herded along with the womenfolks. Delight sat up proudly on her father's knees. Her eyes were brighter than ever since her nap and the wild-rose color stained her cheeks. Her long fair hair had been freshly braided.

The driving was better now than if they'd gone right after dinner. The sun was not so hot, the scrubby trees cast longer shadows, a breeze stirred the dry, intense stillness of the summer air.

Dave took up the reins, ready to give a slap on Mollie's back, while Bertha breathed, "Oh, Mister, be careful!" Clarence always sat primed for this moment, half scared and half proud, knowing that Mollie would settle at once into her customary amble.

Dave shouted, "Now folks, you're going to see a fine little town. The best on earth."

Clarence believed that with utter trustfulness. He always listened and drank in his father's praise of the town in which they lived. But today there was that new brightness over everything.

They would drive through the main residence portion first: all this portion that lay up on the hill. Their own long street sloped down to the bridge across which was the lot where the church and parsonage stood. But the best residences were nearly all on this side. Dave pointed out the houses of leading church members and of other important citizens: The Stiles house, directly across from his own— that was where Mr. Greenwood had been entertained on his earlier visit; the Willis Vance house, with its shingled tower —"Some of our very best members," Dave said; "that wing is where her father lives, a fine old gentleman"; the Harry Harper place, all balconies and porches, and with a conservatory—"they should attend, but they don't; maybe you can persuade them" ("Ja, nobody's going to persuade *her,*" Bertha murmured); and then the Ira Miller place. All the houses were frame and had an air of newness. The Vance and the Murdock houses had been the earliest built. Willis Vance and H. C. Murdock had been the first to move in from the old community. But it was hard to believe that the town of New Hope had been in existence for not much more than fifteen years.

It looked pretty different today, though—Dave Miller exulted—from what it had when he and his brother Ira first landed about fifteen years back. He said it seemed longer ago than that! He'd watched all of these houses go up—and about every other building. You wouldn't believe any town could make so much progress in so short a time! When he first came there wasn't anything but just the railroad. Miller Brothers was the first store. They'd run the store for a while, and then gone into the banking business; it was evident the town was in need of a bank. Well, the railroad had picked a good spot for a town to flourish.

"And we're just at the beginning," Dave said, with a large gesture.

Clarence heard all this, and had heard it before, but he couldn't really believe there was ever a day when New Hope hadn't been here. It seemed to have been established since the beginning of time.

He listened eagerly, though, while his father pointed out the new buildings and told where others were to stand. The schoolhouse wasn't much, Dave admitted; well, they'd needed a school right away and there hadn't been time to think of trimmings. A new stone schoolhouse would be the next thing on the program. This building was already filled to overflowing, he explained with pride: Clarence and Delight would have to go to primary in the Methodist church basement, when they started in this fall. The principal was a fine young man—too bad he was a Methodist, but the Methodists had to have some of the offices. "We've got the bank, and the newspaper, and the lumberyard, and the railroad station, and several of the stores. Can't ask for everything." Oh, Dave went on with booming confidence, 'twouldn't be long before New Hope had all the works. The town had already overtaken all the others around here. It ought to be the county seat. (Clarence nodded his head with great indignation.) It was a shame to have the courthouse located away off there in Fox Center that wasn't a center at all—just a slowpoke town that had already seen its best days, didn't have anything like the same growth ahead of it. But those old settlers thought the county belonged to them.

Everywhere building was going on. Everywhere was that same smell, raw and fresh, from weedy lots and new-cut lumber.

They drove over the rumbling bridge that separated the hill from the business section. New Hope had no river, only Dry Creek. The river was a mile away, marking the boundary between this state and Dakota. Over in Dakota, there wasn't anything, Clarence thought. Why should any folks want to move over to Dakota? he'd heard his father say— and not only his father, other people too, Mrs. Stiles and Mr. Vance and Cass Story. He pictured all of Dakota as vacant country with maybe one little old shack . . . His father was saying now there was no disadvantage. What good did a river do a town? New Hope had all the water it needed. A few miles northeast, on the Rundle farm, there was a large pond, a small lake almost, that some day might be developed. The old man Rundle wouldn't let anybody get a smell of it now; but he wouldn't live forever, even if it did look as if that was about what he intended. "I'm keeping my eye on that place," Dave said, "right along." If New Hope had a lake and fine woods in its vicinity, he didn't see what more could be asked. Meanwhile, they'd get along with good old Dry Creek—the kids got a lot of enjoyment out of it, anyway.

Even that sluggish summer stream, flowing shallow and all to one side, had a fine fresh glitter as Clarence looked down at it.

Now they were across the bridge and coming to the

church and parsonage. The two buildings were counted as really belonging to the hill even if they were on the other side of the Creek. Mrs. Greenwood leaned out of the buggy, and Delight stood up to see the house where they were going to live. But they mustn't stop now, Dave said. Let the womenfolks get the place fixed up first. Nothing to see in an empty house.

"Ja, nothing for *you* to see," Bertha told him. But he didn't care to hear that. He never heard his wife's mutterings unless he wanted to—nor did Bertha expect them to be heard: they were uttered only as a dark female commentary upon the sanguine big talk of the menfolks.

Mrs. Greenwood had to be content with this first bare glimpse of her house. Dave was heading straight for Main Street. He didn't know whether he was more anxious to show off the town to the new arrivals or to show *them* off to the town!

"Here's our building!" he announced proudly. Mollie had stopped of her own accord in front of the bank. The folks must come in, Dave said, and meet his brother Ira. "Lots of Millers you haven't seen yet," he added to Mrs. Greenwood. "They'll all be on hand Sunday, though. You'll meet the whole tribe."

Clarence swelled with pride as his father led the way into the bank. It was the best red sandstone building in town: the finest material to be had. He was certain there was no such building anywhere, even in Horton.

Uncle Ira and Merrill were behind the shiny counter. Uncle Ira came out through his little gate. Although the Miller brothers had been only a few years in banking, Ira was beginning to hold the chief place here while Dave's interests were spreading out in all sorts of directions. It was a common saying that the two of them were about as unlike as brothers could be. Dave was stock and ruddy, Ira tall and spare, looking like—folks said—the typical Yankee.

The Millers were not Yankee stock, however, but came of the mixed strains even more common in this Western region: the father "oh, just American, I guess," as Dave had once said vaguely, and the mother of Pennsylvania Dutch origin. Dave and Ira had come to New Hope from Cylinder, a town in the next county east, having seen their opportunity here —so Dave always told the story. Later they had persuaded their youngest brother Andy to come out too and take up farming. The other brother, Albert, was still operating the family farm in Illinois and wouldn't listen to any glowing accounts. The old folks had been dead for some years. Two uncles, two uncles' wives, and two cousins were the only relations that Clarence knew. His mother, when she and his father got married, was an orphan.

Dave cried, "Well, Merrill, what are you so bashful about?"

Clarence's cousin Merrill, who was about Irene's age, was helping in the bank this summer—not entirely to Dave's satisfaction, either, for he foresaw that the Iras were, as he called it, pushing Merrill into the bank, and that when Clarence came along there wouldn't be a place for him. Clarence might not want to be a banker, of course; and Dave always said his children were to choose, he wasn't going to stick 'em in where they didn't want to go. Clarence didn't know yet whether he intended to be a printer like Lute Fairbrother or a farmer like his Uncle Andy. Or he might belong to a circus, like Wes Bibbs.

Merrill came through the gate, giving it a light, easy swing. Dave regarded his nephew with admiration and jealousy mixed—not that Merrill in any way had it over his girls, but he couldn't be so sure in regard to Clarence, although he wouldn't openly admit that. Clarence looked up to Merrill, and didn't look up to him; the girls said Merrill was conceited, but Clarence admired all the big crowd. Now Dave said to Delight, half teasing and half proud:

"Isn't this a pretty handsome young man?"

The little girl stared up at Merrill with intent bright eyes. "Yes, he's *very* handsome," she then said gravely.

The older people laughed. Even Ira's drab face brightened at this praise of his son. Merrill was used to approval, he could carry it off; he had none of the hangback bashfulness that so disturbed Dave in his own boy. Merrill showed his fine teeth in a handsome smile.

"You think he ought to have no trouble getting a girl, then?" Dave asked.

Delight shook her head.

"I'll take *you* for my girl," Merrill told the little girl, laughing.

But she wouldn't have that. She shook her head emphatically; and stepping back, with gracious but imperious confidence she took Clarence's hand.

"I knew this little boy first," she said. "We're going to play together. We're just about of a size."

Clarence's pride, satisfaction, bashfulness, were agonizing. He heard the approving laughter of the older people. His hand was limp in that small confident clasp. But this was something he had known before, although it took him so by surprise—he couldn't have explained the way he felt about it.

Dave cried in high glee, "Merrill, that's one on you!"

But there was more to be seen; they couldn't spend all their time at the bank. They wouldn't stop in at any of the business houses now—the fact was, Dave didn't mind keeping his guests to himself this first day. But he did give the children a nickel each, and stopped the buggy while they went into Donohue's to buy some candy. The Donohue store had been Miller Brothers first.

"My papa used to own this place," Clarence told Delight. Those were the first words he had addressed to her.

Then they must drive out past the new reservoir. It

would be no time before New Hope got all cement sidewalks as well as electric lights and city water; it had been
the first town in the county to put in city water. "But we
can get things done here," Dave said, "as long as we all pull
together." Some folks hadn't made use of the water works,
they still used their pumps. But the pipes would be extended
to every part of town.

They must take a look at the cemetery, which had a fine
location up on the hill. Didn't have much population as yet,
Dave said, but he supposed they'd have to look forward to
the cemetery growing right along with the town! Folks had
bought their lots, and they were getting the place fixed up
and ready. "Oh, Mister, don't joke," Bertha mourned. "It'll
fill up soon enough a'ready."

Even the cemetery looked new, bright, fresh, with its
few clean, shining granite stones. There wasn't even a Civil
War monument, the town was so young; although a few of
its older citizens had fought in the Civil War, John Budd
and Horace Livermore. Decoration Day exercises were held
in town, in the City Hall—there were so few soldiers' graves
on which to put flowers. Young trees had been planted, and
snowball bushes. There was a sunny freshness about this high
airy spot. . .

Dave wanted to take the folks on up to the edge of the
bluff where they could look over into Dakota; but he agreed
to reserve that for another day. The sun was getting lower.
The buildings cast long, unobstructed shadows.

When they stopped at the house Clarence got out and
ran around to the back door again. He still felt so excited,
elated, that he didn't know what to do with himself. He
wanted Bess to know how the little girl had taken hold of
his hand, but he dreaded to have anybody tell about it. He
would beg the folks not to tell. The whole town beyond
the hill was touched with brightness.

Ashamed, but unable to keep from doing it, Clarence

stopped on the back porch and stuffed down two big gum-
drops. He sweated for a moment for fear they'd got stuck
in his throat and he would choke to death. Then he gave a
huge swallow and the sticky lumps went down. He had
saved a beautiful big red gumdrop for Bess, a not quite so
pretty orange one for Irene, and nothing but a plain white
one for that old Edie—he was still mad at her because she
hadn't wanted him to go down to the train.

Mrs. Dave had scurried out at once to the kitchen where
she and Bess held a consultation.

"Do you think we ought to send Clarence downtown
for anything?"

Clarence heard that and hastened to make himself
scarce.

He went and stood in the parlor doorway. Shy as he
was, he couldn't keep far away from the company.

"Come on in here," his father said. "You don't have to
be scared."

Clarence with head hanging, went into the room.

"When is your birthday, Clarence?" Mrs. Greenwood
asked him.

"June the eleven," he answered shyly.

Delight jumped off the rocker of her father's chair. Her
cheeks burned pink. She cried, "That's almost just exactly
the same as mine is! Isn't it, mama? Mine's June the twelfth.
We're almost twins!"

She went dancing through the rooms, singing out that
they were almost twins. "We're almost twins, Edie! Clarence and I are almost twins!" she cried out to Edie who had
come to see what all the excitement was about.

Now everybody said they must see how the twins meas-
ured. They must stand back to back. Delight stood up
proudly, making herself as tall as she could. Clarence tried
to do the same. The erect little back pressed against his. He

could feel the long braids. Clarence felt something ineffable
—a pride that seemed to put him straight in his place in the
world.

The children were nearly of a size, the grown people
were exclaiming. But Clarence was taller!—just a speck
taller. Clarence felt a warm diffusion of triumph. The
agony of his bashfulness dissolved. They were almost twins.
They would play together. But he was one day older than
Delight and a speck taller! He was ready to begin playing
right now.

Bess had come, however, to call them all to supper. The
dining-room windows faced east. The western windows in
the sitting room were shining. The light was clear above the
plants on their stand in the bay window.

Clarence felt happier than ever in his life. Happier even
than if he'd had his pony. The older people were exclaiming
that they didn't see how they could eat after that wonderful
dinner. But the cold chicken, hot biscuits, fresh tomatoes,
cottage cheese, and jelly all looked delicious. Clarence went
over and whispered something to Bess. She smiled and spoke
to her father.

"So that's it!" Dave said in great good humor.

Clarence hid his face. He wanted to sit next to the little
girl. That was what he had whispered to Bess. His mother
was shocked at his boldness but the others were pleased. One
on the dictionary, one on the slippery pile of music, the children ate their supper sitting side by side in the light of the
summer evening.

CHAPTER II

The Church

SUNDAY MORNING BREAKFAST at the Dave Miller house was ordinarily a somewhat messy affair. The girls took pleasure in slopping around in their very worst clothes. Their father declared they wanted to see how homely they could make themselves before putting on their war paint and fooling folks into considering them good-looking.

But on this Sunday morning all that was changed. The girls wore starched summer skirts and clean shirtwaists. The cleanly smell of freshly ironed clothes added to the sense of expectancy that surrounded the breakfast table.

The Millers had talked things over beforehand. They were not quite sure how they ought to act. Maybe they would be expected to serve the minister his meal by himself. But he laughed at the idea of any special fuss being made.

To everyone's relief, Mr. Greenwood seemed just as usual at the table. The only thing that gave him away was the preoccupied look in his eyes. Bertha, sitting on the edge of her chair ready to get up and wait on folks if need be— Mister made her take a seat at the table—had noted those eyes with a mixture of minute curiosity and of awe. They were set keen and deep, and they had in them a peculiar bright intellectual impersonality. That clear, piercing, yet guileless gaze—blue as the cloudless sky—touched Bertha Miller with wonder, making her feel humbled but uplifted. Judge Lewis, a friend of the Greenwoods in the town where they had been living, had given the best description: Mrs. Greenwood told the Millers about it later. He said that William Greenwood had "the eyes of an innocent eagle."

Dave was the most nervous of anybody at the table. More depended upon this first church service than the minister himself understood; and the new minister was Dave's own man. He was the choice of the newer element against the older element. A somewhat peculiar situation existed in the church at New Hope—at least the members regarded it as peculiar. The membership was made up, first of the members of the "original church," who had moved in from the old community, and next of those who had come flocking to New Hope from elsewhere. That had meant some division from the very start. The Millers, of course, belonged to the new element: *were* the new element to a certain extent. Many candidates had come, when the pulpit was open; but Mr. Greenwood was the one on whom all could unite. Some couldn't, some could never give up: the real old-timers, like the Budds and the Livermores. But the more forward-looking—as Dave always said—among the folks from the old community, the Stileses, the Murdocks, the Vances, and Mrs. Vance's father—all these were enthusiastic about what the new minister could do. To have won Electa Stiles was almost enough—she was a legion in herself.

Dave had more personal reasons, as well. He believed that now was the time, if ever, to cut loose from the hold of the old community—a strangle hold, he thought it had 'been at times. Now their church, going ahead united, would assume a leading part in the life of the town. Dave had talked about these things so much and so often, with such faith and enthusiasm, that even Clarence had a childish understanding of them.

Church was held at ten-thirty, Sunday School was called at half past eleven. But today they must be there early —no easy thing for the Dave Millers! As soon as breakfast was over, all scattered to get ready.

The parlor had been made over to Mr. Greenwood for a study. The Millers stood in awe of its closed doors.

Dave warned the girls, "Now you see to it that you make as little clatter as you can. He's looking over his sermon."

That made Edie fume. "Why doesn't papa tell himself to keep quiet? He makes more racket than all the rest of us combined."

But this morning the scurrying around was hushed and breathless. The girls all shared the same large bedroom. It was directly above the sitting room, and also had the bay window, around the length of which ran the window seat. The seat and the chairs were piled high with clean summer clothes. There was scarcely room to step about in the place.

Irene had been commissioned to see that mama got ready. "My getting dressed don't take me long," Bertha protested. The girls were the ones. But she knew she must pass their inspection. So she submitted to having her hair curled on the iron. "Now, mama," Irene said, "hold still or I'll burn you." Bertha was obsessed with the notion that her best clothes were too good to be worn, except on occasions that never came; and that terribly distressed the girls. But today *was* an occasion. And she wouldn't have the excuse of dinner to get, for they were all invited over to the other house. Her best shoes hurt her bunions, but the girls made her wear them just the same.

"It don't matter how I look. Nobody'll be looking at me."

"They'll look at you just as much as they will at Aunt Belle or anybody. Mama, please now, you've just got to hold still."

Since none of the girls seemed to be on hand—and never were when they were wanted!—Dave had taken it upon himself to get Clarence scrubbed at the kitchen sink. It was a thorough process! Now Clarence, red and skinned-looking, with hair plastered, scuttled up the back stairs almost on hands and knees. He burst into the girl's room demanding:

"You have to dress me right away, papa says so."

Edie cried, "Pugh, smell those shoes!" Clarence had tried to do his own shoe-blacking. "Nobody'll want to sit in the seat with you."

Bess gave Edie a warning look. "They'll be all right," she assured Clarence. She rubbed the shoes with an old handkerchief, saying the fresh air would do the rest. Then she told Clarence to go on down now.

The company had been getting ready in the front bedroom. The minister had dressed first, so that he could go down and give one more glance at his sermon.

Now Delight came running, dancing downstairs.

"See my fan, Uncle Dave!" she cried out eagerly. "Look, Aunt Bertha, see my fan. See my best dress with embroidery. I've got my hair hanging."

Dave said, "Well, sir, you're the finest girl I ever saw." He asked, "Don't she look pretty fine, mama?"—and Bertha had to admit she did. Her mother had washed the child's hair yesterday morning—the Miller girls watching and exclaiming—and had braided it in ten tight pigtails at night. This morning it had been combed out, wavy and shining, a wonderful light-gold mass and thickness, hanging far below her waist. Bertha, in spite of fears about such hair using up strength, couldn't keep her eyes from it; while noting at the same time the fine embroidery on the dress, figuring up the hours the mother must have put upon it, wondering if those white kid slippers looked too much like a party. Some of the real old-timers—such as old Mother Livermore—might object.

But even Bertha couldn't dash such radiant enjoyment. And there wasn't any real vanity about it, either. Delight was always dancing, always hither and yon—she didn't have time to be vain!

She had to tell Uncle Dave and Aunt Bertha—they were already aunt and uncle—about her fan. It was a miniature affair of ivory and gauze hand-painted with for-get-me-nots, and she wore it around her neck on a long, fine silver chain. Judge Lewis had given it to her for a present just before she left Ballard. She said her Aunt Marian had given her the white slippers—"Not really my aunt, just like you, Aunt Bertha, but she's mother's very best friend, and she calls me her little girl"; Aunt Marian had given mother her real amber beads.

The Miller girls were crazy over the fan and those white slippers. Clarence was so impressed that for a while he couldn't look at Delight. It was almost as bad as when she'd first arrived. But it didn't take him long, this time, to get over it.

The iron clangor of church bells sounded through the Sunday streets.

"Listen to that old Methodist bell," Edie grumbled. "It makes such a racket you can't hear ours. They always begin ringing it sooner too. They're smart over there!"

But it stopped; and then they could hear the somewhat higher, thinner clang-clang of the bell from their own wooden tower.

The group had assembled now in the front hall. Mr. Greenwood came out of the sacred precincts of the parlor carrying his sermon and his pastor's handbook. He looked fresh-faced and clean-cut in his Sunday black-and-white. He hated to wear clothes that set him off from other people; refused to wear a really long coat; the white vest was bad enough. Why should he dress himself up to be different from others? he always demanded: that wouldn't change his sermon, or make him anything but what he was. The Millers, however, were proud of his appearance. And Edie was so crazy over Mrs. Greenwood, looking fine and flushed in her thin, stiff-starched garments, that Edie said, "I have to hug you, I don't care if I *do* muss your dress."

The carriage wouldn't hold them all, so it had been agreed that the girls and the children should walk. The children had better start first, since it might take them a little longer.

Delight was ready. She cried, "Come on, Clarence— come on, let's you and me walk together." Confidingly, she took his hand.

The older people smiled, watching those two. They looked small and brave, comical and touching, setting off together down the long boardwalk in the hot July sunshine. They kept their pennies squeezed tightly in their hands. Delight's fan on its long fine chain bumped against her knees as she walked. She switched her starched embroidered skirts. Even on Sunday those little feet could scarcely keep from dancing. But she was careful of her white slippers, going on tiptoe over the crossings. "Look at Clarence!" the girls said —and giggled. With his ears scrubbed red, his biggest ruffled collar, and those awful Sunday shoes that smelled to the skies! But he was walking along just as proudly, eager to show off Delight to the other children. There was a childish innocence in the devotion of the little couple, a pristine quality, that strangely affected the older people watching them. Edie actually had tears in her eyes. But the older people were afraid to call attention or to make any comment. Better leave it just as it was.

The two children reached the church ahead of the older people. The frame building, painted tan and brown, raised its steeple sharply into the turquoise blue sky. On the further side, and down the slope, stood the one-story parsonage painted in the same colors: the house where Delight was going to live.

A number of teams were already there, some in front, some fastened to the hitching boards along the west side. Boys and girls had gathered near the church. When Clarence came up with the new little girl, they silently gave way.

The two children went into the church. Everything seemed different on this first Sunday. The Young Ladies' Society had spent all yesterday afternoon decorating the room, and now the smell of plants and July flowers was diffused through the waiting air. The big room was already partly filled with people. The confident curve of Delight's pink lips trembled into pathetic uncertainty. She slipped her hand into Clarence's again, this time for comfort. They were to wait in the entry until their parents came. Clarence was more proud than he was scared. He had never felt so big and proud in his life.

Now the Dave Miller carriage drew up in front of the church. The minister would enter by his own door, which led into the small vestry room—Bess, too, since she belonged to the choir. The others came up the front steps. All eyes were on them as they entered, Dave red-faced with anxious importance, Bertha with eyes downcast, Edie looking somewhat defiant; Irene, cool and pretty, gave away nothing. Many in the congregation had not had a look at the minister's family until this morning. Now was their chance.

Early as it still was, the church was filling up fast. On such a fine day people ought all to be able to get in from the country. Teams were now thick around the building—some had to be tied even as far away as Main Street. Two ushers were ordinarily enough, Merrill Miller and Dean Robinson. But today a group of young men had been pressed into service. Smiling, heated, with collars wilting, they were all kept busy. The auditorium, it was soon apparent, wouldn't seat this crowd. The tall doors into the primary room were opened, and folding chairs were placed in there. Even so, by the time the service started, latecomers had to stand outside on the porch and on the steps.

"An awful lot of folks out today," Dave whispered loudly, leaning across Bertha to speak to Mrs. Greenwood. "Looks like everybody's here."

If he had sat next to the minister's wife he would have told her about people in the congregation. Bertha might whisper a few names, but that would be all. It was good to see so many out. Folks seemed to realize how much hung upon this occasion. Dave felt a personal anxiety and took a personal pride. The Iras, always ahead of time, were settled in their usual place. Belle leaned forward, smiled, and nodded. Large-bosomed, confidently assured, in her well-trimmed hat and rustling summer clothes, Dave's brother's wife was in notable contrast to his own. Bertha's hands, with the knuckles enlarged from early hard work, were folded in her lap like those of some old peasant woman. The Andys were here, too, but Dave couldn't catch Andy's eye. Neither Andy nor Mary would be caught stealing a glance at the newcomers. They were too self-conscious and too shy—and anyway they were what Dave called "funny" about all such things. Andy, for example, thought there was no place like the farm he'd taken up and was working, but you'd never know it from what *he* said; or from what Mary said, either.

Dave noted triumphantly that the Budds were here in spite of all their complaints. Couldn't stand it to remain away. He had to poke Bertha, and whisper to her to tell Mrs. Greenwood where the Budds were sitting. Old John Budd pulled gloomily at his beard. None of the Harpers

seemed to be present. That was to be expected, however—
and they were about the only ones!

The other members, the good, solid, reliable members,
were certainly out in force: the Vances, the Wrights, the
two Murdock families, the H. C.'s and the A. D.'s. The
Stileses were sitting well toward the front, a striking couple:
he with his impassive hunter's look that Cass Story said made
him resemble Daniel Boone or Leather Stocking; she tall and
upright, very New England, with bright resolute eyes. Dave
did want Mrs. Greenwood to notice old Mr. Broadwater,
Mrs. Vance's father: the fine-looking old gentleman in the
Prince Albert coat, Dave whispered; wears the only plug hat
in town; always puts it down underneath the pew—"you'll
notice that's where he's putting it right now." The other
man wearing a frock coat was Cass Story, editor of the New
Hope *Citizen,* and one of the strongest members. But Mrs.
Greenwood had met the Storys.

Grandma Story, in her little bonnet, with its fresh lawn
ties and its nodding blossoms, was one of the most beloved
persons in town. She wasn't with the family, however, but
was seated in the pew directly in front of the pulpit that
was reserved for the hard of hearing. Even the old people
were out today. But in general—as the new minister's wife
could see, and as she mentioned later—this was a congregation of young people. The town was too new for its early
settlers to have grown old. The few aged held the status of
relatives: they were Mrs. Murdock's Uncle Rob, old Mother
Livermore, Grandma Story. There were many children. The
atmosphere, Mrs. Greenwood could feel—and she spoke of
this too—was quite different from that of the faded church
on the shady side street in Ballard, the small rural town
where the Greenwoods had been living. This church, with its
plain furnishings, its uncolored windows, was bare. But the
bareness was redeemed by the exciting atmosphere of youth,
of communal fellowship, and of faith in achievement.

The people in the congregation had their eyes upon the newcomers—as Mrs. Greenwood was well aware.

"Mama," Delight breathed, "are you scared?"

"Sh!" she gave the little girl's hand a quick pressure.

"Papa isn't scared, though, is he?" Delight whispered trustingly.

"No, of course papa isn't."

The little girl's bright eyes were fixed upon the empty pulpit chair behind the blooming bank of flowers. As soon as her father stepped into the pulpit, everything would be right. Her faith was unlimited; her bright confidence shone in her face. Now, seeing the ladies take up drugstore souvenir fans from the hymnbook holders, Delight opened her own pretty miniature and began to fan herself with eager self-possession. People noticed and had to smile.

Bertha had heard the whispers between the two, the mother and child. Bertha could see that Mrs. Greenwood was very nervous. She breathed quickly, so that her amber beads moved slightly against the crisply ironed lace of her yoke. The palms of her hands were wet in their thin silk gloves. But her eyes too, although so anxious, were confident. She had faith in her husband. She expected him to do well. She thinks everything of those two, was what Bertha thought— what she had already said several times to Bess and Edie; she thinks the sun rises and sets in him and in the little girl.

The last bell rang, loud, hard, and close at hand.

A solemn expectancy was everywhere felt as the time came for the opening of the service. People moved in their seats. Dave Miller loudly cleared his throat. Clarence felt this atmosphere of waiting. He stared around him. The flowers bloomed in the hot stillness around the empty platform.

Dora Palmer, the organist, came out from the vestry room, looking very nice in white organdie, with her braids of fair hair wound smoothly around her head. Dora never did her hair any other way. She took her place on the bench, with her back to the audience, manipulated the stops that Clarence always regarded with great curiosity and longed to monkey with himself, and began to play. She had chosen Schubert's "Hark! Hark! the Lark." The joyous burst of music suited the summer morning; it gave the service its background. But people were too excited to listen much.

The choir members filed into the loft and took their places behind the low railing. Bess, soft and smiling, was among the altos. Franklin Story had left his post as usher and joined the choir. He had a fine tenor voice that would be greatly missed when he went back to college in the fall.

The minister stepped briskly in from the vestry room. He parted his coattails—he hated those coattails!—and sat down in the tall pulpit chair.

Mrs. Greenwood's eyes grew blurred. A pulse beat in her neck, under the lace-edged collar of her starched dress. Then her sight cleared.

The minister was looking out over the congregation. His own natural self-possession put everyone else at ease. But even while gazing directly at the people, there was that crystalline blue distance in his eyes. Delight smiled up at her father in confident pride. But his wife moved uneasily. She felt his remoteness. She had confided to Bess Miller that when her husband was in the pulpit she felt humble. For he really was different from most men, so she believed—in his unworldliness that yet was salted with good sense and good judgment, his intellectual and spiritual ardor, the simplicity and loftiness together which so strangely marked him. It seemed to her that everyone must feel that. Bess did feel it, of course. Bess fervently agreed.

Dora finished the prelude. The minister stepped forward.

"Let us unite in singing the Doxology."

With great rustling and scraping, the congregation rose

—all but Grandma Story who, tremulous and frail, remained devoutly, smilingly, in her place.

"Praise God, from whom all blessings flow!
Praise Him, all creatures here below!"

The familiar music had new volume and meaning sung today by this large congregation. It overflowed the room, sounding through open doors and windows, and was heard far out upon the streets—the almost empty Sunday streets of the town, small and raw in the midst of the great countryside, where the corn was ripening, where late summer wildflowers grew ragged and thick along the dusty country roads. Mrs. Stiles sang with strict ardor, her head proudly lifted. John Budd could be seen to move his dour lips with the music but he could not bring himself to sing. The minister's clear, strong tenor could be heard throughout. People standing outside joined in, not needing their hymnbooks. The horses switched their tails, under the biting of the flies and the burning of the sunshine.

The congregation took seats again. The service went on simply and without innovations. Dave Miller had thought some striking change should be introduced; but the minister hadn't wanted that. It would rile up the old-timers, he said to Dave, and do no particular good. No, all he cared to do was get rid of a few embellishments. What he asked of his services was to strip them to the core. Yet he didn't want too bleak an austerity. Although he had chosen to preach in the Puritan church—he had left the church of his immigrant parents, and made his own choice—it was not for the old stern theology: rather for its simplicity, its freedom and community of action. The Puritan faith of New England, carried westward, had lost the narrow stringency of the mountain valleys and become diffused with the open prairie light.

That day there seemed significance in every part of the

service: in the duet that Bess and Franklin sang, standing together, sharing their music, representing the finest of the
young people; even in the offering, heartily responded to
with the feeling that this marked the beginning of a new
day. All seemed invigorated by the minister's clean energy,
his lean, youthful figure, the force of his gestures, his voice,
his sincerity.

His wife smiled at his terseness. He wasted few words.
Judge Lewis had said that to hear William Greenwood was
an intellectual joy, for when he had finished, he stopped.
And that from the Judge, who loved the grand manner, the
flourishes of old Virginian oratory! Let us give our morning
offering. Let us unite in prayer. Let us stand and be dismissed.
Everything was contained in that opening phrase of union
with his congregation: Let us. He was their leader, not because he was put over them, but because they had selected
him. He took no other authority.

His vigorous voice in prayer, in the firm self-respecting
tones in which he addressed even deity, rang out over the
bowed heads. A hymn followed. Then came the sermon.

The minister took his time. But it was only to make sure
of the attention of his audience. There was no play acting
about him: people could see that. He was too direct, too
essentially single-minded. His face had its firm keen look.
His hand was steady as he opened the large Bible upon the
pulpit stand. He began with that same directness, looking
straight at, and beyond, his congregation, with his gaze of
crystalline clarity.

"I take my text from the words of Jesus, to be found
in the New Testament, in the third chapter of the Gospel
according to John, the nineteenth verse: 'Light is come into
the world.'"

The house was still from the opening sentence, held by
that authority which sometimes—but rarely!—takes a

listening audience when the speaker is in full possession and has reached the center of his theme.

"To be found in the New Testament." That sounded the new note. That marked the difference in the preaching they would hear now from the doctrine they had been listening to, carried over from the original church in the old community. People sensed now, and came to know better, how characteristic was that phrase. This was what Mr. Greenwood would stand for in his preaching: for the New Testament, its brightness of hope, its promise of new life, its creative spirit, turning away from the dark historic involutions of the old books. Often he said to his wife impatiently—and she told it to a few of the others: "I don't care for all those Old Testament kings, don't care about kings anyway, all those wars and battles, and those superstitions. Jesus came into the world to change all that. Why preach them over and over? I intend to skip the lot." It was the New Testament that Mr. Greenwood preached and believed in—the doctrine, not of power and might and darkness, but of goodwill, of love, of communal not tribal effort, and of light, more light. The words sounded with a peculiar relevancy that came home to people, here in the bare frame building in the new town just beginning its growth in the great opening country.

Everyone felt that significant stillness. But the expressions varied. Edie Miller could scarcely contain her pride. Even Ira's face showed a dry satisfaction. John Budd's long countenance was stubbornly impassive. He looked down at his hands, one folded over the other on his bony knee. Mrs. Stiles' sparkling eyes were exultant. James Stiles was listening—a thing that rarely happened. He was accustomed to diverting himself in many ways—by a soundless whistling, a tapping of his knee, finally blowing his nose with a mighty blast. Now his glass eye stared, profoundly vacant, but the other eye was intent. Old Mr. Broadwater leaned forward, his hand cupped at his ear, from which the silvery long hair was pushed back. Mrs. Vance's face was prettily flushed with pleasure. But Dave Miller's ruddy color had paled. He was moved by something beyond expectation.

Clarence sat in awe, his mouth slightly open and his lower lip hanging, his eyes raised to Mr. Greenwood's face. Even to Clarence, the sermon, in its directness and brevity, had meaning. The words sank down into him and through him, although he was too young for realization. He could not have been said to comprehend; but there was something about the words as they were spoken that heightened the sunshine in the dry summer air, that made the country round about still wider and more open, the sky more immense and of a more exultant blue. Delight sat next to him. He saw her lifted profile, confident and eager. Her long hair shimmered in the morning brightness. The children listened together to the minister's clear, firm voice—telling them what this church could be, what the town could be, in the great continent, the new nation "conceived in liberty," in the New World—where all were to share equally in the boundlessness of light and hope.

CHAPTER III

The Town

THE MINISTER'S FAMILY stayed with the Dave Millers for over two weeks. The car with their goods had got sidetracked at the next town of Tucker.

"That railroad, you never can count on it," Bertha sighed.

"Now don't blame the railroad," Dave protested vigorously. "What can you expect of Tucker, a little burg like that? They've got some old jay for a stationmaster. We don't have any such trouble here."

The three girls exchanged glances.

Mrs. Greenwood apologized anxiously for the trouble they must be causing. But Bertha told her, "Ach, if it wasn't you folks it'd be somebody else, and I'd rather it was you."

The Miller house was always full of company. Bertha and the girls never knew whether they would have to feed six, or sixteen. Country people made the house their stopping place, even those who had no special claim on Dave; and he would bring home men with whom he was making some deal. Bertha said, "Ja, I don't know who all—I don't even know their names."

"Yes," Edie sputtered, "and as if that wasn't enough,

entertaining every old Tom, Dick, and Harry that drives into town, we've got all the bums to feed besides!"

Tramps didn't ride even as far as the water tank. They dropped off the freight and cut across lots on a beeline for this house. And that wasn't papa's fault, Edie added. That was mama's.

"Ja, they don't know where to find their food," Bertha murmured. "They ain't got anywhere to look to."

"Well, they get plenty from us!"

There was plenty of food in that house anyway. Such cooking as went on! Every day was baking day. And when the regular baking was done, one of the girls would cry, "Do you know we haven't a bit of candy in this whole house?" There seemed to be always at least one great batch of fudge set out in long baking pans in the back kitchen to cool. All three of the Miller girls were famous fudge makers. "Bess's fudge," "Edie's fudge," "Irene's fudge"— each kind had its defenders among the connoisseurs of the town. Mrs. Greenwood, however, couldn't be prevailed upon to give any opinion; she would only laugh and say, "I like all of them better than is good for me!" She said with some anxiety she never saw the two children when they weren't licking candy spoons.

In the hot summer noons they might all sit down to a table that reached the length of the dining room; and no matter how many extras they'd had during the morning, samples and tastes of this and that, they were ready for the steaming chicken and dumplings or the fine big steak and Bess's great, rich, melting, white coconut cake.

Then in the evenings they would have to finish up with ice cream!

"Run across and get Mr. and Mrs. Stiles," Dave would tell Clarence. "Tell 'em to come over, we've got some *ice cream.*"

If the Stileses weren't at home he would say:

"Then run up to the other house and get the folks."

They tried to eat out on the porch, were driven in by mosquitoes, finished happily and sloppily in the dining room. If any ice cream was left over, somebody had to take it to Dora Palmer and her mother.

Bertha protested, scandalized, "Why, Mister, they'll be gone to bed."

"Get 'em up then. They can sleep any time. Don't make 'em miss their ice cream."

Bertha would never let her company stay and help clean up the table. She made excuses: the water wasn't hot, the girls would see to it, she had to wait up anyway and get her biscuits set. When everybody else was safely upstairs, Bertha would go trudging around the dining room, mopping up little spillings of ice cream on the golden oak.

Everybody else, that is, except Clarence. He stayed down with his mother. He loved to hang around. She liked to have him, too; she liked to have somebody to help her decide what to do with the remains of the cake, whether to keep it or not. "Maybe one of 'them,' " she said, "would eat it," meaning one of the tramps—"mama's old bums," as Edie called them. Clarence was eager to help save some cake for the tramps.

Bertha took off her shoes and padded around in her stocking feet, with a scared glance at the door, not wanting the girls to catch her. Clarence glanced at the door too—in fact, it was all his mother could do to keep him from peeking out. The voices and laughter sounded from the porch or from the lawn swing. Bertha would stand and listen in acute concentration, trying to make out what fellows were with the girls out there. They had so many fellows she couldn't keep track. But she wouldn't look, or let Clarence look; and he was as interested as she was. She listened to the gay sounds, and Clarence heard her sigh, "Ach, ja . . ."

The Millers worried at first because their household might be too noisy for the Greenwoods. The minister might think there was too much going on. But it was soon apparent that he spoke the truth when he said nothing like that ever bothered him. If he wanted to work on his sermons, he would just go upstairs and shut the door.

"Oh, you don't need to worry about Will," Mrs. Greenwood assured them. "The house might burn down and he wouldn't know it until his own clothes caught fire."

She was the one who really might have been worried —by doors banging, voices yelling, stormy duets on the much-abused piano. Bess could see that, and spoke about it. Mrs. Greenwood confessed that she hadn't been quite accustomed to it at first. But now, she said, she was in the swing of it, and enjoying herself completely.

And why not? She hadn't had so much petting and spoiling in years. In Ballard, she confided, there had been so many elderly people that she had grown to feel elderly herself. The Miller girls fussed over her, fastened flowers in her dress, begged to be allowed to comb her hair; and Edie, hugging her, would whisper intensely, "You're too sweet to *live*."

She couldn't understand it. But the others understood it well enough. The girls told her, "You'd know why if you'd ever seen Miss Hannah Barbour!" They wanted to expatiate —Edie particularly—on the subject of Miss Barbour, the spinster sister of the former minister. But Mrs. Greenwood didn't let them say much. She even suggested that they might be a little hard on Miss Barbour. "Girls often are," she said, "when it comes to someone they think of as an old maid." Edie didn't believe so—she wouldn't have that. "Well, she was hard," Edie said, "on all us girls. Always snooping and— oh, well, I guess she's gone now." That last was a great concession for Edie! The other two girls remarked it. But they'd never seen Edie so ready to listen to anyone as to Mrs. Greenwood.

They were all ready to listen to Mrs. Greenwood and to talk to her. They could feel how much she liked and enjoyed them: all their activities, their beaux, their goings-on, their different kinds of prettiness. The Miller girls were the most popular girls in town. Bess was the oldest, tall and full-figured, with brilliant cheeks, and a silky dark mass and fuzz of hair. Edie was small, light-haired and intense; not so attractive as the other two; yet in some ways the stand-by. It was a highly disputed question in New Hope, which was prettier—Bess or Irene. Irene's fair coloring was lovely, her clear features, her immaculate look; like that of a clean, hard, scarcely opened, white-pink rose from the greenhouse. But Bess had a radiant, exuberant bloom.

The girls were excited and subdued by the perception of a different degree of family harmony from any they had ever come in contact with before. There was a delicate intensity in Alice Greenwood; her everyday life seemed to be lived in another, more shining dimension. The girls talked about it. They disagreed on just what it was. Edie cried:

"Well, I don't care, when I get married I want my marriage to be just exactly like Mr. and Mrs. Greenwood's."

The other two girls kept silence. But when Edie had flounced out of the room, Irene observed, in her cool voice:

"She'd better call it quits, then, with Leroy Chesborough."

There was a good deal confided to Mrs. Greenwood while she was there. Edie dropped dark hints about "a fellow I've been going with—the folks don't like him. The other girls don't. Well, I don't care whether they do or not. They can have the pick of fellows in this town, so I don't think they're the ones to talk." Irene, of course, kept her doings to herself. Edie once let out with considerable sharpness: "Irene's up to more things than any one of us girls but nobody would ever know it. She covers it all up. Nobody ever gets onto Irene." Mrs. Greenwood said gently, "Irene's independent." Edie shrugged her shoulders, but kept back whatever else she might have liked to say.

Bess gave a few, rather oblique confidences in regard to her engagement to Franklin Story. She had gone with Franklin Story ever since they were in the eighth grade. People all took it for granted that Bess and Franklin were engaged; or that if they weren't now, they would be.

"But you said you are engaged, didn't you?"

"Well—not just exactly."

Mrs. Greenwood smiled. She was sitting in the small cane rocker near the bay window, and Bess was on the floor at her feet. Nobody else was in the room—for a wonder!—except the two children. They, of course, didn't count. Delight was completely absorbed in making ladies out of petunias. Clarence didn't care about that kind of game—he just pretended to, because of Delight. He listened more to the grown-up people talking. He took an endless interest in his sisters' affairs; thought anything "the girls" did was wonderful.

"What does *he* think?" Mrs. Greenwood asked.

"Oh, *he* thinks—" Bess didn't finish, to Clarence's great disappointment. Bess switched over to something else. "His folks think I belong to them. Well, they're awfully nice to me. His mother gave me one of his baby curls." Bess glanced up through her thick eyelashes; but Mrs. Greenwood didn't reply. "Of course, *my* folks think there couldn't be anybody else. Papa does anyway. Mama never says anything to us girls. She always says, 'Why do you ask me, you'll do what you like anyway.' Oh, I know Franklin's a grand fellow," Bess said quickly, before there could be time for any comment. "I know he's the grandest fellow in New Hope."

"Well, you just aren't quite settled yet," Mrs. Greenwood told her gently. "Isn't that it?"

"Yes . . . Did you ever hear of a person going with other fellows just to torment another person?"

Clarence's mouth hung open. But Mrs. Greenwood laughed again, gently. "Oh yes, but I don't think you're going to do anything like that."

Bess didn't answer for a while. Her soft face had a stubborn and yet fractious, flighty expression that came over it only once in a long, long while. "Yes, but when the other person doesn't even notice," she muttered.

Mrs. Greenwood didn't seem to hear. Her eyes, pretty, but even now slightly faded, as though from an intensity too concentrated, seemed to be looking at something else. She told Bess a woman must care for the man she married the very most she was capable of caring for anyone. "There isn't anything that can take the place of that," she said, with conviction. "Nothing else on earth."

Delight threw down her flowers just then and said— her eyes, so intent a moment before, now eagerly shining —"Come on, Clarence, let's you and me go play something else outside. We don't want to play this game any more, do we?"

Clarence told her "No," and was of course ready to run outside; but he hadn't been playing much all along. She would be ready to play one of his games, though. She was so quick to think of things; but before she had a chance Clarence cried out, "All right, we'll play hit-the-mark with our wood thrower."

"All right."

Bertha felt some of the same things that the girls did. She made her own comments: "They're so close, the two of them, they seem so kind of close together. He talks everything over with her, his sermons even. He takes care of her just as much as she does of him. He's always looking out for her, too. Ach, I don't know. I never see two just like them before. Well, ja, he's a minister though."

"Well, he's a man, mama," Bess cried with considerable indignation. "Men don't all have to be just alike."

"Ja, but it ain't the same."

The Millers told the new family a good many things about the town and about the people in their own church. Edie knew everything that had ever happened in this place. The minister didn't care for long, minute life histories— only, as he said, for a few essential facts. But Mrs. Greenwood was always ready to listen. Her interest lay in personal relationships. "Ja, that's her side," Bertha commented wisely; "that's where she comes in." The girls had never enjoyed talking to anybody as they did to Mrs. Greenwood. She had a quality of intense sympathy; it often revealed something that put the whole story in a different light. And then she was a newcomer—she was someone from away.

They told her about the Stileses, how they did and didn't get along; what Mr. Stiles had been like, according to reports, before Mrs. Stiles married him. He had spent his young days out in the old wild West, in the cattle country, and in mining towns. He'd had to promise that he would never drink or gamble and would never carry a gun. He would attend church, but he wouldn't consent to become a member. He'd told Willis Vance that "Lecty was a hard woman for a plain mortal cuss to live with, because no mortal could live up to her, but he'd rather take a scolding from her than a kiss from any other woman." That was just his talk, Bertha said, wisely nodding. 'Twasn't all scoldings!

They talked about the Donohues—Bess with easygoing tolerance, but Edie from a standpoint of fierce partisanship. Mr. and Mrs. Donohue were of different religions. They fought over their children. *He* wanted the children brought up as Catholics and *she* was determined they should be Protestants. The household was split two ways.

Edie let out a few things about "the other family." Aunt Belle could never forget that she was a Merrill and had been brought up in one of the older towns in the eastern part of the state; she thought she was everlastingly superior because a Merrill had been lieutenant governor. "I suppose Millers have held offices too," Edie said sharply, "if we cared to go to the trouble to look up every Miller in the country."

It was about the Harper family that local legend gathered. They lived in that big house—"that real fancy place," Bertha said, "the one we drove past." It wasn't Harry's law practice, however, that had built the house! His law practice alone would never keep that family going. The money came from the old man. The old man Harper was the first person to come out to this part of the county and try to start up a town. He'd bought up land when land was going for almost nothing; and owned farms now all through this section.

The Harry Harpers didn't care to mingle with the community. All their friends were outside: in Horton, or over in Wilton, where there was an English colony—or had been; only a few families were left. Mrs. Harry Harper didn't call on the ladies here. Not even Mrs. Vance or Mrs. Stiles. She spoke to Aunt Belle on the street but that was as far as acquaintance went; she seemed not to have heard about the Merrills! The children all went East to school. Floss Harper, the oldest daughter, was the town's one heroine of romantic scandal. Although only a few years older than Bess, Floss had been twice married and twice divorced. The first marriage was an elopement when she was still in boarding school. When Mrs. Greenwood asked, "Where is she now?" Edie said, "Nobody really knows. She's supposed to have gone to Paris. Anyway, she never comes back here."

But when the girls got to a certain point in their revelations, Mrs. Greenwood's eyes would take on an absent look.

Bertha remarked once, "Ja, there's lots you can't say to her." She sighed. "Ja, she ain't had to know."

Nevertheless, these times were pleasant, the afternoons

when the womenfolks sat and talked things over together. Outside in the yard the sweet peas on their wire trellis grew limp and faded under the burning late-summer sun. In the sitting room the smell of the freshly watered plants was cooling. Scissors clicked lightly, cloth rustled, someone broke off a thread with a tiny snap. At times Irene or Bess dashed to the piano and played or sang. Edie brought in a big pitcher of lemonade; and just at that moment, the children—if they hadn't been in the room all along—were sure to come running in from outdoors, flushed and heated, demanding "Give *us* some."

Dave Miller's satisfaction in the new minister increased. *He* was responsible for bringing Mr. Greenwood to New Hope. Oh, of course he'd had good backing, from Mrs. Stiles and others. But if the Millers hadn't banded together, he said, and taken a firm stand, even threatening to withdraw their support if things were to go on in the same old way, the Vances and the Murdocks and others of the old families might have given in to John Budd. And what progress could the church have hoped to make under that droning old-time preacher whom the Budds had favored? Why, the Methodist man had far more drawing power.

During the early part of the visit Dave suggested that he would like to take Mr. Greenwood into the stores and introduce him to the businessmen, even to those who didn't belong to their own congregation. ("Ja," Bertha said later, "he'd rather show off the preacher to the Methodists and Baptists than he would to our own!") Clarence at once cried:

"Let me go along!"

"You don't want to go along," his father scoffed. "What do you want to go along for?"

"Oh, let him come!" Mr. Greenwood said heartily. "Let them both come if they like. They won't make any trouble."

This was one time, however, when Delight wanted to stay at home. Bess and Edie, and Trixie Donohue who was coming over, were going to wash her hair and then comb it to suit themselves. Delight—to Clarence's impatience—was more than pleased. He couldn't see what fun there'd be in that.

The men started off down the hill to town, and Clarence trotted along too—sometimes walking with them, sometimes lagging behind, often making short side excursions of his own and then running to catch up. He liked to go into the stores under his father's protection. It made him feel important—and then he liked to get into all these places, too.

They went into the Murdock hardware store, Day's drugstore, Vance's lumberyard; into the creamery where Hans Larssen came across the damp floor to meet them through clouds of smelly steam; into the office of the *Citizen* where Cass Story held forth, sitting at a big untidy desk under flag-draped pictures of Washington, Lincoln, and Benjamin Franklin; and out to the printing shop for a moment to speak to Lute Fairbrother; up the outside stairway to the photograph gallery to call on Mr. and Mrs. LeValley; and finally into those smaller establishments, little one-story buildings, harness shop and blacksmith shop, which formed the petering out of Main Street at the further end.

"Say," Dave cried, "we better make a stop at the marble works. Won't do to leave that out!"

Ollie would never forgive them, Dave added; even though you couldn't ever get him inside the church. Dave told about Ollie as they walked along; and Clarence, who had been getting tired and ready to quit, pricked up his ears. He was an Englishman—Oliver Jenks, but Ollie was what he went by—kind of odd in some ways, Dave explained, but not such a bad little fellow. Well, you would call him a character. He was a bachelor and lived by himself—ate, worked, and slept in the gray-painted two-room shack at the marble works. Ollie'd come out here from nobody knew where and wouldn't say a word when folks asked him about his life in the old country. Some said he'd had to leave home. But as long as he behaved himself here, and was a good marble cutter, made good tombstones, his early life, whatever it was, oughtn't to be held against him.

"Of course not," Mr. Greenwood vigorously agreed. "No use paying attention to that kind of talk anyway. I don't give it a thought."

"That's right," Dave said. "That's the way I feel."

In fact, he continued, he wouldn't shut out anybody—unless it might be the Groundhogs. All were fellow citizens, all had their share in helping to build up the town. Ten years ago half these businesses hadn't even been established! Well, Dave said, you have to have all kinds. Even the Groundhogs—he laughed—might have their uses, since they were the only folks here really poor enough to welcome charity. Otherwise the womenfolks wouldn't have any place to take their basket at Thanksgiving time!

"I want to meet the Groundhogs," Mr. Greenwood said, stepping along briskly.

"Oh, you'll meet 'em," Dave said. "You can't help it. They'll be around!"

Now they had reached the marble works: a place that to Clarence held both dread and fascination. The polished surfaces of the tombstones glittered in stark sunlight. All the same, they were tombstones. They were meant for the cemetery.

Ollie Jenks came forward and stared at his visitors with bright sharp eyes, keen but furtive; his glance was oblique. But he proceeded to act out his role of a character. If they hadn't met now, he told the minister, they'd have met later. Both were in much the same business—getting folks buried. He would furnish the labor and the minister the praying. Dave thought the minister might be shocked. But he wasn't.

"Well, there's a good deal to that," he said. "I guess we're both needed."

Clarence was right there, but Ollie Jenks didn't look at him. Ollie seemed to be looking at him, and yet wouldn't pay any attention. Clarence wondered why his father had once said, "You'd better stay away from the marble works. I don't want you hanging around there." But he could go to the lumberyard any time.

As they went away, Dave remarked: "I don't know what kind of a dialect that is he's got. Supposed to be English, but it's not like any English I ever heard! Yorkshur, or some such thing—ever hear of that? I can understand Ole Thorkelson, out in the country, better'n I can this fellow. Does have kind of a queer look, don't he? Well, it takes all kinds."

That was one of Dave Miller's favorite expressions—"It takes all kinds." It always pleased and excited Clarence to hear the way his father said that.

When they got back to the house Mrs. Greenwood asked, "Did you have a good morning?"

"We had a fine morning!" Mr. Greenwood answered heartily.

"Then you'll have a good appetite for your dinner maybe," Bertha said. She couldn't get it out of her head that the minister's appetite needed to be "favored"; "This'll be good for him, it'll favor his appetite," she was constantly saying.

"I'm in the market for one of your dinners right now," he told her.

His color was high; his eyes sparkled with fresh vigor. He was better pleased with the town the more he saw of it, was what he said. Oh, it was new yet, some of it put up in a hurry, it had to be given time for development. But he had known from the first that he would like both the place and the people.

"We've got a mighty fine class of people here," Dave boasted.

New Hope had still the rawness of a new community where bedrock showed, hadn't been covered up yet by layers of classes and customs. All trades were needed, and folks could see that, so all were on something of an equality. The blacksmith was needed just the same as the banker and counted for as much.

"And that's what we need. That's the way to keep it. That's the way things ought to be."

"Ja, if things ever stayed that way," Bertha sighed.

Everywhere could be felt the sense of natural comradeship, of being all together at the start and working together for the future. Even in Ballard, social lines had been drawn, in a rural village like that, smaller and more rural than New Hope. There Judge Lewis had the big house and was the head citizen—one might almost call him the squire. Red brick, with spreading white porches, the Judge's house stood manorial and apart. Judge Lewis used to ask Mr. Greenwood into the library occasionally to have a talk, in that dim atmosphere, both rustic and stately, thick with stale tobacco smoke and the smell of law books in their dingy black and yellowish calf bindings. The Judge was a member of the Circuit Court. He hobnobbed with other state worthies, other judges, officials, men of wealth, "the bigwigs"; if he had not been a Democrat, in a dyed-in-the-wool Republican region, he might have been State Supreme Justice by this time. His abilities entitled him to such a position. The Judge was by birth a Virginian; and although he himself was an old-fashioned patriot and a Jeffersonian Democrat, the aristocratic tradition was a part of his make-up. Socially, he was aloof from his neighbors. The night, just before they were to leave Ballard, when he had asked the Greenwoods to dinner—served in his lofty dining room, by the only colored man in the county—was an event and marked an occasion.

But the people of New Hope, Mr. Greenwood went on to say, came from everywhere. None stood apart—

"None but the Harpers," Bess put in, with a mischievous smile.

"Yes," Dave said testily, "but they'll find out they don't gain much. They're flying high now but there'll be a fall. Just wait till some new lawyer comes in here—and there's sure to be one. Harry'll find out a lot of these folks just go to him because they have to: there's been nobody else. 'Tain't because they like him."

"*She'll* find out," Edie said. "She's really the one."

Mr. Greenwood frowned impatiently. He didn't care for this kind of personal talk. But he continued with his own subject: Here was that atmosphere of freedom and equality which Judge Lewis had expounded as an academic idea, sitting in his smoky library with the bust of Plato and the portrait of Thomas Jefferson. These things might not be actual subjects of discussion in New Hope, but they were in the living air of everyday.

Dave, of course, liked to hear that. What the minister said was exactly what he himself had often thought and couldn't put so well.

"But I want to get out in the country," the minister continued. "The country's what we depend on here."

"Oh, we'll get out there," Dave promised. "Any time you say so. We'll hitch up Mollie and drive out. She needs the exercise. She'll just stand around eating if we let her have her way."

They did take that drive very soon to the high bluff beyond the cemetery from which they could look over into Dakota. Delight was much impressed to think she was looking over into another state.

Then they drove on country roads for a while just to get the general lay of the land. It was harvesttime; some of the farmers had begun their threshing. Thick black smoke went up from the threshing machines. Corn was a good crop this year, and nearly ripe. All felt excited by the fertility that lay around them, in the smooth high billows of dark-brown loessal soil: the deep fresh fertility, for centuries undisturbed—waiting for their own plows, so Dave said—while across from the Dakotas blew the dry, pure, limitless air of the West.

The two families, although so different, became well acquainted during the visit. But the children enjoyed this time most of all.

The Miller place, so Mrs. Stiles often said, was meant for kids to run around in: with the good-sized yard, the barn, the open pastures behind the lot. Clarence had had all this ever since he could remember. But it was as if he had been playing in his sleep. "What does that boy do with himself!" the family used to ask in helpless exasperation, when he couldn't be located, answered to no call—and *he* scarcely knew. He would lie out under the sunflowers and dig at the ground with a piece of dry board. In the house he was always at somebody's heels. "Why don't you go outdoors?" his father would demand. Clarence would whine, "I don't know what to do out there." Dave was so exasperated by that whining! When he was a baby, Clarence had been sickly—"a puny little mite," Grandma Story had called him, tenderly shaking her head; and he had never seemed to learn how to play. But now that he had Delight to play with him, this was all changed.

The two of them were in and out from the time they got up until bedtime. Even at bedtime they didn't want to be separated. They were allowed to say their prayers together.

Delight had her own way of doing everything. Clarence listened to her prayer in admiring wonder. It was better than hearing a story. She wouldn't fold her hands, but held them out, palms down, the way her father did in pronouncing the benediction. She had to pray for everybody she'd ever known; it would be mean, she thought, to leave out *any*body. This included the animals. She had just one accusation against her father: he didn't put in any of the animals when he got up to pray in the pulpit, and the horses were all standing out there waiting to take folks home. Her Uncle Dave told her she mustn't forget the lightning bugs or the mosquitoes! If that prayer got much longer, he liked to tease her by saying, she'd have to start it before six o'clock!

"Bless papa-mama"—she always said those two names right together so neither one would seem to come first—"and bless Aunt Marian who sent me my white kid slippers, and mama her real amber beads, and Judge Lewis for giving me my fan—well, bless them *any*way," she generously conceded. "And everybody we knew in Ballard, especially Grandma Pettibone, and the grocery horse, and Judge Lewis's big dog that wouldn't chase cats, and *all* the cats, and the humming bird and all the birds, and Grandma Pettibone's Hamburg rooster, and the other roosters, and the big chickens and the little chickens. . . ."

When she was through with Ballard she took a long breath. Clarence's mouth hung open in anxiety. He was waiting for her to reach New Hope. She began in a pretty tone of gracious politeness:

"Bless Aunt Bertha Miller and Uncle Dave Miller and the girls—and bless *Clarence*."

When she said that, so firmly, in her clear treble, Clarence blushed and could scarcely listen to what came next. He felt relief, shame, deep pleasure—but she was going on with the prayer and he didn't want to miss anything.

"—And old Mollie, and the petunias and the sweet peas, and the ornamental birch tree and let it not dry up; and the nice conductor on the train coming, and all the people on the train, especially that big fat man that gave me the candy hearts; and the whole town of New Hope— and even the old community—and let Mr. Rodney Harper move here and start a better store, and not be mad at people, and the daughters not ever use their shotgun, and come into this town to do their buying; and bless the Groundhogs and cause them to clean up. . . ."

When at last she said "Amen" she gave a prodigious sigh.

Clarence was so impressed he didn't know what to do. He'd wanted his turn, but now that it had come, and they were all waiting, he was almost ready to back out. He was ashamed just to repeat the "Now I lay me" that was the only prayer he'd ever learned. But he heard Irene's amused whisper, "He can't think of anything!" and fiercely told her:

"I can too!"

"He can pray for their new teacher," Bess suggested helpfully.

"Pray for himself, when he starts in to school!"

"Ach, let him do his own praying," his mother said.

Clarence hung his head. He did have a prayer that he wanted to make. He remembered how his father had told mama not to feed any more tramps because the last one was such a smart aleck and had thrown away good home-made bread and butter. He had thrown it right into the road and somebody's old bulldog had found it and gone off with it. Clarence felt he couldn't endure the shame if they should have to tell the next tramp they hadn't anything to give him. Both of them, Clarence and his mother, had been worrying about that ever since. What if all the tramps would have to go hungry? Clarence said in a scared little voice that could barely be heard:

"God bless the tramps and tell them not to be smart alecks. Jesus' sake. Amen."

CHAPTER IV

The Countryside

THE OLD COMMUNITY

THERE WERE MANY drives on which Dave hoped to take the newcomers, before they moved into the parsonage and got settled down to work: out to the woods beside Rundle's Pond, if the old man Rundle would let them in there; over to see the big sand pits on the flats beyond the bridge— Dave said a real business could be developed out of those beds of sand and gravel, although Bertha looked upon that as just one of Mister's big ideas; and of course he intended to take them all out to his brother Andy's. But Mrs. Greenwood wanted first of all to visit the old community.

"You won't see much of anything out there," Dave warned her.

No, maybe not, but she had heard so much about it; she was curious, she said. She had been hearing mention of the old community ever since she came to New Hope. And then, it was there many of their members had started out: the Vances, the Murdocks, Mrs. Stiles, the Budds, and the Livermores—all came from the old community.

"Yes," Dave admitted grudgingly, "they came from

there. But they all knew enough not to stick there. Oh, some of them of course have hankerings back—the Budds have, even Addie Murdock. You might think to hear *them* talk, there was no such place before nor since. But Electa Stiles has better sense. She says when the old has served its purpose, folks have to go ahead and take up the new—and when they once decide on that, they've got to do it with all their might. Yes, sir, Electa Stiles is a mighty smart woman. There aren't many like her."

The minister agreed.

"You ought to get her to play for you someday," Dave said to Mr. and Mrs. Greenwood. "Play the piano. She studied in the East when she was a girl. She was studying the piano when she met Jim Stiles and decided to marry him. He followed her back home and finally got her consent. Or that's the way folks tell it."

"Ja, they won't get her to play for them," Bertha scoffed. "She won't play for folks. Just for herself and sometimes for him. Just when the notion takes her. She's awful funny about it."

Irene said, she wasn't funny. If she couldn't be a great musician, and devote her life to that, Mrs. Stiles had resolved that she wouldn't play at all, except for her own pleasure. She didn't care to do things halfway. Irene thought that was a very sensible way to feel. Well, she's a married woman, Bertha agreed. It would be funny, too, for a married woman to keep up her music.

Dave still maintained that there was nothing to see out in that little old burg. What was there out there but a few old buildings? A few old cellar holes and a graveyard! He couldn't see why the womenfolks were so anxious to go out there. Bertha was almost as curious about it as the minister's wife; and the girls would have gone along, if there'd been room for all of them in the carriage. It beat all, Dave remarked, how womenfolks liked to poke around through a lot of old stuff—the older the better. For his part, he couldn't see what the attraction was.

But he'd be glad to take them out there for the sake of the drive and what they'd see on the way. It was all nice countryside; although he preferred the section on the other side of town, where his brother Andy's farm was located. That was where he could show them some real country. But when they went out to the farm, they wanted to make a day of it, not merely drive out and back. It called for a real visit.

The old community lay only three miles beyond the new town—just far enough, Dave Miller said with considerable satisfaction, to be left high and dry by the railroad.

Mr. Greenwood wanted to know if the place hadn't a name.

Oh yes, Dave said, the post office name was Canaan. It was still marked Canaan on the map. "Nobody ever calls it that any more, though. Folks just refer to it as the old community."

"What's Canaan, papa?" Clarence demanded. Oh, 'twas just a name, his father replied. A name from the Bible, Mrs. Greenwood added; from the Old Testament. Clarence's eyes grew big. He had always accepted his father's view of the old community. But he hadn't known it got its name from the Bible. Now the old cellar holes and few, dilapidated buildings took on a melancholy glory.

It was strange that, in country which seemed so new, this locality should have gathered already a feeling of age. Even this road on which they were driving seemed a road going back to the past. "The old south road," it was called in New Hope. Thickets of early fall flowers stood tall and dusty in the August weather. More trees grew out this way—the newcomers remarked on that; some were native, but most of them the early settlers had planted. Distant groves on the swelling waves of land here and there showed dark against the sky. A sense of mournful dignity lay over the whole region, on this day that was sunny and yet unsettled, with a feeling of fall already in the air.

But only a few years ago the place had been flourishing! Although it had never boasted many houses, the old community—Canaan, in those days—had stood as the center for a considerable neighborhood. It had looked forward to a fine future, as New Hope did now. But of course with less reason. The location of a town here had been a mistake. First, as Dave told it, 'twas too far from the river—too far out in the countryside and off by itself—could serve no purpose except as a center for rural trade, and the railroad spoiled all that. These folks hadn't had sense enough to get the railroad to come through here. The old man Harper was too set in his ways; he had thought it wouldn't matter. Then after the tracks had been laid, and the new town started, the cyclone had come along and torn down church, school, and most of the houses—leaving only the store, the now deserted post office, and the ruins of a few other buildings. Part of the roof was torn off from the old town hall but the main structure left standing.

They drove past the town hall now. It stood near what had been the edge of town. It was a good-sized frame building—plain, but Dave admitted that some folks said it was good architecture, if you liked the old New England sort. They'd had big gatherings here in the early days. The Grange used to hold its meetings here. Now the roof covered only the front portion of the building and the window-panes were shattered. Birds, as the children watched, flew in and out; they had their nests inside among the old rafters. Mrs. Greenwood thought it a shame that the building should go to ruin. Couldn't something be made of it? she asked. But the others asked, What? Nobody wanted to drive away out here. The City Hall, up above the Fire Station, was able to accommodate all gatherings. No, what they should do, the minister asserted vigorously, was pull down this old wreck. It was worth nothing, standing here. It merely cluttered up the landscape. Then where would the birds go? Delight cried piteously. She didn't want the birds disturbed! "Don't worry," her father told her, laughing. "*I'm* not going to tear down the hall, and probably nobody else is. If it's stood this long, it'll keep on standing, until the walls cave in of their own accord." Delight was satisfied.

"We ought to stop at the store," Dave said to the others. "Except that the old man might refuse to wait on us! He's never forgiven Ira and me for starting up storekeeping in the new town. He blames us, instead of the railroad and the cyclone, for taking away his trade."

"Does he have any trade these days?" Mr. Greenwood asked.

"Oh yes, a little," Dave conceded, "from right around here in the country. Not enough to amount to anything by itself. But his money comes from land. Oh, the old codger won't give up!" Dave continued. "He'll keep on as long as he's alive, whether anybody comes here to buy or not. He keeps the same old stock from year to year. It'd be a sight, I guess, if I was to take you in there. Folks say there's junk from forty years back, all jumbled up together, in the regular old-time way. But I guess it wouldn't do to go in."

The children wanted to see the junk. "We want to get some candy, papa!" Clarence cried. Whenever they went downtown with him, Dave let them buy candy.

But he said now, "No, you don't want to get any candy there. It'd be so hard it'd break your teeth. You kids wait until we get back to town, and then you can go into Donohue's."

Clarence said, "All right." His father thought everything they got in their own town was better, was more to be trusted; and Clarence accepted that with perfect faith.

Dave did let Mollie take her time while the visitors looked at the shabby white frame store. One forlorn team was tied outside. Delight said, "Poor horses!" because they were hanging their heads. But Dave told her that didn't mean anything, the horses were just resting and letting go while they had the chance; horses were smart. There was a gaping cellar hole close by the store into which the children tried to stare; but without seeing anything but big weeds and nettles. That was where the post office used to stand. The only post office now was in one corner of the store. The Harpers must be about the only ones still to get their mail here, Dave said. Maybe a few other folks from farms nearby.

He slapped the reins and told Mollie to "*Gid*-dap." He didn't care to have old man Harper look out and catch them all staring; didn't want to give the old curmudgeon that much satisfaction.

But he promised that he would drive them past the Harper place. Bertha had kept insisting that the folks would want to see that. The girls had been telling Mrs. Greenwood all sorts of stories. Dave said there was nothing so much to see. The Harry Harper place was bigger. But the women-folks always seemed to be impressed by any old house no matter if it had gone to rack and ruin. Or all the more, if it had gone to rack and ruin! He couldn't see the point of that. Bertha protested: the house hadn't gone to ruin. No, Dave said, but it was headed that way. Nobody else would want to live out here when the Harpers were gone. Who'd want to keep up such a place? It was getting more and more run-down.

A funny thing, Dave added, that it should have been this house and the store building to survive the cyclone! Jim Stiles said even a cyclone had to bow to the old man's authority. You ought to hear Jim on the subject of the old community! ("Yes," Bertha put in, "but that's to tease her. He likes to see if he can't get her riled up.") Well, he was a tyrant—Dave said with relish—old Rodney Harper. He was a genuine autocrat. Time was when he'd ruled the whole community. He ruled his own family still—lorded it even over Harry. If Harry'd had his own way—or his wife's way, at least—he'd have moved to some other place long ago; back East, probably. But the old man held the money reins.

"Watch when we go past," Dave said, "and you may catch a sight of the girls. Nobody ever sees them in town. He won't let them go there."

Delight asked in awe, did their father lock them up? Dave laughed and said, that was about what it amounted to!

"How can we see the girls, then?"

"Oh, he lets 'em out in their own yard."

"Just like princesses!" Delight breathed.

The large white house, in the style of the seventies, was set back at some distance from the road. It was one of the oldest houses in the county. With its cupola, and its stately windows, it seemed to give a different character to the landscape in the midst of which it stood: the western bareness. There was a grove of big cottonwoods along the north edge of the grounds, which the old man had planted to mark his boundary line. He was a stickler for property rights, had got involved in several lawsuits; and since things had gone against him he'd grown terribly crusty. People said he kept a shotgun loaded, and gave the girls instructions to use it on any trespasser if he wasn't around. But there were so many stories, you couldn't believe them all. Still, Dave admitted, he wouldn't care to make the test!

Dave had slackened the reins and let Mollie saunter. Although he laughed at the womenfolks for their interest, he didn't mind a good look at the place himself. Mrs. Greenwood's friend Marian (the "Aunt Marian" who had given Delight her white kid slippers) was a talented painter in both water color and oil. She taught in an art school in Cleveland, Ohio. If Marian ever saw this house, Mrs. Greenwood said, she would want to paint a picture of it. This was just the kind of scene that would appeal to her.

Mrs. Greenwood said she wished they could see what the place was like inside. Mrs. Stiles had told her something about how the house was built, with lumber hauled from the woods along the river bottom; and Nellie Vance had described the rooms to the Miller girls. There were black marble fireplaces in three of the downstairs rooms—the front and back parlors, and library. The tall doors between the parlors, and the railing of the staircase, were made of black walnut, and carved by hand. Nellie said the carpets were beautiful. The girls kept the blinds closed in both parlors in order to preserve those carpets. There was a huge old curio cabinet in the library, standing almost as high as the ceiling, filled with things the girls had brought back from abroad; and there was one whole shelfful of little bottles, all the same size, and with labels: honey from Mt. Hymettus, grass from the Coliseum, water from the Jordan, earth from the Garden of Gethsemane—they had made a tour of the Holy Land while they were across the water.

"Well," Dave told her, "I'm afraid you'll never get in there! Hardly anybody gets in any more. The last time Nellie Vance drove out here to see the girls, she told me— and Nellie used to be one of their very best friends, when she first came out here as a bride!—Caroline, or whichever one it was, I forget the other's name" (Bertha said, "Amelia"), "would only talk to her from the front door. Nellie said she went away from there in a hurry, and Willis, when she told him about it, said she was never to go again." Why was it? "Oh, the old man's sore at everybody for moving away. He's even sore at Harry. As if a lawyer could spend his time driving back and forth—or as if any clients were going to hunt him up out here in the country! But the old man's never admitted the place was done for. He sticks here, and he makes his daughters stick here."

Delight was up on her knees staring in eagerness and wonder. Maybe the two daughters were locked up in the cupola! Delight was greatly impressed by that cupola; she wished she could live in a little room like that, all windows, up on top of a house. She thought the two daughters might be looking down at them now, seeing a horse and carriage, and wanting to be rescued.

Her Uncle Dave laughed at that idea. He didn't think they cared about being rescued! They were as queer, from all reports, as the old man himself. If anybody was going to undertake a rescue, it should have been done long ago.

"Look!" Bertha said quickly, in a low voice. "There goes one of them now."

One of the two daughters!—she was crossing the lawn. Bertha had never seen them close, so she couldn't be sure which one it was; but she thought it must be Caroline. She was the younger one, and not quite so queer as the other. Folks did get a look at her now and then.

Delight scrunched back in her place, asking fearfully, will she shoot us? But her Uncle Dave reassured her: they were safe out here in the road. He took up the reins again, just to make it look as if they had no intention of stopping; but he was as curious now as the womenfolks. The Harper girls, although not so far past their youth, were already becoming legendary. They were never seen in New Hope. They didn't even come to Harry's. The younger one used to visit now and then; but even she didn't venture out any more. If they did any shopping, outside their own store, it must be in Horton or some other town.

Dave, telling about the two sisters, had sunk his voice to a hoarse whisper. Even that made Bertha uneasy. She was the one now who was anxious to drive on.

The old man, Dave related, had sent both daughters

East to school, to study fancy subjects, and he'd considered them too good for anybody in Canaan—even when there'd *been* anybody. They never went out except with old Rodney himself. He'd taken them on trips; taken them both abroad with him. Oh, they were well educated, no doubt of that— for all the good it was likely to do them. Folks told how he used to sit in church with his arm around one or the other of them. "Just as if he had to keep them guarded!" Mrs. Murdock said. "I don't know from what," Dave added, "or who'd ever have wanted to run away with them." They were both tall and skinny as scarecrows. Old Rodney himself was well over six feet, and wore a beard longer than John Budd's. Harry was the runt of that family. Folks said the girls were accomplished. Electa Stiles said they were among the most accomplished women she knew. Amelia was supposed to be a painter, and Caroline to sing and play the piano. But nobody ever got the benefit of their wonderful accomplishments, except themselves, and the old man.

The visitors couldn't any of them, from out here in the road, get a really good sight of the daughter; more than to see that she was very tall and thin, wore a big old-fashioned summer hat, and seemed to be carrying a basket. She was going out to the garden. But her figure, even at this distance, and still more her bearing, conveyed an impression of odd, angular distinction. Was that the one who played the piano?—Delight asked in her breathy little whisper. Or was she going out into the garden to paint pictures? "*I'm* going to paint a picture some day," Delight informed the grown people, "and put in the house, and the big tall trees, and the two daughters out in the garden picking bouquets." She was going to paint the inside of the house, too, she said—she was going to imagine what it looked like. She would have one daughter singing and playing at the piano—it would be a big old dark mahogany grand piano, like the one in Judge Lewis's house—and the other sister painting a picture at an easel; it would be a picture of a castle. "Aren't you, Clarence?" she begged, turning to her confederate. "We'll both of us come out and paint pictures." Clarence wouldn't say; although he stared at the house, fascinated, afraid the other daughter might be pointing her gun. "I guess he wouldn't know how to paint a picture," his mother murmured.

"Drive along, Mister," she pleaded, shivering.

"What's the matter? What are you so worried about? We've got a right to be out here on the road, haven't we? We have as much right to the road as anybody."

"Ja, but I wish you'd drive along."

The only other place to see was the cemetery. They'd looked at all the other ruins, so they might as well have a glimpse of that. Dave said they'd drive on a ways, past the old burying ground, and then turn around and go back.

"Not for me," Mr. Greenwood announced. "The rest of you can look at the tombstones but I'll look at the view." He said he got enough of cemeteries. He didn't care to visit one for pleasure! In Ballard, where so many old people had lived retired, he used to have funerals to conduct almost every week.

"But this is an *old* graveyard," Mrs. Greenwood said to him.

"What difference does that make? I'd just as soon see a new graveyard as an old one. People are exactly as dead whether they've been buried one year or a thousand. I prefer to make my travels among the living."

People died, and were buried—well, what of it? Their lives were what counted, not their graves. He never could understand what there was so romantic about tombstones. The man wasn't beneath them—not what he considered the man.

Dave, although impressed by the minister's viewpoint,

was more inclined to agree with the womenfolks. It wasn't so much because this cemetery was older than the one on the hill, that he wanted to go past it, as to see what was left of it—in what condition the place was now.

"Well, we might as well see it now we're here," he said.

The old community burying ground lay beyond the Harper grounds. There was pasture land on the other side, and then a cornfield. Although the old families still contributed toward its upkeep, the spot had an air of neglect. The grass was long—the old wild grass that belonged to this region. There wouldn't be much of that left pretty soon. A black iron fence surrounded the little graveyard to set it apart from the farming land. Dave pointed out some of the lots and monuments; while Bertha kept up her murmured interpolations.

"That big tall monument belongs to the Harpers, of course. The old lady's buried here. She died a good while ago, before any of us came into this region. Well, it gives Rodney a nice view from his windows!—to be able to look out and see his own monument. That stone over there is for Mrs. Stiles's parents. Their name was Kent. Father Kent —that was what people called her father. He was the first preacher anywhere in this locality, used to go through the country on horseback, so they say. Folks have a good many stories about him. I guess he was one parson even old Rodney couldn't boss! He did some farming as well as preaching. That was the way they used to do. Well, she takes after him, I guess—Mrs. Stiles does. She has her own ways. She's an awful good woman, though." That was what Dave Miller always added, whenever he said anything about Mrs. Stiles. She might have her ways, but she was as good a woman as ever lived. "They say the mother was Quaker; or came of Quaker stock. Maybe that's where some of 'Lecta's ways and beliefs come from. But I don't know how far back that might be."

"Ja," Bertha murmured, "she's been out here. There's some of her flowers. Some of her red dahlias."

"The Murdocks have a lot here, both families. But the A.D.'s moved their little girl's coffin into our cemetery."

"Ja, they wanted to be closer for Decoration Day. Addie wanted to have the child closer. She takes flowers out nearly every Sunday."

"Well," Dave continued, "old Father Kent preached out around here, so I suppose it's all right to leave him. He preached in the old church. The only preacher it ever had. I expect the Harpers'll have to be laid here! It'll be a joke on Mrs. Harry, if she should have to get buried out here—the way she turns up her nose at the country. One reason she didn't care to attend church, so they tell it, is because she thinks we have too many from the country."

"Turn around now, Mister," Bertha begged.

"What are you so anxious to turn around for?"

"I don't want to look any more. It looks too sad."

Dave turned around—since he'd intended to do so anyway. As soon as they were back on the main road Bertha said she could breathe better. It was all so queer, she didn't think after all she'd care to go inside that house. You never could tell what crazy folks might do. To her notion, the Harpers must be crazy. Clarence didn't say anything, but he too was scared of the shotgun. But he'd like to have tried it out, run fast across the lawn, just to see if anybody would shoot.

Mrs. Greenwood kept repeating how interesting the whole place was! This was the most interesting drive they'd taken since they'd been here. Mr. Greenwood took issue with that. What was there so interesting, he'd like to know, in an old house, and two foolish women who let their lives be run for them by a still more foolish and morbid old man? He didn't consider morbidity as interesting as health! His wife admitted all that, but just the same for her the old community had a special appeal. It was like some old ballad.

"Some old ballad!" Mr. Greenwood repeated. He scoffed at her. Yes, some old ballad that threw a romantic light over a lot of mean actions and dirty deeds that must have seemed sordid enough to the people closely involved in them—"Would seem sordid to you too if they hadn't been set to music!"

No, he must admit, that kind of thing made little appeal to him! He preferred a going concern to one that was run down and disintegrating. He hadn't much patience with any such sentiment as that of clinging to old surroundings when the life had gone out of them.

"I do," Mrs. Greenwood sighed. "I've hated to leave every place we've ever left, even when I wanted to go."

"Why, you're the one," he said, "who's always first to decide on the move!"

"I know it," she admitted.

"Well, Alice, that doesn't make sense to me."

It made sense, however, to Bertha. She's the ambitious one—Bertha had surmised that long ago. She's the one who does the pushing. She wants to see him rise. She thinks nothing's too good.

He found far more pleasure, Mr. Greenwood said, in looking at this fine country through which they were driving now. Dave acknowledged there were some nice-looking farms out this way, but he preferred the country north of town where his brother Andy had settled. "Just wait till you see how it looks around there." The Palmers owned a farm in this locality, one of the best in this section; but it was off on a different road. There was a fine old house for you! He'd take that house any time in preference to the Harper place. It had been quite a show place in Captain Palmer's time. They'd raised fine-blooded stock; and the Captain used to keep peacocks on the lawn. The farm still belonged to Dora and Mrs. Palmer, and brought a good income.

The two women mourned over the desolation of the old community. But Dave wouldn't hear to that. He asserted that Canaan had never had a real future. Not with old Rodney Harper running things! His whole idea was to keep everything old-timey. The community had reached a standstill long ago. Otherwise, they'd have managed to get the railroad to come through—or at least to hook up with it! But oh no, they wouldn't have the railroad; not unless it was on old Rodney's terms that were too high to be met. He'd actually doomed the place right then. Of course, the cyclone had finished it. But cyclones had hit other towns, and the towns had been rebuilt. People always could rebuild if they felt real faith in the future.

"Ach, that must have been terrible," Bertha said shivering. "That cyclone. I hope we don't get one."

"Oh, we won't get one!" Dave promised largely. "We don't have any such bad storms any more. Cyclones or blizzards either. Those were in the early days. They're past and over."

"Ja, that's what *you* say," Bertha sighed.

Folks could thank the cyclone, anyway. It had given the new town not only its first rapid growth but its very name. Taylorsburg was what the railroad had called the new station—just another burg! That would have been a handicap from the beginning. But when this terrible cyclone struck the other community, and took nearly everything with it, so the old families had to move out, they changed the name of the railroad settlement to New Hope. Mr. Broadwater was the one who'd suggested it. The town was incorporated under that name since the railroad made no objections.

"So that's the way the town got its name!"

"Yes, sir, that's the way."

Dave said that was soon after he and Ira had come there. They'd come first just to look the ground over. But it didn't take them long to see that this was the coming place. How it had grown in just this short while!

Dave had already forgotten about the old community and was launched on the subject of New Hope: its prospects, favorable location, and its fine class of people. He did acknowledge that the old community had contributed some of its finest people. Oh, there'd be a real city some day! Horton would be left far behind. Fox Center was already a back number.

The two children listened eagerly. This time they had refused to be separated. Since there wasn't room for both of them in the back seat, they were sitting down on the buggy floor—to the anxiety of the two mothers, for whenever the children wanted to look out they rose precariously to their knees and sat jolting and swaying. They were up on their knees to see the last of the old community: to get their last sight of the ruined Hall where the birds flew in and out of the empty windows. They had a feeling of awe, and of romantic respect, and yet of great superiority. *They* belonged to the new town.

THE FARM

The drive to the Andy Miller farm had to be put off until later in the season. "When we go out there," Dave kept saying, "we'll want to spend the whole day." So he thought it would be better to wait until Andy was through with thrashing and had got some of his fall work out of the way. Andy didn't hire any help. He was sole man out there.

The visit took place early in October: on a Monday,

because that was the best time for the minister to get away. He took off Mondays instead of Saturdays; because Sunday, for him, was no day of rest. The children had started to school by that time, but the parents could ask for them to be excused. They had been promised this trip and it wouldn't do to leave them behind.

Clarence went running up the parsonage steps. The minister's family had been settled for some time in their own house. They were no longer "the company." Clarence shouted:

"Rev'rend Greenwood. Mrs. Greenwood. The folks are out here."

"You tell them we'll be right along."

The carriage waited in the October sunshine. Mollie lazily switched her heavy black tail across her warm brown flanks. There was still a little glittering swarm of flies. The usual discussion ensued as to how the folks were all to find room. But the children settled that. They had to be together. They would sit on the floor again.

"Down there on that hard buggy floor? All the way?"

"Yes! We want to."

The old buggy robe was folded and put down to help ease the jolts. Bertha still worried—ach, their poor little bottoms, they would be all bruises—but Dave laughed. The children were lifted up over the wheels and settled down into their small compartment. "Don't sit on our feet," Bertha protested feebly. "Clarence," she added. They must watch out for things stowed under the seat. Bertha was taking along some extras for Mary: a few jars of pickles and preserves, and one of Bess's cakes. Mary didn't have so much time for putting up, Bertha explained. "I want to take a little something. But *you* wouldn't need to," she protested, seeing the beautiful fresh cinnamon rolls Mrs. Greenwood had brought. According to Bertha's code, minister's folks should receive, not give. She was scandalized when

Mrs. Greenwood contributed to suppers the same as the other ladies; although in her heart she approved.

"All fixed back there? *Get* a move on, Mollie!"

The children braced themselves for Mollie's lunge. They shouted with pleasure, while the women held their breath—Bertha moaning faintly, "Ach, Mister, that's the way he always has to start up."

"Well, we've got a fine day for it, folks," Dave proclaimed exultantly.

The trees had begun to lose their leaves. Shriveled and curled, leaves lay along the sidewalks, some caught in cobwebs, some piled in dusty drifts. Box elder trees didn't turn well.

"Out in the country we'll see the colors," Dave promised.

"Ja," Bertha put in, "if we were going the other way."

"Oh, there'll be plenty out this way too."

The Greenwoods had not driven out in this direction before. The region was less settled than that where the old community was located; but Dave said that out here was some of the best farming land.

There was a different atmosphere about this locality. The road seemed always to be rising, ahead of them, in the distance, toward some far hilltop that was never reached. When they came to what should have been the hilltop, all they could see before them was more and more swelling land. This was "new" country—Cass Story, who studied into such things, often said that on this land men had never before had a settled habitation: the way the bones of animals were left behind showed that. The Indians had only hunted here and roamed, making campfires, or putting up temporary shelters. Yet a savage roughness underlay the newness. This region was at once a brand-new thriving habitation for young people, and the far interior of an ancient mighty continent belonging to a prehistoric race and age. Farm-

houses were set at far intervals. Small, plain, uncompromising, so fixed and yet so temporary—in the very unmitigated
character of these qualities, lay both exhilaration and loneliness.

It was the exhilaration which Mr. Greenwood seemed
to feel. He took off his hat and lifted his head, looking out
over the smoothly rolling expanses of land—rough nearby
—with his innocent eagle gaze; off toward the lift of the
horizon.

But there was a homeliness, too, in the fall. The newly
planted windbreaks of soft maple and cottonwood had a
look that was scraggily local. Some of the trees were nothing
more than switches. Chickens crouched or scratched about
the roots. Wagons stood out in the fields, partly loaded with
corn stalks. In some places husking had just begun. The
shocks made the children think of Indian wigwams—they
were studying the Hiawatha Primer now in school; but the
big hard pumpkins, turning from green to orange, belonged
to the Pilgrims and Thanksgiving.

Mollie jogged along, slowly enough to suit even Bertha.
She knew this road—knew there would be a good feed for
her at the end. There was something tolerant and kindly in
the sound of her hoofbeats, in the way she tossed her head
occasionally and shook her heavy mane, looking back to see
that the folks she was carrying were all right.

The two men in front were talking about the crops
and the weather. Mr. Barbour, the former minister, had
cared little about such things; but William Greenwood came
of farmer stock, he had never lost his interest. Dave pointed
out the different farms. "Mister knows where they all live,"
Bertha sighed. Andy had one of the best quarter sections in
the township. "I had my eye on that piece for him before
he ever made the move," Dave boasted. The bank owned
some of the best land out this way; and Dave thought it

should own more. There was no better investment. Ira was so cautious, Dave had to buy on his own hook.

The murmur of the women's voices was low, intimate, and continuous, both a comment upon, a deference to, a withdrawal from the conversation of the men. The men's talk seemed to spread out, the women's to draw tightly to center. By this time, in spite of the marked differences between them, the two women had grown very friendly. Bertha felt she could confide some things to Alice Greenwood that she had kept silent about until now.

"Ja, I always like to go out to Andy and Mary's. It's one place I like to go. She was a teacher back there—Andy he went back and got her. But she seems to like it real well on their place. Only she don't like not having trees. Someday, when they get to where they can retire, Andy told her, they can go and live where there's lots of trees. That's looking a long ways ahead! They're just started. I don't know, I think the work's hard on her. But she won't say so. Andy is an awful good farmer. Mister, he don't care much for farming, though he talks a lot. He don't like to keep too much to one place. Ja, I don't know, maybe sometimes she gets lonely. They're anxious for a baby. I tell her that'll come soon enough a'ready. Once you have one, then you're started."

Bertha sighed. She glanced at Mrs. Greenwood. There were some things it wouldn't do to say to her, after all. Her own marriage, and her early married life, Bertha had to keep to herself. She began to talk instead about the children. The three girls had all been fat, healthy babies. The doctor said Irene was about the most perfect child he'd ever helped to bring into the world. But Clarence was so small and poor she'd never thought they'd be able to raise him. Mister was so crazy for a boy, and then, when they got the boy, it seemed as if he had to turn out to be the sickly one. Mister could hardly get over that. But now here he was, as strong a child as any other. Ja, nobody ever knew. Those that started slow might get farthest in the long run.

The children were having too good a time to listen much to anybody although they heard. They liked their crowded space down on the buggy floor, avoiding their mothers' feet, finding room for their own. They laughed about everything. Everything was a secret. The country looked different, seeing it all unrolled backwards, when they looked out over the buggy wheels. An occasional hard jolt threw them against their mothers' knees and made them gasp joyously.

Delight cried, "Come on, Clarence, let's sing." She warned him, "Wait, though. I have to get the pitch."

She struck one forefinger sharply with the other, held up the finger anxiously squinting at it, listened, and hummed to imitate the pitch pipe their teacher used. Clarence tried to hum along with her, although he didn't quite get the key. This was the song they had just learned in school: the one they now sang.

"October ha-ad a party,
The leaves by hundreds came."

There weren't many trees near them on this road. But far off on a rounded knoll stood a group of trees, colored and hazy, like a great fall bouquet.

"The beeches, oa-oaks, and maples,
And lea-eaves of ev'ry name."

The older people became aware of the singing. Delight's small treble was clear and assured. Clarence's voice was breathy, uncertain, and shy. The moment he discovered they were being listened to, he stopped.

"That's fine!" Dave boomed heartily. "You'll have to

sing that for Uncle Andy and Aunt Mary when we get out to the farm."

Delight was willing, but Clarence instantly shook his head.

"Ja, he won't go on if anybody hears him," Bertha murmured.

It didn't matter about the singing, not to the children, there were so many other things they could play. Clarence, although his bottom did hurt with the jolting of the carriage, and he couldn't find any good place for his feet, felt a tingling intoxication of happiness. There was always this excitement in being with Delight—a naturalness that was touched with magic. Whatever they did together was fun. They didn't need anybody else if they could be together. Delight said they must count all the fence posts or the Old Witch would get them. Clarence had never quite dared to ask what the Old Witch was like. But it seemed to him she was somewhere now, in a darkness like a storm cloud, in the golden dusty air above the faded cornfields. A shiver went down his backbone. He and Delight were always on the lookout for places where it would be fun to hide and keep house. Now she whispered:

"There! Up in that haymow where the window's open."

Clarence looked. After a while he said, "I see a house. That haystack, where it's caved in down under."

"Oh yes! Nobody'd ever find us down there."

When they reached the farm, Mollie turned into the driveway and stopped of her own accord.

The children were already up on their knees looking out eagerly over the buggy wheels. A shaggy young dog came racing, but stopped at the corner of the house and barked. That was the only sound in the whole great country—that, and the drone of the windmill in the intervals between the barks.

But Uncle Andy came out to meet them now.

The Greenwoods had seen Andy Miller at church, of course. He and Mary had been at the Ira's for dinner that first Sunday. But the young couple had had little to say; it took a while to get to know them. Except for his father, and now for Mr. Greenwood, Clarence thought his uncle Andy was the greatest man in the world. Andy, the youngest of the Miller brothers, was taller than Dave, but not so tall as Ira—harder and better-built than either of them. Now he was smiling, and his blue-gray eyes were squinted against the sun. As he reached over to swing down the children the golden bush of hair on his wrists and hands glittered in the light. His arms were so strong that Delight, when he had set her down, looked up at him in wonder. He was even stronger than her papa! she told Clarence afterwards—she hadn't supposed there could be any other man in the world that strong.

"Hello, Andy. Vee gates?"

"Hello. Glad to see everybody."

"Where's Mary?" Bertha asked—then cried with timid pleasure: "Ja, I see her!"

Mary was on the doorstep waiting for them. She was a small, dark woman with softly glowing eyes. The deeply tanned strength of her hands, showing clumsily dark against her light summer dress, was oddly out of keeping with her pretty delicacy. It made people feel sorry for her in some way they couldn't just understand. She greeted her guests with an eagerness that was fluttering and yet shyly reserved, proud to welcome them to her new home, but fearful of her own deficiencies as a housewife. Mary and Andy had been married just a little over a year.

"Did it seem awfully far out here?"

"Oh, we enjoyed the drive."

"I guess maybe the children got awful bumped down where they was," Bertha said.

"*They* didn't mind that," Dave boomed. "Helped to shake up their stummicks. They'll be ready for dinner now."

"Won't you folks all step inside?"

The house had been built just before Mary and Andy were married. It had an elemental newness about it still. The front step shone woodenly bare in the sun. When Mary opened the screen door, blue flypaper streamers waved slightly. The company stepped into the clean, cool sparseness of the front room.

Saying "Maybe you'd like to go in and take off your hats," Mary led the womenfolks into the bedroom just off the parlor. The shades were pulled down there, making an empty-feeling semidarkness. Clarence started to go along, then decided to stay with the menfolks. He didn't have any hat and he didn't want to give his mother a chance to get at him and brush his hair.

When they all came out again, Mrs. Greenwood looked pleased and smiling, but Delight had grown silent and strange, almost as if she wished she hadn't come. Mrs. Greenwood seemed to make friends at once with Mary. There was something about Mary that was very appealing— some quaintly indefinite charm, a delicate originality. Aunt Belle always said, though, that she ought to speak up for herself. Her black hair curled around her forehead with a softly pretty naturalness.

Bertha remembered the presents. "Mister," she cried, "those things we brought. Under the back seat. I hope they didn't get squashed a'ready," she added anxiously. "I told Clarence he should be careful about his feet."

He said, "I *was* careful."

The things were all right, nothing broken, nothing spilled, just the frosting on Bess's cake a little smashed in places.

Mary cried, "Oh, you folks shouldn't have brought anything."

"Why, sure," Dave told her. "You're still a bride. Anyway, we didn't know how good you could cook. We were worried, thought we'd better bring our dinner right along."

He squeezed Mary's arm, and winked at the others. Mary's eyes had a dark, happy glow. It was the thick lashes —Mrs. Greenwood saw now, and said afterwards to Bess, who adored Mary—the lashes, and the curling hair, that made her think of ferns. She thought of ferns, and a secret spring of cold, clear water. Mary didn't seem quite to belong to this bare open country. Although she and her husband were happy together: that was apparent too; most apparent of all.

Mary hurried to dispose of her gifts. The two older women offered to help with the dinner, but with the pride of a young housewife Mary must do it all herself. The womenfolks sat down in the front room to wait. The men had gone outside. Clarence went out with them, but Delight chose to stay with her mother. Clarence could see her now and then when he looked through the screen. She rocked in her new, hard, shiny chair, sitting well toward the edge so that her feet would reach the floor.

All through the house there was that same fresh emptiness, as if a breeze were just about to stir. But the great countryside spread in motionless stillness in the autumn sunshine.

Mrs. Greenwood said afterwards, also, that the house showed it belonged to a newly married couple. "When you're married, Bess, you'll be able to notice that too." The furniture was new, and there was just enough and no more. But Mrs. Greenwood remarked with pleasure how even this bareness showed touches of Mary's elusive individuality. On the varnished stand were some pine cones, odd pebbles, a pearly clamshell; and a big brown crock in a corner held a branchy bouquet of oak leaves in their polished autumn colors. In that hint of fresh breeze, always about to stir, lay the secret happiness of the young couple, the hope of all that was beginning, manifesting itself with reserve and yet with candor—the thought of the hidden spring in the great stern, yet sunlit, solitude of this new-old country.

Now all the menfolks came back into the room bearing cold, dripping glasses of water. Clarence carried his with elaborate care. His chin still had a dribble of wet, which his mother made as if to wipe off with a gesture, although he wasn't near her. Andy followed the others, silent and smiling.

"Alice, you must taste this water," Mr. Greenwood said, eagerly handing her the glass.

Dave insisted that Bertha must have a glass, too, although she protested that she didn't care for a drink.

"Clarence, did you get yours in here without spilling it? Pretty good! You go give it to Delight, then. Let 'em all have a taste."

The women accepted their glasses a little gingerly. The men waited expectantly while they took their first sips.

Mr. Greenwood cried, "Now, isn't that about the finest water you've ever tasted?"

"It's wonderful," Mrs. Greenwood said.

"I always think it's too cold," Bertha complained feebly. She held her glass after the first drink.

"Too cold!" Dave roared in disgust. "What do you want water to be—lukewarm? Here," he said, "I'll finish your glass for you. Holy Moses." He glanced at the minister and Mrs. Greenwood but neither seemed worried. "Delight, what do *you* say? Pretty good?"

But for once Delight wouldn't commit herself. She held her glass with both hands, slowly sipping.

"We got a good well," Andy admitted.

Mary called them to dinner now. She'd made Andy

promise not to tell how early she'd got up to get everything ready; but he did tell later on. Mary was flustered over preparing a dinner for matrons so much more experienced than herself. Her brunette cheeks were stained with rose. The customary company meal of fried chicken, mashed potatoes and cream gravy, vegetables, coleslaw, pickles, pie, was set out on the best wedding-present tablecloth—the one, in fact, that Belle had given. But Mary always had something a little different!—as Bertha exclaimed admiringly. At each place, on each white napkin, she had put a beautifully colored leaf. She was serving a wild brambleberry jam from a recipe that she had made up herself. The leaves—the drink of cold water just before the meal—seemed to bring a strange element, delicate and wild, into the plain new-smelling dining room in its setting of bare country quiet.

"She always finds something," Andy said with pride.

But all could feel now the stern influence of the country silence. Beneath the bright, soft glow of Mary's eyes lay a look that was solitary and shy. Even Dave was at first subdued. There was not much talking at the table. In the intervals, the windmill could again be heard; and then each one of the persons at the table seemed to feel suddenly detached and lonely. Delight seemed to feel this most of all. Her wild rose cheeks were pale. She could scarcely eat her dinner.

It was not until after dinner that the real pleasure of being out in the country began.

The company again divided itself into two groups, the menfolks and the womenfolks. The men went outside and sat down on the doorstep to take their ease and recover from the meal. Dave couldn't be content long with sitting still, however.

"Well, s'pose we go and take a look around," he proposed. "How about it, Andy? Like to see the place, Reverend?"

"Oh yes," Mr. Greenwood answered alertly.

"I don't know as there's much to see," Andy felt that he must add. The place didn't look as he intended it should some day. He and Mary were just starting out. There wasn't much to show folks now except land—and most townsfolk, he said, didn't know enough about that to think it was worth seeing.

"It's worth seeing to me," Mr. Greenwood assured him. "Nothing more so."

Dave could show off anything, even a pigpen. Andy walked along with the other two men, mostly silent, but with an expression between exasperation and secret amusement in his eyes. You would certainly have thought, to hear Dave talk, that he himself was going to do all the work of development! Andy had sometimes remarked, even to Dave, that Dave didn't care about farming. "You look upon this piece of land," Andy had told his brother, "as an investment first of all." And when Dave had then demanded, "Well, don't you? Isn't that the way you look at it?" Andy had replied shortly, "No, I don't. I look at it as the place where we live and are going to raise our crops."

Clarence went trotting along with the men, keeping close beside his Uncle Andy. For the time being he had almost forgotten Delight, and had gone back to his old insatiable interest in the conversation of older people. The minister's blue gaze, sometimes brightly alert, and then again so strangely remote, seemed to link all that he saw around him with something far beyond.

The windmill kept barely turning up in the wide blue air, until all at once a breeze struck it and it began going at a great rate.

"Ah, I must stop and have a taste of that water again!" Mr. Greenwood said.

He insisted on doing the pumping himself. The breeze had come up and died right down. Andy looked as if he felt rather foolish standing back; but it seemed to amuse and please him to see the minister working vigorously away, his face keen with concentration. The pump was new, it still had its green paint. It gave its first harsh metallic gasps, then the bright water came rushing. Clarence had to have another drink too. He'd never thought anything much about his Uncle Andy's well water before, except that it was good and cold; his mother said it hurt her teeth; but now, from what Mr. Greenwood had said, it seemed to him there was something mysteriously different in the taste. He realized that this was country water. The earth out here was bigger, and the well must be deeper, it must almost reach to the center of the earth. He got dizzy trying to imagine.

"Isn't this fine, Clarence?"

Clarence solemnly nodded his head.

"Wipe off your chin now," his father told him.

Andy grinned; he was more pleased and proud than he cared to show. Clarence had often heard Uncle Andy say that this was one reason he had chosen this place—because of the water. Dave might say now *he* was the one who'd made the selection, but the fact was Dave had had another piece picked out, nearer town. Uncle Andy had done his own selecting, going at it very carefully, trying to take everything into consideration. Now he was satisfied. If Dave, he said, should ever take it into his head to pull up stakes again and go on further, this time Andy knew *he* wasn't going to budge. He liked it right where he was. But Dave scoffed at the idea of ever pulling up stakes, and Clarence couldn't even conceive of such a possibility.

"Funny how the wind always seems to go down right when you want it," Dave grumbled.

"Oh well," the minister said confidently, "we'll soon have machinery to beat the wind."

"Sure," Dave said, "to beat the whole business."

Andy grinned again, but not so the other men could see him. Those two could talk, but Andy had the hard-bitten skepticism of a grower and outdoor worker, who had to take the seasons as they came. Still, he seemed somewhat moved and even doubtful. He had a farmer's diffidence, as well as a farmer's skepticism, with those who could put things into words.

The pump still made harsh, remonstrating noises after the men had turned away. A few last drops trickled, running off the new board platform, then crawling in dusty runlets that soaked slowly into the hard bare ground.

"Think they'll ever get machinery to make it rain, Reverend?" Dave was asking.

Clarence looked first at his father and then at Mr. Greenwood. His lower lip hung slightly.

"Mankind will solve all those problems in time," Mr. Greenwood firmly replied.

"Yep, they will all right," Dave agreed. "They're on the track right now. Inventors are."

"Well, yah, I guess we ain't there yet," Andy put in.

"Not there," Mr. Greenwood said, "but we'll reach it some day."

Clarence's eyes shone. He broke away from his Uncle Andy, picked up a stick and threw it. The stick traveled through a great bright arc of space before it landed on rough ground. Clarence felt the immensity of the prairie sky. The dog barked, but kept to his place near the back door, sullen and wary—he didn't see enough people to learn to be friendly, Uncle Andy said. "He's all right with us, though. You ought to see how he follows Mary." The barking sounded tiny and distant; ominous but futile.

The men were going now to have a look at the barn.

"That's something I *am* going to have," Andy remarked. "A good barn. This one ain't much to look at."

"Oh, you'll have everything fixed up in time," Dave assured him.

"Yah, maybe, I guess so."

The barn seemed big to Clarence. It was a lot bigger than the stable at home. He sniffed the boardy newness, the smells of straw and manure, and of hay, dusty and fragrant. Their footsteps made hollow sounds.

"You get a good view from here, Reverend," Dave said.

He was standing in the open doorway at the back of the barn; Mr. Greenwood joined him and looked out eagerly. Across the trampled barnyard, hard and dry in autumn sunshine, they had a view of fields brown or dark gold, slowly rising toward that limitless horizon. Cass Story had once written, of his first entrance into this countryside, that he had felt himself out of sight of water just as on the sea people got out of sight of land.

"Yes, this is a fine prospect."

They looked over tramped stubble, plowed earth, uncultivated pastures, here and there the brushy softness of a planted grove—all rough and new, yet thriving; hazy in the dusty, golden air; and beneath the freshly turned soil, that ancientness, archaic, inscrutable; kind, but with a savage mystery, almost hidden.

"A wonderful prospect," Mr. Greenwood repeated. He ran his hand through his rumpled hair. "Oh, I tell you," he said with characteristic firmness, "we people can make anything of this country here, if we go about it, make actual use of our opportunities."

"That's right," Dave agreed. "Oh, we're going right ahead."

"It's a great endowment," the minister said. "The richest endowment any people ever had given them."

"That's it," Dave cried eagerly. "That's the way to state it."

"When you think of this—that right here and now we people have the chance to work out one of the greatest experiments in mankind's history. The forefathers gave us the theme, when they wrote the Declaration of Independence and the Preamble to the Constitution."

"I don't know as I've ever read those documents," Dave said, abashed. "I s'pose everybody should."

Clarence was thrilled by the grand-sounding titles.

Andy had come up and was standing near the others. He said he didn't know about "given" them—he thought folks had to work for what they got. When it came down to that, he guessed they'd taken this land, not had it handed over to them. There was a pile of buffalo horns, the Indians had left, right over there on Wes Peeble's place above the river. Yet he admitted some truth in what the minister said; his pride and satisfaction were deepened.

"It's a good piece of land," he said soberly. "I don't ask for much better. If grasshoppers don't come again. Or it don't get too dry."

Dave said those times were over—drought, grasshopper plagues, blizzards: those hardships belonged to the early days. But Andy said in farming you never could be sure; you might rid yourself of weeds one year, but they'd come back just when you thought you had them licked; things had a way of coming 'round again—like one of those Ferris wheels. A farmer always had to be on the lookout.

"But then," he added, "I guess there'd be something you'd find against you, everywhere. I guess there's no place that don't have something."

The three men looked out at the country together. To each one of them it bore a different significance.

Clarence was right there, too. He didn't know just what Mr. Greenwood meant, when he said "endowment," but he felt the same excitement that had made him throw his stick a little while ago. Now he jumped from the doorsill down onto rough ground, hearing through a dazzled glitter of elation, that came partly from the stubble and the sun, his father shouting at him:

"Hey there! What you doing? Look out!"

The two women had insisted on helping Mary with the dishes; but now they had all come back to the front room and taken out their sewing. Delight had been keeping so quiet all this while they had almost forgotten she was anywhere nearby. Now she came softly over to her mother's chair.

"I guess she's set still as long as she could," Bertha observed. "You should have brought your sewing like the rest of us."

Delight shook her head.

Her mother said, "I'm afraid she doesn't care much about sewing. She used to like to make doll hats. But now she and Clarence are too busy playing most of the time. I wonder where Clarence can be."

"He's gone off with the menfolks. They're nobody knows where by this time."

"Do you want to try and find him?"

Delight shook her head again. But she was beginning to look forlorn. She was wearing her blue percale dress, and her worst scuffed shoes, so that she could play as hard as she liked out in the country. Her mother said that once she would have been able to occupy herself all day long. But now she and Clarence must do everything together.

"There he is," Bertha said suddenly. "I thought he'd be around." She told him, "Come in if you're coming. Don't hang on the screen that way. You'll let all the flies in for Aunt Mary."

Clarence let the door bang shut.

When they asked him where he'd been—"Around," he said vaguely.

"Ja, he never knows."

He wanted Delight to come out and play with him now. But they had both grown shy in this interval of being apart. Delight wouldn't give any answer at first. Then suddenly she shook back her braids and went running off.

Even when they were outside, Clarence couldn't get her to play. The yard was big and empty; she felt even more strange than in the house.

"Come on, Delight. I'll take you. I know lots of places where we can live."

"I don't want to live anywhere."

"*I* do."

She went slowly off across the yard and Clarence trailed after her. The sun burned down on their bare heads. The windmill turned lonesomely up above them. One of those queer little winds came up suddenly, from nowhere, and whirled the dust. Delight was scared.

"Maybe it's a cyclone!"

"No, it 'tain't a cyclone!"

The windmill had started going loud and fast. Grit blew into their eyes until they couldn't see. Delight caught hold of Clarence's hand, and he stood protecting her, braced stoutly. Strands of her hair blew against his face and even got into his mouth when he shouted to her that this was just the wind. Clarence wasn't afraid of any cyclone out on his Uncle Andy's place.

The wind died down almost as suddenly as it had started. Then the children both began to laugh. The noise of the windmill was slowly fading out, like the swing when they let the old cat die.

"Come on, Delight, let's go out and see the corn shocks. Should we? Come on."

Delight picked her way daintily, then crying suddenly

"I'm going to run!" she spread out her arms and went running ahead. Clarence wasn't going to have her beat him, and he ran as fast as he could pound, with his fists doubled up, and face red and determined. He got to the edge of the cornfield first. "I beat you!" he started to yell. But Delight looked so innocent of any thought of a contest that he was ashamed. She never could go long at a walk. She always had to run or skip or hippity-hop.

Uncle Andy had got his shocking done out here, so as to have one field out of the way. Again the corn shocks seemed to the children like little wigwams. The sun shone down on their weathered gold from the Indian blue of the sky.

"Let's play Hiawatha and Minnehaha!"

Last summer, before they'd started to school and got their primers, they had played fairies and brownies or queens and kings. But now they liked Indians best. It troubled Clarence that Delight was ahead of the story. She knew how to read before she started to school. While the other children were laboriously repeating "Hiawatha was an Indian boy, Nokomis was his grandmother," she had gone skipping far ahead. She knew how Hiawatha had gone out to the land of the Dakotas and brought back Minnehaha for his bride. Another thing that impressed Clarence was her blithe daring in making over any story to suit herself. Now she said:

"We'll play Hiawatha and Minnehaha knew each other when they were children. We don't want any Nokomis. I don't want to be a grandmother. We'll play Hiawatha and Minnehaha always lived together in the wigwam."

They picked out the best and biggest of the shocks and burrowed out a little place for themselves. They couldn't really crawl into it, but Delight said they could pretend. The long dry corn leaves crackled and the sharp points scratched their faces. They looked at each other, bright-eyed. Clarence remembered the brush of her hair against his skin, and the glossy taste of it in his mouth. They could hear each other breathing.

Delight said in a breathless voice, "This is *our* wigwam. Nobody knows where we are."

It was the best of all the places they had found: better than the haymow, or the sunflower patch, or the little corner in the choir loft beside the organ. They were out here all by themselves in the golden freedom of the October afternoon.

But the shock was too scratchy, they came wriggling out again. The sun was so brilliant after the brief crackling darkness that at first they had to shut their eyes.

"Now let's play."

Delight was going to stay and keep house in the wigwam and Clarence would go out roaming and bring home things. Then she would cook their feast over the fire. He wasn't to shoot any animals, though.

"Hiawatha did. He shot the roebuck."

Delight said with airy imperiousness, "We'll play he didn't. Because I don't *like* things to be shot." She wanted everything in the world to go on living.

Clarence felt a sneaking disappointment. The book showed a colored picture of Hiawatha with the roebuck over his shoulder. He wanted to play he had a bow and arrows. If he couldn't use his bow and arrows, what was there to bring back? Delight told him, oh lots of things. Corn, and pumpkins—the Indians ate everything like that. They discovered the corn. Mr. Story said so.

"And while you're gone, Hiawatha, *I'll* have to be making the fire. Because Indian ladies do that. Papa always does it for mama, but we're Indians. I won't make it *in*side the wigwam, I'll make it *out*side. And then we can have a big Indian feast."

Clarence set off, pretending he had on moccasins, and feeling anxious, important, and alert. He could play he had his bow and arrows anyway. There might be wild animals, mean ones, like wolves. *They* wouldn't be Hiawatha's brothers, like the beavers and squirrels in the picture. The sun burned down, making the top of his head feel hot and shiny. Far up in the sky he saw something flying—a hawk! Hawks were mean to other birds, worse even than blue jays, those old pesky blue jays, so he guessed he had to bring down that old hawk. He took his bow from his shoulder and pulled an arrow out of the quiver, selecting one carefully and feeling of the point. When he'd found the right one, he fitted it to the string, drew his bow with a mighty effort, squinted up toward the sky and shouting "Whang!" let fly. The sky dazzled his eyes, but this time it was an empty dazzle. He ran a little way and made believe to pick up his hawk. He couldn't take it back, though, so he threw it away. He walked stealthily in his moccasins because there were enemies on all sides—now and then taking aim with his bow and arrow.

Ducks were out on the moist sloppy ground near the water tank. Clarence pointed his arrow at them and they went waddling. "Aw, I wasn't going to shoot you." He picked up some mottled gray feathers, and a little fluffy one, and a pure white one—he would give that one to Delight. He leaned over the rim of the tank and looked down into the silent water. In the corncrib, where the walls showed cracks of gold in the dusty light, he took two hard yellow ears of corn. Uncle Andy wouldn't care. There wasn't any orchard yet, so he couldn't find apples. Maybe Uncle Andy wouldn't like it if he was to pick a pumpkin. But Aunt Mary had some gourds piled up outside the shed. He did take one of those.

It seemed as if he had been away for a long, long time. He was glad to come in sight of the wigwam. Delight was out in front of the wigwam sitting cross-legged and rocking back and forth and singing. Her braids had been looped up hammock fashion, but now she had let them down to look more like Minnehaha. She was singing the song the class had learned from the primer. Her treble sounded clear but strangely distant. Clarence could see the sun on her long shining braids, her long fair hair.

"Ea-wah-yea, my little owlet,
With your big eyes, light the wigwam,
With your big eyes, light the wigwam,
Ea-wah-yea, my little owlet."

Clarence felt the same dazzling golden happiness as on that first day when Delight was visiting at his house and he had run outside when he heard the girls talking about her. Everything had a glittering edge, like the rough corn shocks out in the sunshine. Clarence didn't care if the other kids teased him, saying, "I bet you're going to marry Delight! Ha ha." He *was* going to marry her, Clarence thought with perfect confidence. They were always partners. All the boys wanted the new little girl. But they couldn't have her for long. Playing Needles-Eye on the vacant lot behind the church, Delight wouldn't let down her hands until she could catch Clarence—"Because I wanted *you*." Clarence hurried to give her his plunder. They could stick the feathers in their hair. It seemed perfectly natural that they should be living in their wigwam. It was the most natural thing that could be.

Mary had insisted on setting out an early supper. It would be too late, she told the folks, when they got home. The chicken tasted even better cold, along with Mary's homemade bread.

But the children were so sleepy they could scarcely eat. Clarence's loose tooth had come out when he was trying to gnaw that hard corn at their feast. He didn't want his mother to notice. The children had decided that their wigwam would always be a secret. They had taken their feathers out of their hair and Clarence had them hidden inside his blouse. Whenever they played Hiawatha and Minnehaha, they would wear these same feathers.

Now, when everybody went outdoors again, the sun was low. The windmill threw its shadow long and straight across bare ground. The crickets shrilled all through the fields. Their great autumnal chorus made that in town, in the vacant lots, seem only the small chirping of a local band. Nighttime sounded in this great music. The cows were near the barn now, wanting to be milked, and the pigs set up a terrible squealing.

"Mollie's getting impatient, folks," Dave warned. "We'll have to hurry. She won't stand much longer."

Bertha believed that. Dave winked at the others. Mollie turned her head to look at the folks. Her kind brown eyes tried to see past her blinders. She had been staked out all afternoon and had enjoyed herself as much as anybody. But she was willing to get back to her stable now.

The women had come out laden with packages again, things Mary in her turn had insisted on giving them: a pint of cream each, and half a dozen big duck eggs. Bertha kept up an anxious twitter as Dave took the packages from her.

"Look out, Mister. Those are eggs. Be careful, that's cream, ach, that'll spill."

The children refused to sit anywhere but on the floor of the carriage. "No, we *like* it there," they insisted. Andy and Mary stood together watching the company leave. The dog came as far as the corner of the house, growling, until Andy said to him, "Haven't you got any sense, you ought to be acquainted by this time." Then the dog came slouching slowly forward and lay down just behind Mary. She reached back to pat his head and he accepted that gratefully. The chickens had all crossed the farmyard. But when the carriage started they ran crazily strutting and clucking. Delight thought they were going to get run over, but Dave said:

"*They'll* skedaddle, don't you worry."

It was time for last good-byes. The children were up on their knees looking back and waving.

"Good-bye, good-bye!" they shouted as the carriage turned into the road.

Dusk came over the country long before they reached home. The two women in the back seat talked contentedly. The men had done most of their talking this afternoon. The children were played out. Their heads rested against their mothers' knees, and the mothers moved their feet in cautious discomfort. The farmhouses seemed to stand farther apart than ever. Lamplight here and there looked almost more lonely than the dusk. Fresh odors of evening came up from the ground and from the partly withered thickets of asters and goldenrod along the roadsides. The road was narrow and intimate between great reaches of fields.

When they came to the railroad tracks, the carriage bumped going over, and the children were jolted half awake.

"Nothing," their mothers told them. "Just the tracks."

But they sat up again because they were coming to New Hope. With all the lights, it looked like quite a city. They were proud and excited to think this was home.

CHAPTER V

The Parsonage

THE MINISTER'S FAMILY had moved into the parsonage the
week before school began. The members of the Young
Ladies' Society had been there the day before giving the
floors and woodwork a final going-over. The rooms smelled
of paint, wallpaper, and scrubbing. The doors were open to
let out this smell; and through the blank glisten of the screens
vacancy showed. There were no near neighbors. On one side
stood the church, on the other stretched an empty lot rank
with tough-stemmed weeds. A boardwalk ran beside it leading to Main Street. The boards had a shimmer of blue-gray-
silver in the dry August heat. The one-story frame house was
surrounded by the shrilling of katydids. It seemed lonely at
first after the turmoil of the Miller household. There was
something almost somber in this vacancy. The Greenwoods
were all glad to go back up the hill to the Miller's for supper
that first evening.

The settling itself had turned out to be not so much of
a job. People came in to help. "Many hands made light
labor." It wasn't so long since *they'd* been getting settled
here, people said, and they knew what it involved. Mr. Stiles
and old Mr. Broadwater came over to lay the carpets. Folks

could always count on plenty of fun whenever Jim Stiles was around! Mrs. Stiles had to be there too, keeping her bright, sharp eyes on the business. "James, have you taken the exact measurements? Are you sure that's being cut to fit?" Mr. Stiles was as unperturbed as his own glass eye. When he was ready with a strip of carpet, he shouted, "Woman, out of my path!" and sent Mrs. Stiles scurrying before him. She was both pleased and indignant. Old Mr. Broadwater did the tacking. But this was in his own line of business, he took pains to explain, courteously refusing any thanks. Mr. Broadwater—as the two families agreed, talking the day's work over at the supper table—was as much of a character in his way as James Stiles. A Southerner—like Judge Lewis—he had come North with his family about the time of the Civil War, when he had taken the side of the Union.

"No, he didn't take the side of the Union, papa," Bess interrupted. "He just couldn't be in favor of slavery and secession."

"What's the difference?" Dave demanded, glaring. "I don't see any difference."

"Well, that's what Nellie said. I don't just know, but Nellie Vance explained it to Dora and me."

Well, anyway, when Nellie and Willis were married and moved to New Hope, the old gentleman had come to make his home with them. He had then taken up the trade of paper hanging, as—this was the way he put it—"a needed and useful calling": first to help out his daughter, in the establishment of her new home, but afterwards consenting to make a business of it on the request of fellow citizens.

Entering the parsonage that morning, with an air that was both modest and formal, saying to Mrs. Greenwood with a bow, "At your service, ma'am—I beg your pardon," he had taken off his frock coat, folded it, laid it in a corner, and set his stovepipe hat upon it: his customary proceeding before starting to work.

The children had been in and out all that morning—
driven out when they got too much in the way, but always
appearing soon again; wandering down to the Creek, and
finally up the hill to the Miller house. At noon Clarence was
sent running back to the parsonage to tell the folks they
were all to come up the hill to dinner.

"Mama says to. She's got everything ready."

The Young Ladies' Society had undertaken to hem the
new curtains. They had met at Dora Palmer's for a sewing
bee. Mrs. Greenwood and Mrs. Dave Miller had been asked to
come too; and Dora had asked the children to come in for
refreshments. Everybody enjoyed being entertained at the
Palmers'. The house was new; Dora and her mother kept it
Swedishly bright and spick-and-span. Nowhere else—and
there were many good coffee makers in New Hope—was
such coffee as Mrs. Palmer served, or such rolls and cookies.
Dave had said, "If old Captain Palmer had married her just
for her cookies I wouldn't have blamed him!" That was another interest for Mrs. Greenwood—that she would see
Dora's mother. She had been hearing many stories from the
Miller girls. Dora Palmer's mother, a Swedish woman, had
taken care of Captain Orlando Palmer's first wife in her
long illness. Nobody would at first believe it, so Mrs. Vance
and Mrs. Murdock had said, when Captain Palmer had married this girl "right after." Oh, she was good as gold, but
at that time a young girl, just over from the old country,
scarcely knowing a word of English; and Captain Palmer,
Mrs. Murdock said, was a *very* cultured man, and had three
grown sons. Two of these sons would never "acknowledge"
the marriage; but the other, a rich man now, in business out
in San Francisco, was good to the second wife and treated
Dora like his own sister. He was always sending Dora lovely
things. He had paid for her musical education.

But the girls never could persuade Mrs. Palmer to come
in and eat with them—not on this afternoon nor at any

other time. They could get her only as far as the door. There
she held back, laughing and shaking her head until her small,
round gold earrings jingled.

As soon as the curtains were up, and the rooms in order,
the ladies in town made visits, of combined welcome and inspection, at the parsonage. The girls particularly—the Miller
girls, Dora, Trixie, Ella Murdock, and the others—admired
the way that Mrs. Greenwood had arranged the house; saying among themselves, "Do you remember how Hannah
Barbour had this room, wasn't it *awful?*" The parsonage was
certainly not highly furnished now. But Mrs. Greenwood
gave a peculiar daintiness to whatever she touched. The girls
all wanted to copy her plain, sheer curtains, and the little
draped and ruffled dressing table she had made out of dimity
and packing boxes for Delight. Even her economies had
turned out to be virtues in the eyes of these girls!

There was plenty of work to be done about the place
before winter began. Mr. Barbour had possessed no knack
for tinkering; and of course he had been in poor health. But
it soon appeared that Mr. Greenwood was the kind who must
have everything shipshape. Almost his first act had been to
fix every lock and catch throughout the house. Bertha Miller
couldn't get over that. To think a minister should be able to
fix the locks and all like that!—he could do it, and Mister
was no good at such things, always had to fall back on hiring
somebody.

The backyard work was what the children enjoyed.
Clarence, at any rate, did. Some of the country members
paid in wood. The children were allowed to pile up the wood
after it had been chopped—or to carry over the pieces and
fling them down near where the winter woodpile was to
stand. Mr. Greenwood's woodpiles were marvels of precision;
he wouldn't have tolerated another hand in the actual building. He must have Yankee blood in him, Mrs. Stiles asserted;
although Mr. Stiles teased her, saying there'd been good

woodsmen before there'd been Yankees, believe it or not. The children loved the freshly cut sticks, with their crisp, clean edges, the swaths of shiny pale surface and the splintery brown streaks, the curly knots that were like taffy candy. Later it was their work to pick up the chips, digging grubby fingers into moist brown dirt and fresh sawdust and withered grass. Lugging the piled-up bushel basket between them, they trudged importantly to the kitchen. It wasn't so easy getting Clarence to work at home! He was better at sliding out of jobs there, so the family said. But he liked everything that went on at the parsonage. He was on hand as soon as he'd finished his breakfast.

Mrs. Stiles, when she was over at the Millers' one day, remarked that she liked to hear the minister out in his backyard chopping or sawing. He brought the same clear-cut energy to bear in work of this kind as he put into the organization and delivery of his sermons. His ax always rang true. If he gave up the ministry, once he said, he'd go into carpentry and woodcutting. Jesus never would have spoken as he did, Mr. Greenwood maintained, if he hadn't worked earlier at the carpenter's trade.

The first time she had seen the parsonage, that first afternoon when Dave Miller had taken them on a drive through town, it had seemed to Mrs. Greenwood the house couldn't ever be made home. This was what she confided to some of her friends, to Mrs. Stiles, and to Bess and Edie. But now that feeling was gone. On Sunday mornings, when people were always running over, when country women came in to rest and to get the babies changed before the service began, the parsonage seemed only an offshoot of the church. But on Monday morning, the church stood closed-up and empty on its rise of ground, and the one-story parsonage down the slope detached itself and became the family dwelling place.

During their first days in the parsonage Mrs. Greenwood had been almost afraid of the emptiness, the rawness, the harsh and weedy lots, the long, bare boardwalk shining in the heat. But in the fall sunshine there was exhilaration in the bareness itself. It gave them the chance to do whatever they liked and to make the place their own. The surrounding shrilling of the katydids and crickets rose above the minor chorus of the evening and in the early daytime had a golden sound. It seemed to mean that this was morning, not that night and winter were close at hand. They were living in a morning world.

The long, dry, beautiful autumn season, filled from horizon to horizon with sunshine, seemed to have endowed the young couple in the parsonage with exhilarating energy. Mr. Greenwood declared with keen satisfaction that his wife hadn't been so well in years. As soon as they were settled in their new home, they threw themselves wholeheartedly into the work of building up the church.

This church, founded by families from the old community, and for a long time dominated by the "old element," had kept the stern Calvinism that Rodney Harper had fastened upon the early establishment. Old Father Kent himself had preached an austere doctrine. The former minister in New Hope, the Reverend Abel Barbour, had suited that part of the congregation represented by John Budd. Coming West because of poor health, Mr. Barbour, himself quite elderly, had taken the young struggling church at New Hope as a home missionary charge. But dissatisfaction had long been growing. The new minister had caught the church at the very point of transition: when it could reorganize, make itself independent, and choose its own man.

This was the time!—Dave Miller went around saying, with pride and elation, because he had foreseen it; and his hopes and prophecies were right. The town was growing so rapidly that if their church didn't get a move on itself and take the lead, some other church would. The younger people must cut loose, once and for all, from the early community. Its day was done. To want to rebuild, as the Harpers held out for doing, on the site of the first meetinghouse—that would simply have meant that the Methodists and Baptists could take over the town. As if folks were going to drive four miles, for sentimental reasons, when there were other churches right at their door! The fact was, Harry Harper knew that just as well as anybody; the only reason he advocated such an idea was to give himself an excuse for not attending church. But the Vances and the Murdocks and Electa Stiles had just about had their fill of the Harper domination; although they too seemed to Dave Miller sentimental about the early days. Old Rodney's hand had been heavy over them in their early youth. Now they were ready to join hands with those who—after nine, ten, a dozen years —were still called "the new families": the Millers, the Storys, the Wrights and Staleys, the Shafers, the Wards.

The town itself—Dave Miller had seen this too—had just been waiting for a real preacher. A lot of these folks, Dave admitted, were natural rovers, they would go wherever the crowd was heading. Mr. Greenwood was able to draw in some who had never attended before, some of the stragglers, "the doubtful ones": Lute Fairbrother, the printer who worked for Cass Story, Wes Bibbs who traveled in summer with a circus, young people who were undecided.

A perplexing problem had come up at the very start. The children listened in awe when it was talked over among the older people. The problem concerned Mrs. Donohue's brother. No one had known until he suddenly appeared—his name was Clayt Hetherington—that Mrs. Donohue *had* a brother. Then folks could see why the brother hadn't been mentioned: he had been serving a term in state's prison back in Pennsylvania. He had come out here to make a new start. Mrs. Donohue, it seemed, had gone over to the parsonage

to tell the whole story and to interest the new minister in
her brother's reformation. Mr. Greenwood asked at an early
meeting of his trustees, held at the Dave Miller house, why
should not Clayt Hetherington be given the position of
janitor? Really taken at his word and helped along? The
church had come to the place where a janitor was needed. It
couldn't depend upon voluntary efforts much longer. Some
were against the idea—that was to be expected; but more
were for it. Mrs. Stiles was reported as saying grimly that if
this church refused the man a chance, it had no right to grow
—it might better close its doors. There was sympathy for Mrs.
Donohue, on close sectarian grounds—her husband, Barney
Donohue, was a strong Catholic (although even Lowell
Livermore, who blamed the Miller brothers for "selling out
to a Catholic," couldn't deny that Barney was a good fellow). The oldest daughter Trixie attended church with her
mother; Alicia was devoutly her father's child; the youngest, Winifred, went to Sunday school but not to church. Mr.
Greenwood wouldn't listen to long tales about this part of
the matter—he brushed them aside. Sectarian motives
shouldn't enter into the decision; shouldn't be allowed to
count one way or the other. Whether they did count or did
not, the motion to appoint Clayt Hetherington janitor won
through; and the church felt with awe that it had a real
potential convert. It was this action which led Lute Fairbrother to attend—a matter for wonder. Until now, in spite
of Grandma Story's coaxings and wistful head shakings, Lute
had never set foot inside any church in New Hope.

Dave Miller kept saying with pride that every sermon
was better than the last. Mr. Greenwood himself told others
that it was inspiring to him, after the small old-fashioned
church in Ballard, with the same few families sitting Sunday
after Sunday in the same pews, to look out over these big
congregations. If a man couldn't do well under such condi-
tions, he wouldn't amount to much! Many of these people

had driven in from miles away. All through the prolonged
sunny weather the church doors stood open, as on that first
Sunday. The air kept the tang of goldenrod. The feeling of
growth submerged differences and gave all a desire to work
together. In spite of the threat of division at the beginning
of the new pastorate, the church had never been so united
as now.

The young people turned out in full force. The moment
the Christian Endeavor let out, almost before they finished
saying in unison, "When we are absent one from another,"
the boys began a scuffle for the back row of chairs in the
primary room. The girls sat just in front of them. Some of
the older members didn't like this arrangement. John Budd
for a while took to standing near the door of the primary,
waiting for the meeting to be over, and warning in his
cold, deep voice, "Guess you young men better find seats
farther front." But the minister said he'd rather stand the
commotion than be too severe with the young people. Only
once did he have to pause in his sermon and briefly suggest
that there might be more quiet in the rear of the church.
The whisperings and gigglings stopped so short it seemed as
if the girls were holding their breath. Some had tears in
their eyes. There was a clear-cut incisiveness in the minister's
voice more intimidating than the direst thundering from Mr.
Barbour. The girls' faces burned as they stared straight ahead
of them. They paid no attention to the boys. But later on,
during the last song, slips of paper began circulating, torn
out of the backs of hymn books and smudgily pencil-marked
with girls' names: "Irene," "Trix," "Mamie W." The girls
pretended not to know they had received the notes. Then
they would read the papers, hastily fold them up again, and
crush the hard little squares in warm hands. After a while,
looking stealthily around as they began putting on coats,
each would give one quick nod and glance toward a certain
face in the back row, hastily turn and be absorbed in the

benediction—flushed, with glowing eyes, lightly pleased or tumultuously happy.

During the final hymn the boys would have begun edging toward the door; and even before the singing was over they would have started slipping out into the entry. Then when church let out with a burst of music, on these autumn nights under great skies of stars, the girls would come outside giggling and huddled together for protection, torturingly aware of the dark, significant, waiting rows, lined up all down the walk, through which they must pass. They had to endure the helplessness of deferred expectation, until figures detaching themselves from the lines saying gruffly, "See you home," turned fear into high security. At the end, there would always be a little residue of boys to fade insignificantly away into the darkness, a little knot of girls to go off clinging together, laughing and pretending they didn't care. Voices for a while rang with shrill animation. Footsteps were loud on the board sidewalks.

The older people had their excitements too. There were many things to be talked over, the size of the congregation, the plans for the coming week; and there was the collection to be counted. The leading families often stayed for some time after the service had closed, until sleepy children began to wail, mothers said they simply must get these children home to bed. The janitor, diligent but not quite at ease, gathered up the hymnbooks and closed the primary-room doors. The minister, and the others who remained, said, "Good night, Clayt," and left him to lock up the building. Lights shone in the parsonage while the minister had his lunch of milk and cinnamon rolls out in the kitchen. Finally both the house and the church were dark. The houses were dark up on the hill. Another big Sunday was over. Occasionally a buggy went past, some young fellow driving home after kissing his girl in the dark shelter of her porch. Then the town settled into the great stillness of the prairie night, broken only by the whistle of a train on its way across the continent.

The September morning seemed faraway, when—with new tablets, new pencil boxes, new pencils with erasers—Delight and Clarence had started in to school together. They became seasoned school children. Mr. Broadwater would say to them, meeting them on the street:

"Good morning, young scholars."

Saturdays were the big days now. On the other days, they played after school with the rest of the children. But Saturdays they spent together.

Clarence put in his appearance at the parsonage as early as possible. Sometimes he had errands downtown for his mother and the girls, and he wanted Delight to go with him. When they were through with errands, and with gathering the chips, they could do whatever they pleased.

The parsonage as it was then had a little square front porch with two wide, shallow steps leading down to the sidewalk. Delight tried to balance herself on the iron foot scraper attached to the lower step. She swayed with her arms outstretched in a poised, eager gesture. Clarence waited anxiously for her to say what they should do first. She could think of more things than he could. But he would begin to think of things later. They played her kind of games part of the time and part of the time they played his. Her eyes were bright now with all the possibilities of the long day before them.

"Let's just start out!" she cried. She jumped lightly to the ground.

No matter in which direction they did go they could have good times: in town, where they could see the teams and stamp for white horses, look into store windows and say which things they would buy first, finally wander into the bank and wait for the pennies Clarence's father would give them to spend at Donohue's. Wherever they appeared they were sure of a welcome. They could play among the piles of boards in Mr. Vance's lumberyard, which smelled of planed woods, of fresh shingles, of resin getting sticky in the sun; or crawl through long tiles that had an earthy odor, scared of getting stuck, but wriggling through to daylight again. They made friends with the new man who was working for Mr. Vance, and he saved clean little blocks of wood for Clarence and long shaving curls for Delight. Clarence always wanted to go into Mr. Story's office in the small frame building of the *Citizen*. He liked this building one of the best. The floors were shaken by the racket of the printing presses in the other room where Lute Fairbrother was boss. "Do you know who that represents?" Mr. Story asked, pointing to one of the pictures over his desk. "That is Benjamin Franklin. He was the first great editor in America." Clarence looked with awe, but Delight giggled because Franklin wore his hair in curls like Bonita Button in their grade; Bonita's mother put Bonita's hair up on curlers every night but the curls didn't stay. Clarence could have spent all morning in and around the shop, watching the machines, and shouting questions at Lute Fairbrother; but Delight wouldn't stay long, she liked houses better. The whole town lay open to them in the autumn sunshine, with its wide, brown, dusty streets, the bluish shimmer of the boardwalks, the empty lots with paths trodden through harsh, dry, glittering weeds.

The church was open. The janitor was getting it ready for Sunday. They could hear banging sounds inside as he swept between the long rows of wooden pews. Delight said *she* wasn't afraid to go in, and Clarence said he wasn't either. *They* weren't scared of the janitor because he had once been in jail, the way some kids were; Delight's father said that would be wrong and foolish. All the same, they preferred to go into the church when more people were there.

"We'll decide on the way," Delight said.

They stopped for some time on the bridge. It was fun when teams went over with a great rumble of planks. They were safe, on the raised footwalk at the side. The bridge had an iron railing. The old wooden one, carved all over with hearts and initials, had been carried away in the overflow three years ago last spring. Clarence's father always called it "the overflow"—never the flood. New Hope had never had a real flood. Trees grew scrubbily down the rough sides of the gully. The children leaned with both hands on the iron railing, warm from the sun, and stared down into the brushy treetops. The stream was all dried up this fall. They could see in patches the dusty glint of the stream bed. If they followed along, on and on between cracked dry banks, they would come into strange, far country. They would reach at last the ramshackle hut of the Groundhogs, standing in the open lot, in the midst of rusty old glinting tin cans. The children stared up the Creek in dreamy, delicious fear. They always talked about going to see the Groundhogs, but they hadn't quite dared. When they took their hands from the railing, the palms were smudged with reddish rust.

Clarence said, "If you have a cut, it can give you lock-jaw."

They searched their hands. Clarence had one tiny sore spot near the ball of his thumb.

"Spit on it," Delight told him.

Clarence spat, and rubbed the place with his other thumb.

"Now it'll be all right," Delight said confidently.

The loose heavy boards joggled when they ran across. But the bridge was safe. The town had put up new supports after the overflow. Clarence's father said the bridge was safe. Someday soon the town would build a wonderful new bridge: like London Bridge, Delight said, but even more wonderful.

They took the long boardwalk that led up the hill. They

could see the Miller house standing in the sunshine. The lightning rods glittered in the blue fall air. The slender branches of the ornamental birch tree were delicate without their leaves.

They weren't hungry yet, and so they didn't want to go into the house. Edie would give Clarence some errand. They ran through the yard and up the stable stairs to the haymow. Clarence's father had pushed all the hay over to one side and made a nice little room. It was going to be their playhouse and carpenter shop next spring. They were going to move all their furniture up there, Clarence's tools, Delight's little dishes and all her books. She had a whole row of fairy stories: the *Blue Fairy Book* and the *Gold* and the *Silver, The Little Lame Prince,* and *The Adventures of a Brownie.* Then they would come up here whenever it rained. Delight had told most of the stories to Clarence, in her eager voice, speaking for all the characters, deep and awful for the Old Witch and the ogre, in sweet, tiny tones for Tom Thumb and Thumbelinda, in squeaky tones for the brownies and marvelous whispers for the fairies. Delight was steeped in fairy tales. She moved surrounded by the gilded and starlit glimmer of their enchantment even on the long, straight boardwalks of New Hope; and the characters, Snow White, the Easter Rabbit, the Snow Queen, were just as familiar to her as Ollie Jenks and Mr. Groundhog and the "characters" in town were to Clarence. He knew the fairy and legend people too now; but only when he was with Delight. They were real to him when she told him about them. Sometimes she would tell him instead about Ballard: about Grandma Pettibone and the Hamburg rooster, and Judge Lewis and his colored man. Her bird treble would become a breathy whisper, her eyes would have their excited shine. Ecstatic shivers would go down Clarence's backbone, as he listened, with his lips apart. Everything was enhanced in the vividness of her bright fancy—and yet so clear, clearer than the daylight outside. The characters—Joan of Arc, Queen Isabella and Columbus, Sir Philip Sidney, Alice-through-the-looking-glass, Judge Lewis's big dog Prince, the hummingbird in the Judge's garden—all moved together in that shining enchantment.

But it was too cold up in the bare haymow on this day. It was warm now only in the sun. The two children decided they would make calls, like Delight's mother and father.

They considered their places. They could go to see Mrs. Vance, and old Mr. Broadwater if he was at home today. The Vances' house was as fancy inside as outside; and the children were impressed by the silken fringed draperies and the vases and the pictures in carved gold frames. Mrs. Vance and Mrs. Harry Harper were the only ladies in town who kept hired girls regularly. The children were flattered by Mrs. Vance's welcome, her voice that kept a lingering Southern slur; although Nellie Vance was born—Edie said—after her folks had left the South. They believed trustingly that no lady was ever more lovely than Mrs. Vance, in her soft dressing sacque trimmed with deep lace, her heirloom gold bracelet and her opal ring. She would seat them in cushioned rockers and talk and talk to them with her soft loquacity. Old Mr. Broadwater lived in his own wing of the house, although he took his meals with the Vances. He had two rooms. In one were his cot, his stove, his tall secretary desk; and the other, littered with big rolls of wallpaper and buckets of paste, was his workshop. His courtly greeting was almost more flattering than Mrs. Vance's talkative welcome; and while the children were calling upon him, and being asked what they had learned in school, they sat decorously in hard windsor chairs and nibbled on the white peppermints Mr. Broadwater gave them.

They went often to Dora Palmer's house, mostly to see the tiger cat that had broad black stripes like the watered silk ribbon Irene used for a girdle with her brown cashmere dress. They would go all through the yard calling the cat, not able to locate the faintly annoyed "Miaow" in answer; until they found him at last sitting stately and calm on the peak of the woodshed roof or on the cool, sun-spattered ground of the neat grape arbor.

They liked that house, too, with its bright windows and light, shining floors; the kitchen that smelled fresh of hard Swedish scrubbing. Mrs. Palmer, tiny and wrinkled in her immaculate kitchen dress, said things in a funny language they couldn't understand, always laughing, nodding so that her earrings jingled. Dora would call them into the parlor before they left and get them to sing for her while she made up accompaniments on her shining grand piano. First she let them sing the songs they learned in school, "October's Party" and "Over the River," which their teacher was giving them in preparation for Thanksgiving. But now Dora was teaching them other songs out of a big flat songbook with green covers stamped with a garland of gold.

"You pretty miller's maiden,
Come bring your boat to land."

Even Clarence wasn't afraid to sing in that light atmosphere, with Dora comforting and encouraging at the piano, humming along with them to show them the tune. Over the piano hung the picture of Mozart, with his fine keen face, making them think of Delight's father, except for the white curly wig like colonial days. They well knew, too, that Mrs. Palmer would come to the door, beckoning them out to the kitchen to get those fine, crisp-edged, Swedish cookies, light-colored to go with this house, that no other ladies could get to turn out so well in spite of having taken down the recipe.

Then there was Grandma Story's; Aunt Belle's; Mrs. Donohue's. But the children liked best of all to call on Mr. and Mrs. Stiles.

The Stiles's white house looked older and more settled than the other houses on the street. New England austerity had shaped the uncompromising front gable. Running up the front steps, then standing on the narrow porch, the children held a whispered conference.

"Shall we ring the bell?"

"No, let's knock on the door."

"*You* knock, Clarence."

Clarence gave one bold rap that hurt his knuckles against the doorframe, hard and minutely knobby. Although they expected a welcome, they always stood a little in awe. They waited, staring through the tightly hooked screen into the dark hall from which the staircase with its walnut railing mounted severely. The silence made a setting for the slow, stern ticking of the big old clock.

"Rap again," Delight whispered.

But Mr. Stiles had heard them. He was coming now to the front door. He had on slippers, and his glasses were set halfway down his nose. One lens was only window glass. Mr. Stiles didn't keep that one polished. He looked at the children over the glasses with his one good eye. They waited, expectant and uncertain.

"Well, see who's here! Come in, strangers." Mr. Stiles turned and shouted, "Lecty! Got some callers! Better come and see who they be."

Winking at the children, as if to say Mrs. Stiles would be fooled and think they were grown folks, he took them into the sitting room.

This room seemed to Clarence and Delight very spacious; and although it was on the other side of the house from the row of planted poplar trees, there was a gloom about it too. Maybe that came from the smell. Once when they were playing Guess Smells instead of Guess Colors, Delight had made up the name of one smell that Clarence couldn't guess, he had to give up: Mr. and Mrs. Stiles's Sitting-Room Smell.

They looked at each other now as they solemnly breathed that odor. It seemed to come from woodwork, wainscoting, faded ingrain carpet the color of withered leaves, from the clean, smooth nickel and iron of the unlighted stove, and the cold glassiness over the big picture of the Signing of the Declaration of Independence, in blackish gray, with a brown water stain in one corner. Delight said the smell was dark brown—chair-brown, she said, because in Mrs. Stiles's sitting room the chairs were dark walnut and had flat, squashed-down cushions. The footstools were made of carpet, but with undersides of shiny black oilcloth, so that they slid a little on the floor. Ferns, faded and brown, delicately brittle, were pressed and framed under the same cold glass, that seemed cold even in the summertime. The furniture had come from the old Kent house that was now only a nettle-grown cellar hole out in the old community.

Mr. Stiles said, "Well, Mehitabel Long-locks and Thomas Teedlebum, be seated."

"Those aren't our names."

"Then what are your names?"

"*You* know."

Delight had got all over her shyness. She cried, "I know where *I'm* going to sit," and ran over to the low rocking chair with the featherstitched red cushion tied to the back. It had belonged to Mrs. Stiles when she was a little girl. Mr. Stiles sat down in the swivel chair at his desk and put his feet on one of the footstools, reaching for it with his long legs and drawing it up to him. Mr. Stiles didn't have any store or office downtown. He looked after his own interests. Mrs. Stiles owned land near here and Mr. Stiles had property here and in the West.

"Coming, Lecty?"

"Oh, I know who 'tis," Mrs. Stiles called out from the kitchen. But her voice had a briskly welcoming sound. "You tell 'em to wait and I'll be in."

"She says, tell 'em to wait and she'll be in," Mr. Stiles solemnly repeated.

He swung his chair around to the desk, settled his glasses, and began looking over his papers.

"Mr. Stiles. Can we look at the specimens?"

"Look at anything you like, so the Missus don't know it."

They laughed. They knew that was supposed to be a joke.

First they tiptoed over to look at the specimens; kept in a tall cabinet with glass doors. Every time they came to the house, the children must stare with the same wonder at the dusty chunks that showed planes of glassy color, sparkly gleams of golden brightness, thick turquoise masses that looked as if they could be broken off and crumbled. Mr. Stiles had been connected with mining in the West. On top of the cabinet were the three cones that came from the biggest trees on the face of the earth. "How big are they, Mr. Stiles?" the children had asked. "So big, that if I was to set you down at the foot of any one of them, you couldn't see up to the top." Delight put back her head and squinted up with bright eyes. Clarence was so overawed he couldn't even imagine.

"None like that around here," Mr. Stiles had said with satisfaction.

"No, trees here are for shade, not to see how high they can get," Mrs. Stiles had retorted.

When they had seen the specimens, the children went softly out to the hall to look at the deer. The deer's head was fastened up on the wall in the dark place under the stairs so that Mrs. Stiles wouldn't have to see it. She couldn't abide the thing. It was velvety but hard in that solemn gloom. The round, dark eyes looked out unmoving. Clarence liked the branching antlers, stony-pale, looking as if they were petrified. Delight loved the deer, next to Dora Palmer's cat and

Judge Lewis's big dog, better than Grandma Pettibone's Hamburg rooster. She didn't think of putting Mollie in this list because Mollie was almost the same as a real person.

The children went back to the sitting room.

"See the deer?" Both solemnly nodded. "Pretty big fellow, wasn't he? I shot him with this gun right up here above my desk."

Clarence was greatly impressed. But Delight stared at Mr. Stiles. She turned for help to Clarence. Was the deer *shot?* Was it *killed?* She hadn't known the deer was killed!

Suddenly she clenched her fists at Mr. Stiles, just as she had done at that horrid Willie Schnitts when she had met him carrying a gopher by the tail. Her eyes were bright with fury, but her soft little mouth trembled. She broke into a storm of crying, and she stamped her foot, saying, "I don't like you, I don't *like* you any more." Clarence was scared. He didn't know how he felt. He didn't know what it was all about.

Mrs. Stiles came hurrying. She exclaimed in dour triumph, "There, James Stiles!"

"Why, she's threatening *me,* not me her."

Mr. Stiles tried to make a joke of it. But Mrs. Stiles wouldn't listen.

"Yes, your old guns and things. Come," she said to Delight, "we'll get away from these menfolks."

Mrs. Stiles took Delight into her sacred parlor. Neither of the children had ever been allowed in that room. She sat down in the horsehair chair, lifted the little girl onto her lap, and firmly rocked. She told Delight never to look at that old deer's head again. *She* never did.

"Men think it's smart to shoot things."

Mr. Stiles said the womenfolks depended on the menfolks to do their shooting for them. The womenfolks were great ones to talk! "Where'd we all be if the menfolks hadn't shot the Indians?" How'd she like to have been massacred, like those settlers over there at the Lake? There was a massacre not a hundred miles from this spot.

" 'Twas the white folks started the massacring," Mrs. Stiles retorted. " 'Twa'an't the Indians."

"Oh, it 'twa'an't, hey?"

"No, it 'twa'an't!"

Mr. and Mrs. Stiles were glaring at each other.

Then Mr. Stiles scratched his head and gave a slow whistle. He said ruefully. "Well, Clarence, it don't seem to be the place for us here. S'pose you and me go out and feed the turkey birds. Help fatten 'em up for Thanksgiving dinner. *That's* all right. Good New England festival."

If Mrs. Stiles heard she disdained to reply. She rocked harder. Mr. Stiles paused to show Clarence the gun fastened up over the desk. It had brought down deer, and bear, and maybe a few Indians. Mr. Stiles whispered that to Clarence, and let him in on the secret, nodded, as if they two were in cahoots. Mr. Stiles stealthily took down the gun and let Clarence feel of the smooth wooden handle and the cold, round, metal barrel.

Then they went outdoors and wandered around through the yard together. "Well, Clarence," Mr. Stiles said, "the womenfolks are funny. They've got some funny ideas." Clarence nodded. But—although he was proud to be taken into companionship by Mr. Stiles, who had lived out West and fought Indians, and who had lied about his age so he could get into the Civil War—he felt a painful estrangement from Delight. He didn't want the deer to be killed any more than she did. Or not much more. This was the first time that he had felt himself separated, as one of the menfolks, from the womenfolks, a wholly different tribe. He was at the edge of, but didn't quite enter into, that secret, hard, contemptuous masculine glory.

Mrs. Stiles had known what they were up to in there, but she wouldn't give them the satisfaction of a scolding.

She sat up straight and spare, with tightly closed lips, and bright black eyes. She smoothed Delight's shining braids— that was going far for Mrs. Stiles, she wasn't given to caresses.

"You've cried enough now," she then stated firmly, and set the little girl on her feet.

And she was to remember—Mrs. Stiles added sternly— the womenfolks hadn't anything to brag about. Menfolks liked to shoot and kill, but all womenfolks ever did was cry about it—unless they were the kind that urged the menfolks on; those were the worst of all.

Mr. Stiles and Clarence had come into the house to make their peace. "Well, maybe we better go back," Mr. Stiles had said. "Got to make up with the womenfolks or they won't give us our dinner. Everybody's got to eat—can't get around *that* fact."

The parlor door was open. Clarence stared at the darkened room in wonder. Mr. Stiles said *he* wasn't allowed in the parlor, either! The room had an air both frugal and stately. There was a cold, stale fragrance—it might come from the feathery grasses in the tall vase. It didn't seem as if the familiar street lay so close outside.

Mrs. Stiles went to the rosewood piano and lifted the dark, polished lid. The piano was kept scrupulously in tune but seldom opened. Mrs. Stiles wouldn't consent just to "play something" when people asked her. She cared little for any composers but Bach. Beethoven was "too passionate." She would play a few pieces of separate music that her stern taste accepted. What was the use of fooling with any but the noble and great? Her playing had become almost legendary. She sat down on the red velvet stool—straightened her skirts, found the pedals, held her hands above the keys. This piano had been shipped from the East and given to Mrs. Stiles on her seventeenth birthday—she was then Electa Kent.

Her hands came down in firm attack. "Ein Feste Burg"

sounded out strong, solemn, grand, in the darkened room. There was nobility in that uncompromising force.

Delight stood close to the piano, listening. The wild-rose color came and went in her cheeks. Out in the hall, Clarence and Mr. Stiles were listening.

Mrs. Stiles stood up and closed the piano. Her eyes were solemn and bright.

"There. We'll let them have their old guns."

Mr. Stiles went into the parlor, and Clarence after him. He said, "That was fine, Lecta," and took hold of Mrs. Stiles's arm. "You might play for me now and then. It might help convert the reprobate."

Mrs. Stiles didn't answer. But the sternness of her face was mollified. Her straight lips softened.

They went into the other room, forgetting to close the parlor door. Clarence stole another glance into that mysterious room. On the wall opposite hung two pictures in dark oval frames. They were of Mrs. Stiles's parents, Father and Mother Kent. Both faces seemed to stare at him from out of past time: the old preacher with gaze fiery but stern under fierce, heavy eyebrows; the mother with luminous sweetness.

Mr. Stiles still kept hold of Mrs. Stiles's arm. After he had let it go, he squeezed her hand.

"Come, make up," he said to Delight. "I promise you I'll never shoot a deer in these parts."

"Oh, you!" Mrs. Stiles said.

Clarence went over and stood near Delight. He wondered whether they were mad. *He* wasn't mad but he wondered whether she was. They had never been mad at each other. There was a pain that spoiled everything when he thought she might be mad. She didn't look at him at first. Her face was pale now and her eyes tearstained. But nobody was mad any more.

Mr. Stiles said, "Well, Lecty, are we going to have any

dinner today? Or are you going to sit and play the piano. I was thinking it might be nice to have some company for a change. That is, if there was going to be anything besides a little hard tack and cold water."

"Oh, I guess you can count on a little more than *that*."

Mr. Stiles winked soberly with his deep-set gray eye. He didn't mind if the children stared at the glass eye—told 'em to go ahead, see if they could make out whether *'twas* glass, he might just be fooling folks. Clarence couldn't help staring, and wondering if what his mother said was true, that Mr. Stiles had got his glass eye from a shooting match with another man out West. ("Duel, mama," Irene impatiently corrected her. "Not a *shooting* match. Nobody says that." "Ach, whatever you call it.") The eye never moved— or . . . maybe it did. The children were afraid to commit themselves. They wouldn't give any opinion.

Mrs. Stiles now said as always, "They can stay if their mothers say they can."

"Our mothers don't care," Clarence anxiously assured her.

"Well, anyway, you scamper across and ask."

What was the fascination of these meals? Maybe they were the embodiment of the Mr. and Mrs. Stiles's Sitting-Room Smell. There was the thinness of the tablecloth on the hard table; the darkening shade of the row of planted trees that scraped the window glass; the vinegar cruet, always faintly stained; and Mrs. Stiles's kind of beefsteak, fried dark brown and thin, the pieces with their sizzles of fat lying in blackish pan gravy that had a taste of scorch. Dinner would have been better at either of their own houses. Mrs. Stiles wouldn't carry off any prizes as a cook. ("No, she's too smart to cook," Clarence's mother said with dark ambiguity.) But it seemed as if the children must taste this kind of meal over and over again, just as they must run barefooted over the rough planks of the bridge, to feel, Delight said, that the bridge was like what it was like. "There! See if that isn't the size of your mouths." They wanted to pour dark pan gravy over the boiled potatoes, and watch some of it soak in, some run over on the cold white plate. They wanted to hear Mr. Stiles ask a blessing, in sonorous tones, and to see Mrs. Stiles flush as if somehow he was making fun of her.

"And, O Lord, change the hearts of the sinners and make them walk in the straight and narrow way!"

But—bright-eyed, her lips compressed—she would never admit any hurt; merely say, with austere sedateness: "James, will you please serve our company the meat."

This noon, however, Mr. Stiles was on his best behavior. He asked Mrs. Stiles to say grace, and almost sternly bowed his head. He served Delight in the most courtly manner— James Stiles could be very courtly when he pleased; that was often said of him—and he put the best pieces of everything on her plate. She was polite to him, but she wouldn't smile.

She wanted to go home soon after dinner was over. Clarence said anxiously, "Should I go over to the parsonage with you, Delight?" She told him yes. But when they got there, she didn't want to play any games; she sat down at the piano and said she was going to play like Mrs. Stiles. Clarence hung around wistfully. Delight didn't really play anything, she merely brought her hands down hard—sitting with her head sharply lifted, her long braids hanging: the attitude of Mrs. Stiles, as Clarence could recognize. But he felt as if he heard again the strains of that music: its simplicity and noble strength. Clarence and Delight had always trustingly believed that there was no piano player in the world so fine as Dora Palmer. There was something else, however, in Mrs. Stiles's playing; a touch quite different from Dora's tender, singing tones. Clarence felt almost afraid of this different music. But it was best.

He didn't want the deer killed—and yet he couldn't

entirely go back on his companionship with Mr. Stiles. Finally he couldn't stand it any longer. He had to make up with Delight.

"I wouldn't uv shot it," he told her earnestly. "Honest I wouldn't."

She accepted that. She said, "I know you wouldn't uv."

When Mrs. Ira Miller entertained the Missionary Society, Clarence and Delight were asked to come over for refreshments.

Poor Clarence!—how he used to be dragged to these affairs, whiny and unwilling, because the girls were all at school and his mother wouldn't leave him at home alone. He would have to sit close beside her and feel her restraining hand upon him. Occasionally a pitying hostess found him a few toys. But he was imbued with his mother's timidity, and he was afraid to handle things that didn't belong to him.

Now that he had Delight, all that was changed. The two of them ran over to Uncle Ira's the moment school let out, proud of being the only children invited. It was still too early for refreshments. The meeting was held in the front room and the children had the dining room to themselves. They were almost hidden behind the hanging bead and leather portieres. One of the bookcases stood in the dining room; and Aunt Belle had come tiptoeing out to tell them they could look at any books they pleased just so they were careful. Aunt Belle owned the whole set of Stoddard's *Lectures,* twelve volumes. Clarence and Delight took out the volumes one by one. They had two little chairs, a straight chair and a rocker, that had belonged to Merrill and Marguerite when they were small. Heat reached them from the kitchen range. Mrs. Zissler was out in the kitchen looking after the coffee for Aunt Belle. Their cheeks burned in the heated air. The lace curtains veiled the cool window glass through which they could see the side yard, now bare.

Clarence held the volume they were looking at on his knees, sitting pigeontoed, like the men at church socials. Delight hitched her little rocker closer to his chair. He looked at the pictures themselves, with respect and wonder, but Delight always saw the two of them, herself and Clarence, in the midst of foreign scenes. Clarence listened to her breathy whisper.

"Look, this is where we go riding on our big high horses, clappity-clappity, that's your horse and this is mine. We both have to wear silk stovepipe hats, like Mr. Broadwater's only lots nicer, and we have on shiny boots. Only *I* have on a long, long skirt and looped up over my wrist with a ribbon. We have whips but we don't use them because our horses *like* us, and we like them. They'll go for us anyway. We're the Prince and Princess out riding."

Clarence listened, his mouth slightly open, his pale face sensitively responsive. He had never thought about foreign scenes until now, and he was lost among the turreted castles, and the stately avenues through which Delight seemed to thread her way with such airy lightness, as if she remembered the way from long ago. But when she told him the castle was where they lived, he believed her; just as at other times he believed they were Hiawatha and Minnehaha in the wigwam, John Alden and Priscilla in the log cabin, or the President and First Lady in the White House. Now they were the Prince and Princess.

All the time he was conscious of Delight beside him—of her soft breathing, her small hand turning the pages with eager deftness, her long braid that hung down and brushed his knee. The pictures were in dark, clear print on glossy pages that still smelled new. Clarence had no doubt at all of their future together somewhere grand and faraway; and at the same time no doubt that they would always live together here in New Hope. Once when Mr. Vance had asked them what they were going to do someday, Delight had cried, spreading out her arms in a sweeping gesture:

"Everything!" They were going to do everything, and live everywhere!

Mr. Vance said, "Well, that's a big program!" But they both had stared up at him with shining, confident eyes.

In the other room now, a missionary hymn was droning, led by Aunt Belle, assured, but slightly off-key, with Marguerite playing a reluctant accompaniment; and out in the kitchen, Mrs. Zissler lifted the stove lid and poured in a big rattle of coal.

Sometimes, even after Delight had come, the stale blankness of the old Sunday afternoon tedium would steal over Clarence, like a dream he had once dreamed. He would remember how it used to be in the summer, when they were all invited over to the other house for dinner; how the grown people would go to sleep, or get to talking, and he wouldn't know what to do with himself. He would lean against his mother, burying his face in the cottony fullness of her sleeve, giving little whines when she suggested, worried, that he try to take a nap, hanging his head when Aunt Belle tried to find some diversion for him, with her mixture of real kindness and false bright cheer—finally to go wandering disconsolately about the yard in the slumberous heat, pulling at the leaves of the snowball bush, stopping to dig bits of things from out the cracks of the wooden walk in the back yard, lying flat on his stomach on the dreariness of the sun-heated boards. Merrill and the girls always went off somewhere the minute the dishes were washed. They managed to slip off without his seeing them. He would be just in time to catch them going off down the street, Merrill walking between Irene and Bess, and Edie and Marguerite having to console each other.

Sunday afternoons were full enough, since Mrs. Greenwood had organized the Junior Endeavor for "the little
ones." "And thank heaven," Irene declared, "even if they
did have to spoil dinner trying to teach him his verse for
roll call, they needn't have that kid teasing to go along to
the Senior meetings!"

Clarence could scarcely wait to get his dinner eaten. He
went over to the church early with Mrs. Greenwood and
Delight to get the primary room ready for the meeting. His
family wouldn't have known him, he was so busy and gallant
in the role of right-hand man.

They set the small red chairs in a semicircle; took down
the big Sunday school chart and put up instead the white
cloth stretched between two standards on which they were
tracing the journeys of the young Jesus; and then Mrs.
Greenwood unlocked the tall cupboard and let the children
get out the large flat links of cardboard, pasted over with
gold paper, which formed the chain. Those links had a
marvelous mystical value—like something in a fairy story,
but more sacred. The golden chain, stretching unbroken,
dipping slightly in the middle like a necklace, was the magic
center of the whole meeting.

"Should we ring the bell?"

"No, we must let the janitor do that."

The children were beginning to come. Some entered
boldly. Others were self-conscious. Little Amber Day was
too small to belong; and besides her folks were Methodists.
But she had cried so hard to come that Mrs. Greenwood said
the older ones might bring her; Mrs. Day wrote out her
verse for her, and Dosia Murdock read it when Amber's
name was called. Mrs. Stiles said the children should bring in
the Groundhogs. But no one had ever got the Groundhogs
to attend.

"Now we will begin our meeting."

The children sat down noisily in the small red chairs.

Mrs. Greenwood stood waiting for the coughing to subside.
Then she sat down to the organ and sounded the opening
chord. There were still some who forgot, but most of them
stood up proudly. The smallest ones were pulled to their
feet.

The ritual of this meeting was marvelous to Clarence.
He and Delight stood side by side. They felt that the whole
success rested on their shoulders. Delight's fearless treble
carried Clarence along in the opening song. Sometimes Willie
Schnitts didn't sing at all. Then at other times he roared and
made the kids giggle. Delight held up her head with disdain
and wouldn't even smile.

> "When He com-uth, when ·He com-uth,
> To make up his jew-ulls,
> All His jew-ulls, precious jew-ulls,
> His loved and His own."

But when they had got that far into the song, the nervous torment that his busyness had kept subdued began to
rise to the surface, until Clarence was barely able to keep it
from breaking into panic.

> "*Like* the stars of the morning,
> His bright crown adorning—"

What if he should forget his verse! The joyous ringing
of Delight's bird treble seemed to drown out remembrance.
He couldn't fail her and Mrs. Greenwood and all the others.
He would bring some awful calamity if he broke the golden
chain. Sweat came out all over him. Then in the comforting, repeating cadences of the final line, the splendid-sound-
ing "Wherefore" with which his verse began, the verse Bess
had picked out for him and taught him at breakfast, returned into the safe confines of his memory; and the sweat
of fear became a heated glow of relief.

> "*His* loved and His own."

When they all sat down, Clarence's legs were trembling. Mrs. Greenwood left the organ. She opened the roll call book that held all their names: the boys and girls who were starting out together. Clarence's heart began to thud under the wide ruffled collar of his Sunday blouse. He didn't mind having Jamie Murdock and Bonita Button called to the front to hold up the chain. Clarence and Delight let their names come at the end of roll call, because Delight's mother had charge. It was more honorable for them to come last.

"Now we will have our roll call. And I hope you have all learned your verses, for we want our chain to be perfect today."

Jamie stood with alert readiness to put up the first link on the boys' side. Bonita put up the links for the girls. The two sides were just about equal.

The children sat on the edges of their chairs, waiting— some eagerly, some fearfully—for their own names. The little ones had to be prompted. But that was considered fair. Every verse safely given was followed by a long-drawn sigh —then the eyes turned brightly to the next child called. Clarence was torn between eager listening and horror of losing his verse again. He kept up the silent repetition of the first "Wherefore" like an incantation—feeling through the mounting anxiety of the group the tense pulling of his own, single torture. Now they had almost reached Willie Schnitts! What would Willie do this time? He sat there naughty and cheerful, with his hair sticking up smartly from his cowlick, enjoying the suspense.

"Willie Schnitts."

Heads were motionless in the painful hush. Willie got up easy and swaggering. Delight kept her little nose in the air. But Clarence felt a guilty admiration. Willie's eyes shone with impish brightness under the cocky crest of hair. He intoned loudly:

" 'I press toward the mark!' "

A long-drawn "O-oh!" went through the room. Hands beat the air. Shocked eyes were turned toward Mrs. Greenwood. He had given that one before! Willie had given it last time. But to break the chain . . . Alta clasped her hands, imploring the leader. Mrs. Greenwood was flushed. He was daring her to let him off, he actually *wanted*—that child— to spoil the meeting! She knew what the minister would have done. He would have put down Willie in short order. But how could she disappoint those beseeching faces?

"Willie, I'm afraid—didn't you give that verse last Sunday?"

Willie swaggered. He said with easy malice, "Oh, uh guess uh did." His little bright eyes glanced—he wasn't disturbed to have everyone against him. It would have killed Clarence to have everyone against him. "Here's the one uh meant." He rolled it off glibly. " 'Suffer little children tuh come untuh me.' "

That was Dosia's verse! The little rascal was so smart— he could have learned that from hearing Dosia! But there was no way of proving it, and Mrs. Greenwood hastily accepted the way out, looking ashamed of her weakness, but unable to betray the imploring eyes. Moans of relief sounded when Jamie put up the link.

But now if he should be the one to forget! Clarence sat in burning agony. It was no help now to see Delight beside him, poised and fleetingly eager; to hear her bright bird tones repeating her verse. The eyes turned trustingly upon him made him sick. It was his turn. He had to speak. Clarence got up shaking. But to his amazement, the words said themselves—the whole long verse, even the part Bess had said he needn't commit to memory.

" 'Wherefore thou art great, O Lord; for there is none like thee.' "

He sat down in the midst of admiring murmurs. Roaring filled his ears, scattering his wits, so that he couldn't pay attention to anything. Jamie and Bonita were taking their seats. The chain hung, golden and completed, swinging a little, before the eyes of the whole meeting. The children were all united. Clarence had remembered his verse and it was the longest of any. Now he could be perfectly happy.

"Clarence, you'll come over to the parsonage with us, won't you, and have supper?" Mrs. Greenwood always would say that, and Clarence would always answer:

"Yes, ma'am."

It was what he used to look forward to all through the week. Everything tasted better because he was eating at the parsonage. They would have supper at the small table in the kitchen. Clarence and Delight would drink their milk out of the gilded cups and use the tiny souvenir spoons. They felt at such times an intimacy so close that it created for them their own small world within the big world. The bell ringing loud and hard for the Senior Endeavor warned them the precious time was getting short. At the evening service they would have to be separated. Clarence would sit down in the audience with his folks, and Delight would be up in the choir loft with her mother. She sat on a small red stool at her mother's feet. She was privileged. She was the minister's daughter. During the service she drew pictures on small pieces of white paper cut just her size and fastened with gold tacks to a square of cardboard: drew the Bible ladies when they were little girls, a tiny Ruth, a pretty Mary. Then she drew herself and Clarence wearing Bible robes and sandals.

But for Clarence himself, sitting fretfully between his mother and his father, there wasn't anything to do. He could barely see Delight's head beyond the railing. Only when she stood up with the choir to sing, he could see her, the eager little face and the long hanging hair that was brushed out and left unbraided on Sundays; and it seemed to him that she was now far from him, in an unattainable region, while he had been put back among mortals down in the audience.

CHAPTER VI

Festivals

IN NOVEMBER, before Thanksgiving, came the Harvest
Dinner, the first of the great church festivals of the early
days. This had been carried over from the church in the
old community.

The dinner was held on Saturday, to make it easier for
the country people to attend. But preparations used to begin
a day ahead. Early on Friday morning, Clayt Hetherington
came over to open the church and get the fires started. He
was proving very faithful. By nine o'clock, smoke was coming out of the chimneys, drifting blue across the parsonage
yard that was frosty and wet, with its faded grass matted
close to the ground. The ladies would be working at the
church all day with the help of such males as were available:
Mr. Stiles, old Mr. Broadwater, the janitor, and the minister.
There was more than the janitor could do alone. The building had to be swept and scrubbed, the pews taken out and
stacked in the parsonage barn; and long table boards set up
on sawhorses. The Young Ladies had charge of the decorations. Mr. Vance had let his helper have the use of the lumberyard wagon and team to take a group out to the country—Bess, Mamie Wright, and Dora Palmer—to gather

pumpkins and corn stalks. Autumn leaves were gone by now. Mrs. H. C. Murdock headed the dinner committee, assisted by Mrs. A. D., Mrs. Ira Miller, and Mrs. Stiles. But the first one on hand at the church on Saturday was Mrs. Dave Miller. She would have been, as Mrs. Ira put it, too timid and hang-back to have taken charge; but when it came to actual downright hard work, Mrs. Dave was the stand-by. Clarence trailed after his mother, carrying one of the baskets, restive until he could put it down and run over to the parsonage to find Delight.

"Now you keep out of the kitchen," she warned him. "You aren't needed out here."

Keep those children out of the kitchen! Let anybody try it. The whole pack was underfoot all morning long. Baskets began coming in early. The children had to see the baskets unpacked. They were shooed out in great bursts of impatience, but it was like driving out flies in flytime. In a moment they were back, clustering thick around the long table where the food was set out before being taken into the other room: in china dishes, granite pans, big cake pans —all the different kinds of baked beans, the rich, dark, Boston beans with molasses that Mrs. Livermore brought over in a deep earthen crock, the pale, close-packed loaf kind that Mrs. Story made, the dishpanful that somebody had brought in from somewhere . . . the cakes, the loaf cake the children scorned because it had no frosting, the good kinds with chocolate frosting rich and deep, Grandma Story's whipped cream cake with Jersey cream an old-fashioned-looking yellow, the angel foods, Bess Miller's white cake with glistening coconut icing. The children gazed in hungry gloating. "Mama, we want *this* cake on our table. Can we have *this* cake? Ma*h*muh!"

"Can't somebody keep those youngsters out of here?"

They ran into the auditorium where the long tables were being set. But they weren't wanted in this room either.

Every now and then they would be discovered helping themselves. Long finger-scoopings showed in the frosting.
"Now you young ones clear out and stay out!"
When Mrs. Stiles spoke, it was time to mind.
Dinnertime came. Clayt Hetherington rang the bell.
The welcome clangor sounded through the blue Indian summer air. The children, who had all gone scurrying like a
flock of scared chickens, now rushed back pell-mell into
the church. Some of the ladies—Mrs. Ira Miller in particular
—thought the children ought to wait until the grownups
were through. But Mr. Stiles said, "Send 'em to me." He'd
rounded up wild horses in his time. He couldn't be scared
out by a bunch of youngsters now. He stood at the head
of their table shouting:
"All kids under twelve this way!"
Some of the ladies were scandalized. But the children,
overjoyed, ran pushing their way to the table. Mr. Stiles
wouldn't let them lose out on the good things. He could
stretch out his long arm over their heads, to beckon wait-
resses, while he shouted:
"This way! This way!"
Every so often he would stand up and roar:
"Don't forget the children's table!"
But he knew how to keep order. No mistake about
that. His glass eye had a baleful brightness. Mr. Stiles could
make even Willie Schnitts toe—if not "press toward"—the
mark. No grabbing was allowed. No exchanging after
they'd once made their choices. But every child to eat until
his belly could hold no more.
First, though, came the blessing. All proceedings must
halt until that was over. Mr. Barbour's blessings were only
too well remembered. They had been a bugbear even to the
grown folks; even to John Budd who could himself go on
and on until everybody went home late from the Prayer
Meetings. The women had stood silently fuming while all

the food got cold. But the new minister wouldn't take so long. He had a good appetite himself!—Lizzie Murdock remarked. Mr. Greenwood could make even the children give him their attention.

Dave Miller pounded on the table making the dishes jump. There came a startled hush.

The minister's clear voice sounded through the crowded room . . . blue Indian sky showing beyond the long windows. Delight couldn't keep her head bowed. She stared at her father with shining pride. Clarence looked at Delight.

"Our Father, we are thankful we can gather on this Indian summer day. The labor has been ours but the Almighty gives the harvest. When we eat of these foods we share in your abundance. Some of us have come from older lands, from poverty, from failure, or disaster over which we had little control, but all drawn by that spirit for which our town is named, all ready in some manner to start our lives anew. Others of us have known good fortune which it is our desire to share. We have entered these fields, still fresh to the plough. These woods, where the ax has never sounded. We have come from the ends of the earth to this new land, which may never have been more than a temporary dwelling place for men, but where we now establish our homes. It is the land which we praise today. Make us worthy of its mighty grandeur."

Cass Story said that prayer should be printed, framed, and put up in every home in New Hope.

The children played outdoors through the long afternoon. The kitchen lost its charm for them when it came dishwashing time. The weather, blue and bright, was warm enough so that the backs of the tied horses were shiny. The children could play without their jackets through the best hours of the day. They trampled the tall, bright, with-

ered weeds in the vacant lots. Their calls sounded through
the sunny air.

> "Engine engine number nine
> Running on Chicago line!"

The grown people heard that eager chanting as an accompaniment to the sunny day.

Delight's clear treble rang out above the other voices.
In every game she was the first one chosen. She ran the
fastest and played the hardest. She could be picked out by
the long sweep of her shining hair. But Clarence could run
as fast as she could—sometimes faster. He could keep going
longer, but it took him longer to get started.

There was a period during the afternoon when some
of the children got mad at others. The games dwindled,
nothing was fun any more. Delight and Clarence and Alta
and Dosia and Jamie Murdock were the only ones who didn't
want to stop. They sneaked into the barn, and sat in one
of the pews, and played Tin-tin. Then Jamie got mad because Clarence wouldn't accept the name of any girl but
Delight. Alta giggled at all of them.

But later in the day the November chill drew back
into the air. The horses began to stamp and whinny. Some
of the young people came out, in couples, to give the horses
a little exercise. Irene had two fellows: Ray Putnam and
Dean Robinson. Neither one was able to crowd out the
other. Bess was with Tom Burchard, the lumberyard
helper, and some of the kids shouted, "We're going to tell
Franklin Story!" Clarence didn't like that. Bess could do
what she pleased. The women, sitting together and talking
and resting their feet, now said they supposed it was time
to get busy again. "No rest for sinners," said Mrs. Stiles.
"And I guess that's where we most of us belong." The
sleepiness and the crossness wore off. The crowd gathered

again in the vacant lot behind the church, after raids on the kitchen for crumbled pieces of cake; and then cries of Pom-pom-pullaway sounded far through growing cold and darkness—until the tables were all reset, the food steamed and coffee smelled good, and everybody was called in to supper.

At last, when it was over for another year, when the women were sorting out dishes and silverware and dividing the leftovers—with a basket set aside to take to the Ground-hogs—the tired children could scarcely keep on their feet. They could only whine, "Why don't we go home?"

The young people that winter were organized into a large chorus choir to take charge of the music at the evening services. They practiced in the evenings for a Christmas Eve cantata. At first they had met at the church; but John Budd and a few others had complained about the use of so much fuel, and Dave Miller said, "Send 'em over to our house. Let 'em make all the racket they please. We don't care, we can stand it. House has to be heated anyway!"

This evening they came to the Miller house for the last time. John Budd or no John Budd, the final rehearsal must be held at the church.

Bess and Edie had spent most of that morning getting ready. The great pans of fudge were cooling out in the back kitchen. Now Edie was fussing, saying it might have been nicer to serve oyster stew on such a cold night. But it was too late to change. All morning it had been snowing. Bertha mourned: ach, all that snow would be tracked into her clean house. Never mind, they could put down rag rugs in the front hall, Bess said. Clarence could have the job of sweeping off the overshoes.

Laughter and stamping sounded from the porch. The young folks came in with red cheeks and made a dive for

the sitting room to warm their hands at the big register.
Snowflakes melted into shining drops in the meshes of the
girls' hair. They laughed when Bertha feared they would
all catch cold; and Dave said robustly, a little snow wouldn't
hurt 'em, 'twould just make their hair curl more. There
wasn't room for everybody around the register. Paul Staley
pulled Mamie Wright down onto his knees. That was a
signal for all the boys!—followed by scrambling, scurrying,
shrieks and laughter.

"Here comes the minister!"

The minister and his wife came into the room, looking,
as Bertha told them, as young as any of the others. Mrs.
Greenwood's cheeks were as pink as Delight's. Warm up?—
Mr. Greenwood said. That's what they *had* been doing, walking through this fine snowfall. The Greenwoods put no
such damper on the enjoyment as Mr. Barbour and Miss
Hannah used to do. Nevertheless, the very presence of the
minister, with his keen face ruddy from the cold, meant
that it was time to get down to practice. In a few minutes
the sitting room was almost deserted; the young people
were grouped around the piano. Dora sounded the opening
chords.

Bertha and Dave Miller and Mrs. Greenwood remained
in the sitting room to watch and to listen. Mrs. Greenwood sang with the chorus in the regular services, but she
wouldn't join the cantata and be the only married lady.
Bertha marveled over the minister—how he could find time
to lead the singing, with so many sermons to preach and
all—how he could stand up there and direct, just like the
leader of the band!

"Come now. Opening chorus. Everybody in unison."

The two women talked at intervals, Mrs. Greenwood
cheering Bertha's lugubrious fears—that there would be too
much snow for the countryfolks to get in for the program,
that maybe the old members wouldn't approve of the can-

tata; in spite of the mournful strain, Bertha's voice had a contented sound. Both paused to listen to the final stanzas of the chorus.

"Ach, ain't it wonderful how they can sing, just our own young people?"

"Why shouldn't our young folks be able to sing!" Dave demanded.

The young people themselves paused, elated by their own success. There were more quick footsteps, more hasty stamping on the porch. "Who's that?" somebody asked. "Who isn't here?" Bess looked down at her music—she was sharing a booklet with Tom Burchard; he was shy, just beginning to get acquainted in town, and Bess had taken him under her wing. She let Edie go to the door. "It's Franklin!" now they were all exclaiming. They thought he wasn't expected until tomorrow. Mr. Greenwood cried heartily:

"Just in time!"

Franklin Story entered handsome and laughing, trying to answer all the questions. How had he got here? By train. "We knew that," Edie said. He'd heard they were practicing tonight, and didn't want to lose out, thought they might forget to save him his part, so he'd just caught the train and come along. His handsome eyes, from the very first moment, had sought out Bess. He went over to her with an air of taking possession.

Mr. Greenwood repeated that he was just in time. "Here, Franklin, this gentleman has been acting as your substitute. Now you can take over your job. We're just ready for that duet."

Franklin said, all right, he was ready. Let Dora play over the air. "Fine to see you, Dora!" He patted her smooth braids. He hummed along while Dora played, taking hold of the booklet that Tom Burchard had at once relinquished, and giving him an easy "Thanks." Tom retreated to the edge of the group.

"Well, I think I have it. Let's get going. Ready, Bess?" He gave Bess a quick smile. Her hand, holding one corner of the booklet, was nervously stiff; but Franklin's hand, large and well made, mottled from the cold, was steady. With easy confidence he entered at once into his part. His strong tenor seemed to override her lovely alto. The others had withdrawn, leaving these two together at the piano.

Applause followed the duet. All said how grand it was to have Franklin back at home. His voice had been the only one lacking. Good looking and well dressed, carrying off easily his college splendor, Franklin laughed and joked and praised their musical efforts. He had heard that chorus when he was away off down the hill and it had sounded better than the Glee Club. Franklin's sudden arrival gave the final enthusiasm to the rehearsal.

Mrs. Stiles, hearing the music, had come over to the Millers, and had joined the group in the sitting room. Sitting and listening at times, and at other times talking together, the older people were enjoying themselves. Mrs. Stiles said, "I think our town has the finest group of young people that can be found. What a handsome couple Bess and Franklin make!" Here Bertha sighed. Dave, joining in, demanded to know where else you'd see as many pretty girls in one room? "Nowhere!" Mrs. Stiles briskly answered. The only trouble would be in picking the prettiest. They looked most often at Bess, however—in her dark-red cashmere, with the satin ribbon around her neck, her puffs of silky, dark hair, her brilliant color. Although Irene was just as pretty in her way—maybe prettier. "Irene isn't going to let any one man take first place with *her*," Mrs. Stiles observed with satisfaction. "Not until she chooses!"

The children had stayed out in the sitting room, too. "I see *they're* on hand," Mrs. Stiles said, nodding. "Oh yes, nothing can go on without them!"

These evenings when the chorus practiced were as much fun for them as for the young people. Although Clarence and Delight weren't supposed to go into the parlor and make nuisances of themselves, they were in and out just the same. They ran scraping their feet across the carpets to give folks a shock—running away laughing when they'd been successful. Franklin Story caught Delight, and said, should he kiss her, or should he spank her? Clarence, which? "Not either!" Clarence shouted boldly, and pulled Delight away.

"Ach, they get beside themselves," Bertha murmured.

They ran out to the back kitchen to steal the good nutty crumbles from the top of the fudge, which Edie had cut while it was still warm. These rich bites always tasted better than the regular pieces. But they heard somebody coming out to get the candy, and they ran and hid behind the brooms.

Bess entered the cold back room by herself. The children peeped out and saw her. They saw Franklin come in and put his hands on Bess's shoulders. Bess stood still. Wan snowy light filled the small window space. They saw the cold, dull gleam of an old flatiron on the window sill.

"I haven't seen you alone yet," they heard Franklin whisper.

The children poked each other and scarcely dared breathe. There was silence in the small room. Then they heard the sound of a kiss. Bess said in a confused tone:

"I must get back. Take the candy. . . ."

"Are you glad to see me? Are you? Tell me before I let you go."

His voice was exuberant, and he laughed. There was silence again. Bess cried, "It's cold here!" and ran out with the candy pan. Edie had come out to the kitchen, crying, "Aren't you ever going to bring in that candy? Oh, ex-

cuse me!" Franklin said laughing, "No excuses needed!"
The kitchen seemed all at once full of voices.

The two children at last came out stealthily from their
hiding place.

"He *kissed* Bess!" Delight breathed. She marveled.

Her bright eyes shone in that dim snowy light. Her
long hair hanging made Clarence think of fairy tales. He
said, "So can I," and put his arm around her. His lips
touched her cheek, and he felt the brush of her hair. "I can
too," she whispered, and kissed him back.

"We're playing we're Bess and Franklin," she told him.

But they were only half playing.

They weren't going to miss out on the candy, though.
Bess was passing it around. Franklin took one of the plates
from her. It was he who offered the fudge to Tom Burchard
saying carelessly "Have some?" Tom, pale and meek, accepted his piece. Franklin's eyes shone with careless triumph
and his voice was jubilant.

The crowd went out into the hall to find wraps and
put on overshoes. Edie tied Mrs. Greenwood's fascinator
and said, "Do you know how sweet you look?" Delight
and Clarence wanted to wait and see if Franklin would kiss
Bess again. "What are you two skeezickses laughing about?"
Clarence's father said. They laughed still more. In the hall
were smells of melted snow, cold wraps, and overshoes—
snowy draughts of fresh air when somebody opened the
door.

It looked as though Franklin might be intending to
stay longer. He hadn't put on his coat. But the children
heard Bess ask him—greatly to their disappointment—if he'd
walk home with Dora. The last time, Dora had gone home
alone. Everybody liked Dora and admired her, but the
boys seemed never quite at ease with her, nor she with them.
("Ja, all that piano playing, that scares them," Bertha said
wisely.) Franklin smiled at Bess for her thoughtfulness. The

children got a little reward when they saw him squeeze her
hand. Clarence squeezed Delight's hand then, and she went
running and wildly laughing, until her father brought her
back. He said:

"Now you two, call a halt!"

Bertha cried anxiously to the girls to come back where
it was warm, but they waited, and Clarence with them, to
watch the others go down the walk: going in couples, making fresh tracks through the dry, soft snow. The light from
the doorway showed the shadows of scanty trees with
branches interwoven. Mrs. Stiles, tall and spare, with a shawl
drawn around her, went plunging straight across the road.
The minister's folks were the last to leave; and Delight,
with her bright eyes shining from under her kitty hood, and
her long hair hidden beneath her coat, turned to wave, and
went skipping backwards; until her father caught hold of
one hand, her mother of the other hand, forcing her to
turn around and walk the way she should.

The ladies worked in the church most of that day—
the day before Christmas. The children were supposed to
keep out; but Clarence and Delight, hanging about the parsonage, watching people go into the church with presents,
couldn't stand it. They put on their wraps and went out
to play in the snow. Dean Robinson, who was working at
Donohue's during the holidays, came along with two big
sacks of apples, and said:

"Hey, you kids, want to take these in for me?"

"Uh-huh!"

The bare floor of the chilly entry was already smudged
with melting pads of snow from overshoes. The children
pushed open the swinging doors with elbows and knees because they needed both hands for the sacks of apples. The
Christmas Tree was the first thing they saw when they
came into the audience room. Its glitter of tinsel and green

and flimmery red hurt their eyes coming in from the soft snowy atmosphere outdoors.

They ran toward it down the sloping aisle.

"Where do you youngsters come from? Thought you weren't to be allowed in here!"

"Well, we have to. We have to bring in these apples," Clarence explained, feeling very righteous. Delight added: "We're messengers!"

"Messengers, are you! Well, hand over the apples and skedaddle."

They couldn't do that, not right away. Mr. Stiles was up on a stepladder, trimming the top of the tree, and he shouted down:

"Climb up here, Susan Long-locks! I want that hair to trim the tree."

"You called me Me-*hit*-abel Long-locks!" Delight cried, dancing back out of range.

"Well, Susan-Mehitabel, one and the same, come let me snip off those long braids."

"James, don't tease the young ones," Mrs. Stiles said. "And for goodness sake, don't encourage them to stay."

"Oh Lecta, let them see the tree now they're here," Mrs. Vance coaxed prettily.

"Well, see it, and then scoot."

The children stayed just as long as they dared. They picked up the long festoons of popcorn, and when the ladies weren't looking, ate off some of the white kernels that tasted stale and soft. They had a right to!—Bess and Edie and Irene, and Trixie, and Mamie, and the other Young Ladies, had strung all this popcorn and all the cranberries. Pasteboard boxes were packed with glimmery tinsel. They drew out some of the long, shiny, prickly strands. The stepladder wobbled when Mr. Stiles reached up to pin the gold star on the tip of the Christmas Tree; and all the ladies except Mrs. Stiles let out shrieks. *She* wasn't scared, as Mr.

Stiles said; his wife didn't expect he'd come to any such good end as falling off a Christmas Tree! He brushed against the branches while he fastened on the star, and spicy fragrance went through the air.

"Scoot now, you two—scoot!"

"*Let* them stay," Mrs. Vance coaxed. "Lecta, you're mean."

"No, if it's fair for them to be here, it's fair for everybody," Mrs. Stiles answered inexorably.

The children ran up the sloping aisle, with backward looks, and out through the swinging doors again. Delight wanted to play Shepherds Watching Their Flocks by Night —Clarence to be the Shepherds, she the Chorus of Angels —but Clarence was so excited he couldn't settle down to playing anything. They ran down the Creek bank, making tracks that at last were shiny, so that they could slide away down to the surface of shallow ice.

The packed church, on that wonderful Christmas Eve, was scented with evergreen, with wax and tinsel, heat from the registers and cold air from outside, snow melted on coats and furs, melted on buffalo coats from the country. The pile of packages around the Christmas Tree grew mysteriously higher and higher, and children could hardly endure it to stay in their places.

The members of the chorus, who were to put on the cantata, gathered out in the vestry, packed together so tightly it was all they could do to breathe. The girls were in winter dresses, since some of the older element might not approve of costumes; but they looked their best. Mr. Greenwood gave them their last instructions.

Strong above the continuous buzzing and shrill occasional sounds in the audience room, rose the opening music from the organ. The chorus members took their places. There were too many for the loft. They filled both the loft and the platform. First must come the opening prayer, then the song by the whole congregation. Dave Miller, helping out as usher, since most of the young men were singing in the cantata, noted triumphantly how many outsiders were here, some from other congregations. That cantata was New Hope's first musical attempt on a large scale.

Mr. Greenwood took his place, facing the chorus, with his back to the audience. At his sharp gesture, the members rose. The opening chorus went well, better even than at rehearsals. The other members sat down, leaving Bess and Franklin standing together.

"When shepherds watched—"
"*When* shepherds watched—"

The voices set each other off—the strong tenor, the rich alto.

Many in the audience were saying, what a splendid couple! Dave Miller cleared his throat in pride. All the Storys beamed with satisfaction; Grandma Story nodding her head in time to the music. Clarence and Delight gave each other looks, remembering their secret about the back kitchen. They almost laughed out loud. Bess always had a radiant quality, but she was brilliant tonight. There was an intense note in her luscious alto, over which Franklin's tenor rose jubilant and assured.

All went well, but passed too swiftly! So it must have seemed to those who were taking part. They had practiced the cantata for weeks, and now they were presenting it, and it was almost over. The closing chorus had been reached. If any portion of the cantata could be called better than the duet, it was this: when the company of young people rose in full force, their fresh voices ringing through the Christmas-scented air.

A pause followed the ending of the cantata—if it could be called a pause, when there was so much whispering and moving about. Willis Vance dressed as Santa Claus came forward to take charge. The great distribution of presents began. The boys and girls of Marguerite Miller's age, summoned as helpers—those in between, neither children nor young people—sped about through the big room and out to the primary. Every child who ever attended Sunday school received a present: the ladies always saw to that. But the helpers were sent oftenest into the choir loft. Clarence and Delight were almost as interested in those presents as in their own.

"Irene Miller!" "Irene Miller!"

It kept one girl busy just taking things to Irene. That was what a girl got by keeping the whole bunch of fellows guessing! Serene and cool, Irene accepted each gift with her charming smile. Her lap by now was full of presents. Bess's name was called out often enough. But it was generally admitted by then that Franklin Story had the inside track; so the other boys held off. Clarence felt very important because his sisters were so popular.

"*Miss* Bess Miller!" Mr. Vance shouted.

When the children heard that, they exchanged glances. Delight pinched Clarence's wrist. They knew a secret—Mrs. Story couldn't keep from telling. They knew that Bess was going to get her diamond ring. Delight had been talking about "diamond rings" for the last two days; saying what she was going to do when *she* got a diamond ring. "Who's going to give it to you?" her Uncle Dave had asked. "Oh, Clarence will," she answered with airy confidence. Clarence, she said; or else papa. When Bess got Franklin's first present, the one he was pretending to give her—a handsome bottle of perfume—the children laughed and giggled; because they knew that her real present was in Franklin's pocket, and it wouldn't be given to her until after the exercises, maybe on the way home.

But the present wasn't from Franklin—it was something unexpected: the huge box of candy, tied with pink ribbons, the one the children had admired in the drugstore. Bess took out the card, and Franklin read it; his handsome face broke into a smile of amusement. He gave a brief sparkling glance toward the end of the row where Tom Burchard was meekly seated, wearing a high collar, and with his light hair slicked down. The present didn't bother Franklin. He seemed rather pleased! Tom Burchard had bought the candy. *He* was giving the candy to Bess. The children wondered and were excited. Later, Clarence saw Bess lean forward and deliberately smile at Tom: her most radiant smile.

The apples and sacks of hard candy were passed. There the children of the primary department came in strong. They were all packed into the front pews; the old people had to take back seats tonight. Clarence and Delight, as usual, were sitting side by side. This was a different Christmas—Clarence had felt that from the very first—and the feeling had grown. All was marvelous, beginning with the walk down the hill through the soft, thick snow. Uncle Andy and Aunt Mary had driven to town in a bobsled, and at supper they had told what the country looked like on a night such as this. Delight had on a red plaid dress; but the color in her cheeks was almost deeper. On her lap she held proudly the three Japanese silk handkerchiefs that Clarence had given her—one yellow, one blue, one pink—and he held the present from *her,* the new copy of *Huckleberry Finn.* The church, trimmed with tinsel and evergreen, filled with laughter and shouting, seemed to reverberate with the closing chorus of the cantata.

Mr. Greenwood stepped forward at last and raised his hand for silence. Commands to "Sh!" went through the audience. The minister began to read then, in his firm clear voice—looking up occasionally from his New Testament, and over the congregation, with his far-seeing, blue, impersonal gaze:

". . . 'For, behold, I bring you good tidings of great joy . . . Glory to God in the highest, and on earth peace, good will toward men.' "

Clarence listened, wiggled in his seat. For the first time, this was not just a reading from the scriptures that came at a certain point in the program. Meaning shone from the words, and shone around them, in the scent of the evergreens and the unsteady candlelight—surrounded by the white silent glitter of great snowfields, great smooth billowing acres of winter snow. Clarence felt the awesomeness of that shining immensity that lay all around them outside the windows. But he and Delight were here together, in the midst of their own community—Delight in her warm, red dress, with her light gold hair; and from their happy closeness, holding their presents, the meaning of the words spread out to everyone in the church. It was true, Clarence thought with joyous wonder—he was happy, he hated nobody, not even Willie Schnitts. He felt "on earth peace, good will toward men."

The children had agreed that they would pray for good weather on Washington's Birthday. Clarence was to pray to God, and Delight to Jesus, in order to make doubly sure. It was no surprise to them to see the sun out on that day. The church was to hold the third of its festivals, the Washington's Birthday Bazaar. Clarence and Delight would have their chance to shine: they were to be George and Martha Washington.

They couldn't wait to get into their costumes. Clarence was to bring his suit over to the parsonage, and they were both to get ready there. The mothers would be too busy to look after them. The girls were to see that they got dressed. Clarence would have no one but Bess; so Edie and Irene took charge of Delight.

Irene said, "We can make her look just simply darling."

Edie said loyally, "He'll look cute too."

Delight had taken off her dress right after dinner. She was in her little cream-colored woolen petticoat with scalloped edge and grayish thick winter underwear—she was such a dance-about, it was all the girls could do to keep her from running all through the house like that, in spite of its being full of people. The sleeves of the underwear had been washed so often they were getting too short and didn't reach her little soft wrists. She looked funny and unfledged.

But wait until she saw herself in costume! Restless though she was, it was easier to dress her than to do anything for Clarence. He was like a switchy little minnow, Edie always complained—you thought you had him, and then he slid right out of your hands. Irene said that dressing up Delight was like having a beautiful big doll. Unlike Clarence, she *wanted* to get dressed. She held up her arms trustingly so that Edie could slip over her head the shiny pink cambric skirt with its ruffled train. Over that came puffed panniers of pink-flowered muslin. The girls carefully rolled up the sleeves of the winter underwear. The costume was short-sleeved and low-necked—to their mother's dismay, of course. The two girls talked in low, intent voices. "Now your slippers," they said. "Now wait and we'll get your fan."

Their doll looked so sweet they couldn't wait to have other people see her. But first, Irene must put up her hair. It made a marvelous great coil on top of her head. "My, don't you hope you keep that when you grow up," Edie said enviously. One strand had been put up on rags the night before so that she could have a colonial curl over her shoulder. Mrs. Vance had lent the big tortoise-shell comb that had belonged to her great-grandmother. Irene thrust in the comb just behind the shining topknot.

"Now go in and show everybody!"

Delight went dancing away.

The girls had been giggling about Clarence—what he would look like in those shiny pink pants! They'd never thought he would actually consent to wear that costume.

But he did; and to his sisters' amazement and pride, he looked as striking as Delight. They hadn't known Clarence *could* look so handsome. He wore a little long-tailed coat, an old one of Mr. Broadwater's that Mrs. Vance had dug out for Bess to make over. Bess had trimmed it with pink shiny cambric and gold braid. He wore a flowered waist-coat to match Delight's flowered panniers; a ruffled stock made from Irene's old white silk dress; buckles and sword of cardboard covered with silver paper; and a little cocked hat which he was to carry in his hand.

Mil Anderson exclaimed: "Why, Clarence Miller! I'm in love with you myself. I believe I'll have to wait until you grow up."

"Ah!" Mrs. Murdock said coyly. "Somebody wouldn't like that!"

The children had their hair powdered just before they went over to the church. Irene was best when it came to anything of that kind. She had the cornstarch ready.

"Do you have to do that to them?" Bertha said.

"Of course. They all had their hair powdered in those days."

"It'll get all over the floor a'ready."

"Why, mama, it won't either. Don't you see we've put papers down?"

The children stood shyly radiant in the midst of an admiring circle. Even Clarence made no resistance to being fussed over; it couldn't bother him, so long as he was with Delight. Most of the cornstarch brushed right out of his smooth hair. He should have a wig, Mrs. Murdock said. Bess said she knew it, and they had tried to make one for him, but they couldn't get it to look right.

"You give him gray hair," his mother protested. "Make him an old man a'ready."

"Mama, we told you, *every*body had powdered hair!"

"Ach, well, that was a queer way."

Enough of the powder stayed in Delight's hair to frost the pale gold, to make her eyes more starlike, her cheeks pinker. But her cheeks were no brighter than Clarence's today.

"They don't know each other!" Mrs. Donohue said.

They must see themselves. The girls took them both into the bedroom to look into the large mirror. They stared at their own shining eyes. They were just the right size—one enhanced the charm of the other: Delight's eagerness lit up Clarence's shyness, his quietness supported her radiant assurance.

"What do you think of yourselves?"

But they wouldn't say.

Now came the business of getting them warmly wrapped without spoiling either costumes or hair. Delight had a shawl, and Mrs. Vance had brought her plaid golf cape for Clarence. Capes were what soldiers wore in the Revolution, so he needn't mind. And shawls were what Revolutionary *ladies* wore, weren't they, Delight said.

"Don't trip on your sword. Hold up your train, darling."

The children crossed the yard together. They felt the shivering chill and joy of that brief journey. They were themselves but they were above themselves. Their feet slipped on the icy patches that brilliantly shone in the February sunshine. The girls came hurrying after them. There was a secretive shedding of wraps in the vestry room. Then the little couple were sent out to make their first appearance on the platform.

The pulpit had been moved back for the occasion and they stood in that sacred spot. The big American flag had been borrowed from the G.A.R. room, and was spread above them, held up by two tall standards. Clarence felt dizzy. His knees trembled. But being in costume was different, and with Delight beside him. He was George and she was Martha: it was like their games. The grown folks all had to pass in line and shake hands with little George and Martha Washington; and Martha and George must distribute the little souvenir hatchets the Young Ladies had made of red blotting paper with bows of red baby ribbon and pins attached.

The children felt their joint responsibility, their dependence on each other. Everybody in town seemed to be here at the church, and many people from out of town. A group had come over that morning on the freight from Tucker. The children looked out over faces familiar and strange. Other children stared at them with distant respect. They felt the marvelous eminence of holding the center of the occasion. Conscious and unconscious, thrilled and shy, they experienced this glory together.

People said what a fine little couple they made, "just right for each other." They could hear the approving murmurs.

When Mr. Broadwater accepted his hatchet, he put his hand on his heart, and said, "Thank you, Your Excellencies."

Delight, much elated, answered, "Oh yes, indeed!"

Mrs. Stiles made a wonderful curtsey ("Didn't know she could bend her back that much," one woman whispered), holding out her skirts and sinking away down to the floor. Mr. Stiles said, "That's showing 'em, Lecty!" and beaued her gallantly away, to the sound of much applause—

so that, for the moment, they made a dashing couple, folks could see why they had chosen each other, after all.

The children stood and met the admiring stares of strangers, the fond exclamations of old ladies, the teasing of the men, the awe and admiration and jealousy of other children, the jeers of Willie Schnitts who said "Who's the Pink Pants?"—all in an entrancement of royal dignity.

Then it was over. They were helped down from their station; down from their glory. They were just to have a good time.

It seemed queer to them at first, being down on the floor with everybody else; like getting off a boat or a railroad train. They had to find their floor legs. Now they were shorter, not taller, than other people. But they still felt themselves apart. They were still George and Martha Washington. Strangers tried to stop them. Some asked for kisses, and the children ran away, Clarence with his hand on his sword, and Delight holding up her train.

"Think that old sword'll cut anybody?" Willie Schnitts asked, putting himself in an attitude of cocky defense.

"Here, here, what's this!" Mr. Stiles demanded. "A Britisher?"

Willie looked scared, made a snoot, and disappeared.

Delight and Clarence wandered hand in hand among the booths, in delicious self-consciousness and freedom— stopping at Edie's booth for candy, at Mrs. Vance's to look at fancywork, at Mrs. A. D. Murdock's to stare at the baked goods. The other children had to go and get their own plates, but *they* had their supper brought to them. They ate together.

Next day the excitement was not quite over.

"They must get their pictures taken in those costumes," people had said at the Bazaar.

Right away, before all the powder came out of their

hair! They went downtown immediately after breakfast on Saturday morning when the gallery was likely to be empty. Mr. LeValley would be ready for them.

The Millers had all been prepared for what they called "a time" persuading Clarence to wear his costume. But instead, he didn't want to take the costume off! He looked at himself for a long while in the mirror in the girls' room. He felt that the costume belonged to him, more than his own short pants and ruffled blouses and scuffed shoes. His appearance astonished him, and was at the same time a confirmation of something secret. He was glad that lots of people had seen how he looked in his costume.

Delight was ready when Clarence got to the parsonage. Now *she* had a cape, so they both had capes—she had Grandma Story's best black cape all heavy with jet; and her mother had tied a gray fascinator lightly over her hair. She looked like a funny little bright-eyed, lively old lady.

The children wouldn't let anyone else go with them. They said, "We want to get our pictures taken all by ourselves." The morning light made them more self-conscious. The cornstarch showed in their hair. But they felt important and happy. Delight remembered to be Martha Washington. She walked daintily, and at the crossings held up her skirts with both hands. The cape nearly weighed her down, but she wouldn't admit it. They were very proud when they reached Main Street, and everybody, farmers and everybody, turned to look at them.

"We're going to have our pictures taken," Delight explained.

"Oh, you are!" A traveling man said, "You must save one for me."

"No."

"You won't? Then what'll I do?"

"You can go and look at our picture in the gallery."

Clarence enjoyed being noticed when he had on his costume.

The photograph gallery was up over the hardware store. The frame building stood gaunt in the dull winter light. An outside wooden staircase led up to the gallery. There were dingy crusts of snow in the corners of the stairs. Delight held up her pink skirts with both hands and couldn't take hold of the railing. She had to go up step by step. Both had a solemn feeling when they stood on the wooden platform at the top of the stairs and saw the alleyway down below them.

"You open the door," Delight pleaded.

Clarence liked to have her ask him to do things like that. In some ways she was the bravest. She would rush with eager confidence into new enterprises while he hung back. But all at once she would turn scary, the wild-rose color would ebb from her cheeks, and she would want Clarence to take the lead. Nothing seemed hard for him to do when they were together.

Clarence opened the door of the gallery. That made a bell tinkle with a queer, empty sound.

The gallery was at the back of the building. Mr. and Mrs. LeValley lived in rooms at the front. Their son was away at school, at that time. Other mysterious rooms opened off from the studio. The children stepped inside. They waited in the wan snow-light, in the softened wintry gloom.

Mr. LeValley came out from the front part.

"Well! Here's our President's folks. Father and Mother of their country. Is that right? Minty! Come out here!" he trumpeted.

Mrs. LeValley came tripping out, just through with breakfast, wiping egg from her lips with a fringed napkin.

"Won't we get a lovely picture!" she said.

Mr. LeValley was tall, thin, and bald-headed. His name was French, but he said if his family was, it must have been a long time back. All Americans, so far as they'd kept any count. But Mrs. LeValley intended to have the family looked up some day. The LeValleys had come to New Hope among the first and had taken pictures in Mr. Vance's barn until the gallery was built. Clarence had heard that, but it seemed to him the gallery must always have been here. Mr. and Mrs. LeValley took pictures together. He was slow and careful, she was the artistic one. Mrs. LeValley got the subjects ready and Mr. LeValley took the photographs. Clarence had always been in awe of the couple, they seemed to him like wizards; but that day—another of those far-away joyous days—he was secretly eager to get his picture taken. Mrs. LeValley fluttered about the two children glee-fully, taking off Delight's fascinator and exclaiming over her hair, saying what a beautiful picture the two would make.

Clarence had started out so bravely that it was no time to get frightened now. But he began to feel funny. The preparations were solemn. To the children they seemed august. Mr. LeValley was setting up the big screens at the back of the gallery. The wintry light was ghostly beneath the skylight where the children were to stand. They could hear teams pulling wagons through the alley. But this place seemed hushed and faraway.

"Now they'd both better come," Mrs. LeValley said, "and let me fix them up a bit. Always do that before taking a picture."

Mrs. LeValley took them into the small dressing room. The walls were covered with photographs. There was a beautiful portrait picture of Irene with gauze around her shoulders, and one large rose. Mr. LeValley had taken that for an exhibit. If Irene didn't give him one of those photo-graphs, Chick Bostrup was reported to have said, he was going to steal this one from the gallery; but nobody could get Irene to tell whether she'd let Chick have her picture or not. Chick Bostrup was sporty; he followed all the horse races. Clarence was too excited now to look at the photographs. She would just sprinkle a little talcum in their hair, Mrs. LeValley said, to give the effect. She shook the powder from a tall can with a picture of carnations, and the spicy scent was in the air. Her little hands fluttered . . . the children saw themselves again in the mirror, with their eyes strangely bright and their faces rosy under their whitened hair.

They could step into the studio now, Mr. LeValley was ready.

The room seemed awesomely big as they crossed it. Clarence heard the solemn clumping of his shoes and the tapping of Delight's on the wooden floor. Mr. LeValley had set up the big screen with pictures of blurry trees on one side and a draped marble column on the other. He placed them in front of the screen. He used the marble column because it was in keeping with George Washington. Mrs. LeValley darted over, settled Delight's colonial curl, tipped Clarence's head to one side. She said: "Be using your fan, darling. Hold it just as though you were using it. Now, deary boy, you put your hand on your sword. That's lovely." Mr. LeValley had retreated to his camera and his bald head disappeared under the black cloth.

They heard his muffled voice. "That's it. That's the ticket. Now neither of you move."

The children stood side by side in the wintry wan glow from the skylight. Mrs. LeValley had tiptoed away and was standing carefully out of sight. They could hear the wagons far below. Once again they held the center. They were George and Martha Washington. The moment was tense, it would never be over . . . Clarence's face felt stiff and his breath wouldn't come . . . Then it *was* over, and he felt sorry, and felt exultant. Mr. LeValley came out from under the black cloth.

"That's all. Well, Minty, I think we got a good one." The children wished it could happen all over again.

CHAPTER VII

The Big Crowd

NEW HOPE in those days had a splendid crowd of young people: the finest crop of young folks, people boasted, of any town around. The crowd was big and liberal, with no tight limits, taking in boys and girls who ranged in age from barely sixteen to over twenty. Now, right now, it had reached its most interesting stage. Its couples—some of them, like Paul and Mamie, and Bess and Franklin, had been going together since childhood—were at the point of open engagement. But the first wedding was still to come. The crowd at that period was still intact.

The gay good times went on but they were changing. The older ones were too grown up for their wild games of Beckon and Run-Sheep-Run in the long spring twilights, all over town, on the vacant lots. There were still the big parties, the bob-rides; in summer, picnics. But most of the meetings were not planned in advance. Soon after supper a group would get together—to sing, make candy, go out for hastily thought-up excursions. Before the evening was over the party might turn into almost anything.

The two children, Clarence and Delight, got in on much of the excitement; the crowd's chief center was the

Miller house. "Where shall we meet?" "Oh, we can go to Millers'," people would say: everybody, the church ladies, the trustees, committees in charge of exercises for Decoration Day. A stranger fainted on the street—one of the Tucker baseball players was knocked out—a young wife from the country was seized with premature labor pains . . . the answer was always the same: "Let's take 'em over to Millers'." When the crowd met, the children were in and out, around and about, coaxed and made much of, shooed off as nuisances. They didn't much care how they were treated so long as they could be on hand.

Clarence used to worship the big crowd. He had always gone tagging after his sisters. Half his small life had been lived vicariously in the drama of the big crowd's doings. But when Delight came, he was no longer a wistful hanger-on. Together they were watchers, mockers, gleeful imitators—half in wild fun and half in admiration. When they got that old, they said, they would belong to a crowd just like the big crowd. They would do just the same things. They would go together like Bess and Franklin. But they never could be that old; never could themselves attain a status so marvelously and irrevocably, glitteringly adult. None of those who were then children could ever rise to be so adult as the big crowd.

Sunday morning breakfast was the time when the three girls took pleasure in being sloppy. If those fellows, their father liked to tell them, could take a look now, it might make 'em think twice before getting to the point.

Edie demanded pertly, "What point?"

"What point do you suppose? What point is there where girls and young fellows are concerned?"

"None!—that any of us have ever reached," Irene said with airy impudence.

Edie was the worst. She would come down to breakfast with her hair skewered, and tricked out in the oldest patched underskirt that she could find. And where she dug up those stockings! They were some on which she had experimented with dyes, and which had come out the colors of unsuccessful Easter eggs. Since her legs were large in contrast to the taut thinness of her neck and shoulders, the effect, as Irene hastened to point out, was rare. Edie never stopped lamenting over her big legs! Bess had slender ankles in spite of the womanly amplitude of her breast and thighs. Her feet looked childishly small in Turkish slippers with pompons on pointed toes. Bess achieved picturesqueness in deshabille—with her fluffy braids, her bangle bracelet jingling faintly on her tapering wrist with its baby-textured skin. Irene couldn't be sloppy even on Sunday mornings. Her last-summer's dress, neatly starched though faded, gave merely an austere subduing of her decorative prettiness, that was almost more becoming than the long flounced dress and flower-trimmed hat she wore to church.

The family used to straggle to the breakfast table one by one. Bess seemed to be the tardy one on that particular morning—there was always a tardy one who couldn't be got down until the last minute. "Where is that Bess?" Edie had kept demanding, biting every word. "Well, she'll have to fry her own cakes. I'm not going to stand at this stove all morning. I'm going to get ready for church. And she'd better, too. She has to sing."

"Whoops!" Irene exclaimed when Bess did come in. "Who, pray, are we?"

Clarence had eaten one griddle cake and run off—now he came back with appetite renewed for another. His father didn't like that habit, tried to keep him in his place; but his mother pampered him in all such ways. She would be right there to wait on him, Dave grumbled, whenever he might choose to show himself!

But Clarence had to find out what Irene meant.

Bess asked sweetly, as she sat down at the table, shook

out her napkin, wrinkled her nose fastidiously at some faded berry juice stains, and reached behind her to open the sideboard drawer and get out another, "Can't I dress before breakfast as well as after?"

"You can. We all can. But we never do."

"Well then, this morning I did."

Bess had put on her new flowered spring challis, the one she had made for Easter. On an ordinary Sunday morning, bad weather at that! Why should she want to spring it now, Edie marveled, and rush the season? What was the big event?

"Oh, I know!" Edie crowed. "Franklin dear has come home for over Sunday."

"He has not come home for over Sunday," Bess icily replied.

Dave got up from the table. Why such fuss, he demanded, over a new dress? Seemed to him they were always appearing in new dresses. You could hardly step around in this house most of the time there was so much cutting and sewing going on all over.

"I see! I spy!" Irene sang out in clear high tones.

"Spy what?" Edie demanded.

Edie stared at Bess with fierce intentness. Clarence stared too. Nobody at first could make out what Irene was talking about. Then they all saw! Bess tried to go on eating calmly but her cheeks burned.

"Well, I meant you to see," she defended herself finally. "Why else do you suppose I wore it?"

"See what? Wore what?" Clarence was still loudly wailing; until to shut him up, Edie grabbed his head between both her hands and forced him to look straight at Bess's left hand.

"See *that*. Now do you see?"

It was the diamond ring. Franklin *had* given her the diamond ring. Everybody had suspected at Christmas time.

Mrs. Story had told them. But that sly, deceitful Bess hadn't given anybody a single glimpse until that morning.

There wasn't time then for more than a glimpse. With an exclamation—"Oh, you all make me so everlastingly tired!"—Bess threw down her napkin and left the table. Her mother mourned. "She's got to eat more than that if she's going to have anything to sing on. Go on, one of you. Make her come back." Bess had fled upstairs and wouldn't answer when Irene yelled up to her to come down.

"You go up," Bertha said finally to Clarence. "You go and take her this doughnut and cup of coffee. She'll have it from you. She won't care if you go up a'ready."

Clarence was eager enough to go upstairs to Bess, but he hated to leave the dining room. The others were speculating about the ring: why Bess had kept it hidden, why she should choose to bring it out this morning. Bertha sighed, "Ach, I can't make her out. Who knows." Irene said there wasn't any reason—Bess had just taken it into her head to do things this way. "She's like that." Edie wouldn't have it that Bess was like that. She said there was something behind it. Clarence wanted to hear everything they were talking about.

But he wanted still more to take Bess her coffee. He wanted to find out whether he had a sister engaged. Delight had been talking and talking about folks being "engaged." Delight and Clarence hadn't quite decided whether they were themselves engaged. Clarence rapped on the bedroom door.

"You needn't bring me anything," Bess cried out. But when she discovered that it was Clarence outside, she relented. "Oh, I don't care about you, *you* can come in."

She wouldn't let even him stay. "Set down the cup," she told him.

"Mama says for you to drink it."

"I will when I get ready but I won't until I please."

Clarence hung around for a while but Bess wouldn't look at him; finally he left. Ever since that last rehearsal for the Christmas Eve cantata, Clarence and Delight had cherished their secret about Franklin Story and Bess. They had been waiting for Bess to wear her diamond ring. Delight thought it would be almost too marvelous to come true that somebody belonging to one of their own families should get engaged and wear a diamond ring. The ring didn't matter so much to Clarence; rings themselves didn't, diamond or any kind. Delight couldn't get him very much excited about rings and precious stones, any more than he could get her stirred up about baseball mitts—she'd just give a snippy glance, toss her head, and go on. But this ring took on iridescent glory, because it was part of their secret, and because his sister Bess wore it.

At Sunday school he told Delight, "I know something. It's about Somebody."

"What?" she breathed. Her eyes gleamed—oddly, one set a little more slanting than the other. "Is it D. R.? Is that the something?"

"How did you know?"

"*Is* it? Oh, it is!" She bounced on her seat.

The two children sat together at the morning service hardly able to contain themselves until Bess appeared in the choir loft. But the older people were as bad, or worse. Bertha had whispered the news to Mrs. Greenwood the moment they sat down: "She's got her diamond on—Bess has. She wore it down this morning." "Oh he *did* give it to her then. I'm so glad." Bertha sighed and said, "Ja, if she's still wearing it. Who knows." Clarence was indignant. Of course she was still wearing it!

The choir members filed into the loft, took their places, turned and faced the audience. Bess was too far away for anyone in the audience to see the ring. But she looked different that morning. She stood out from the others. Her

light challis dress sprinkled with rosebuds was springlike
among the dark winter dresses the other women were still
wearing. Although it was the beginning of March, and the
snow had turned into water and thaw, the air kept its chill
and the sky that morning was dark.

"Ja, I don't know why she put on that dress a'ready,"
Clarence's mother complained.

"Why, to go with her ring!" Delight's mother said.

The special music was presented by a quartette: composed of Lulu Jones soprano, Bess Miller alto, Tom Burchard
tenor, and Willis Vance bass. Tom Burchard took Franklin's place while Franklin was away. Tom sang a pure sweet
tenor—his voice had a purer quality, so Mrs. Stiles said,
than Franklin's; but it did lack strength in comparison.
Some thought that was what was bothering Bess; in their
short duet, Tom didn't give her the right support. Lulu and
Willis had to carry the whole burden that day.

"That dress is too light," Bertha whispered again in
protest.

The two children stared and listened. They knew that
Tom Burchard had somehow entered the drama. But they
didn't suppose he actually counted. He was a third character—put in to make it more thrilling. The singing made
Clarence uneasy. He would never admit that Bess could be
anything but perfect, and once when she came in late he
turned and glared at the audience. He began to feel that
he was developing a cold.

The moment the service was over, Mrs. Greenwood
started down the aisle. Delight followed so eagerly that she
almost stepped on her mother's skirt. Clarence trailed along
after them trying to feel as excited as before. The members
of the choir were still in the loft. They still surrounded
Bess. But they made way for the minister's wife.

Mrs. Greenwood took Bess's hand and cried, "I must
see it too!" She was glad about engagements and weddings;

always rejoiced over brides, expecting each one to find in marriage the same happiness she had found in her own.

Bess smiled, and let her hand lie on the delicate palm, with its many fine lines; while the other women clustered again to look at the ring. Delight tried to squeeze in, first one place, and then another, until finally Mrs. Jones noticed and pushed both children into the circle, saying:

"Here's two others who want to see."

"What do they want to see for?" Willis Vance boomed. "What object have they got? *They* aren't thinking about rings, are they?"

Mrs. Vance said gaily, "You never know."

The children saw it now—they saw the diamond ring: the sparkling, glittering stone of fiery, light, clear colors— a stone so precious that its hard clarity held all colors— clasped in prongs of gold.

"Is it a *di*'mond ring?" Delight breathed. She looked down at the ring and then up at Bess.

The grown people laughed—they were always laughing at Delight; but in approval, not in scorn.

Lulu Jones asked her, "Is that the kind you're going to wear some day?"

Delight nodded in careless confidence.

The children turned and ran down the steps. They had seen. Delight said Tom Burchard looked "vay-ry sad. Do you know it?" Clarence nodded solemnly. They were both sorry, because Tom was so nice to them when they went to the lumberyard, saving the scraps for them, and letting them play on the brand-new boards. They liked Tom better than they did Franklin Story. Tom paid more attention to them, he said he enjoyed kids. But Bess and Franklin belonged together. That was something they didn't question. Bess and Franklin were the ideal couple.

The Daves had invited the Iras for Sunday dinner. The

Andys hadn't driven in to church that morning; roads were too bad out their way. Clarence wanted Delight to come to his house for dinner too, but her mother laughed and said, oh no. Didn't they see each other often enough? Clarence wanted Delight there to share with him his pride and curiosity: to hear the way the grown folks talked at the table, the questions, comments, and congratulations.

Bess had become calm and self-possessed. Her Uncle Ira said to her, "That's right, don't you let anybody bother you."

She answered, "I'm not bothered in the least."

She smiled when Merrill attempted to tease her, hinting that he should be first choice for best man. He'd have to speak to Franklin about that, she said.

Mrs. Ira seemed very pleased. When she praised the ring, her tone was complacent. She approved of the engagement—and she didn't always approve of Bess; she was one of the few people in town who ever had a word of criticism for Bess Miller. Aunt Belle considered Bess frivolous for not going away to college; for being content with a few lessons in china painting, and a few scattering piano lessons, enough to play popular music by ear. She said that Bess had a "wayward streak"—that remark had come back to the other family, and made them all furious (especially Mrs. Dave and Edie, who often made the same accusation themselves). Mrs. Ira had a great deal of criticism to offer, too, on the grounds that Dave and Bertha (although she considered Bertha didn't count) allowed those three girls to run around at their own sweet pleasure—something that couldn't be said of Aunt Belle and Marguerite!

But that day the atmosphere was benign. Mrs. Ira thought highly of Franklin Story—in spite of some jealousy where Merrill was concerned. She said now:

"Well, I'm very glad your engagement is announced, Bess. We were wondering. But this is good news for all."

Bess said afterwards, when the others remarked that Aunt Belle seemed satisfied for once, "Oh yes, she sees me right now where I ought to be, among the town's worthy matrons."

"Where would you want to be?" Irene demanded.

"Oh, there of course!" Bess answered, with a dry note in her voice. She went upstairs.

"What makes her so funny?" her father asked.

"Girls are all funny about their engagements," Edie pronounced.

"Ja, it's that flighty streak," her mother murmured. That made Dave indignant. "Flighty streak! Bess hasn't any flighty streak. What are you talking about? No more than any other girl. All girls are more or less flighty—until they get married."

Bertha rocked, saying nothing, her faded but still pretty eyes looking away, her lips closed. Edie started to say something—that mama was talking just like Aunt Belle, and papa thought girls had nothing to do but get married; but she thought better of it, and went to carry out the dishes.

Clarence had listened to all this with solemn eagerness mixed with unconcern—his customary attitude toward older people talking. Now, as he had in church, he felt uneasy and cast down. The excitement of the morning was darkened. It made him indignant, too, to hear anyone so much as suggest that his sister Bess could be less than perfect.

By that time his cold had really developed, and the folks decided that he was not to go to his Junior meeting or to church at night. For a wonder Clarence didn't protest. Even when Edie reappeared in the sitting room, wiping the big platter, and said, "That kid shouldn't be allowed to go *any*where until he's over his cold," Clarence was meek. He didn't ask to see Delight again. He didn't want to talk about the diamond ring. His pride had become confused and overcast.

After supper the folks made him go up to bed. Edie insisted on it. She said that was the new way to treat colds. "You don't let kids go around giving their colds to other kids." "Ach, why should he give his cold?" their mother asked vaguely. Clarence was a child—it seemed to her even his colds must therefore be harmless. But their father agreed with Edie this time. Clarence protested, but only feebly, out of duty. He was glad to consent; and all the more so when Bess announced that she wasn't going to church either. She didn't want to sing in the choir tonight. She'd done enough singing this morning.

Clarence was half asleep when Bess came up to his room. It was the little room at the end of the hall.

"Are you awake, Clarence?"

Then he shook off his drowsiness. He always liked it when Bess came up to his room. Bess sat on his bed and put her head down on the pillow. Clarence could smell the cleanly fragrance of her dark mass of hair; could feel its crinkled silkiness.

"Bess, what?" he pleaded.

At first she wouldn't say anything. Then she sat up and laughed. " 'What?' " she mimicked. "Nothing." She squeezed his wrist. Her gentle, mirthful, teasing voice was just the same.

Clarence felt warm with relief. It seemed to him that even his cold was better. Her presence, motherly, big-sisterly, yet lovely and exciting, was just as he had always felt it. Bess had been the one who had looked after him from the time he could first remember. She was almost as much his mother as his mother herself. There was no doubt in Clarence's mind over that old question as to which of the Miller girls was the prettiest! He admired Irene, and took pride in her popularity—she could get any man she wanted, was what the other girls said of Irene. But Bess was the big sister, beautiful, dramatic, who shone above them all.

"Do you like my ring?" Bess asked. Her voice had an exciting, half-teasing note; but petulant too, as she turned the ring, held the diamond between her thumb and forefinger, making Clarence look at it.

"Gee, it's awful pretty," Clarence said earnestly.

"Do you want me to get married?" Her voice was really petulant now.

"No, I guess not." Clarence was doubtful. "I don't want you to go away from our house."

"Yes, you do."

"I don't either!"

"All right then, I won't."

Bess laughed. She started to take off her ring, but Clarence, scared, cried, "No, don't!" Now he saw she *was* teasing. But her teasing was never mean, as Irene's could be. Irene could be cool and mean.

Bess leaned over and hugged Clarence before she got up from the bed. Clarence tried to hold tight to her and make her stay.

"You don't have to go, Bess. You don't have to."

She told him, yes, she did; she'd decided to go to church after all.

Clarence wailed, "You can't! I'm not going to stay here all alone in this house."

"You won't be alone. Mama's downstairs. She didn't go."

Bess forced open his fingers and got away; while Clarence, sniffling and half sick, lay feebly protesting, "No sir, no sir, you can't, I won't let you go." After she was gone, however, he lay there happy and excited, with his cheek on his hand, because he was proud of Bess—radiance shone upon her. Her teasing and her flightiness made her all the more radiant. She was the most beautiful grown-up person who had ever lived.

Clarence came home from school alone one afternoon. Delight had to stay and practice her Easter song with Alta and Bonita.

"The little birds with joy do sing
On Easter Day, on Easter Day."

The little girls were to present this song as their number on the first-grade program before the spring vacation. The boys made fun because this song was just for girls. The boys stood outside the Methodist basement window and mimicked the girls singing, until the teacher came out and told them to go straight home or they'd be reported. Then they ran.

Clarence and Jamie and Harvey played around near the schoolhouse for a while. But the ground in the school-yard was soft and muddy, and they got tired of dragging around great clumps of brownish mud on their shoes. They all sat down on the edge of the board sidewalk and cleaned the mud off with sticks. Jamie wanted to go downtown to the hardware store. He said Mr. Groundhog was working for his father now. "You ought to listen to him talk. He talks awful funny." Clarence wanted to hear Mr. Ground-hog talk; but he was cold, and the thought of the hardware store, with the dull gleam of the stoves in a double row down the length of the barnlike room, made him shudder. He was hungry.

"No I guess maybe I *got* to go home."

Over the bridge, and up the hill, seemed a long way— as it often did in those days when he was a small boy— through the fine chill mist that was almost rain. The mist silvered the boardwalks and hung in cold drops from the railing of the bridge. When Clarence came in sight of his own house he started to run in a fresh burst of energy. Smoke from the kitchen chimney spread thick and low through the cloudy dark air. The yard at this time of year had a raw, empty look.

He gave his shoes a hasty wipe on the crumpled rag on the porch. The front hall was empty, and the doors were closed, the door that opened into the dining room, and the folding doors that shut off the parlor. But the coffee smell and cake smell were fragrant in that cheerless, shut-off atmosphere. Clarence yanked off his jacket and tossed his cap toward the newel post. In the dining room he squeezed himself between the table and the clotheshorse; the whole dining room was spread with still-damp, freshly ironed clothes. Clarence said "Bla-ah" to the dangling legs of his own long underwear. He burst into the kitchen shouting: "Gimme something to eat. I'm hungry."

Then he halted and said, "Gee."

The room was dark on that lowering spring day. At first it all seemed blurred—it was like looking through steamed-up windowpanes. Clarence blinked. Coming from outside, as he did, the room seemed to him like a cave, thick with warm odors, aroma of coffee and fresh spicecake, and the scorching smell of ironing. The cave was full of women-folks gathered around the kitchen table. In that close atmosphere the sense of female was enough to knock anybody down. Clarence started to beat a retreat.

But they all cried, "Come in. Don't let us scare you out." His mother said anxiously, "Come and get warm a'ready."

His sight seemed to clear. The room settled at once into its familiar aspect. There was just the regular old crowd, mama's cronies as Irene called them with disgust, the women who got together to gossip and drink coffee when they had nothing else to do: Mrs. Wright, Mrs. Staley, Mrs. Donohue, and the new neighbor woman from across the road, Mrs.

Tipp. "I don't know why they always have to come *here* to pick everyone to pieces," Irene had once said. "They might do that at their own houses sometimes." Clarence was used to these gatherings—the talk, both furtive and intent, full of dire relish, and with sudden bursts of jollity. When he had been smaller still he was often a part of the conclaves—quiet, not much noticed, playing by himself with pieces of wood, or tagging his mother around.

Bess and Edie were both in the kitchen that afternoon, so Clarence, lured by hunger, entered boldly. He was sure of protection with his sisters at hand. The two older girls were at home all the time that spring. Bess had finished school and Edie had quit—she'd refused to go back after staying out two weeks with tonsillitis. Aunt Belle thought that was terrible, and talked to the folks about it; which made Edie furious. Papa had stormed around a while and had several set-tos with Edie. But he'd said finally he wasn't going to make *his* life miserable forcing Edie to do what she didn't want. He guessed a few weeks of school more or less wouldn't make much difference. If a girl did lose out on her diploma that wouldn't keep her from getting married. Edie said she hated school. She couldn't bear the principal. His wife was so afraid he'd be decent to the high school girls that he just favored the boys. Only boys could get good marks in that high school. Irene said that was because Edie thought she wasn't going to pass in geometry. "He's decent to me." Edie said, "Oh well, *you*." Anyway, it was better having Edie here at home. The family had to stand more of her fussing but they profited on the whole. Edie's energies had to go somewhere and when she was out of school they were spent on cooking.

The womenfolks welcomed Clarence and made much of him.

"Look at his cheeks, how red! It must be getting colder outside."

His mother felt of his coat to see if it was damp and Edie told him to go change those awful shoes. Clarence pulled away from his mother and ignored Edie. Bess said let him sit in his stocking feet awhile, the room was warm enough. In fact it was so warm she was going to get out, of here in a minute. Where'd he pick up so much mud? the neighbor woman asked, marveling. The girls both laughed. They said that was nothing new! There had to be no mud at all for Clarence not to find any!

Clarence squeezed in a chair at the end of the table, next to where Edie sat, and closest to the stove. Edie had got up to frost her freshly baked spicecake. It was too warm to frost, she told the women, but she wanted them to have some of it, they could eat it with forks.

"Yes, we can be swell like Mrs. Harry Harper," Mrs. Wright said. "She puts forks even for olives."

"Yes, for olives, and then it ain't right to take your fork for bread!" Mrs. Staley cried. "Ain't that some note?"

Mrs. Wright declared the cake was worth waiting for, no matter how long. "I got all afternoon," she said, shaking with laughter. "Nobody's going to shake me loose until that cake comes 'round."

The gabble went on over Clarence's head: the hints, scraps of information, speculation, the rich mournful relishing of the worst. Those afternoon conclaves of womenfolks in the kitchen were different from decorous meetings in front rooms with other folks, menfolks, around. Then often if they didn't agree with the menfolks the womenfolks kept still. Now they let things out. They told what they really thought of the menfolks, and things the menfolks said. *We're not through yet, this is just the beginning. You'll see. Folks'll see. It never rains but it pours. They'll see. The menfolks they always talk but their big talk don't always pan out. They'll see.* The singsong repetitions sounded a dark refrain through the homely kitchen comfort, with the mist, turned half to sleet, slanting against the window-panes. Edie joined in vociferously; Edie was right in on these meetings. Bess added a word when she felt like it and kept still when she didn't. (Irene utterly disdained such company.) Clarence didn't know what all the gabble was about and didn't want to know. Sometimes he listened and sometimes not. He both despised these meetings and felt a zestful enjoyment. He sat in the dimness of the cave, the one small, admitted male in the huddle of females, waiting for his cake and soaking in heat from the stove.

"Give him some coffee too," Mrs. Wright begged. Edie was passing Clarence. "Don't leave him out."

"Ja, that's what I say," his mother put in. "Coffee won't hurt him. She's got that notion lately. She gets that from the minister's wife. She won't ever give the little girl coffee."

"Why, what does coffee hurt!" Mrs. Wright exclaimed; obese and jovial. "Mine had coffee from the start. I don't see it ever hurt 'em. They don't show it, do they?"

Mrs. Staley said, "Mamie sure don't."

"He can have some today," Edie conceded, "to get warmed up on. He's just over his cold. But he isn't going to have it right along, I don't care what anybody says."

Mrs. Dave gave the other women a meaning look. Edie couldn't hear one word that might sound like criticism of the minister's folks. She flared right up if there seemed to be so much as a hint. Mrs. Staley showed that she understood, put her finger on her lips and nodded. Mrs. Wright shook with silent laughter.

Clarence accepted his coffee. The less he called attention to himself the better he would fare. The cake was what he wanted anyway, and he knew he'd get a big piece from Edie.

But he couldn't entirely escape.

"Where is that little girl?" Mrs. Wright asked him. "I

thought you and her was never apart." She winked at the other women.

"Ja, where *is* Delight?" his mother echoed.

"She stayed after school," Clarence mumbled, his mouth full of cake.

"Stayed after school!" Mrs. Staley repeated. "Then she must have been a bad girl!"

"She was not a bad girl!" Clarence swallowed his cake, gulped, and glowered.

"That ain't the way to answer," his mother murmured.

"She wasn't either bad," Clarence repeated. "She stayed because the girls practiced their song."

"The girls did! Ain't the boys got a song too?" Mrs. Wright nudged Mrs. Staley.

"No," Clarence said briefly.

"The boys don't care to sing, do they?" Mrs. Donohue put in for comfort, in her sad, gentle, brooding voice—a voice full of muted grievance. "They let the girls do that."

Clarence scowled and said nothing.

"You can't say nothing against *her*," his mother warned the other women. Clarence heard, but he wasn't going to show those women that he did.

"Oh, we wouldn't say anything against *her*," Mrs. Staley silkily agreed. "She's a real cute little girl, that's all anybody would say."

Clarence took big bites of cake and then a gulp of coffee. The womenfolks seemed to think it funny to watch him glower! He glanced over at Edie. In any situation like this, Edie would be on his side. The mere suggestion that the Greenwood family could meet the same kind of comment as other folks made Edie just as mad as it did him. But Edie gave him a look that said, take no notice. "Consider the source," was what she was telling herself.

Edie came back to the table, announcing abruptly, "I think I'll stop and have something my own self!" The women all welcomed her. They wanted Bess to sit down with them too, but Bess said the ironing was done, and she was going to get cleaned up. They called to her not to forget to put on that diamond ring—they'd missed that ring this afternoon.

"She don't wear it when she works," her mother explained.

"It might get lost," Mrs. Donohue soothingly added.

That set the women off on a new tack. "When's somebody in *your* family going to get their diamond? Looks to me like there's some candidates there."

"What about in your family?" Mrs. Donohue weakly countered.

"Oh, in my family! Everybody knows that. How about it, old lady?" Mrs. Wright poked Mrs. Staley. "You should know! You furnished the other half! You and me are joint producers."

"Oh, we don't make any secrets!" Mrs. Staley archly replied.

Mrs. Donohue looked down at her plate in discomfort. She well knew that was directed at her. There wasn't much of a secret regarding Trixie and Emmett, except that they hadn't announced they were out-and-out engaged. But it was considered mysterious that Alicia, whom some people thought even prettier than Bess and Irene Miller—who had been called by such an authority as Vincent Harper the "only genuine beauty" in New Hope—never seemed to go with any of the boys.

But the women took another tack again.

"Edie," Mrs. Wright said, "when are *you* coming out with your di'mond? I don't know about this quitting school, just what it means!"

"You needn't bother about *me* having any diamond!" Edie retorted.

"Ja, I don't know," her mother sighed.

Clarence—with his coffee cup raised to his lips—looked from one to the other. He had been listening to this. He had his ears pricked up now. Mrs. Staley was saying:

"You don't mean to tell us you haven't got any beau!"

"I'm not telling you anything," Edie answered smartly.

"No, that's just what we hear," Mrs. Staley slily murmured, while the neighbor woman's eyes glistened. "You don't tell anybody much of anything. So we hear."

"Because there's nothing to tell!" Edie snapped. But her whole face burned.

"Oh, oh, Edie! Now be careful what you say!"

Clarence looked from one to the other again. He could safely do that since their attention was off him. He hoped that maybe he was going to hear something about Edie's fellow. There were rumors all the time, but nobody ever saw that fellow around. "That fellow" was what the folks always called him, in a tone of suspicious disgust. For a while Clarence hadn't even known that "that fellow" had any other name! But he knew the name now: it was Leroy Chesborough.

He didn't know much else, however, beyond the fact that the folks didn't approve; and nobody seemed to be certain whether Edie was actually going with that fellow or not. If she was, she took pains not to bring him into the house where anybody could get a look at him!—so her father said. Who was that fellow, anyway, who were his folks, and where did they come from? Why didn't they ever show themselves at church? "Because there isn't any of their kind of church here," Edie retorted. Her father said that was no excuse. Lots of folks didn't have their own kind of denomination, but they went to church anyway. "They'd be welcome at our church, you know it, whether they belonged or not." Edie wouldn't go on with the argument. "Well, why talk to me about it? I'm not married to him, am I?" Her father growled, and said no, and she'd better

not be. Irene laughed at that, and Bess tried to get papa
calmed down, while Edie banged out of the room. And that
was all anybody had found out! The folks tried to get something out of Bess or Irene about that fellow but all they
ever said was: "Don't ask us!" Clarence was off-and-on curious—especially when his father said that fellow didn't have
a good reputation. "I can tell you this much, he don't have
a very good reputation around town." Clarence pondered
that; tried to think up things that made a reputation "not
very good"—smoking maybe, or hanging around freight
cars, or being seen around the marble works. He couldn't
get Delight interested in regard to Leroy Chesborough.
Leroy and Edie weren't a romantic story-book couple, like
Bess and Franklin. It wouldn't be any fun for her and Clarence to pretend they were Edie and Leroy Chesborough
walking down the street together.

Once Clarence had gone over to the other part of
town past the house where Edie's fellow lived, just to see—
what, he didn't know, and he hadn't seen much! It was just
a house—a small, new frame house on bare, rutty, brown-
black ground. Two planks, still shiny, although mud-
tracked, led up to the front steps.

Clarence's curiosity was all awake again.

The women couldn't pry a word out of Edie, however, in spite of her flaming cheeks. All at once Clarence
felt himself Edie's partisan. He was fiercely and loyally on
her side. He scowled at the women; they were what Irene
called them, a set of old gabby-hens, they gave Irene the
pip. If they said one other word Clarence was going to
tell them to let his sister alone.

He hitched over closer to Edie. His anger against her
fussing and stewing, always keeping after him about rubbers, could suddenly evaporate. Edie was in the middle and
got the worst of it from both sides—that was what she herself said; she always felt herself aggrieved; and there was

an asperity, a sense of defraudment, in the way she faced
the world. The folks talked against that, and scolded Edie
for it—"Well, you needn't take it out on us," they said.
Clarence felt that way too, and he wouldn't mind Edie; and
yet he had some childish comprehension of Edie's side.
There was a remark he'd once heard Mrs. Murdock make
—that really it was hard on Edie, she'd have a better chance
if she stood by herself. Bess and Irene always got the pick.
It made Clarence ashamed, to think his sister should go
around with a fellow who didn't have a good reputation
and whom she didn't want to bring into the house and introduce to her folks. But he felt somewhat the way Bess
said she did: they oughtn't to blame Edie too much. Irene
had said nastily, no, Edie'd probably rather go with somebody better if she could get him.

Clarence didn't want anybody else to blame Edie, at
least! He clenched his hands under the table and looked
around, warily on guard, at the womenfolks. They didn't
notice him. But it made him feel big and protective. If
Edie went with Leroy Chesborough, Clarence didn't care
if she did; he sided with Edie, and not with the folks.

Easter came early that year—not in spring, but at the
tag-end of a drawn-out, snowy winter. Plants had to be
carefully wrapped when they were taken over to the church
to be used for decoration: the callas, ferns, gloxinias, and
Easter lilies. Several ladies made a point of lily culture so
that the church could have lilies at Easter time. New Hope
didn't have a greenhouse then—of course there would be
a greenhouse before long. Meanwhile the ladies raised their
own decorations.

The morning service had been well attended, but even
more would come at night. Because a crowd was expected,
and the primary room would be in use, the meeting of the
Juniors had been postponed. The order of Sunday was re-

versed. Delight came over to play with Clarence. She stayed at the Miller house for Sunday supper and she was going to sit with Clarence in the Miller pew.

The girls had some of their friends over for supper: they had Trixie Donohue, Mil Anderson, and Ella Murdock. Trix was Edie's bosom friend, and the other two girls were Irene's age. Bess was absent from the table. "Invited over to the Storys'," Edie said, "if you please!" Mama Story had asked her even before Franklin came home for vacation. Bess lived in a more glorious region than the other girls, because she was engaged.

As soon as the meal was over, all the girls went upstairs to get ready for the evening service. Edie consented to let her mother carry out the dishes if she would promise to let them stand over until morning. Somebody could wash dishes while the others were washing clothes. It didn't take three to get out the laundry.

"Those kids are standing right in the doorway watching us," Ella Murdock said, shocked.

"Who cares?" Irene asked flippantly.

"Goodness, *my* brothers wouldn't come up to my room on a bet."

"Oh, he just does it for smartness."

The two children acted as if they didn't hear. When they saw a chance, they slipped quietly into the room. With respect, spiced with mischief, they watched the big girls getting ready—ready themselves, at an instant's notice, to turn and run. Edie and Mil and Ella and Trixie crowded in front of the big dresser, taking turns at the mirror; Mil and Trixie, who were tallest, sometimes standing on tiptoe and peeking over the others' heads. They brushed up their pompadours, resettled their side combs, put on powder and leaned forward to rub it out of their eyebrows with wetted forefingers. Clarence imitated them, licking both his little fingers and rubbing both eyebrows at once; and Delight wanted to laugh so hard that she had to press her fists against her mouth.

But Irene was the one to watch. She wasn't satisfied with any such hasty preparations. The moment she entered the bedroom Irene had taken her china-backed comb and brush set (the one Ray Putnam had given her at the Christmas Tree) and gone swiftly over to the small commode which she kept fastidiously apart as her own: Irene wasn't going to have any of *her* things mixed up with others. Clarence could run in and use Bess's comb or Edie's nail scissors if he felt like it; but he didn't dare so much as approach Irene's sacred dressing table. The tall bottles of perfume that she had also received for Christmas—from Dean Robinson—guarded the immaculate small objects on the commode top with their remote sparkle.

Irene had taken off the waist of her new changeable silk dress and put on her dressing sacque of thin cream-white nun's veiling. She had let down her hair. The children watched the scrupulous unhurried care with which Irene was brushing her thick locks. Irene's hair wasn't as long as Edie's nor so curly as Bess's. But some people thought Irene's hair the prettiest: it was of such nice texture, they said, slightly wavy, easily arranged, and a light brown-gold. Irene's hair grew prettily and looked loveliest when brushed straight back from the face—something that even Bess couldn't stand. Bess didn't look well unless her hair was fluffy.

"Look at that Irene Miller!" Trix exclaimed. "If she isn't dressing all over again. Irene, what are you up to?"

"Up to? Nothing. Just combing my hair."

But the children, eagerly watching, could see the smile lurking in the corners of Irene's thin rose-pink lips.

The girls were through at the big dresser and they came over and gathered around Irene. Was it true, Mil demanded, what everybody had been hearing? What had everybody been hearing?—Irene asked with delicate disdain. Oh, Mil said, about Vincent Harper. How you got Vincent Harper to bring you home. Irene leaned toward the mirror and carefully thrust an amber side comb into her hair. Her eyes sparkled. Then she laughed outright.

It *was* true! Mil cried in lusty triumph. What was?—the others demanded. "Oh, that this little wretch here made a bet she could get Vincent Harper out of his house—Irene, you tell it," Mil finished impatiently.

Irene didn't seem to mind telling the story. Her voice had a note of subdued sweet malice. The children had heard that note before; they admired, and were wary of that tone. But they listened eagerly to the story. Dear Vincent was at home for the spring vacation, home from Harvard. It was a long way to come but mother must have him here. You know dear Papa Harry had bought that beautiful red-wheeled trap. Reports were all around that Vincent had said he had no time to waste on any girl brought up in the atmosphere of New Hope, although Alicia Donohue *was* a beauty in her way—here Irene gave a slight smirk and glanced slily up at Trixie. It seemed too bad, when here was Vincent, dear Vincent with such a beautiful high collar, and the new trap stuck in the stable—

"Well, I simply got tired of hearing all that," Irene said.

Yes, she *had* made the bet, and it was with Chick Bostrup. Chick had bet her a pair of new spring gloves. She was going to hold him to it! She would have those gloves, Irene said with satisfaction.

To the children listening, taking it all in, the story sounded like the most exciting romance: and Irene, cool, ethereal in her cream-white nun's veiling, brushing back the thick hair that curled golden at the ends, lifting her round arms, from which the sleeves fell back, to pin the smooth coil in a figure 8—Irene was the heroine. She was part of the story and scarcely seemed real.

She knew dear Vincent was at home, Irene continued, and she knew he was in the house. So she merely decided to walk past there. When she was just in line with the big front window she decided again that she would have to cross the street. "In all that mud!" Mil shrieked. "Why, that's right where that puddle is!" Irene murmured, "You don't say so." Well, right there she slipped, and her feet went *into* the puddle, and she was stuck! Irene told this part of the story with a serene, soft nonchalance that made the listeners' eyes bug out. And did he come out of the house?—the girls were asking in excitement. Why of course he came out. Wasn't Vincent Harper a perfect gentleman? "Ask *him* if you don't believe it. He's the only gentleman in town." And what was more, he asked Irene to come inside. Under the circumstances there wasn't anything else she could do. Vincent built a fire in their fireplace—not a very good one, though, it smoked a lot—and brought Irene a pair of his mother's slippers, and seemed terribly impressed because the slippers were too large for her, and they both sat in front of the fire until Irene's shoes were partly dry. The hired girl had to clean off those dreadful shoes!

Edie said, "Yes, and what's more, I bet you spoiled them."

Then? Oh then, nothing much, except that Vincent took her home when the shoes were dry enough so that she could put them on again. Of course home wasn't very far. She *might* have walked home in wet shoes.

"But didn't you have any rubbers?" Ella asked suddenly.

That smile curved Irene's lips. A dimple showed faintly in one cheek. "Look under the sidewalk near Vance's crossing," she said demurely, as she took up her silk waist to put it on.

"Irene *Miller!*" the girls breathed in awe.

Edie turned. She said, "You kids run off now . . . They don't have to hear everything, the little snips," the children heard her grumbling as they turned and made for the stairs. Wasn't it wonderful?—Delight breathed, her eyes gleaming. Oh, she cried, dancing, she couldn't wait to see if Vincent Harper came to church tonight and if he was going to take Irene home! "Clarence, can you?" Clarence wasn't going to admit that he cared much. But he did care. His sister Irene could get any fellow she wanted; that was what people said and it made Clarence more than ever proud.

Going to church, they were both in such spirits that Dave grumbled there was no holding them back. Delight danced and skipped on the wet boardwalk going down the long hill until once she would have fallen if Clarence hadn't caught hold of her. They slid a ways together, ending up with shrill laughter from Delight, shouts from Clarence.

"Here, here, here, you kids!" Dave was scolding. "You've got to act better than that."

Tonight, they had a secret! Delight didn't dare give Clarence one glance or she would have burst out into wild giggling. Again they watched the chorus choir. Bess was wearing her challis dress and they knew she had on her diamond. Bess and Franklin were together. But it wasn't Bess who was their heroine that night: it was Irene. When Irene stood up, in her changeable blue silk dress shot with golden glints, like the gold in her hair, Delight breathed: "Isn't she *beau*tiful?" Irene was just beautiful. She was as beautiful, Delight whispered, as the White Cat after she'd been turned into a princess. Or as Queen Isabella.

"Bess is too," Clarence loyally maintained.

Delight stared at him with her oddly set bright eyes. She murmured dreamily, "I'm going to brush *my* hair, I'm going to brush it back just the way Irene does, and have dressing sacque sleeves that fall back just the same way from my arms." She slightly lifted her arms.

Clarence listened, in pride for Irene and jealousy for Bess—until his father leaned over to mutter sternly:

"Now, you children, both calm down."

After that Delight for a while sat primly upright. But then she had to twist her neck trying to see if Vincent Harper had come to church. Vincent Harper! He was almost as legendary a figure to Delight and Clarence—although he had grown up in New Hope—as the Harper girls, his aunts, Miss Caroline and Miss Amelia, out in the old community. Vincent Harper was the only young man in town who had been sent East to school. Mrs. Story had wanted to send Franklin but Mr. Story preferred, he said, the progressive schools of our great West; and Merrill Miller would go to the college where all the Merrills had gone. The children knew the community tales about Vincent Harper: he wore high collars, and gave a high handshake—the children practiced the high handshake. He wore buttonhole bouquets from his mother's conservatory. No other man in New Hope would wear a buttonhole bouquet. Although Vincent Harper was the same age as Franklin Story, he had never associated with the big crowd. That riled Aunt Belle Miller particularly: that Vincent Harper should be too good, if her Merrill wasn't too good! People said the trap had been purchased so that Vincent Harper could take visiting girls driving—he never had looked at any girls except girls from away! The triumph, if Irene Miller walked off with him, would be a triumph for the town.

He had come to church. Vincent Harper had come to church! When folks stood up for the last hymn, and some people were bending down for rubbers, the children saw him.

They couldn't wait after that for the service to be over. The moment the "Amen" sounded they darted for

the aisle. Clarence ran butting through the crowd, trying
to keep up with Delight who made her way between people,
when it seemed there *was* no between, like a sharp little
needle. Finally they both reached the back of the room
where Vincent Harper was standing with a sort of elegant
inconspicuousness. They had to get there before he went
outside. But he wasn't going outside; wasn't going to join
the lowly line-up. If he was waiting for Irene he was going
to do it here inside the church.

The children halted. When the folks came past and
asked, "Are you coming home with us?" Clarence impatiently shook his head. He said he was waiting for the girls.
He was going home with Edie and Dora. The folks gave
their consent.

Delight's eyes were fixed on Vincent Harper with such
bright intentness that Clarence almost felt embarrassed. But
now that she saw Vincent Harper "close to," Delight didn't
know whether to be impressed or disappointed. He *did* wear
a buttonhole bouquet. His hair was parted in the middle.
His trousers had a wonderful crease. But he was slight, and
rather pale looking; hadn't Franklin's fine broad shoulders
and easy strength, or Merrill's pleasing features. There were
several better-looking young men in the big crowd! But
Vincent Harper would have to be the hero of the romance
since Irene was the heroine.

Many people were trying to make out why Vincent
Harper should have come to church that night! If it was
Irene who had drawn him there, she was taking her time.

But at last she came walking up the aisle with Merrill—the two cousins were often together. She had put on
her winter coat; Clarence remembered how the girls had
stormed around that morning because Easter was too cold
for their new spring jackets; but even a dark winter coat,
at the end of the season, could look well on Irene. The coat
hung nonchalantly open, showing the blue and gleaming

gold of the changeable silk dress. Her wisp of a white silk fascinator trailed softly from her arm. When Irene came up to where Vincent Harper was standing, she stopped, and smiled with vague sweetness. The children held their breath. Unperturbed, exquisitely pretty, Irene for a moment paused. Clarence's mouth was open. He felt as if he had never seen his sister Irene before, not to know what she was like: the charming harmony and compactness of her looks, neither too tall nor too short, but exactly right—and her coloring, the brown-gold hair, and the eyes blue-gray and changeable like the silk dress—not one feature standing out from the others, but all cunningly blended, and exactly right. At this moment she was the prettiest.

Vincent Harper stepped forward and claimed Irene. The children witnessed her smiling assent. Had the meeting been prearranged? That was something no one would ever find out from Irene unless she chose to tell. Bending her head slightly, she threw over her hair the web of white silky stuff and tied the ends under her smooth chin. She put the tips of her fingers on Vincent's proffered arm and they went up the last space of aisle together.

Amazement shone all around them. Everybody could see Merrill's astonishment. Ed Saltonstall was streaking over toward Irene—he stopped—his jaw dropped ludicrously. Clarence was almost overcome by his rapture of embarrassment and pride.

But Delight was running on ahead of him. She must be on hand to see the wonderful couple leave the church. Clarence ran after her. On the steps they halted. Was the trap outside? Yes, it was there. They saw the loftiness of its neat, fine outline in the rainy dusk. Irene would ride away in the red-wheeled trap! The children saw it all: saw Vincent Harper untie the mare, saw the frisky switch of the blowing mane, the pawing of the hoof and fine toss of the head—"Whoa, girl, whoa, Kate," Vincent was saying soothingly. At that moment Clarence wanted a slender, black-brown mare more than he had ever wanted a pony. He wanted to sit up high and drive a fine-stepping creature like Kate. Now they saw the gesture of final elegance, as Vincent Harper stepped forward, the reins held in one hand, while with the other lifted high to grasp Irene's, he helped her lightly up into the trap. They drove off past the vacant lots into the misty chill of the March evening.

"Oh!" Delight turned to Clarence. "Did you see how Vincent Harper did that? Oh!" She jumped up and down.

But it was too much. She suddenly cried "Good night!" and went running home to the parsonage.

Clarence was left standing there alone; bewildered, too, because he didn't know whether to make fun of Vincent Harper or to admire him. Boys outside the church were saying "Oh my!" in mincing voices; but some of the voices held envy too.

The folks had gone home and Clarence couldn't find anybody. He couldn't even find Edie. Maybe that fellow had been waiting for her outside!—"skulking around," as the folks said. But he wasn't afraid to go home alone if it *was* nighttime.

Clarence ran across the echoing bridge and then went more slowly on up the hill. When he got nearly home he began to gallop, and to flourish a thin tasseled whip, pretending he was sitting up high in his red-wheeled trap driving his black-brown mare, and with Delight, of course, sitting up high beside him. He could see the tilt of Delight's head and the eager complacency of her little profile. He felt heavy with satisfaction; exalted with pride. He wouldn't confess it but he knew his sisters were the most beautiful in the world. They were like three beautiful princesses— three sisters; always three sisters!—in the *Gold* and *Silver* and *Blue Fairy Books*.

Snow faded away—first the soggy drifts, then the soft, dirty patches, and at last there was only rich, bare earth. Early in April that spring there came a spell of warm weather that dried the surface of the ground. But underneath, the deep, brown, close-packed soil, full of tough fibrous roots, kept its moisture. Farmers cautiously admitted that the outlook was good, so far.

Town changed from its winter to its springtime aspect. Boardwalks dried out from their seasonal soaking. Crossings became passable again. The Creek went foaming and rushing; the water seemed just underneath the heavy planks of the bridge. But the snow had melted gradually enough to give little danger of an overflow. Clarence and Delight stood on the raised footwalk, looking over the railing, and Clarence told about the last overflow: how the water had covered all the flats, as far as could be seen, and had carried off the Groundhog shanty. Men went out in rowboats—Lute Fairbrother and Mr. LeValley—and got the Groundhogs and took them all up on the hill. Mrs. Stiles had invited all the Groundhogs to spend the night at her house; and she kept them until they found another home.

"But it wasn't a flood," Clarence assured Delight. "Just an overflow."

Mr. Greenwood took advantage of this fine weather to make some of his country calls. The children hoped he would accept Dave Miller's offer of Mollie and the one-seated rig, because they wanted to go along. But Mr. Greenwood said he wouldn't bother with a horse. He preferred his bicycle. Some of his best thoughts for sermons came to him when he was pedaling fast along the country roads. Several times, he admitted, he had ridden on past the place for which he was headed and he'd had to turn around a mile or so farther on and ride back! He would take off his hat, holding it in one hand while the other grasped the cork handle of his bright steel handle bar, and let the wind blow his hair.

"I like to get out where I can see all around me!" he exulted.

The roads were almost empty. Only once in a while he would meet some wagon and team. Local marks—houses, barns, barbed-wire fences—were scantily defined upon the rolling immensity of the land. No matter in what direction he looked there was nothing to come between his sight and the pale, distant meeting of great earth and great sky. He would feel drunk with the sense of boundlessness. One might believe the country still unoccupied, still unsettled— scarcely known to mankind. And it was easy to understand, Mr. Greenwood said, riding along on those lofty open stretches, with the breeze that came suddenly out of no- where, and that sang in the telegraph wires long after the wind was gone—easy to comprehend that these great smooth mounds were wind-blown soil, for all they were so close-packed and solid.

"But we don't want the land unoccupied," Dave Miller had protested. "We want to get this country settled. That's what we're after."

"It's a fine feeling, all the same," Mr. Greenwood said firmly.

Clarence looked from one man to the other: the two men in the whole world whom he admired most. He was scared at the thought of living on wind-blown soil. It gave him the strange feeling he'd had sometimes driving out in the country, when it had seemed to him it wasn't themselves that were moving—but the great smooth billows of land were going up and down like the ocean.

Why, Mr. Greenwood went on to say, that was the best of it! That was what gave the particular value to this soil. The plow cut down through fine, even, brown-black soil and came out almost as sharp and clean as it entered, with a few moist particles clinging. "You've seen it." Ages had gone into the making of the cornfield where a few days ago he'd watched Andy Miller plowing: centuries of steaming heat and of crushing glacial cold, rotting and grinding to make a deep, rich foundation before the top soil was brought and deposited. Out there, one could feel the swing of the great weather cycles—periods of dryness and wind when the surface of soil was in motion, followed by long ages of settled quiet that allowed the grasses to root and grow.

But it was the past of nature, not the human past, that had filled his imagination: as he'd watched the young farmer, in faded blue overalls, cutting the long-accumulated soil with his bright steel plow that had come wrapped and crated from the implement factory. The smell of the earth was new. The light-blue sky had the freshness of morning.

Just as the fact that this site had never been used for settled dwellings gave it its own virtue. New Hope wasn't built upon ruins, he said—except on those of the old community. Their town was the first. It started history here.

Clarence had always supposed that history meant something that was over, not something starting; at the same time he fully believed that real living began and ended with New Hope. Even life in the old community had never been anything more than a legend.

There was too much going on in town that spring for the children to think long about the country. The great pastime for everybody, young and old, was to stroll through town in the evenings and look at all the new houses. Most of these were going up on the hill. The streets that seemed so long already were lengthening. Town was spreading out mostly in that direction.

Along with the boom in houses, Mr. Greenwood predicted, would come a boom in weddings. That had been his experience. Unless they let some other couple steal a march on them, Mrs. H. C. Murdock said, Mamie Wright and Paul

Staley would be the first. Their house was almost completed; and the moment it was ready for them, she had it on good authority, they would get married and move in. That would be the first wedding in the big crowd. But others were sure to follow.

"Oh, don't say that," Mrs. Vance protested.

"Why, Nellie," Mr. Vance said, "you aren't against weddings?"

"Oh, not against *wed*dings, but. everything's just right the way it is."

Wishes like that, no matter who did and didn't share them, had no effect upon time and events. They didn't keep the carpenters from going ahead. The young people had to see every day how the house was getting on: Paul and Mamie's cottage with one upstairs bedroom they called "the house."

The older people had to see too. Not to mention the children. A group set out early one evening, right after supper. The women had left their supper dishes. Well, Lizzie Murdock said in defense, weather like this didn't come every night in the year. Folks couldn't spend all their waking hours in kitchens. If they didn't hurry, too, the house would be finished before ever they got there.

"You don't have to persuade the menfolks it's all right for you to leave your dishes, Lizzie," Willis Vance told her, winking at the others. "We're willing. We haven't said a word."

"I'm not talking to the menfolks. I don't care whether they're persuaded. I was just *saying*, that was all."

"Oh, that was all!"

The children tagged after the older people.

"In fact, you know, folks, Clarence is the real cause of this." Mr. Vance winked again. "He thinks it's about time he was planning on a house of his own. So he got us all to come out and see this one. That right, Clarence?"

"We have got a house," Clarence innocently answered. "Up in our barn."

Well, well, Mr. Vance assured him, there was nothing like beginning early. That was the way to provide.

"Don't tease him, Willis."

"That wasn't teasing, my love. That was hearty commendation. I was speaking as one responsible man to another."

Clarence and Delight were both pleased—they thought that was exactly right.

The company set out in two main detachments, men together and women together—with the children following, and then scampering ahead. The women began to complain that it was a long way up the hill. But houses had to go up somewhere, and it was nicer on the hill than on those flat streets over across the bridge. "Where *we* have to live," Lizzie Murdock said sharply, with a glance directed at H. C. The H. C.'s lived in town and the A. D.'s on the hill. The menfolks paid no attention. They were talking among themselves. The voice of Dave Miller boomed out above the rest: saying yes, it might look kind of bare now, without lawns or trees, but those things could be planted. Wait a few years and this would be the best part of town.

The house Paul and Mamie were building was the last on the street. The road went on beyond it to meet the crossroad along the heights. Building would have to stop there: the river was down below. The bridge leading over into Dakota was a mile away on the lower road.

April air softened the blank new structure on its bare lot, where digging had left rough heaps of clodded yellowish dirt. Voices and laughter sounded from inside the house; and going up the two shiny planks to the open doorway, and looking inside, the older folks discovered the whole crowd of young people.

"What is this?" Mr. Vance asked. "A housewarming?"

A prehousewarming, Mamie said; everybody was invited.

"If we can get in," H. C. Murdock said dubiously.

"Oh," Mrs. H. C. cried, "we're still spry enough for that, I should hope!"

The children stood back while the older people stepped gingerly up to the doorsill; the front steps weren't put up; and then they themselves scrambled in through the open windows.

The floors had not been laid, only planks had been put down. People had to stand where they could find footing. Mrs. Vance seemed to need help from all the menfolks. The other women looked down at her pretty feet in pointed shoes as she stepped out daintily and perilously, clinging to Willis's hand on one side and Dave Miller's on the other. Nellie Vance had to send away for her shoes. The stores didn't carry ladies' sizes small enough to fit her. "I'd like to see *our* menfolks helping *us* around—without us asking!" Lizzie Murdock said to one of the women. She thought she was whispering but the children heard. H. C. wouldn't think of ever helping *her*—the old Scotchman. She could fall down and break her neck first, she said cheerfully. The children giggled. But Jamie didn't want to hear his uncle called a "Scotchman" even if it was his own aunt who said it. And Clarence and Delight wouldn't have a word spoken against Mrs. Vance. They thought her little feet were beautiful. Delight said *she* was always going to have little feet too. Her feet were always going to stay as little as Mrs. Vance's. *She* was going to send away for *her* shoes.

Mamie led the whole crowd through the house on an inspection tour. The children, however, were in and out. Clarence held his hand up elegantly high to help Delight over the window sill. Jamie and Dosia did the same in imitation, but they didn't know what it meant—where the other two had seen such a gesture, and that it was a secret.

Jamie said Clarence had to let *him* help Delight part of the time, and change 'round; 'twasn't any fun just helping his own sister. Clarence agreed; but warily.

"Let's not help anybody any more," he finally said. Dosia was disappointed.

Clarence kept snooping about and picking up small shiny blocks of wood, to use for the playhouse up in the barn. He wanted to use them for his workshop. This wasn't strange territory to the children. Nearly every day after school they went through the new houses as eager scavengers. They brought home treasures: shingles, pieces of screen, shiny nails a little bent, handfuls of clean sawdust.

Dusk was settling down. It began to get dangerous walking about on tipping planks. Folks all decided they would go out and see the back yard where Mamie would hang her washing and where Paul would put in his garden.

There was nothing much to see, when they got out there, except bare ground and a litter of boards. The pink afterglow was slowly fading from the wide, pale sky.

Clarence had gone tagging along at the end of the procession. But he had to snoop everywhere; his curiosity was boundless. He heard voices in the small pantry room off the kitchen and he went over to peek in at the door. He was going to yell "Hey there!" But he stopped. His mouth opened. He stood uncertainly.

It was his own sister Bess who was talking in there—it was Bess and Tom Burchard, Mr. Vance's helper. They weren't saying anything now, just standing together in the pale light from the small high window. They didn't know anyone was at the door. Tom wasn't looking at Bess. His face had a strange, disturbed expression. But she was looking at him. Clarence saw Bess lift her hand and gently push back the lock of fair hair that hung over Tom's forehead. Tom did look at her then. His eyes seemed fearful, perplexed, and hopeful. He caught hold of Bess's hand.

Clarence stayed there a moment longer, hardly breathing. He felt excited and perturbed. He knew it couldn't mean anything, because Bess was engaged—engaged girls didn't flirt with other men. But he didn't want anybody else to find out. He wasn't even going to tell Delight. He was going to get away as fast as he could, without seeing anything more.

CHAPTER VIII

May Day

THE DRY MARCH, and that first dry week of April, were followed by a spell of rain. Mornings began with soft, dark skies, with smells of muddy freshness through misty air. Clarence complained every morning because "they" made him put on rubbers. But he liked those days—liked putting up the big umbrella, so that he could take Delight to school; running down the long, sodden boardwalk and across the hollow-sounding bridge; waiting in the warm parsonage kitchen while Delight put on her hooded mackintosh; and then both of them hearing the drum and drip of raindrops on the cotton umbrella as they started out for school. When they came to crossings, they tried to act like Mr. and Mrs. Vance—Clarence gallantly holding out his hand while he tried to keep the umbrella tipped the right way, and Delight arching her wrist as she gave him her right hand, holding her short skirts daintily with the left, mincing as if she had on high-heeled shoes; but taking the last of the crossing in a hop and jump. Buggies splattered the liquid mud that smelled so good—it seemed as if all the rainy darkness held the fragrance of grass and violets and leaves.

The children were all thinking about May baskets.

Dave Miller said, how would the kids like it if he were to drive out in the country and take them along to pick wildflowers? The first of May came on a Saturday that year, so 'twould be just right. There was a fellow he'd been wanting to talk to, and this would be as good a time for it, he guessed, as any. He would let the children out where there was a nice patch of timber; and then on his way back pick them up again.

"Not if it rains!" Mrs. Dave put in fearfully.

Dave said largely, "*It* won't rain."

Bertha Miller always felt a sense of secret triumph over Mister and all he represented when the weather carried out her predictions instead of his. But that time he was right. The skies started to clear about the middle of the week and by Saturday everything was shining clear.

Mister hadn't told where he intended taking the children or who the man was he wanted to see. Bertha, all week, had been wondering and surmising; but she would no more have thought of asking Dave outright than of demanding to know how much he had in the bank.

Delight came over before Clarence had finished his breakfast.

"Now see," Edie said, "she's got on *her* rubbers."

Irene gave an enormous sigh. Edie had been going on about rubbers from the moment they sat down to breakfast. But if Delight was wearing hers, thank heaven that ended it! Clarence got up from the table without another word and went off to dig out his own from the wooden box in the back kitchen where shoe polish, overshoes, and rags were kept in one big jumble. "Next time we clean, somebody's got to get after that box!" the girls were always fuming. But no one of them was willing to consider it *her* business and to tackle it alone—so the jumble remained. They could hear Clarence rooting around in it now. He came with rubbers dangling from his hand. He hadn't cleaned them off since the last time he'd worn them and they were crusted with dried yellow mud from down near the Creek.

"Don't you bring those rubbers into this dining room!" Edie shrieked.

Dave came in just then. "Here, what's all this to-do?"

"His rubbers. Just look at those *rubbers.*"

"Oh, what's a little mud."

"You'd say that, if you had to clean off the carpet!"

"Go on, then! Out in the kitchen! Go on!"

"I guess you don't have all this fuss at your house, do you, Delight?" Bess asked.

"Oh no, but I enjoy it," Delight assured her seriously.

Whatever happened at the Millers', Delight accepted— shouting and all. Dave had gone out to hitch up Mollie, and Delight skipped after him, crying, "I'm going to help Uncle Dave!" She called eagerly for Clarence, and he came running, stamping down his feet into his shiny, washed-off rubbers, and pulling at one jacket sleeve.

"Here, you kids, are you ready?"

Even Mollie seemed anxious to start. She looked around, straining to see past her blinders, then began to walk off. Dave shouted "Whoa!" and the children shouted "Whoa!" until he had to tell them, "That'll do."

Mrs. Dave and the girls came out to see them off. Nobody could ever get away from this house without having the whole family on hand, Irene often said in great impatience. Irene stayed in the dining room to pour herself another cup of coffee and to disassociate herself from the family turmoil. But she couldn't stand her elegant isolation. Hastily drinking the coffee, and giving a look at herself in the glass, she took a cookie and went out to the back yard —making an excuse of taking the kids their baskets. Edie was shrieking at that moment:

"Oh, their baskets! Papa, don't go yet. Their *baskets*."

"I've got their baskets. So you needn't yell your head off."

Mrs. Miller came hurrying, carrying a shoe box.

"More stuff?"

"Ja, it's their lunch."

"*They* don't need any lunch."

"Ja, but they'll get hungry, though," Bertha insisted.

She stood submissive but stubborn, holding up the shoe box until Dave had to take it. He handed it over to Clarence.

"Here, stick this thing away then. Now let's see if we can get off."

He roared "*Gid*-dap!" and slapped the reins. The children hung on thrilled, looking back as the buggy went rocking out to the road, waving and shouting good-bye.

Mrs. Dave and the girls stood watching. Then Mrs. Dave, sighing, and muttering "Ja, who knows," went back into the house. The girls looked at each other with resigned impatience, which burst finally into laughter.

"Oh, I want to stay out here," Bess said. She sat down on the step, stretching her arms above her head. The loose sleeves of her dressing sacque fell back showing her white arms to the shoulders. In the armpits were curls of soft dark hair.

"Well, why don't you?"

"Oh . . . I suppose we ought to go inside."

"There's plenty to do out here for anybody that wants to stay," Edie reminded her. "When are we going to get those seeds planted, of those flowers?"

Bess and Irene groaned.

"I wonder where papa *is* taking those kids," Edie said with sudden curiosity.

"Ja, who knows," Irene mimicked.

Then all three girls sat down on the back step.

The children sat tight, holding their baskets on their laps: old grape baskets they were, with darkish stains and rough handles.

Clarence began to snuffle. He never quite got over his winter cold until summer. As soon as he got into the open air, his nose would start running. That sound always irritated his father.

"Here, where's your handkerchief? Don't snuff that way. How does that sound?"

Clarence sat as stiff as he could, staring straight ahead, holding his head back so the mucous wouldn't run down to his upper lip, knowing his father would roar if he dared use his hand.

"I've got one!" Delight cried anxiously. "An extra one —oh, just wait a *min*ute!"

The extra one was pinned under the ruffle of her yoke. She bit her bright pink underlip as she worked to open the safety pin. Clarence's eyes were glazed with the effort of waiting.

Delight gave Clarence the handkerchief and watched with motherly interest while he wiped his nose. His father watched too in order to see that Clarence did the thing right.

"You ought to remember hankies yourself," he grumbled. "You're big enough. Look at Delight, she remembers hers."

"Oh no, I didn't remember, Uncle Dave," Delight said very seriously. "Mama pinned it on me. I would have forgot."

"Well, you didn't come off without it, anyway."

Dave had to smile, though. It tickled him, how those kids stood up for each other.

Clarence wiped his nose in a last luxury of relief.

Already they were beginning to feel the elation of the wide May morning. The buggy went rattling over the bridge, the loose boards rumbling, and they both drew in their breath to get the full smell of the rushing spring waters. Delight's father was out in the back yard of the parsonage working in his garden, but he was so absorbed he didn't know they were going past. Houses stood drenched in the spacious sunshine of Saturday. But town was full of teams.

"Papa, can we have a nickel?"

"Oh, I guess so."

They ran as fast as they could to Donohue's while Dave went into the bank. They bought big white hearts of paraffin gum with colored pictures pasted on top.

"Well, it didn't take you long, did it?"

"No, we knew what we wanted to buy."

It was exciting to go through town. But both children waited for the great moment when they should get beyond the city limits. "Clear out beyond the city limits." That was where they were now.

The fields lay wide in morning sunshine. Level near town, they grew more rolling further on. The air was so good the children lifted their heads to sniff it in, coming to them fresh and damp with the odors of new plowing. The roads were just right, dry enough for good driving, but with the dirt well packed down. Pools, blue and flashing, still remained here and there beside the road. Some of this land could stand drainage, Dave said. But that would all come in time. A meadow lark sang liquid cadences from the fence. The barbed wire glittered. There was a humming from the telegraph wires.

"Where are we going, papa?"

"Oh—we'll see."

The children accepted that. They were busy getting the pictures off the paraffin hearts. Delight's picture was a bouquet with a big red rose in the center. Clarence's was a Newfoundland dog. They were keeping all these pictures.

They had almost two dozen stowed away in one of Irene's old candy boxes, along with a queer little hoard—agate stones from down along the Creek, red stones they called "cornelians," bluebird feathers, beautiful white dove feathers from Mrs. Vance's dovecot, and all their Valentines. Conscientiously, they offered Clarence's father one of the hearts, but were relieved when he refused. They could never quite get the pictures off the paraffin, there was always a little fuzziness of paper remaining. But that made better chewing. Delight whispered "Now!" and they both started to chew at exactly the same time. There was the ecstatic first moment when the powdery sweetness of confectioner's sugar dusted over the hearts could be tasted—after a while it was gone, there was only the paraffin.

Dave reached into his pocket and got out some tobacco.

"This is my gum. Now you kids needn't tell."

"We won't," they promised solemnly.

When they heard papa chewing, they looked at each other round-eyed, and made their own jaws work harder.

They knew the road out to Clarence's Uncle Andy's; but that morning of May Day they were going a different way. No woods were visible yet except the planted groves near farmhouses, standing thin-stemmed, the tops blurred with new leaves, against the great blue silent sky. But there must be woods out here.

Clarence looked at Delight, at her eager little profile—he knew its outline so well, and yet he always felt as if he *didn't* know, he must steal another glance. When she had come to the house that morning, in the dark-blue cap and old clothes she had on for the woods, she had seemed colorless and small. Now she was vivid. Her long fair braids glinted in the sunshine. The wild-rose color stained her cheeks. It seemed to waver almost with her breathing—with her eager glances out across the fields. Her eyes, when she was excited, were all coal-black shining pupils. But at that moment in bright sunlight the pupils were small—and the eyes were transparent blue, like the pools beside the road, when suddenly she turned toward Clarence.

"Uncle Dave, are those the woods?"

"We'll come to 'em."

The children leaned out to look at the thick brushes against blue sky, stretching long and distant now over high rolling land. Close around town there was not much timber; just the scraggly little wood beside their hill where they went sliding down at the Creek, and the thick tangled trees growing rank near the river. "The woods" had a dark, mysterious, fairy-tale sound.

Dave had good reason for not telling where he was taking the kids. It pleased him to think that Bertha would have been horrified if she had known. But this was the spot that he'd had in mind from the first, these woods that belonged to the Old Man Rundle, the finest stand of virgin timber anywhere around. "Will he allow you?" Dave could hear Bertha's scared voice asking that. No, he wouldn't allow anybody, the consarned old skinflint! The Sunday school had wanted to come to this timber for their picnic and had been refused. There was a pond away off in the woods, the only water around that was good for anything. And to think that old buzzard fenced it off for the sole benefit of his cows! Well, the place would be up for sale some day. Old Rundle had nobody but his wife to leave it to, and they couldn't either of them live forever. Dave was well aware that Harry Harper had his eye on this place also, but he didn't intend to let any Harpers get in ahead of him. Dave knew the old man's renter, Hans Gunderson, a Norwegian; he'd done business with Hans at the bank. Hans was "the fellow" he'd spoken of coming out to talk to. Not that his business just now was anything in particular. He wanted to look things over again, that was all. And he felt a sly pleasure in letting the kids get a few of the old man's flowers, instead of giving them all to the cows. That in itself was worth the drive.

"Is this where we're going, Uncle Dave?"

"I guess so."

"Where is this? Whose farm?"

"Oh, Hans Gunderson lives here," Dave said.

They turned into the narrow driveway, that was muddy still. The small bleak house stood a short distance from the driveway, needing paint—the old man was too mean to put on paint for a renter, would hardly do it for himself. That riled Dave too. He himself was generous, liked to do things in a big way. He and Ira disagreed on that point, in regard to farms they owned jointly, Ira always wanting to make each item pay for itself before he spent more. Dave detested Ira's small tight ways. He couldn't say too much, though, for he was well aware that Ira didn't always approve of *his* methods, thinking Dave played fast and loose with people and property. Dave noted with satisfaction that the place looked trim. The Norwegians and Danes who were beginning to come into the region were some of the best farmers to be found—although to Ira's wife they were "the foreign element." Dave hoped to get Hans Gunderson for a renter himself. He'd suggested it once to Hans, in connection with a farm that had come into his hands on a trade. Hans had said, yah, the old man was hard to work for, but he liked the place, he'd put in plenty of work there, didn't care to move. All the same, Dave believed he'd put an idea into the fellow's head. Another time Hans might be willing to consider. Dave enjoyed the feeling of having schemes started, lines laid down, here and there all over the country. It was what made him exuberant that morning. The children felt and enjoyed his exuberance.

Just as they drove up, Hans Gunderson came out of the barn.

"Hello there! Thought we might find you out in the field."

"Yah, Ay had to come up to the barn."

"How are you this morning?"

"Pretty good."

Hans looked at the children.

"I've brought my twins out," Dave said. "Know I had twins?"

"We are almost," Delight explained eagerly. "Our birthdays are one day apart."

"Yah?" Hans answered.

"This is my boy and this is the minister's little girl. Think the boss'll start proceedings if these kids pick a few wildflowers out in the woods? They want to fill their May baskets."

Hans grinned, saying with a slyness that admitted his knowledge of the old man's characteristics, "Yah, Ay can't tell."

"Well, I'm prepared to take the risk."

Dave said if Hans didn't object he'd drive the children out and leave them to fill their baskets, and maybe meantime Hans would let him have a look at that new stallion he'd been hearing about. "Hear you've got a champeen." Dave thought it wouldn't be a bad notion to get a squint at this farm again, perhaps make an estimate in his own mind of the worth of the buildings.

"How's the road out there?" he asked.

"Maybe pretty wet."

"Well, I'll drive as far as I can."

Dave drove carefully down the narrow wagon road that led first through a meadow, soggy where a little stream flowed through, so shallow it hadn't made a bed for itself and seemed only to pour over flattened grass.

That part of the timber wasn't fenced. It was where

Hans cut his wood. The cattle were in the further stretch where the pond lay.

"Now you kids get out."

They scrambled down from the buggy.

"Our baskets!"

Yes, and that lunch box, too. Can you take it all? Dave asked. They said they could. Clarence held the lunch box squeezed against him, with the cover partly off. Dave couldn't help thinking they looked kind of small to go off and leave. But there was nothing that could hurt them. They couldn't go farther than the fence and that wasn't far. Dave knew this timber pretty well, he'd looked at it more than once. To most people in town, the existence of the pond wasn't much more than a legend. In fact there wasn't much about this whole countryside that Dave Miller didn't know!

"Now pick all you can," he told the children. "Make use of your time. Keep sight of the wagon tracks and you can't lose your way."

They promised.

"You take care of Delight, now, Clarence."

Clarence said he would—standing there solemn and small.

"And set down that lunch box. You needn't go lugging that."

There were curving tracks where Hans had turned his wagon. Dave backed the buggy until he'd got headed toward the house again. The children listened to the rattle and squash of the iron-rimmed wheels on the narrow road.

Both stood silent, clutching their baskets. They had been wild to get here, "out to the woods," all week they had been repeating that. But they were prairie children; they played in the open. The sunlight shone only in scattered intervals here from among the trees.

"C'mon, Delight," Clarence said bravely.

She came up closer and slipped her hand into his.

"C'mon, let's find the flowers, should we?"

She let him keep her hand and pull her after him. Clarence felt a pride in the clinging of those small chilly fingers. Even if the cattle *were* in here, if they'd broken through the fence, he would just pick up a stick and—and go right after those old cattle.

They followed the wagon tracks that were two sunken ruts pressed down on old matted leaves. They weren't far from the road, but it felt far. It was strange and damp and still, in among the tall trunks of oaks and elms and soft maples. Old last year's acorns, discolored and small, lay among leaves and sticks on the ground. Looking up, the children saw blue sky far above. They felt like Hansel and Gretel; only there wasn't any witch. They knew there wouldn't be any witch.

"I see one!" Delight breathed. "I see a wildflower!"

Clarence peered anxiously, seeing at first nothing but old leaves. Then—oh, everywhere! Bluebells, great pools of them, scattered all through the cleared spaces. Delight let go of Clarence's hand.

"Look! Just look! You pick over there and I'll pick over here."

They set down their baskets—squatted . . . they had promised not to get down on the ground, not even on their knees. Children took cold that way. Now they were absorbed in the flowers. They forgot everything else. The bluebells were like the pools of blue water along the roadside, reflecting the faraway sky. The leaves were green, wet, and chill. Their hands got wet and cold as they went on picking. The ground was cold when their fingers touched it.

"Look—violets! Clarence, come over here, *please.*"

The violets grew long-stemmed and dark-petaled, dark blue like spring thunderclouds. The children picked in rapturous excitement—set their baskets down, made excursions away from them and came running back to heap in flowers: bluebells that had a pinkish cast and veins of lilac, anemones radiant like stars. Sometimes they picked together, bent over as they squatted; sometimes they were far apart. But Clarence didn't want Delight to get too far from him. When she was by herself, and he could see her head bent over the flowers, one long braid dangling, he wanted to make her aware of him again. If for a second he lost sight of her, his heart stood still. Birds flew—there was chattering from the branches above them, a sharp whir of wings. Sometimes there were only their movements, the rustle of their fingers among the thick wet leaves. Clarence kept an eye on the wagon tracks—he must watch out, he was the one.

"Oh, Clarence, come here, come here!"

He went running over to where Delight was now. They had come to the fence, of boards, with barbed wire stretched above. They could just, by climbing, sticking their toes in the cracks between the boards, look over. There was the pond, the blue water sparkling and remote. They clung with fingers clamped on the top of the boards and looked over the barbed wire.

Finally they let themselves down. They shook their fingers that felt numb.

Delight whispered then, "Where are we?"

For an awful moment they were lost. They ran wildly over the squashy leaves, twigs breaking—until they saw their baskets left lonely on the ground. They found the dim tracks of the wagon road. They were safe.

Delight held out her hands, breathing:

"They're cold. Are yours?"

Clarence said valiantly, "Do this way." He rubbed the palms of his hands against his pants legs. The cloth was scratchy. Delight tried to rub *her* palms but her skirt was so full it got in the way. Clarence said "Here," and took her hands between his, rubbing and squeezing. He remembered that time when he had kissed her out in the back kitchen. But she drew away her hands, telling him:

"Now they're warm."

Their feet were cold now. Even in rubbers, their feet felt cold and damp. Clarence had begun to jiggle. Delight looked at him and said with motherly seriousness, "You can go off, Clarence, I won't look, truly." Shamefaced but relieved, he trotted away. In deep privacy he watched the stream trickle over dead leaves. He stared into the woods, still and mysterious, the tall trees, the bluebells, as many as before they'd started picking. He thought of the sparkle of blue water. When he came back he felt fine. Delight said to him with the same gentle seriousness, "I went too."

Now they saw the lunch box. All at once they were ravenous. They tossed away the broken smashed-in cover and grabbed sandwiches of homemade bread. They bit great chunks out, almost choked with laughter to see each other's cheeks stuck out like gopher's. They stopped, alert, like Indians surprised. They heard shouting.

"Hey, kids. Where are you?"

It was only papa—only Uncle Dave. They laughed with joyous relief.

They picked up their baskets, grabbed cookies, yelled "We're *com*ing!" They ran back toward the farmhouse. Their feet were so cold it felt as if they didn't have toes. They stuffed cookies into their mouths as they ran clumping, hanging on to their baskets. A few flowers spilled out— a stalk of bluebells with green leaves partly trodden into damp mud—a violet that for a while lay dark and fresh. . . .

Clarence kept going out to the back kitchen to see if the flowers were all right: "picking up," as his mother said they should do. The girls had taken them out of the baskets in careful handfuls, filled the big dishpan with water, and set it on the laundry table under the back window. Clarence

buried his face in the great fresh mass—wet, Irene had
sprinkled water. The blue made him think of the flower
pools, the sky through branches, the distant sparkle of the
pond, fenced off—blue water they couldn't reach. In the
farmhouse kitchen, they had sat with their feet on the open
door of the oven, drinking big cups of coffee to get warm
—papa said they could; and children had stood off staring
at them, three small silent children with white hair, almost
as white as Grandma Story's. They were like the woodchop-
per's children in the fairy story.

Now the May baskets were ready on the little sewing
table in the sitting room. Bess had been working on their
May baskets all week. There was one that Delight didn't
know about. It was woven of pink and blue tissue paper, and
had a braided handle, and a beautiful fringe curled up with
the shears.

Clarence went into the sitting room and stood beside
Bess's chair. He put his cheek against her silky dark head,
breathing in the fragrance of her thick hair.

"Bess . . . what I asked you, *you* know."

"Yes, I remember."

The girls had promised they would fill the baskets.
They left their suppers and went out to the back kitchen.
They drew flowers carefully out of the fragrant mass, so
that the stems wouldn't get injured. Bess and Edie threw
away wilted blossoms, and cut the stems the right length,
while Irene with smooth, deft fingers made up the bouquets.
The small back room with its one window was filled with
fading sunlight and the mysterious freshness of the flowers
—as the girls clipped, shook off moisture, arranged.

Clarence leaned against Bess, silently reminding her. She
smiled at him, arched her black eyebrows, went softly
through the kitchen. He followed her. They went into the
parlor and closed the folding doors behind them. The calla
lily stood tall and aloof in the early evening light. Clarence

watched in awe as Bess cut off the blossom, holding the stem carefully. This was what she had promised him. She cut some lacy ferns and made a little nest inside the pink-and-blue basket, then put the calla lily in the center of the fresh delicate green.

"Keep it for me," Clarence whispered.

He ran out to the back kitchen. Edie and Irene had finished packing all the little baskets into big market baskets. Now they gave these to Clarence, telling him to take one in each hand, and to be careful. He was going to take them over to the parsonage, and he and Delight would start out from there. Bess was waiting in the front hall. Without a word, but smiling, she set Delight's basket in among the others.

Clarence went down the walk, carrying his delicate burden with sacred care. Everything was fragrant, spring-like—the growing grass, the leaves small and new on the box elder trees. Going over the bridge he looked through the crossbars of the iron railing down at the muddy shine of swollen waters with little crests and swirls of foam.

A big honeysuckle bush grew on the slope between the church and the parsonage. Clarence knelt down behind it, parted the shoots, and hid Delight's basket in there. Nobody was in sight. He got up, brushed off his knees, and ran over to the parsonage. Delight was ready. She came running to the door. She had on her blue jacket and blue hair ribbons.

"I know something," he couldn't help saying.

"I know something too!" Delight cried eagerly, skipping backwards. "I'll bet it's the same as you know—almost. Only mine's for you and yours is for me. Isn't it?"

He looked aside and wouldn't say.

The big kids would come out later, with their mean old snatch baskets. This was the hour when the little kids were abroad. Doorbells were rung, feet went scampering. In the new town, with its bare yards and scrubby trees, there wasn't much place to hide. Blue sky showed at the end of the long boardwalk. They breathed the fresh, pure air of the empty lots. They were giving their baskets together. The little cards that Bess had written for them said: From Delight and Clarence.

They had baskets for all their little friends, and their teacher, and for Grandma Story, and for Mr. and Mrs. Stiles. Now the only basket left was the cornucopia for the Groundhog girl.

Clarence and Delight had never yet followed the Creek beyond the clump of poplar trees. They had never quite dared. This evening they had to cross the bridge and take the narrow path along the top of the clay bank, where the rush of the Creek seemed far below them.

The light was fading. They saw its dreary flash on the windows of the Groundhog shanty. Mr. Murdock, not long ago, had offered Mr. Groundhog a job, out of concern for the family; but after enduring it a week or so, he had made Mr. Groundhog wash himself at the granite basin out in the back room of the hardware store, and Mr. Groundhog hadn't come back next morning. This small shanty, standing bleakly by itself, was the only real slums that New Hope possessed. Whether the Groundhogs should be "helped" or run out as a disgrace to the town, was a matter of controversy. Mrs. Stiles said that they "constituted a challenge." New Hope must admit defeat if it could do nothing better for the Groundhogs than run them out of town. The children had listened in awe. They were on Mrs. Stiles's side.

Clarence's father had said the Groundhogs were harmless.

"They're harmless," Clarence repeated now.

But even Clarence hadn't quite the courage to go up to the house, although what he feared he certainly didn't know. He set the May basket down on a broken plank that led to the door, saying hastily, "They'll find it"; and both children turned and fled. They didn't stop running until they came in sight of the bridge.

The blue sky had deepened, there was one clear star. They got the smell of the water, dark, muddy, rushing, fresh: it was the smell that meant springtime. Clarence took Delight across the bridge and as far as the church. He always did that. Then they said good night. Irene had something for him, Delight said—he would find "something" at home.

Delight went skipping along the boardwalk, shaking back her long fair braids. Clarence was scared when she passed the honeysuckle bush; but she didn't see the basket. He waited until she was safely inside her house . . . waited a little longer. Then he went over to the bush. What if some other kid—what if Willie Schnitts, had found it? But the basket was still there. The calla lily in its purity of white and gold lay fringed about by the soft green ferns.

Clarence went across the short grass of the sloping lawn with great caution. The long windows of the church had a solemn shine. The front door of the parsonage was open, through the screen he could see the parlor, dim and orderly. He set his May basket down carefully on the wire door mat, pulled the bell handle—jumped down from the steps, scuttled back across the yard, and hid, crouching and panting, behind the honeysuckle bush. Peeking around the bush, he saw Delight pick up the basket. He felt the proud, thrilling, painful moment when she picked up the basket that he had given her. He knew in secret that he loved her, she was his girl, he loved Delight.

She was looking all around for him, innocent and eager, calling "Clarence!" He heard the clearness of her voice in that clarity of springtime air. But he stayed crouching. One foot began to hurt. Finally he got up, his leg aching, hopped a few steps, and then ran as fast as he could go. His own footfalls were hollow and loud on the boardwalk. When he got as far as the bridge he lingered in the dusk, wishing that after all he had let himself be caught.

CHAPTER IX

The Turn of the Year

SUMMER CAME, with dry spells and rainy spells, interspersed
with periods of dense muggy heat: a normal summer, Cass
Story pronounced it. The box elder leaves unfolded and fat
green worms dropped splash on the sidewalks. Women going to town held up their skirts and stepped disgustedly over
the worms. They shooed black and red box elder bugs out
of their houses. But those were clean bugs, so Clarence assured Delight—he'd heard his father say that; not dirty
bugs, like bedbugs and cockroaches. Nobody had dirty bugs
in New Hope except maybe the Groundhogs. Violets were
gone, bluebells were gone; there were clean-colored petunias
against staring white house walls and many-tinted sweet peas
slowly fading on trellises, clinging to the wires with tough
stems intertwined. The Creek was drying up; the river was
sluggish and muddy. You could walk on some of the river
bed under the big bridge. Hot precious stones glinted down
in the sandy stream bed of the Creek, and the cracked banks
were rank with weeds. Out in the country the corn was
changing from green two-leaved plants in patterned rows
on dark-brown earth and growing steadily through the hot
moist nights until all the fields were packed with dark-

green masses. Cass Story wrote a wonderful editorial in praise of the corn. He said folks should drive out into the country. The countryside now was a sight to behold.

Summer passed into autumn. The box elder leaves grew dry and curled and were wrapped in cobwebs. Purple thistle flowers and yellow goldenrod stood thick along the roads. The crickets sang their evening chorus: a golden anthem, long sustained into the great dark night.

Winter came: a normal winter. Old Mollie liked to draw the light trim cutter; she frisked and switched her tail. She shook her hoofs to loosen packed clods of snow. After January, the snow drifts melted. Lacy snow palaces, like pictures of the Alhambra, formed again in the sides of drifts. Delight said if she could have her best wish now, she would be a little tiny snow princess, and live in one of the lacy glittering rooms; she would eat snow ice cream and drink snow water from ice goblets; and her royal robes would be all glittery, and she'd wear a diamond crown, besides a diamond ring.

All the winter activities went into full swing. The Relief Corps ladies held their bean supper in the Opera House; and once a month there were suppers at the church. The suppers were never so well attended; the congregations never so large. Business was growing; stores were full; A. D. Murdock figured so closely that he ran out of stock; town was packed with teams on Saturday nights. At six-fifteen the big flyer came through and the golden windows flashed on westward through the wintry dusk. New Hope increased its population by more than two hundred, counting babies born. Cass Story published a fine editorial calling New Hope the growing metropolis of the growing West.

The turn of the year came, in lingering cold, and rainy darkness; and it seemed then as if spring could never make up its mind to arrive.

It was the minister's custom, after the Sunday morning service, to take the collection plates into the vestry room and count the offering; he would then put the money in a tin box, to which he kept the key, and lock the box away in the lower part of the cupboard in the upper shelves of which the music for the chorus choir was kept. When the evening service was over, the minister would make the count again with one of his trustees; and the evening offering would then be counted and added to the first amount. The minister would take the tin box to the parsonage and keep it in his study during the night. Ira Miller would step by for it next morning on his way to the bank. Ira Miller was the treasurer of the church. Folks made him treasurer of almost every organization. He was one of those men, Mr. Stiles said, who was born into this world a treasurer full-fledged.

Clarence always was glad when it was his father's turn to be the trustee who helped with the counting. It lengthened out the evening, and gave Clarence and Delight that much more time together. They could stand out on the church steps, and watch the boys step out of line and claim their girls; or they could stay in the auditorium and run up and down the aisles. The mothers were too tired by then to stop them. The sleepiness of the evening service evaporated and was succeeded by high spirits. Clarence liked to have his family the last to leave the church. That made him feel important.

On that Sunday evening it was all the more fun because outside it was raining. Folks had gone home as soon as church was over. The two men did their counting up in the choir loft; and the two wives, and the children, and the janitor, were the only other people left in the church.

That night the counting took so long that even the children got tired. Delight did, anyway. Her mother decided to take her home and put her to bed; and Clarence's mother said, "Ja, I'm going too. Mister won't ever be ready." She'd brought her own umbrella just in case.

Clarence refused to go along. "No, sir, I can stay and wait for papa because I always do." He liked to see the money being counted. Delight didn't think that was any fun. Clarence stood behind his father's chair and counted along with the men. He was in second-grade arithmetic— he was better in arithmetic than Delight. She was better in reading, spelling, drawing, and music.

Mr. Greenwood said, "What's that again?" His tone was sharp.

"Don't our counts tally? Here, I'll add up again."

"No, no," Mr. Greenwood said hastily. "No need of that. I don't doubt you're right. I must have made the mistake this morning."

"I don't know as I'm any more likely to be right than you are."

"You're the banker. You're the money expert."

"Not according to Iry."

Anyway, it was time to go home. Mr. Greenwood scorned an umbrella and even a hat. If his hair got wet he'd rub it dry, he said.

"Well, rain water's good for hair. That's what my girls are always after. Always sticking pans around to catch rain water," Dave said.

The janitor went quietly through the room picking up hymnbooks.

"You'll lock up, Clayt," the minister said.

He told the others good night absent-mindedly. They saw him cross the sloping yard, bareheaded, hugging the tin box under his arm. Clarence wanted to go bareheaded too, but his father said no, not a boy that's got a cold all winter. Clarence had to hustle keeping up with his father going up the hill.

His mother asked fretfully, when they got home, "What made you take so long?"

"We didn't take long."

"Ach, what a thing to say."

Mr. Greenwood came over to the Miller house the next evening when they were all sitting down to supper. He wouldn't let the girls set a place for him, however. No, no, he said he'd just stopped in for a moment. Supper would be waiting for him at home. All he wanted now was to ask if Dave could stop in at the parsonage along about seven-thirty. There was going to be a short meeting of the trustees.

"No, thanks, Bess, I know how good your cake is—"

Edie had already run out to the kitchen, however, to wrap up three large pieces of chocolate cake for the minister to take home with him—"for you folks's supper as long as we can't persuade you to stay." People seldom went away from the Miller house empty-handed. But then—as Aunt Belle had said—the girls had to dispose of all their cookery somehow.

"Ja, I wonder what's the matter," Bertha said, the moment the minister was out of the house.

"Who said anything was the matter? Can't we have a trustee meeting without something being the matter?"

She stubbornly closed her lips, but looked wise.

"I want to go along, take me, papa."

"Ja, that's the next thing," Bertha said.

"Well, why shouldn't he go?" Dave wiped his lips with his napkin and glared.

"Can I go, papa?"

"Oh, I guess so. If you want."

Clarence gave a triumphant glance at Edie, although she hadn't so far said a word.

It was raining still, harder even than the day before.

The boardwalk was slippery going down the long hill. Dave kept telling Clarence to stay under the umbrella. "You don't want to get there all soaked, do you?" The parsonage was lighted up for the meeting. The parlor chairs were arranged in a large semicircle. In the largest one, sat John Budd, staring gloomy-eyed, and stroking his long gray beard. Clarence made a wide detour, so he wouldn't have to pass Mr. Budd.

The womenfolks were "in the other part," Mr. Greenwood said. Clarence could run out and stay with them. He was glad enough to get out of the parlor, because he was afraid of Mr. Budd. Delight and her mother were sitting out in the kitchen. Mrs. Greenwood had drawn her rocker up beside the stove, and was sewing. Delight was coloring the pictures in the seed catalogue. She offered Clarence some of her crayons, and they both sat and colored.

"We don't care if we *are* in the kitchen," Delight said. "We *want* to be in the kitchen, because it's nicest and warmest here."

The children couldn't sit still all evening, of course. They were in and out of the dining room, drawn by the mystery of the closed folding doors. They lay down flat and tried to look underneath the doors, and then tried to peek through the crack at the side. They couldn't see much of anything, but they could hear the men's voices—they could hear the deep tones of John Budd, and the dry voice of Uncle Ira, the minister's occasional incisive sentences. Looking around, they saw Mrs. Greenwood shaking her head at them; and they scampered back to the kitchen.

The meeting lasted a long time; which, of course, suited the children. When it was finally over, Dave Miller came out to get Clarence. Mrs. Greenwood rose. Looking up, startled, Clarence saw her anxious face. That was the first moment he had thought anything was wrong.

"What about it?" she asked in a low voice.

The minister nodded. Mrs. Greenwood kept looking at him, and Clarence saw tears in her eyes.

"You mustn't feel too bad about it, Alice. If it's true, it can't be helped—"

"Oh, then you think it *is* true."

"I'm not going to say so until we find out for sure," Dave asserted loudly.

"What's true? Find out what? What for sure?" the children were clamoring.

The grown people became aware of them. "You children keep out, go into the front room a minute," Dave said. With reluctance, and backward looks, the children went.

They were almost scared by the solemn semicircle of empty chairs. Clarence looked at the rocker where John Budd had sat, and was afraid to sit there. Now they were conscious that all the evening there had been an atmosphere of mystery. "We don't care if we *don't* know," Delight breathed. "We don't want to know." But that wasn't true. They sat down together on the green velvet sofa; sharing their alarm, their interest, and conjectures. They suggested wild things. Maybe old Mr. Harper had shot somebody with his shotgun! Maybe there was scarlet fever and the whole town was going to close up. Maybe there was going to be an overflow from all the rains. Delight's eyes gleamed as she whispered these things to Clarence; and he answered with suggestions still more fantastic. They were giggling when the grown folks came into the room.

"Here," Dave said, "get your things on, it's time to go."

Going up the hill, they walked faster than ever. Clarence was so breathless he could scarcely ask questions. "What was it, papa? What was the meeting about?" It wasn't about anything, his father answered crossly. Clarence's eyes grew big because he knew *that* wasn't true.

Mama and Edie and Bess were all in the dining room waiting for them. Haven't you folks gone to bed yet? Dave crossly asked. No, they said, they were waiting for him. "I might have known it!" But he might as well tell them—they wouldn't be satisfied unless he did; only it wasn't to go any further! Mama wasn't to tell any of those womenfolks that came here for their coffee—as if they didn't know how to make any at home. There'd been a little trouble with the collection—he began.

"It's that janitor!" Bertha instantly said.

Her voice had a sound of deep conviction. She dropped her hands in her lap.

"What makes you say that, all at once?" Dave demanded.

She wouldn't answer. She only nodded her head.

That made Dave so angry, at first he wasn't going to tell them. How did that woman find out things? She beat the Dutch. Edie was clamoring to hear more. "Go on, papa. Now go on and tell us." Oh, he supposed he'd have to give them the whole story. Bess looked reluctant and distressed. She would almost prefer not to hear. "What good will that do you?" Edie demanded sharply. Her curiosity was on edge. Her eyes had a sharp, boring light. "Papa, go on."

Well, it seemed there was some trouble about the collection. The minister had counted the morning offering, and they'd both of them counted it over again at night, and the two accounts didn't tally. Maybe the minister had made a mistake, Bess suggested. Edie looked at her disgustedly. "Don't you suppose Mr. Greenwood knows arithmetic?" No, there couldn't very well be a mistake. The minister had gone over his accounts too often. Anyway—well, it seemed something like this had happened before.

"Ja, I knew it," Bertha was murmuring, shaking her head. "I knew last night when you took so long."

"You didn't know it!" Dave roared.

Anyway, he said stubbornly, they weren't sure yet. Maybe the thing could all be explained. Mama was saying, ach, they never should have had him. Papa turned on her and wouldn't let her say a thing like that. He turned on Clarence, too, suddenly becoming aware that Clarence was listening, and said sternly:

"You're not to repeat a word of this. You understand?"

Clarence nodded. He had felt joyful and excited, until he saw how disturbed the others were; and then a sense of fear and disappointment came over him. Papa said it was time for him to get to bed. But he was afraid to go upstairs alone. Bess had to go with him, he said. He was afraid of the janitor's face, as he remembered it from last night—as, silently, with head down, lips expressionless, Clayt Hetherington went through the auditorium picking up the hymn-books.

At breakfast they could talk of nothing else—although Dave kept saying, "I don't want to hear any more of this." Irene said she didn't know yet what it was!

"Well, you *will* know," Edie told her. "Our janitor's been stealing the collection. That's what."

Edie was almost crying, in disappointment and chagrin. She said she was thinking of how Trixie would feel—this was Trix's uncle. Poor Mrs. Donohue. How would *she* feel? "I ought to go right over." Her father turned on her sternly, and said she was to do nothing of the kind. They weren't even sure yet that this was the man.

"Ja, I guess we're sure," Bertha murmured—but she didn't dare say it aloud.

Edie suddenly turned. What made her maddest, she said, was that now that old element would say they were right! They had been against hiring Mrs. Donohue's brother from the first. John Budd must be licking his old chops in satisfaction this morning.

"Shut up!" Dave roared. "Haven't we heard enough? Look at that boy," he added. "Taking this all in. Do you want him to tell it all around school this morning?"

That kept the girls still for a while. He might do that, Edie said, scared. Clarence wailed that he wouldn't either! Well, he might not mean to do it, and yet let something out. Then why not let him stay home? Irene asked, with a shrug of the shoulders. To Clarence's amazement, his mother and the girls agreed. Well, he *could* stay home, they said. It wouldn't hurt him. He had that loose tooth—they could pull that loose tooth this morning. Clarence wailed that he would rather go to school. But Bess said to him comfortingly that maybe they wouldn't pull it; she thought 'twould come out of its own accord.

"What'll we write on his excuse, though?" Bertha asked.

"We can say he hasn't got over his cold yet. He hasn't."

Clarence got tired of hearing about the janitor before the day was over. Mama and the girls couldn't let the subject alone. Papa said at noon, "Now I suppose we'll have to eat this with every meal."

"Ja," mama moaned, sitting on at the table when dinner was over, "and this won't be all of it a'ready. There'll be more. Other things will come too. That's the way."

In the evening the folks were going to the parsonage, to talk the whole thing over again, and Clarence cried that he was going along.

"Oh well, come then. I suppose you'll have to come."

Clarence was all elated, because he could play with Delight two nights in succession. But when they went into the parsonage, his high spirits fell. The grown folks sat in the parlor, where the trustees had sat last night; and the children, frightened and big eyed, sat on footstools and listened. Mrs. Stiles was there, and Aunt Belle and Uncle Ira. Aunt Belle said just what Edie had said: now that old element would gloat. They would say more than ever that a man with a jail record never should have been hired; and they would have a talking point. "It gives them a talking point." Mrs. Stiles said nonsense—who cared about their talking points? "We hired him because it was the right thing to do." That was enough for her.

The children begged, "Why did he? Why did he steal?"

Mrs. Stiles answered soberly, "We don't understand much better than you children."

But the folks had come to hear the minister tell about his talk with Clayt Hetherington that morning. The minister said that the most grinding task he'd ever faced in his preaching career was that interview. Willis Vance, always kind-hearted, had suggested that the trustees might spare him the task. But Mr. Greenwood wouldn't accept the offer. He was the pastor, he said, and he was responsible.

The interview had taken place in his study, at an hour when everyone else would be out of the house. Alice hadn't wanted to go—she hadn't wanted to leave him there alone. But he had laughed at her. Did she suppose Clayt was going to bring a pistol? And suppose he did—what could Alice do about it? No, he'd decided that the best way was to have the house clear; and so he'd persuaded his wife to go up the hill and spend the morning with "our good friend here"—he nodded at Mrs. Stiles. He could feel more at ease if he conducted the thing by himself.

He wasn't actually alone, at that—although he'd supposed so. Willis Vance and "Ira here" had gone over to Donohue's earlier that morning, before Clayt could get wind of what had happened and clear out, and had confronted him with their evidence. He hadn't tried to hedge. Well, it wouldn't have been any use. The two men had brought Clayt over to the parsonage, to the study door; and then, not liking the idea of leaving the minister alone with him, they'd sat down to wait on the front doorstep, where they'd be at hand if need should arise.

"Weren't you afraid?" the women asked.

No, he wasn't afraid, the minister said. He was dis-

gusted. And then the whole thing had seemed unreal. There
he was in his own study, with the bookshelves he'd made
himself, and his own desk, and his snug little air-tight stove:
the room where he had worked, studied, eaten apples, and
talked with young couples about to be married. But this
was the first bitter, rankling task of his whole pastorate in
New Hope: the first event which, as he said, "worked the
other way." That was what hurt him the most.

And then how to go at it, he told them: he didn't want
to make a personal appeal; didn't want to put the matter on
a personal plane; and yet he wanted to touch the man's best
feelings if he could.

"So I asked him, how could you do such a thing? What
did you expect to gain by it? That was what I couldn't make
out. The money could make little difference—the amounts
he had been taking were so small. Then what did he expect to
gain?"

The man seemed unable to answer. In fact, he didn't
even try! He was standing all this time near the desk. "I
asked him to be seated but he refused." There was a look on
his face that the minister couldn't penetrate: an "ancient"
look, Mr. Greenwood said—as if the man had slipped down
to an old low level from which he'd been trying to climb.
"I suppose," the minister said, with a fiery glance, "if I were
the evangelist type, could work all the stops, bring the tears,
get the fellow down on his knees . . . but what I wanted to
get at was the reason."

But he couldn't make any impression. He'd talked as
reasonably himself as he could—made no accusations—said
they didn't want the matter prosecuted. They didn't want
to make things harder for Mrs. Donohue than need be.

"Budd wants it prosecuted," Ira Miller put in.

The minister waved his hand. He'd asked Clayt then—
well, what *were* they to do? If they simply let him go, and

said nothing, would that be fair to others whom he might deceive, just as he'd deceived this church?

"I said to him: 'Look here, man. I didn't get you here simply to accuse you. I want you to talk to me—tell me how this looks from your side. That's fair, isn't it? Now tell me what this is all about.' "

"Perfectly fair," Mrs. Stiles said. "Exactly the way to put it."

Ira Miller sniffed, and scratched his ankle.

Well, the man simply stood there, his shoulders hunched, just taking what came. "As if I were acting the part of an overseer. A kind of Simon Legree." The minister confessed that he'd felt exasperated. He could have dealt better with almost any attitude. This had baffled him. He got nowhere. In the end, he'd had to open the study door and see the man walk away under guard, sullen and silent, with Willis on one side and Ira on the other, as if he were already marching back to prison.

So now the question stood: what was to be done about it?

It was a question that couldn't be decided that night; although this was a time to hear suggestions. Meanwhile, Clayt was still at his sister's, under promise to stay. Would he keep his promise?—Belle Miller asked skeptically. Mrs. Stiles said, At least he had the chance.

The children were at times excited, at other times oppressed and afraid. They heard people call Clayt Hetherington "a jailbird." He was a jailbird; it had never been safe to leave him in the church. When they remembered how they'd talked to the janitor, begged him to let them ring the bell, and set the little red chairs in place, the children were scared. But they were proud of themselves, too. Then when they heard the older people talking, heard them say how dreadfully it hurt Mrs. Donohue, and "what it might do to the church," they knew that this was sorrowful. Their sky was darkened.

They talked in hushed whispers, about why "he" had done it—the janitor had become "he" and the theft was "it." Maybe he'd wanted some money, to buy a gun or something, Clarence said. The church gave him money, though. "I know it." Delight said some folks had a dis-sease—her eyes were big—and they couldn't keep from stealing. They stole anything—oh, she said, even pins. They decided that Clayt Hetherington had this dis-sease.

But in the pleased, scary excitement of the other children, they had a feeling of alarm and defensiveness. It was Delight's father who had wanted Clayt Hetherington made janitor, in spite of all the folks who'd said it wasn't safe. Delight's father wanted to make up the loss to the collection but the trustees had voted against that. Even John Budd had said that wasn't required.

Some people said that this was the worst thing that had ever happened in this town. But Clarence stoutly maintained that wasn't true. This couldn't be worse than when that Tucker baseball player got knocked out. Dr. Day had worked over the baseball player three hours before bringing him to; and if he hadn't come to, then Ray Putnam, who threw the ball that struck him, would have been jailed for a murderer. "A fellow from Tucker said so." Ray would have been worse than the janitor. A murderer was worse than a burglar.

Clarence heard his sisters talking about whether they should go over to the Donohues. Bess and Irene were doubtful. "What could *we* do?" Irene asked. "They might not want us there just now," Bess said. Edie accused them bitterly.

"Those are nothing but excuses. Oh yes, you're sorry for Trixie, but you don't put yourselves out. *I'll* go if you don't. If they don't want me to be there they can send me home."

Clarence admired Edie's fierce championship. When Edie Miller once liked a person, folks said, there was nothing she wouldn't do. But if she *didn't* like you—if you ever got on the wrong side of her—well, look out!

The children in town took an excited interest in the wickedness. They stared at Winifred Donohue when she came to school. Some kids—Willie Schnitts and others—mocked her. "Uncle went to jai-ail, uncle went to jai-ail." Dave Miller heard of it. He said, "If Clarence is in on that he'll get a whipping." Clarence said indignantly he *wasn't* in on it—and the girls were angry at papa for supposing he could be.

But the children didn't play with Winifred, as Edie told them they should. They were afraid to go to the Donohue house and knock on the door. They thought, What if Mrs. Donohue's brother *hadn't* gone away? What if he was in hiding up in the attic. Alta Zissler, going past the house, had thought she saw the curtain in the attic window move. She thought she saw two eyes staring down at her. She was almost sure.

Clarence had again the feeling that the sky was darkened. He looked up—it was not the joyous blue prairie sky. The sense of old things haunted him; when he was alone, he thought of these things. He saw old rusty iron, dead leaves, an empty bird's nest . . . he thought of the gun fastened up over Mr. Stiles's desk. The branching pale antlers and dark eyes of the deer's head haunted him. Then he tried to hear again the sound of Mrs. Stiles's music—the noble, firm harmony of that piece she had played. He whispered over the text of the minister's first sermon—Mr. Greenwood had given the folks a copy of the sermon—"Light is come into the world." He said that over when he thought about the janitor's bent head and downcast eyes . . . when he dug up an old rusted kitchen knife down near the Creek bed, and thought the overflow must have carried it there.

The janitor hadn't waited for the church board to settle his case. He had skipped out of town one night: the news went all over. Many folks thought he shouldn't be allowed to get off like that; Cass Story believed he should be "Apprehended"; it might not be fair to other communities to let him go where he pleased. But nobody wanted to make the Donohues suffer. Official action was not taken. The janitor's disappearance was accepted by many as the best solution.

Or partial solution. For Bertha Miller's mournful reiteration—"Ja, this won't be the last of it"—held only too much truth. People were discussing now the trouble at the Donohue house; the situation there had been worse than anyone had known.

The Greenwoods had gone to call on Mrs. Donohue and she had sobbed out her troubles. Barney, Mrs. Donohue said, had never wanted her brother there; and now he blamed her. The girls had always "taken sides," but this had made it worse. They said they wouldn't hear religion talked back and forth any longer. Trixie asserted that she was going to be baptized and join her mother's church. Alicia was going into a convent. Trixie said she was going to marry Emmett whether they'd have anything to live on or not; she wouldn't stay at home any longer; and Barney said if she did, she'd never set foot in this house again. Mrs. Donohue moaned that she was going to lose them both.

Mrs. Greenwood was sorry for Mrs. Donohue; but the minister had come away from the house divided between pity and exasperation. The church members, he knew, wanted him to uphold Mrs. Donohue and to condemn Barney—to make the whole thing a sectarian matter. This he refused to do. Right and wrong, he said, were above this. He had nobody with him but Mr. Broadwater, it seemed! It astonished him, he declared fiercely, to see such narrowness on every side!

The Greenwoods had come over to the Miller house. Mr. Greenwood told what he had said to Mrs. Donohue. She and Barney ought to respect each other's way—either that, or live apart. (Bertha gasped. A minister advocating "living apart?") No, Mr. Greenwood was saying with energy—*let* the two girls take different paths. Since one stood with one parent, the other with the other, where was the trouble? Both parents should be content.

No, no, it was partisanship that Mrs. Donohue was pleading for. She wasn't suffering from disappointment in her brother—that she accepted with fatalism. She had been all prepared for it—Mr. Greenwood saw that now—he saw that this whole thing had a much older history than he'd known anything about; it must have happened over and over again. "Maybe I was gullible. John Budd may be right about it—probably is. But I can't help that now. Anyway, I'd rather be gullible than suspicious." Mrs. Donohue wanted her minister to condemn one faith and defend another— the very kind of narrow thing that he abominated, what all his preaching was against!

"What's the use of preaching," he demanded, "if folks don't get the point any better than that?"

He defended himself to the company. He expounded his belief: All sects and denominations, he said, were part of a whole. One group emphasized one thing, one another; each had a point, he thought—there was room for them all— maybe even for Calvin! He himself preferred the simplest, most direct approach, with no bother of set creed—"I can make my own creed!" On such grounds he had chosen his own particular denomination, although he hadn't grown up in it. All people, he believed, should have the power of choice. There was no virtue in sticking to any church simply because one's parents had belonged to it. No, what worried him in this whole matter was that lack of faith, the begrudging smallness, stinginess, dissension, suspicion, dark ancient things—these, for the moment, had won out over hopefulness and generosity. Clayt Hetherington's backsliding had given the principle itself a blow. "But *we* needn't for that reason agree"—the minister asserted—"with reactionary forces. We can go on just as we've been going." There were two great principles on which all sects and denominations must take their final stand—"On these two commandments hang all the law and the prophets."

The folks must all believe Mr. Greenwood, Clarence thought. He stared fiercely at the company, just as the minister did, challenging anyone to disagree. His father seemed convinced. But Clarence saw his mother's rocker going softly back and forth; her hands were folded in her lap and her face was downcast; but he knew she was holding with timid stubbornness to her own way.

There was another conversation.

Clarence had been sent over, one morning, on an errand to the Stiles house. He knocked, but no one seemed to have heard. After a moment, he stepped inside. The parlor door was open—the sacred parlor—and voices sounded from that room. In the stillness of the hall, with the slow ticking of the clock, the voices were distinct: those of Mrs. Stiles and Mr. Greenwood. Clarence heard the minister's clear, energetic tones and her decisive replies. He wondered whether to call; and for a few moments he stood hesitating—always a little in awe of this dim, cool hallway, with the deer's head in the recess under the stairs, the velvet stony head and staring eyes that had made Delight cry, when she knew the deer had been shot.

"Yes, yes," Mr. Greenwood was saying—impatiently, firmly—"it's a bad business." For a while, it had made him see the whole town in a different light. "Up until now," he continued, "we've had everything come our way—we people. Everything's seemed to be moving straight ahead." But this, all at once, had brought him right about face. It had made him realize that a fresh start wasn't all that was needed. All these folks hadn't come here for the simple sake of making a fresh start! Some were only running away from their pasts—or carried their pasts along with them. "They've brought us the past as well as the future!" Mr. Greenwood acknowledged. 'Twasn't only John Budd. "When we take in 'all kinds,' it's 'all kinds' that we're getting. The bad as well as the good. It doesn't help any not to recognize that." He hadn't recognized it himself, until Lute Fairbrother showed him how foolish that was.

The minister went on to tell Mrs. Stiles about his talk with Lute Fairbrother. Clarence listened eagerly now, standing just inside the door. Lute had come over to the minister's study, as soon as the Hetherington affair became public knowledge, saying he'd known how bad "the Reverend" would feel. The tall, bony, rusty-looking man—a printer, he couldn't have been anything but a printer! Mr. Stiles said he looked like Mark Twain—was able to offer more genuine consolation than any of the good church brethren. (But Lute was a philosopher. Franklin Story, always somewhat loftily amused over the peculiarities of his father's helper, which he enjoyed because they furnished good anecdotes, had often said to Bess, in amiable derision, "You know, Lute's a great philosopher!") Lute had confessed that he'd always had a notion that fellow was a bad lot. "Still, Reverend," he'd maintained, "the man's feelings toward you *was* sincere, you don't want to go to thinking otherwise. The way I figure it out," Lute said, "you was on kinda too high a plane for him. He couldn't live up to it." Lute gave as his opinion, that the main reason the fellow wouldn't give an answer was, because he thought the minister was too good a man for him to talk to. "You hadn't been a real sinner. You wouldn't

understand." Lute said, "I believe that for a fact. I'm sorry
for the fellow. I know kinda how he felt. It's the way *I*
feel," he added with a twinkle, "when Grandma Story
shakes her head and wonders why I don't mind my ways."
The fellow was bad—he knew that himself better than anybody else did; and he couldn't get on talking terms with
those who didn't know. But—if *this* was any consolation to
hear—the church's treatment of Clayt Hetherington, living
up to its religion in the matter instead of taking it out in
talk, like old man Budd and a few that could be named, was
what had led Lute himself to attend services. "Never done
such a thing in my life before. Except nigger service down
South. *They* meant it."—And in some ways lived up to it,
better than those who'd taught them. *His* religion was the
Golden Rule, and he went where he found that being ap-
plied. "Your bread's due to come back to you, Reverend.
That's scripture. I say that, and I'm a printer. We git around,
in our line o' trade, and we cain't stay softies. Hell, no. But
eventually, in the *long* run—may be awful long, but I believe that's the fact." The minister had Lute Fairbrother's
tones, his slow, soft, Mississippi River drawl, with its Southern flavor. Clarence could see and hear Lute Fairbrother—
knew when Lute pulled his drooping mustache, and at what
point he must have turned aside, looking all around for a
place to spit.

That was fine!—Mrs. Stiles asserted. Yes, that might be
right. Lute was a sensible man. She admired Lute Fairbrother.
"But I don't know as I'd care to have had you more of a
sinner," she added drily. 'Twa'an't just the best way to make
a parson, according to her notion; although it might have its
points.

The minister admitted as reasonable all that Lute Fairbrother had said to him. It made more sense than he'd heard
from anybody else. Yet he couldn't understand, not even
now, how a man could be sincere in his feelings, and at the

same time so false in his actions. Double-dealing was what he couldn't comprehend. But it existed—it was here, and he'd met it—so he'd *have* to understand it.

"We've got to eat our peck of dirt," Mrs. Stiles said, with caustic relish, "like other folks. Might as well swallow it down." Their digestions ought to be strong enough to take it. They'd better be.

Yes, the minister agreed, but this was what he hated to see come back—all the old divisions, the dissensions, the factions. It seemed as if they'd taken on new life. The old persisted beneath the new. It was always there. Even this fine pure air and sun couldn't burn out all the old dross and rubbish.

"The old isn't all bad," Mrs. Stiles reminded him. " '—who bringeth forth out of his treasure things old and things new.' "

"Yes, yes," the minister said. "All true enough." But what he himself was forced to was a reassessment, a retesting of the elements that had made up his belief, to assay out the true value of the metal. But time and experience forced every man to that business. Unless the man preferred to remain a fool.

Clarence started to knock again—thought better of it; set down the plate of angel food cake that Edie had sent over —four big slices, covered with a fringed napkin; went softly out of the door, and down the steps, and then went running across the road.

That summer the two children became absorbed in a marvelous game, one of the best they had ever played. Clarence was the one who had thought of it. They called it "Discovery." Clarence played that he was Christopher Columbus; Delight, of course, was Queen Isabella. (They had cut out the superfluous part of King Ferdinand.) Clarence had never gone so far along the Creek as he did that summer, wading in the warm shallow water or walking gingerly across hot sandy soil . . . past the group of poplars, and away on beyond the Groundhog shack. He wasn't afraid to explore when he could think of himself as Christopher Columbus. He went alone, for Delight was busy collecting precious stones for her royal jewels. Every morning, when Clarence set off, Delight sat down in the shade underneath the bridge and wove a fresh queenly crown of clover blossoms or shiny poplar leaves. It seemed as if this game could go on forever and ever.

On one bright hot Saturday morning Clarence went running over to the parsonage.

"Is Delight here?"

"I think you'll find her in the front room, Clarence."

The shades were down in the parlor, because of the heat, and the room was dim. Clarence stopped short. Delight looked like a queer little ghost, shrouded in a stiff, flimsy wrapping that was patterned all over with lacy white flowers, like frost patterns on winter windowpanes. Her bright eyes stared at Clarence through this white shroud. Her long hair was hanging.

"Hush!" she raised one finger in mysterious warning. "I'm taking the veil."

Clarence's first startled awe gave way to resentment. "Aw, that's just a window curtain," he said.

He waited. "Come on. Don't you want to come and play our game?"

"No, I can't. I've got my veil on. I'm in my ceremony."

"Well gee—you could wear your veil in our game. It could be Queen Isabella's. Queens wear veils."

"Oh no, they don't, Clarence." She corrected him. "They wear *robes*."

"Well, aren't we going to play our game, then?"

"No, *I'm* not. I'm playing something else."

Boys couldn't play the game she was playing, Delight

said in cold, sweet tones. Only girls. This was a girl's game.
She was going to play it all by herself.

Clarence hung around a while—awed, in spite of himself, by her rapt, exalted look.

"I'm going away," he warned her.

She didn't answer.

"I won't come back, either."

He went off finally, and across the yard—stopping now
and then, expecting that at any minute Delight would follow him. He stood all alone on the bank of the Creek. This
was the first time either of them had played any game that
the other couldn't play too. Clarence didn't know what to
think.

But he was mad. He thought he'd go so far up the Creek
that folks would think he was lost. Everybody would go out
looking for him, and they'd ring the church bell.

It was hot, though. Sunlight danced and glittered on
the shallow water. The sand bank shimmered—it hurt his
eyes to look. Clarence went down the little trodden path and
sat in the old place under the bridge, on the flat cool rock,
in the shadow. He felt the way he did when Delight had another partner in one of the games at school. But she didn't
choose to have another partner. When she had a chance to
say, she always chose him. Carlo Klaus made faces to get
Delight to look his way; but she wouldn't.

Disgruntlement resolved itself into resentment against
Alicia Donohue. It was Alicia Donohue whom Delight was
imitating. "I hate Alicia Donohue. She's wicked." Edie said
Alicia Donohue was wicked. Bess had scolded Edie, telling
her that she was narrow. "I wouldn't be so narrow," Bess had
cried. Edie didn't care how other folks took this—she sided
with Trixie and Mrs. Donohue and everybody was welcome
to know it. Not to take sides, Edie thought, was merely
cowardice.

Until now, it had seemed exciting and romantic to

Clarence, that Alicia Donohue should go away to be a nun. Bess and Irene seemed to think it was romantic, and so he did. It was far more exciting than Trixie's wedding even if Mr. Donohue did "disown" Trixie; and anyway that wasn't the truth. Mr. Donohue said there wasn't any truth in it. There wasn't anything very romantic about Trixie and Emmett going to live on Mr. Showalter's farm. Trixie Donohue was just a big fat girl. Alicia was beautiful. She was different; never quite one of the crowd; the boys were all afraid of Alicia Donohue. Even to the children, who ran in and out of the Donohue house almost as easily as the girls did, Alicia had seemed like the heroine of some mysterious story . . . with her Irish looks, her red-and-white skin, black clustering curls, large eyes of a clear deep gray—clear as the glass of marbles—and with long lashes sooty-black and curled. Clarence seemed to see this beauty, awesome and strange, through a flimsy shrouding like Delight's lace curtain.

It scared him to think of Alicia Donohue. He was afraid of her, and afraid of Clayt Hetherington. The Donohue house was changed—the rambling, untidy, easygoing house, with the big kitchen where girls and boys made candy and played spin-the-platter on winter evenings. The house was silent most of the day. Mr. Donohue went earlier to the store—Mr. Donohue, that nice man, who gave lots of corn candy for a penny. The children always wanted Mr. Donohue to wait on them, instead of Dean Robinson. But now he seemed foreign. Clarence was afraid of Mr. Donohue, too. When the neighbors dropped in they would find Mrs. Donohue crying. Perhaps the parents—so the women whispered —would "unite" on Winifred, the youngest. That was what Mrs. Greenwood was hoping. Someday, Mr. Greenwood said, all Christian sects, all religious faiths of the world, would be united: not all one, but united in diversity. Bess agreed. But Edie, when she heard that—even if Mr. Greenwood did say it, had cried, "You won't ever catch *me* joining the Methodists!" It disturbed Clarence to think that "religion" wasn't the church, *their* church, the tan-and-brown frame building with the steeple. "Religion" had far-off, alien mysteries. It meant more than he could comprehend.

Footsteps sounded hollowly on the bridge above Clarence's head. He heard voices, and they seemed the voices of strangers. He was lonesome and his stomach ached. He wanted to get back to his own house, and find Edie hustling around, with her hair up on curlers—scolding, grabbing a dish towel and yanking open the oven door; he could smell the good, warm, cake fragrance from the oven. He remembered his sisters talking about Trixie's wedding. Bess thought she ought to wait a while, for her mother's sake. Edie was the most bitter and partisan, but she was the one who stood by Trixie. She had stood up with Trixie and Emmett at their marriage in the minister's study. Edie and Mrs. Greenwood had been the only witnesses. Clarence thought he wouldn't trade with Mr. Donohue. He would go to the new store. His father wouldn't like that. The minister would be disgusted. In his loneliness and uncertainty, Edie was the one to whom he turned—she was the one who was always *there*. Bess had her fascinating, flighty streak, and Irene was cool and secret; the only one he could be sure of, was Edie.

But he wasn't sure of her, either. There was a time Clarence had almost forgotten—he had hidden it away in his mind, like the spring evening when he had come upon Tom and Bess; and yet different; as if it belonged in another dimension, dark and obscure. He was just getting home from school; the folks had gone for a drive, and he had thought at first the house was empty. Then he had seen Edie and that fellow—Edie had never brought that fellow into the house before, not when any of the folks were there. All Clarence could think about then was to get away without being seen; he was frightened and ashamed, and had never told anybody.

There was what the folks called "something between those two"—Clarence knew that now. He brooded over the memory, sullen and confused; and he felt as if the course of life was swinging out into uncertainties.

It was too solitary down under the bridge. Clarence didn't want to stay there. He climbed up the steep little footpath through the weeds.

"Hi, Miller!"

The call was soft. There was a taunt lurking in it. Startled to be called by his last name, like one of the big boys, wondering if it really was himself who was being spoken to, Clarence got up and stared around. He had been sitting halfway down the bank of the Creek.

A boy stood in the road near the bridge staring down at him. It was Harm Smelzer, a big kid in a higher grade. He belonged to those folks who had just lately moved here. Clarence met and secretly flinched from that hard gaze. One of the Swedish kids was with Harm, a kid they called Whitey, with milky blue eyes and hair that glistened like wisps of milkweed floss silvery in the sunlight. Harm had a slingshot. He was snapping the rubber band.

"What *chu* doing?"

"Nothing."

"Come out in the road then."

Clarence climbed the path and went slowly out to the road. He could feel his heart pounding. He didn't know what this big kid might do to him. Nothing happened. Harm kept looking at him and snapping the rubber on the slingshot. The other kid kept staring.

"We're going over to the woods. Wanta come? I betcha hafta go home and see your mother."

"I don't either."

"If you don't either, then you can come with us."

Clarence was too astonished to know what to think. He

was both scared and flattered. Harm's gang was on the outs with the other kids at school; but the gang didn't pay any attention to the kids in Clarence's grade, because Harm Smelzer wouldn't bother with such small fry. He wouldn't even bother with Willie Schnitts.

Harm looked back. "Are you coming?"

"Sure. I guess so."

The two boys went along the top of the Creek bank, through the vacant lot behind the church, and across the flats. Clarence trotted along just behind them.

"Where are you going to? What woods?"

"River bank. Where's any other?" Harm demanded in sudden belligerence.

"Nowhere I guess," Clarence said weakly. He was thinking of those woods far off beside the blue water of Rundle's Pond.

"Well then, I meant *this* woods, didn't I?"

Clarence nodded. He felt a horrid sense of insecurity; and yet he wanted to go along. He wanted to find out what these kids did. Harm Smelzer was the kind of kid, you never knew how he would take things, or how he would act next. Harm might get sore at anything another kid said, and challenge him with that fearsome belligerency; or he might accept the statement with a kind of grand complacency: either response was alike mysterious. But Clarence could see why the kids looked up to Harm Smelzer, why they tagged after him and let him be boss. His bold swaggering masculinity had a shine to it.

They had crossed the flats, and now the three of them were going trot-trot along the hard dusty road that led out to the river. Clarence kept up with the other two, although they were both of them bigger than he was. He knew with secret guilt that he was pretending. He didn't really belong with Harm Smelzer's gang. But he copied Harm's swagger.

There were a few houses out along this road, at the edge

of town. Mr. Saltonstall's house was one, and the house with the shingle trimming was Dr. Day's. Harm Smelzer glared at the houses in bright, bad-boy challenge. He pointed his slingshot right at Mrs. Day's big geranium plant which had been set out on the front step to get the sunshine. Clarence almost yelled "Look out!" He knew the people who lived in these houses, but the other kids didn't. They weren't friends with these people. To them, plants, porch posts, walls, windows, chickens, cats, were inanimate—merely targets. They looked at these houses only from outside.

"Your dad'll lick you for going down to the river."

"He won't either," Clarence boasted. "I go wherever I want to."

Harm stared at him with hard, bright approval. Whitey glanced at Harm and snickered.

"Shut up, Whitey."

Whitey looked scared. Clarence knew too well how Whitey felt. He despised Whitey. He was fascinated by Harm Smelzer, and hated him; was bewildered by his arrogant caprices, and wanted, just for once, to prove acceptable to big kids like these.

He thought how scared his mother would be if she knew with whom he was running around! His father would scold him but would want him not to be afraid of these kids. He wouldn't think of Delight. He was entering a world that had no knowledge of her. There was a girl's world and a boy's world. He was proud to shut her out.

He wondered what they were going to do in the woods. But he didn't risk asking. He was too unsure of himself in such company to do anything but keep quiet and not give himself away. In his own little crowd he was a leader.

The woods were a strip of rank timber growth down along the river bank. Clarence had seen them from the bridge, when he was out driving with the folks. There was a big bridge compared to the wooden bridges in town—an iron bridge that led over into Dakota. The river was muddy and sluggish. It flowed to one side leaving muddy welts, shiny, but crisscrossed with great cracks. The water was shallow at this time of year; it had a dank, provincial breath. But compared to Dry Creek it seemed a mighty stream. None of the little kids were allowed to come out here. The river was too dirty and unsafe because it had mudholes. People had been drowned there.

Clarence hadn't learned how to swim. If the kids went into the river, they would find out that he didn't know how to swim.

But Harm Smelzer said nothing about going in swimming. He yelled, "Come on!" and plunged into the woods. The strip of river timber, with its scraggly undergrowth, seemed to Clarence a wilderness. He was used to the few little poplars and bushes that grew down near the Creek. He felt lost now. He was in a different existence.

Old weeds, dryly crackling, sent up a smell of stale dust that made the boys sneeze. A long shoot whipped back into Clarence's face with stinging pain. He tried to break it off but it was strong. As he struggled, feeling the tough, slippery, sappy life of the thing opposing him, wanting roughly to put an end to it, he had a sudden, almost homesick shock of remembrance. He thought of that other day in Rundle's Woods—the bluebells, the glimpse of sparkling water . . . he was faraway from that time and scene, he couldn't get back into that time or place any more than into a dream which is fading.

Harm was shouting. Clarence started blindly toward him. He ran smack into a tree. Whitey was going to laugh, but Harm made a lordly gesture.

He said, "Hi—listen!"

There were other kids down here somewhere. Whitey's mouth opened and his pale eyes bugged out. It was almost as if there were Indians around. Clarence was so numb from the shock of running into the tree that he didn't realize other kids had come until they were right around him. They had come running through the timber, snapping twigs and parting weeds and underbrush, shouting to Harm and Whitey . . . when they saw Clarence they all stopped and stared.

"How'd *he* get here?" One kid nodded toward Clarence.

"He come along with us," Harm Smelzer stated calmly.

The boys hesitated. They glanced from Clarence to Harm. Clarence stared back stupidly. His knees felt weak. They were a gang of kids of different ages. None of them came to his Sunday school or were in his grade, although he knew most of them by sight. There was a Groundhog kid among them. One or two were strangers. Clarence hadn't really been aware there *were* any strangers in New Hope!

Harm Smelzer looked back and called him. "Comin' along, Miller?" Harm had taken him in charge. The patronage of the boss felt fine and warm. But at any moment it could be withdrawn. Clarence halfway knew that, and was ashamed of his gratitude.

He went on after the others, feeling reckless and wary both. He was disobeying his folks, going where he was forbidden, with a tough gang of kids, most of them older than he was. Among them were "foreigners"—the word made Clarence's backbone cold. His Aunt Belle was strong against "the foreign element." She said the foreign element had begun to filter in—the old families should make a stand. Swedes were foreigners, and so were the Dutch who'd settled in the township west; but not the English around Wilton. They "dealt in land" or "dealt in stock" instead of regular farming. Aunt Belle thought that was superior. But Dave Miller was disgusted. He said, foreigners, nonsense! Everybody who comes here lives here. It depends on how they behave. Aunt Belle would be still more horrified if she found out Clarence had played with a Groundhog.

But the kids seemed to have accepted him for the time being, although he belonged with the children who attended Sunday school. In that gang were no minor distinctions—nationalities, social levels, had been ground down to the primitive fact that all were boys and all out to have a time together. It wasn't the "takes all kinds" that his father talked about, but something older. Clarence did just as the others did. He felt elated, and the next minute miserable. The boys took him on simple terms. Then, all at once, they would seem to wake up to the fact that he didn't belong to the gang, and would say something to torment him.

"Where's your girl?"

Clarence's heart began to pound. His eyes wavered.

The boy said with languid malice, "He plays with girls. Goes giving May baskets. He takes his girl to school on his sled."

"I do not."

"He kisses his girl. 'I don't like those nasty ole boys, I wanta play with my girl.' His girl's pop's a preacher! He's going to marry his girl."

"You shut up!"

Clarence felt his eyes smarting. Kids like these whom he had barely known by name had all been peeking and noticing and making fun while he was dwelling in happy confidence with his little beloved inside their magic circle! Other kids envied and were spiteful, because of the trusting innocence of that happiness—or else they jeered and snickered. The shock of running up against that other viewpoint was like getting his breath knocked out of him. Clarence tried to act as though he didn't care. He thrust out his chin and spat as far as he could. But if they ever spoke his sweetheart's name, he would fight the whole bunch of them.

But at the same time that they knew so much—they really knew nothing. They saw only from the outside. That fine masculine gesture of spitting had fooled them.

"I can spit further'n that."

"Aw, you can't spit as far. Miller spit the furthest."

All crowded to enter the contest. Clarence tried so hard to exceed his first mark that he felt as if he'd drained himself of all the spit he'd ever be able to work up. He hadn't known until now that he was an extra good spitter. The boys were solemnly appreciative.

But they were getting tired of that now. Harm Smelzer was snapping the rubber of his slingshot. He took a stone out of his pocket, fitted the stone—let go.

"What you shooting at?"

"Just practicing," Harm said calmly.

Now it was the slingshot to which their interest turned; Clarence with the rest. He felt his face frozen into a false look of eager interest. Delight wouldn't speak to Willie Schnitts because he used a slingshot. Willie Schnitts had killed a rabbit once. He had chased the girls all over the school grounds with that old rabbit.

Harm Smelzer said, with a grand carelessness of generosity:

"Want to try, kid?"

Clarence nodded. He couldn't admit to these kids that he had never used a slingshot; had never killed anything except flies and mosquitoes. If he gave away his ignorance he would never survive the disgrace. He had seen himself through the eyes of this other gang, as a nice kid, a good boy, who went to Sunday school—he had never known how he would look to anybody else, had been too happy to think about it, and too innocent, inside his magic circle.

The contraption felt neat in his hands, with its smooth wood and worn leather. He hated it. He saw Delight's outraged eyes and trembling lips when she had clenched her fists at Mr. Stiles. But he wasn't with Delight now. For this hour they were separate and far apart. He would deny his love, and keep it hidden.

"Whatcha going to shoot at?" the kids were asking. The leader motioned to them to shut up, and they subsided.

"There's something you can try on, kid," Harm said grandly.

He motioned to the boys to shut up again, and nodded toward the water. A muskrat was swimming in toward shore. Only the sharp little nose showed above the muddy water but long ripples spread silently. It was making for the bushes a little way downstream.

The boys formed an excited cluster of which Clarence was the center. He suddenly felt cool and quite sure of himself, waiting for the muskrat to come near shore. He knew he wouldn't miss—knew it with a queer sense of fatalism. He felt a pleasure, strange-tasting and perverse, in slowly taking aim and letting fly.

"Got it, by Jesus Christ!"

The boys broke the circle and ran forward. Blood streaked the muddy water. The muskrat was trying to turn and swim away. But the kids yelled and reached in with sticks, and brought it to shore. They beat and pounded until it was dead. The flat tail threshed in the mud more and more feebly. Clarence had joined in wildly with the others. He wanted the thing to be dead. They were all yelling in triumph. One of the kids reached down to pick up the muskrat, but Harm Smelzer ordered:

"Let Miller have it, he was the one that hit it."

The others echoed, "Yeah, that's Miller's."

The blood was seeping warm through the wet, muddy fur. Clarence bent down, pulled between hard triumph and sick aversion. The boys repeated, "Got it the first time!" He could swagger easily among them. He had won Harm Smelzer's approval.

The whistle sounded just then.

"Gee, I gotta go. It's dinnertime."

"I do too," some of the other kids said.

"Hey! Gonna take your muskrat?"

He tossed the dead muskrat away—he had picked it up by the tail—and the small carcass fell messily at the edge of the water. "Hey, don't you want it? It's good fur. You can sell it." The other kids ran to get it. The Groundhog kid 'picked it up. "Naw, you can have it." The fine carelessness of tone and gesture were exactly right. The boys accepted, admired. They were staring after him, open-mouthed. Harm Smelzer shouted after him:

"Suh-long, kid!"

"S-long!"

When he got home the folks were still eating dinner. Clarence went in softly the back way. He had to wash his hands before he entered into the dining room. He had a feeling of elated stealth. Over at the sink, washing his hands under the faucet, he noticed that the dirty water running off them was faintly pink. "Got it first shot, by Jesus Christ." He lived through that moment again and swaggered slightly—the swagger a half-unconscious imitation of Harm Smelzer's. Clarence imagined himself telling the whole story with easy nonchalance to the other boys, Jamie and Walter and Harvey Wright. He had shot and killed a muskrat— hadn't been scared at all—just took aim and let 'er fly. He wanted to tell Mr. Stiles.

The folks asked, "Where've you been?" when he went into the dining room. He answered vaguely, "Playing." He was both relieved and disappointed because they didn't notice anything. "Well, sit down and eat," Edie told him. "The rest of us are through."

Clarence started in hungrily, and then nothing tasted good. As soon as he dared, he left his place and went outdoors.

He hung around the barn, and then went and sat down in his old hiding place among the sunflowers. That sight of the mangled body, with the fur warm, wet and muddy, and with the broken back, the helpless small paws, the sharp, futile nose and dead eyes, was imprinted on his memory, exact, indelible. He saw more clearly than at the actual moment of slaughter, the nasty mess . . . saw it with Delight's eyes, not his own—those outraged, shining eyes. He tried to oppose that gaze with hardy triumph. Muskrats were no good except for fur. It didn't hurt to kill a muskrat.

He could boast about his prowess to Jamie Murdock and Walter Shafer, look down on Willie Schnitts. Willie was just a little shrimp compared to Harm Smelzer. He had played with a Groundhog kid, to his own secret disappointment; because the Groundhog wasn't much different from any other kid except that he was dirtier. Clarence felt he would never again be afraid to go up to the Groundhog shanty.

But the glow of triumph was tarnished. It had somehow turned cheap. Clarence remembered his prayer about the tramps (the folks would never let him forget it!)—"God bless the tramps and help them not to be smart alecks." He felt that he had been a smart aleck. He hadn't really been brave—no braver than Whitey, whom he despised. He had done it to show off—to get in right with the leader and the gang. The joy with which he'd joined in, beating and torturing the dying thing, was false—he could see that, now that it was over. He hadn't wanted to put an end to that small, busy, absorbed life, as the muskrat came swimming toward shore. He didn't even care about being in with that other gang. The glamor of their toughness was gone. He liked his own little crowd better, in which no one fellow had to be boss and lay down the law.

He had got far away from Delight. He saw her little face through the shrouding of the stiff lace veil turned away from him. What he had forfeited seemed better than what he had gained, and all he wanted now was to get back with her into their pristine world. There was a dark place that he had to keep secret from her. It would not be quite the same. But when he started down the hill, he saw her on the bridge, waiting for him. The moment she caught sight of him, she came running towards him, with her fleeting swiftness. The earth took on its old brightness because they were once more together.

CHAPTER X

Commemoration

THE NEWS went rapidly all over town, repeated from person to person—great, solemn news. It reached the Millers before breakfast, from their neighbors across the road. Mrs. Tipp came running over with it the moment she heard it, and told it breathlessly to Bess at the kitchen door.

"Have you folks heard? They say Mr. Budd died. I thought your father would want to know."

Bess went straight into the dining room. But Dave refused at first to believe such news could be true. "How did Mrs. Tipp know?" he scoffed. "John Budd was on the street just yesterday. I saw him." But when Bess ran over to the Stileses, to ask if *they* had heard, she found that Lizzie Murdock had already been over to tell them. Bess came back saying in wonder, "Yes, it's true. He died early this morning."

"Well," her father said, "anyway, we'll eat our breakfasts."

Clarence poured syrup over his pancakes. Irene had made the pancakes that morning, and they were extra good. But Clarence didn't know whether this was to be regarded as good news or bad. The folks didn't like John Budd. With his long gray beard, his stern face, his great arched eyebrows, he was to the children a fearsome character. He was head of the "other element." But now Clarence couldn't make out how the folks were feeling. He looked from one to the other between bites of his syrup-soaked pancakes. What did it mean?—he asked.

"Why, you know what it means to die," his father said.

"Yes," Clarence answered uncertainly.

"Like Uncle Andy's old horse," Bess told him. "Didn't it die?"

"Oh." Clarence pondered. "Oh," he said finally, "that way."

But he still didn't really know. He hadn't seen the horse die—only heard about it. But he liked horses. He didn't like John Budd.

As soon as he could get away from the breakfast table, Clarence skipped out. "Where's that kid going?" he heard his father roar. But he was halfway down the front steps by that time. He could pretend he didn't hear.

The kids met almost every morning that whole summer and played games on the vacant lots behind the church; or, if it was hot, played down beside the Creek. Some of them were already down there.

"Mr. Budd died, Clarence," Alta called out to him brightly.

Clarence said, "I know it."

Alta's eyes shone, and she twirled on her heel and made a pirouette.

"My father's over there now," Delight said.

The children looked at Delight with respect. "Is he over there *now?*" Dosia breathed in awe.

"Of course. He has the funeral."

The news, whatever it meant, couldn't stop the children's playing. They paddled in shallow water, that barely covered their toes, and was almost as hot as the sand. Later they all sat down on the smooth ground under the shadow of the bridge. Horse hoofs thundered, and wagons went rumbling over their heads.

They talked about Mr. Budd. The three little girls did most of the talking. The boys acted smart—Jamie made fun, and splattered water, and Clarence joined in with him, but half-heartedly. Here in the cool shadow he was scared, although he wasn't going to show it.

Jamie said, "Mr. Budd was cranky. I don't care."

Alta giggled. But Dosia was shocked. "You shouldn't say that, because it's very sad."

Alta looked at Dosia—her lip trembled, and she said faintly, "I don't care either."

Delight said, "I do."

"*I* don't," Jamie shouted, and turned a somersault, landing with his feet in the water.

"Do *you* care, Clarence?" Alta asked.

"I don't know."

The little girls talked in hushed tones. Clarence heard them uneasily; and finally even Jamie was listening.

Dosia said, "*I* care, because our little baby sister died. She died before we were either of us—me or Jamie—born. First she was buried in the old community, and then they dug her up and buried her in our cemetery. We didn't ever even see her. I could show you her picture, though. My mama has never got over it."

Jamie said angrily, "She has too."

"That's a story, she has not. Aunt Lizzie says so."

Delight and Clarence listened with grave faces. Alta was impressed, but still recalcitrant. All acknowledged Dosia as the authority, because she'd had a little sister that died. Dosia said, they would put flowers on the door, and everybody would have to send flowers. Mrs. Budd would be a widow, and wear a black veil, and go into mourning.

Alta said unbelievingly, "What's a widow?"

Dosia said it was a lady who didn't have any husband. Lots of ladies didn't have husbands, Jamie retorted, and they weren't widows. They were old maids. Ladies whose husbands died, Dosia said, were widows—adding with earnest kindness, "Your mama isn't, Alta, because your papa didn't die, he just went away."

Alta hung her head. She went and splashed her feet in the water and said, "I don't care." Alta's father had gone off —"merely walked off," Clarence had heard the folks say— and that was why Mrs. Zissler had to do other people's washings. Jamie said, "She's mad"; but Dosia called out, "Come on back, Alta. It doesn't matter. *Every*-body likes your mother." Mrs. Zissler—small, active, with bright-black eyes —was one of the nicest women in New Hope. She made the best coffee of any woman in town; except for Dora Palmer's mother. Mr. Stiles had once said that Bill Zissler was a damned fool, if for no other reason, because he'd run away from the best coffee ever made.

There was talk of nothing else all over town that day except the death of John Budd. New Hope was so young that this was its first loss of an early settler. Whether folks liked John Budd or not, they couldn't deny that he was a leading citizen. In the long, cloudy windows of John Budd's land office above the jewelry store, the shades were pulled down, and there were festoons of black over the windows. Jamie had told Clarence to come on downtown and see. It was "done in honor," Jamie's father said, when the boys asked about it.

Strange happenings in town were all "in honor." The children heard that the flag on the school grounds was at half-mast; but that only meant—when they went to look —that the flag hung sadly part way down the pole. Alta and Harvey Wright stopped at Clarence's house and dared him to go with them past the Budd house and see the flowers. The three of them walked solemnly past the bleak white

house, with its narrow windows, the shades pulled down, on
its glaring treeless lot up on the hill; they saw the bunch
of sweet peas and white summer lilies tied to the doorknob
with purple satin ribbons. As soon as they got past the house,
they began to run, so that they were breathless when they
reached the bottom of the hill; they had to go down under
the bridge again and cool off.

Everywhere in town the same solemn excitement
reigned; and the excitement kept mounting toward the day
of the funeral. That would be a kind of festival day. The
stores were to be closed all afternoon, until just before sup-
pertime. Lute Fairbrother had worked all night in the printing shop to run off special copies of the paper with John
Budd's obituary. The choir practiced in the church. Bess had
washed out her best white dress, and Edie ironed it that
morning, because Mrs. Budd had requested that the quartet sing Mr. Budd's favorite hymn: it was "Rock of Ages."
The girls went over in the morning to decorate the church.
They told at dinner about the wonderful flowers. Wreaths
had come by train from the greenhouse in Horton: a whole
American flag from the G.A.R., a pillow of white roses.
Clarence's mouth opened as he listened. It was going to be a
marvelous funeral, Edie said, with her eyes sparkling. People were coming from all over—a whole caboodle of relatives, she said, from back in Pennsylvania. Clarence thought
Pennsylvania was a town; but Delight told him it was another state. Quakers lived there, people who said "thee" and
"thou"; and the Liberty Bell was there, but it had a big
crack in it. Men Quakers, she said, wore broad-brimmed hats,
and lady Quakers wore little bonnets.

Edie went on to say now that the G.A.R.'s would put
on uniforms and march to church in a body—Clarence
didn't know what "in a body" meant; it scared him; but
Bess said it meant that old soldiers were all coming to the
funeral together.

"You goose," she added.

"I'm not a goose!" Clarence hotly retorted.

"Well, you're a little gander, then."

He nodded his head. He didn't mind that.

The folks were all ready, in their best clothes. They were taking the two-seated rig so that Aunt Belle and Uncle Ira could go with them to the cemetery—Uncle Ira didn't have a rig, "too close to buy one when he can go in ours," Edie had said.

Clarence started before the folks did, however. He was going to stay with Delight, in the parsonage, and his father had told him to start before the crowd began to gather for the funeral. Clarence was dressed up, too, he didn't know just why, since he and Delight weren't allowed to attend the service. His best shoes felt hot and stiff as he went creaking down the long, glaring boardwalk. He didn't know what that day felt like: Easter, or the Fourth of July, or Decoration Day; and yet like none of them. The doors of the church stood open, but there weren't many carriages outside. It was too early. Merrill and Franklin and some of the other young men had gone over in the morning to get the church ready; the church had no regular janitor since Clayt Hetherington had gone; the young men were filling in during the summer holidays.

There was an air of restrained excitement in the parsonage. Delight came running at once to tell Clarence—she said her papa was getting ready, he was going to wear his white vest and sermon coat, because he had to conduct the funeral. "*We* have to stay in here," she said. "We can look out from behind the curtains but we can't go outside. It wouldn't look well." Clarence gravely nodded.

Mr. Greenwood came out from the bedroom, looking as he did on Sundays. He had to wait while Mrs. Greenwood straightened his white piqué tie and gave him a clean handkerchief. There had been some trouble because Mrs. Budd and the Livermores had wanted to bring Mr. Barbour back to conduct the service—slighting our minister deliberately, Aunt Belle had said. But Mr. Barbour, living retired in Colorado, hadn't been able to make the journey. Mr. Greenwood sputtered:

"I wish the old lady *had* got Barbour. I hate like thunder to preach this sermon. They don't want me. And why should they? The old man never liked me. I can't preach the kind of thing they want. Any funeral sermon is hard enough but this one is the limit."

The children listened in wonder. They couldn't imagine that anybody wouldn't want Mr. Greenwood, or that there was any kind of sermon he couldn't preach best.

But soon they were alone in the house. The service was about to begin. They stood at the parlor window and looked out. Teams had begun to drive up. They counted the carriages they knew. But there were many they had never seen before. John Budd had been a part of this region since early days, and families had come into New Hope from all the surrounding country.

The bell rang, hard and loud. Merrill rang the bell now for all services.

"That's tolling and knelling," Delight whispered. "You know." She sang in a small clear treble:

"Tolling and knelling,
    Hear the mournful sound,
    All the day the notes are swelling
    O'er Mount Vernon's holy ground."

Never before had they heard tolling and knelling in New Hope. When the ringing had stopped, the hot air still seemed to quiver with sound.

Music swelled from the open church windows. The

service had begun. But nearly everybody had gone into the building; there wasn't much to watch—only the church itself, looking, to the children's respectful gaze, very impressive on its rise of ground above the Creek. In the hot stillness of the little parlor, the children were down on the floor playing with Delight's Noah's Ark. But they followed the service in a dreamy excitement. They went to the window every now and then. They heard the droning of the hymns in the summer heat—heard the quartet sing "Rock of Ages." Then the sermon began, and they went back to play.

The solemn music of the postlude sounded. They returned to the window, and took their places behind the sheer curtains. It was wonderful to look out from behind the curtains, Delight said—almost like looking through falling snow. Only this was summertime.

People were beginning to leave the church. The people lined up in two rows, down the steps, and down the walk; and then very slowly six men came out bearing the long casket covered with flowers. The men looked strange in their dark coats and white gloves—it was hard to believe that they were just people the children knew: Mr. Vance, Mr. Stiles, Mr. Livermore, Harry Harper, and H. C. and A. D. Murdock. The children watched in hushed awe. They saw the casket being lifted into the hearse; saw the black plumes on the heads of the horses. Some of the meaning came to them now. They still watched eagerly, but they shrank back a little. Delight's fingers pressed down on Clarence's hand. Her pink lips were parted. All the people in the slowly walking procession seemed exalted and strange: Mrs. Budd, a widow in mourning, just as Dosia had said, leaning on the arm of a tall man with a mustache, her stepson from away, the young Mr. Budd. The children were awed by the black, dense draperies that hid the widow's face and weighed down her head. She seemed strangely small, diminished,

didn't look like Mrs. Budd. The relatives followed—the children had been eager to see the relatives from back in Pennsylvania—but they didn't wear Quaker hats and bonnets,
like the pictures in one of Delight's storybooks. They looked
just like other people.

"There's my papa!" Delight breathed. "Isn't he *handsome?*"

Mr. Greenwood was fresh and vigorous in his Sunday
black-and-white, in the stiff white vest that Mrs. Greenwood had spent half the morning getting ironed to her satisfaction. The wind stirred his thick hair. He carried his
hat in his hand.

Then all the other people came streaming out of the
church, townspeople and strangers: the G.A.R. members
"in a body" wearing their faded soldier coats, the members
of the choir, the quartet members who had a special carriage because they were to sing at the cemetery—Bess in
her white summer frock and big hat with white lilacs, her
hand in its decorous silk glove resting on Franklin's arm;
Mrs. Harry Harper, slender, fashionably distinguished, with
her large hat pinned to her pompadour of prematurely white
hair; people from the country, from "out and around," old
settlers with beards, some lame and walking with knobby
canes, old women in small black hats or bonnets and stuffy
black clothes . . . All the people seemed to carry the atmosphere of the wailing hymns. The dry summer air bore
the breath of early days, earlier than the two children had
ever known, but which came to them now with a queer
feeling of recognition.

They watched group after group enter the waiting
carriages, and the slow procession begin to move toward
town, led by the splendid hearse with its black festoons—
something like the kingly procession in a fairy tale; but
sad. They were going out to the cemetery in the old community where John Budd was to be "laid," so Mrs. Murdock

had said, beside his first wife. This Mrs. Budd was his second wife.

The crowd grew more straggling. It dwindled into young people who had attended the funeral because it was a great occasion, and other folks who had come out of curiosity. "Come on," Delight said impatiently, "we can go out, everybody's gone now. It's over." Leaving their Noah's Ark figures scattered over the floor, they both ran out onto the porch.

John Budd's funeral was talked of for days. It took on for the children the color of a great, somber community drama.

Clarence was most impressed by what Mrs. Greenwood said. It was her comment that later held in memory. The scene, when he looked back to it, had become what she described.

In some ways, Mrs. Greenwood had told them, the service reminded her of their very first Sunday. Then, as now, it was summertime. The church was filled to overflowing, and fragrant with flowers. On this day as on that other—which had begun to seem long ago—she had sat waiting anxiously for her husband to speak. The audience which he was to address had seemed a gathering of strangers.

But for the first time he faced a group to whom he and what he stood for were alien. The service which he was to conduct was stamped with tastes and doctrines far opposed to his own. The least he could do, he had said when he learned that Mr. Barbour couldn't be present, was to try to make everything conform to what John Budd himself would have preferred. Every part of the service had been chosen with that in mind. The hymns were the kind the minister detested, words of blood and sin and grief fixed in dreary patterns of wailing singsong. The whole service seemed to have retreated from the light of the New

Testament into the patriarchal darkness of the Old; all the old people present brought a solemn darkness into the church: people who formed the real foundation of the larger community on which the young society of New Hope was built.

When the minister took his place in the pulpit he was as composed as ever. And she need not have doubted—of course she hadn't doubted—that he would find the form for his sermon. He had got from Electa Stiles the outline of John Budd's personal history. The words would have to be his own; but he had fitted the personal details into place to show the relation of the man to the community. He told how, coming from the Eastern seaboard, from the old Commonwealth of Massachusetts, John Budd had met with others who, like himself, were determined to work together in building up a new and more favorable dwelling place. He had taken part and shared in work and events, and his life was woven into the life of the region. The minister didn't say, as no doubt they had wanted to hear, that John Budd was now in glory!—Electa Stiles had drily observed— being of certainty one of God's elect. But the words he spoke were all appropriate, so that even the most grudging must have been satisfied.

That was what she had felt, Mrs. Greenwood said, all through the service: that mere fitness, appropriateness, were lifted into a noble harmony. When she had had to take her place in the long line passing slowly down the aisle, ac- cording to custom, to take the last look at this old member of the community, that was what had upheld her, had made her see things in more just proportion. She had felt this most of all when her turn came to look at that cold, bearded face which she had so often dreaded to see among others more friendly. She wasn't frightened then by its cold severity, although that very quality was accentuated —for she could see that this was a face worn and carved by early hardship, war, storm and plague and flood, by all that was characteristic; a face which, in its hard structure, remained the type of an old stock but little changed—even though the bleak light of the earliest days faded with his passing. She was glad that John Budd had his recognition; a fitting recognition.

She had driven out with others to the burial in the old community. Then she had the dreamlike feeling of having stolen by chance into an earlier world in which she had no rightful share. The place itself belonged to that earlier world: the forlorn old burying ground left behind, only its rusty fence now marking it off from open country. Clarence always remembered, always could picture the scene —as if he himself had been there. The iron gate was pushed back flattening the long tough grass. A hot wind was blowing all afternoon from the plains of Dakota; the long veils of the mourners were blowing. The grave that had been dug showed the close, compact, wind-blown soil.

The people present, Mrs. Greenwood said, were many of them her friends; and yet she had felt that she didn't belong among them. She had stood back with others who had never lived in the old community: with Mrs. Story, Belle and Bertha Miller. In this spot that was itself a survival from a former day, the group clustered about the grave made her feel that she was alien—these people who had shared a youth in which she had no part. Nellie and Willis Vance, the four Murdocks, even the Harry Harpers, had been young people together; and in spite of division that had come later, it was apparent that the old ties still held. Beneath the later ties, like tough old roots they kept their strength. Electa Stiles stood near the monument that marked her father's grave: tall and spare, more than ever a distinguished figure. But although she seemed, by her intellect and personal uprightness, someone marked and apart, in some respects she was the very embodiment of the spirit of the old community. The New England separateness, the New England communal conscience, the Puritan strictness, rigor, and fierce righteousness: these could be felt in her. Even James Stiles, standing beside her—even taller and more spare—was alien too. He didn't belong—never had quite belonged; never would. The old burying ground, when the Greenwoods had first seen it, on the day when Dave Miller had driven them out, had seemed forlorn and deserted; but it still held a place in the lives of all these people. The graves of Willis Vance's parents were there; the parents of Electa Stiles; the family lot of the Murdocks, where the old folks were buried, and where the never-forgotten little first child of A. D. and Addie Murdock had once been laid to sleep.

On that day, the old element and the new, seemingly more and more united, were separate again. The division was deep and on older lines. The sharing of the earliest days wiped out the time that came between. Even the widow was not one of these people—how strange to realize that, she had followed so meekly in her husband's wake! Beside the newly dug grave into which John Budd's handsome coffin would soon be lowered, was the mound, long smooth and grass-grown, under which the first wife lay buried. The widow—suddenly informidable, a shrunken, helpless, small old woman—stared with dim eyes, timid and vacant, from behind the heavy veil which the wind kept lifting. Would she be laid here some day, or alone in the bright cemetery up on the heights that belonged to the new town? She, who had lived as John Budd's wife for thirty years, was today in this place an intruder, a newcomer, and she belonged with the new, not the old element.

But the most dramatic part of Mrs. Greenwood's tale, what impressed the children most, what they talked about for days, was the appearance at the burial ceremony of old Rodney Harper and the Harper girls. They hadn't come near, hadn't spoken to anybody, but had stood at a distance, on the far side of the grave. The picture formed in Clarence's mind and stayed there always, melodramatic, like part of an old chromo—although he himself had not been there to see. In the picture old Rodney Harper, immensely tall, like an ancient prophet, with beard longer than a prophet's beard, longer than Isaiah's or Jeremiah's, with burning eyes under shaggy brows, stood with arms around the two daughters, protecting them from the enemy. The daughters were tall, and strangely distinguished, making one think of old albums and pressed, brown, faded flowers—but their eyes were bright and wild. The dry summer wind whirled the dust around these figures, which seemed to stand alone in the desolate landscape; and in the old man's silence the past was held, dead but still existing, fixed and implacable.

But Clarence's father had looked upon that scene in quite a different way. When Dave got home he unhitched Mollie and gave her her oats, washed his hands lustily at the kitchen sink, came into the dining room cheerful and ruddy, saying that he was starved. "Here, Edie, Irene, what have you got for a man to eat?" He said the town looked better than ever to him, coming back from those old ruins. He had seen the old man Harper not as a prophet, but as merely ridiculous, a scarecrow figure—standing there with his arms around those two old maids, as if anybody could be paid to run away with them! Although the loss of John Budd might be felt in a financial way, Dave wouldn't admit any other. It must be evident that the old element had lost its power. Now, Dave said with great satisfaction, pouring good milk gravy over a great mound of potatoes, and putting off with relief the solemnity of the afternoon, there would be nothing holding them back.

At the time when John Budd had died, Clarence had heard his mother repeating, with that air of doleful wisdom, "Ja, this is only the first." Her cronies, those women around the kitchen table, had joined in, "When one of the old settlers goes, it means others to follow. They've begun to go now." Clarence, feeling indignant—just like his father and Irene—had run out of the house, scowling, and shaking the words from him. But he was affected all the same by his mother's mournful prophecies. When another of the old people actually did die, he couldn't help returning to what she had said, in secret wonder.

In September the solemn drama was re-enacted. The flag on the schoolhouse grounds hung at half-mast; the stores were closed; school had been let out for the whole afternoon. Another leading citizen was gone. Two nights ago old Mr. Broadwater had died in his sleep.

But this was different from that other strange holiday. This was a day of mourning throughout the town: not because Mr. Broadwater had lived here longer than nearly anyone else, had associations, and connections, but because he was honored and loved as a friend. Even people who hadn't known the man himself would miss his presence, as a "character," a picturesque figure upon the streets. The old Prince Albert, and the plug hat, the flowing silvery hair, the smiling bow and courtly manner, would not be seen upon the boardwalks again.

The children knew, and didn't know, what the loss would mean—didn't, as their parents said, realize; and yet beneath their innocence was a kernel of ancient understanding. The flowers, the drooping flag, were not part of a spectacle; but a tribute in which the children felt their share. They had gone themselves to the Vance house, with a great bunch of autumn asters that Bess had picked for them, and Irene made up into a beautiful bouquet; and they had given the bouquet solemnly into the hands of Mrs.

Zissler, who was looking after the house for Mrs. Vance, saying, "These are from us." Mrs. Zissler wanted them to stay and see Mrs. Vance; but they shook their heads.

At first they had wanted to attend the funeral, along with the older ones. But when the time came, they were glad to remain—with Alta Zissler and the Murdock children—in the Miller house, at a distance from the church, across the bridge and up on the hill. They didn't even see the long procession that moved slowly along another street, up toward the heights, toward the sunlit cemetery under the blue September sky.

That evening they all went to call on Mr. Broadwater's son, who had come from Oregon to attend the funeral; he was staying, of course, with Willis and Nellie Vance. The children had begged to go along, and the parents consented.

The folks had talked about Aubrey Broadwater all through supper; when the Greenwoods, the Stileses, and the Iras had been asked to stay and eat with the Dave Millers. No one in town had seen Aubrey Broadwater for years; he didn't come back to visit. People were inclined to blame his wife for that! But everyone, except of course Mr. and Mrs. Greenwood, remembered him as a youth, when for two years he had made his home with Willis and Nellie Vance. He had helped Willis at the lumberyard—the same job that Tom Burchard held today! Imagine that. It wasn't many years ago, either. Now Aubrey Broadwater was regarded with mingled curiosity and respect as the richest man who had ever belonged to New Hope; people still considered him as, in a way, belonging, since it was here in his brother-in-law's business that he had got his start. His career was exactly like a story, Aunt Belle Miller said: when one thought of how he had gone West, with only fifty dollars above his carfare, had got a job as clerk with a lumber firm, married the great lumberman's daughter, and now had risen to be a lumber baron himself. She supposed he must be richer than anyone knew, Aunt Belle remarked with satisfaction.

The children had listened to the whole story. Their eagerness to see a real millionaire—to them any rich man must be a millionaire—overcame their awe of entering a house that was in mourning. And not only a millionaire, Delight said, but a baron!—that meant he must belong to the nobility. Clarence nodded his head sagely. He hadn't the slightest comprehension of what "the nobility" meant; except the vague notion that a baron would be dressed up in fine lace stock and buckled shoes, something like his own George Washington costume. A millionaire, he thought of, however, as wearing a high silk hat and an overcoat with a big fur collar; his expectations were mixed.

The Vance house was on the other street, as Clarence always called it; the other main residence street from the one where his own house stood—both houses about the same distance up the hill. It had a large corner lot. The tower, the balconies, the fancy railings and peaks of the light-green house had a look of sadness tonight in the clear September air. The children nearly always ran scampering on ahead of the older people; but that night they trailed behind. They looked fearfully at the front door. The great bouquet was gone. When they saw that, they hurried to catch up.

Gatherings in that hospitable home were always gay. But the group waiting now, after having pressed the bell, was hushed and subdued. "The other part," where the old gentleman had had his quarters, was closed; the window shades were down. They couldn't bear to look at the other part.

Aubrey Broadwater himself opened the door.

"Come in. Come in, people. Well, this is kind."

"I hope we aren't disturbing you—"

"Oh, no! Nonsense. Come in, all of you. Dave, hello

there. Ira. Belle. Haven't seen you folks. Good evening,
Mrs. Greenwood. Dr. Greenwood, good evening."

"I'm afraid," he added, confidentially, lowering his
voice, "that you'll have to excuse Nellie. She's gone upstairs."

Oh yes, of course, they all said hastily. He mustn't
think of calling Nellie; or Willis, either. And with a sense
of shock, people looked about the familiar parlor, realizing
the hush and gloom that had so recently invaded its ornate
comfort. They had to wonder all over again what this loss
would mean to Nellie, the adored pet of both father and
husband, who couldn't express a wish—so the other women
charged—without having some man go running to see that
it came true. The house seemed empty, although there were
so many people in the room that Aubrey Broadwater could
scarcely find chairs for them all.

The children didn't need chairs. "Oh, don't bring chairs
for them." They could sit on footstools; they'd like that
better, anyway. Nellie Vance's parlor was cluttered with
such things as footstools, silk and satin cushions, knick-
knacks, and draperies.

The children solemnly nodded assent. Jamie had the
Brussels hassock, and Clarence the one of needlework, with
the picture of a curly-haired, brown-and-white dog; and
the two little girls sat together on the fragile love seat,
which they thought the most beautiful piece of furniture
in town. They looked at Aubrey Broadwater. Clarence's expression gave away his disappointment—if anyone had cared
to notice—but Delight's blue-green eyes were like cat's eyes,
with their shining, inscrutable stare.

The grown folks, however, who had no picture in mind
of a millionaire baron, were not disappointed; in fact, they
were much impressed. The slight, sandy-haired youth, whom
most of them remembered, light-hearted and always ready
for fun, had become the stocky, decisive man of affairs. A

young man still, he nevertheless had more the look of middle-age than Willis Vance: with his eyeglasses, his hair decidedly thinned, his firm businessman's mouth. The women had noted at once that Aubrey was very well dressed in conservative style. He sat with legs crossed, nursing a shiny shoe with a well-kept, well-manicured hand. He had stubbed out his cigar when the doorbell rang. Its expensive odor still lingered—making Belle Miller wrinkle her small nose in disapproval. The bankers, the Miller brothers, and the retail merchants, H. C. and A. D. Murdock, listened with respect to what Aubrey Broadwater had to say. Into the parlor of this small-town house, he brought a breath of the great business world: the world of millionaires and barons.

"Yes, I must get back," Aubrey Broadwater repeated.

"Well, we're glad to have you with us even this short while," A. D. Murdock said. "Although we're sorry for the cause that brought you."

The consciousness of loss, for the moment forgotten, came over them all again.

Mrs. Stiles said, "It was a beautiful service."

"Yes it was," Aubrey Broadwater agreed. "In every way fitting."

"That's just what I've been saying," Lizzie Murdock breathed.

"Yes, if anything can console us at such a time, a service like that—" The great man took off his eyeglasses, stared at them, wiped them with a glossy handkerchief, put them on again. All four children watched, unmoving, while he fitted the little gold hook over his ear.

Dave Miller asked, with open pride, "What did you think of our preacher?"

Mr. Greenwood made an impatient gesture—but there was no stopping Dave!

"Oh, he knows what I think!" Aubrey Broadwater answered. "Yes, I've told Dr. Greenwood. That was the finest address I believe I've ever heard."

Delight's eyes stared even more brightly. She interposed now, in a tone of rebuke, "My papa isn't a doctor." She shook her head until her braids shook. "He doesn't practice medicine. He preaches sermons. You should call him reverend."

The company laughed in relief.

"That teaches you, Aubrey," Mr. Stiles said.

"Yes, I stand corrected."

The millionaire took off his eyeglasses, put them on again, tipped back his head and laughed. The four children watched every motion he made.

His face abruptly became solemn again. "Seriously, *Rev*erend Greenwood—" he slightly smiled—"I wasn't half able, out there on the hill, to express my appreciation. I've been thinking about it ever since—your *ad*dress—what you said of my father's life having been heroic. I wondered what you meant at first; but you brought that out."

Aubrey Broadwater told them what he knew of his father's history—many of the details these friends and fellow townsmen heard for the first time. That sermon, Aubrey said earnestly, had made him see the whole story in a different light.

Once he had regarded his father—"Much as I loved him"—as foolish for having given up all that he possessed. "He had wealth of a sort—small wealth—" the financier speaking—"but of a sort. He owned slaves. He had a fine old property back there in the Old Dominion." Then, for the sake of a principle, he'd forfeited the whole thing: left the home where his ancestors had settled, two hundred years ago, and gone to seek his fortune in what was almost a foreign land. He'd never made a go of it in the North— financially speaking; he was unfitted to the life.

"When I was a child," Aubrey confided, with a slight

grimace of pain, "I sided with my mother. You never knew her—any of you people, of course. She died, before Nellie was married; before any of us came out here—long before."

Mrs. Stiles nodded, as if she understood it all.

Aubrey went on, then, to tell them many things they'd never heard from Nellie Vance, loquacious as she seemed. But Nellie's rippling prattle was mostly about unimportant matters. Their mother, Aubrey Broadwater said, had never been reconciled; she'd blamed their father for every misfortune the family suffered after they'd come North— which, by the way, he added, had taken place before he was born. Their father used to tell her, "We'd be no better off there, Vivy. We'd have less than we do here." But the mother wouldn't listen to that. She had been born in the system of slavery, and accepted it as the natural order.

"I took her viewpoint, without knowing more about it. Nellie was always her father's pet, and so of course I was mother's. Even when I came here to New Hope, that was still my viewpoint. I was ashamed of my father—thought it very low that my father, who had started as a gentleman, had come down to paper hanging, in his old age, and in a little raw prairie town."

"Hmp! Was *that* what you thought about New Hope!" Lizzie Murdock sharply ejaculated.

He let that go—perhaps he hadn't heard it. He turned to Mr. Greenwood, and said earnestly:

"But I have a better comprehension of that now, I think. I realize that what you said of it was a larger view."

That this was a man who had listened to his conscience; who had put principle above the tie of home and kinship, although these had been so dear to him, in the place where his family had been settled for generations . . . yes, Aubrey Broadwater asserted, more true, all of it, than anyone outside their family could realize. Nevertheless, when the "awful testing" came, he had made the choice that led to exile.

"I suppose that *was* heroic."

She didn't like that word, Addie Murdock sighed. It sounded "fierce, sort of." Mr. Broadwater was such a gentleman. He had such lovely manners.

"I just loved to meet him on the street, and have him take off his hat and bow. It always made me feel better."

The silence of the other women seemed to say, Why "better?" What was the matter with you?

The idea of not liking that word!—Electa Stiles broke in. Heroic! What better word was there in the language?

"Yes, but it don't seem as if it applies," Addie murmured weakly.

"Of course it applies!" Mrs. Stiles said. Her black eyes sparkled. What was it, if it wasn't heroic, to put truth above everything else? That was moral courage, the rarest kind.

" 'He that loveth father or mother more than me is not worthy of me: and he that loveth son or daughter more than me is not worthy of me.' "

Mrs. Stiles firmly, exultantly, repeated those words. Addie Murdock shuddered. Jim Stiles thoughtfully rubbed his bald head—his good eye almost as expressionless as the glass one. Aubrey Broadwater had blushed slightly at hearing scripture quoted aloud in his sister's own parlor.

The children had been listening all this time. Clarence's lips moved silently: he was repeating the words to himself "moral courage"—"heroic." He felt that same sense of heightened wonder as on the autumn afternoon—years ago, it seemed to him now—when he had been walking across the farmyard, out at Uncle Andy's, and had heard his father and the minister asserting that mankind would solve all problems—would learn to "beat the wind"; when they had talked about "those documents."

Some of the others were embarrassed by the Biblical quotation: it wasn't often Electa Stiles broke out that way. Lizzie Murdock, glancing slily at her, recalled how Father Kent, out in the old community, after sitting and talking about the weather and the crops just like anybody else, would suddenly arise and break out into sonorous prayer. 'Lecta was very much like her father.

Mrs. Stiles herself looked flushed and conscious. She cleared her throat. There was no need to say his father had "started as a gentleman," she protested now to Aubrey Broadwater, and sharply. Hadn't he ended that way, too? Mr. Broadwater was a very great gentleman to the end of his days.

The others nodded vigorous agreement. They all recalled his kindness, his courtliness. Belle Miller said he dignified his calling; it was a joy to have Mr. Broadwater enter the house.

"And this wasn't exile,"she protested. "Why, we feel that he belonged to us. He belonged to New Hope if anyone did."

Aubrey Broadwater replied, yes, he knew that now. This afternoon, when they'd all been standing in that sunlit spot, up there on the heights, with that great view of all the country westward, he'd been glad to think that it was here his father would be laid to rest. His father had found a home at last. Aubrey told the others of the old family burying ground back in Virginia, where several generations of his family lay; he and his wife had gone to see the place (some of the women exchanged discreet glances, meaning: she could go there but she could never come here!)—and they'd felt, both of them, how sad it was that no more Broadwaters would find rest in the ancient spot.

Nevertheless, Aubrey said, it was his firm belief that after his father had come here to stay with Nellie and Willis, he had been more contented than anywhere else; more at home.

Again, the others all agreed; with the sense of loss so deepened that for relief they turned to other things. Small circumstances were recalled: the grand march at the Harvest Supper, led by Mr. Broadwater in his Prince Albert coat, and Mrs. Zissler in her kitchen apron! Mr. Broadwater had gone straight to the kitchen to claim his partner, saying he was proud to offer his arm to the finest coffee maker in the land. They spoke of the early days: so few years past, and yet they were "early days." Dave Miller recalled his first sight of the old gentleman—the glory of that plug hat on the streets of New Hope!—and how Mr. Broadwater had said, in his courtly way, in greeting, that he was proud to cast in his lot with the new town; it would bring back his youth.

The children would miss him! The children looked away, answered nothing.

Mrs. Greenwood said suddenly, in a low voice, "Your father looked so beautiful. I almost wished we had let—" Some of the others nodded agreement.

Aubrey Broadwater told them what Nellie had said: that their father's face had the look of his early photographs, of the old daguerreotypes taken when he and mother were married—but more beautiful, with the beauty of long life added. That look of quiet self-possession, so tranquil, not quite smiling, was his own best look.

But wasn't that true, Mrs. Stiles asked, in most cases when death came, "as we say, naturally? When the life has been lived, and seems ready to go?" However one explained that, whatever science might choose to say, it seemed to be true. She had seen it more than once.

The minister said that he had seen it too.

The children listened in awe so deep that it had brought tears to Delight's shining eyes.

They all felt closely drawn together—as that group in the old burying ground had felt!—these people who had shared the "early days," such a few years past, of the new town. The minister's family had come later, but had been taken in among them. The children felt it too. This was the town where they were born—Clarence, Jamie, and Dosia; the only town they had ever known. But the days talked of were "old times" instead of "early days" to them. Clarence glanced at Delight, a little worried. He hitched his footstool over closer to the love seat.

The conversation grew lighter. Intimacy had been reestablished. Aubrey Broadwater had lost his "baron" look; and again (as some of the grown folks remarked afterwards) he seemed to be the slim, rollicking youth who had been in on all the good times! They recalled the town as it had been at that period—with an effect of great humor: when Miller Brothers was the only store, and the hall above it had served for every kind of community gathering, from a traveling show company's horrible rendition of *East Lynne* to a prayer meeting of Holiness people who had been driven, by a cloudburst, from their campgrounds near the river. Did Aubrey remember that? And did he remember the minstrel show, put on to raise funds for an opera house, in which he and Jim Stiles here had made a hit as end men? Yes, he remembered all of it.

"Do you find the town much changed?" Dave Miller asked proudly.

Changed! It was transformed! Not the same place at all.

That seemed to please everybody except Addie Murdock and Bertha Miller—and who *could* please them.

"And aren't you sorry you left us?" Lizzie Murdock said in pert challenge. "It's so long since you've been back, we began to think you'd forgotten us!"

The great man was slightly confused: trying to say at

one and the same time that no, he hadn't been back often enough, yes, he was sorry he'd left, but no, he wasn't sorry.

"*You* people," he said, "should come out where *I* live."

He spoke now of the wonderful Oregon country; while the others listened with the half-reluctant respect characteristic of inlanders toward a coast dweller—but holding back, resenting the pull of the newer land. He told about the mighty forests, the great rivers, the Pacific Ocean. Jim Stiles chimed in with him, to Electa's disgust.

"Don't you get James started on the West!" she cried.

They had to admit, all of them, that "it must be a great country out there."

But it was time to go. They hadn't intended to stay so long, keeping Aubrey up, when he had that long journey before him. That didn't matter!—he answered heartily. He wouldn't have missed this splendid talk. He must come back much sooner than before—and bring his wife and family with him! Aubrey promised. He stood in the doorway looking after them, lifting his hand in final good-bye.

"He was embarrassed, just the same," Lizzie Murdock whispered, "when I mentioned his wife. That woman'll never come here. You'll never catch *her*."

Good-byes were spoken when the group reached the corner—the Dave Millers and the Stileses and the Greenwoods going one way, and the Iras and the Murdocks the other. The air of the September night was mild and still, but a few leaves had fallen.

After Mr. and Mrs. Stiles had said good night and crossed the street, the Greenwoods still stood talking in front of the Miller house before they started down the hill.

"That was fine praise you got, Reverend," Dave Miller said. "You deserved it. I don't know how you could have spoken better than you did this afternoon."

"It wasn't so hard this time."

"If this only keeps up!" Mrs. Greenwood murmured.
"It feels more like summer than fall."

"There's a change, though," Bertha Miller said.

"How do you know that, mama?"

"I smell it," she said.

"Smell it!" Dave scoffed.

The children looked at each other. Delight lifted her little nose and sniffed the air; and then Clarence did the same thing. The air seemed to him to have no smell at all: only freshness.

But there was the sense of something gone, and tomorrow they would know what it was: tomorrow, when the trees shed more of their dry leaves, and the dust lay thicker. Now the evening light was clear and beautiful; the great sky was full of stars; but tomorrow they would know, they would realize, that an old softness of the South, gently alleviating, had faded out of the harsh, bright, early air.

When Clarence was upstairs in his room, he lay awake reliving the great day; more uplifted than sorrowful. He thought with wonder of the millionaire—he had seen a millionaire! He thought of the new land, breathed the scent of mighty forests. He felt the close common tie of the little group—those who were children together, listening to the tales of an earlier time. He saw the beautiful face of the old man who had died—tranquil, with silvery hair.

CHAPTER XI

The Call

THAT NEXT WINTER was colder than the one before. It was
hard on the country people. Snowfall was heavy and at
times the roads were blocked. Clarence heard his mother
mourning, saying how long the days must seem to poor
Mary, out there on the farm without anybody for company. She didn't call a man real company.

But it was a busy winter in town. The cold weather
drew people together instead of keeping them apart. During
late summer, and the long, almost too mild fall, there'd come
a lull when everything seemed just to be drifting. Then Dave
Miller had gone around fuming, asking what was the matter
with folks, was the whole town asleep? But that period had
been merely a breathing spell. With the first cold snap the
works had all started up again, and throughout the winter
town activities were at their height. Dave rejoiced then because he said everything was progressing, everything seemed
to be going right ahead.

There had been some losses. Even John Budd was missed
in a way—although Dave hated to admit that; and of course
the whole town missed Mr. Broadwater. It was sad to see the
Vance house closed up and standing empty. Nellie and

Willis were spending the winter in Oregon with Aubrey
and his wife; some people shook their heads doubting if
they'd ever see the Vances back here, at least to stay. "You
know how it is," they said, "when folks get out there to
the Coast. They don't return." Lots of folks these days were
beginning to turn their eyes toward the West Coast. But
Dave said that was nonsense. Why should the Vances want
to stay out there? Of course they'd be back. And even if
they weren't, he guessed the town could survive! Dave had
taken Willis Vance's place this winter both as Sunday school
superintendent and as a member of the Board—and the
more Dave Miller had to do the better he liked it. Dave
couldn't be happy unless he kept on the go, was the way
Ira put it. Bertha complained that his family never saw
him any more.

"He comes home for meals yet," she said. "Pretty soon,
when they open up the new dining room, he won't even
need to do that."

Dave had come home quite early—for him. He stopped
on the front porch to unbuckle his overshoes. Clarence
heard him, and yelled, "There's papa!" Edie went rushing
out to tell him not to bring those overshoes into the hall
and dump them. She'd mopped up that hall floor twice today. She took the overshoes and carried them out to the
kitchen, holding them up gingerly to show how sopping wet
they were. "I don't know what papa does, whether he wades
through every puddle—!" Bertha was afraid it must have
soaked right through his shoes, and hurried into the sitting
room to beg Dave to change them; and then came back
saying helplessly he wasn't there. He must have gone upstairs. Somebody should go up after him and tell him, or
he wouldn't think about it.

"Well, mama," Irene said, "papa knows *some*thing. He
can feel it when his own feet are wet."

"Ja, you can't count on that," Bertha sighed.

Irene and Bess exchanged their glances of exasperated amusement. They'd often giggled and marveled together over the way their mother stood in awe of menfolks and at the same time didn't give any of them credit for enough sense to come in out of the rain. This was an example.

"Supper's ready—papa, come!"

"You don't need to holler. I'm coming," Dave said, opening the hall door.

"We thought you'd gone upstairs."

"I did go upstairs. And then I came down again. Ain't that all right?" He spoke good-humoredly, however, and sat down to his supper with great satisfaction. His face was still ruddy from the outdoor air.

Bertha saw with relief that he'd put on his slippers. "It must be awful wet outside, ain't it? You got your overshoes soaked clear through."

"It *is* wet. Sure. It's thawing. Haven't you been out?" Her murmur sounded evasive. "Out as far as the back steps. I'll bet that's how far you went," Dave said to her with good-natured contempt. "Aw, you're just like an old cat—hug the stove, won't go out unless you're put out."

She looked guilty. "I hate it so awful sloppy, though," she sighed.

"Sloppy! That's all you womenfolks think of. Here we get a nice thaw, coming right when it's needed, and you womenfolks have to complain that it's sloppy!"

Why, he said, it was fine outside now, except underfoot—and the ground had to get wet when the snow melted. Nobody ought to mind that! They ought to be glad of it. Unless they didn't want any crops this summer. It was these good soaking snows that made good crops. They ought to go out, all of 'em, and see how good the mud smelled. There wasn't any better smell on earth, Dave proclaimed with gusto, than the smell of good, wet, rich dirt!

The girls were making faces of disgust. Irene said, "No,

thank you. I prefer toilet water for mine." But Clarence's eyes shone. He knew just how his father felt.

Dave went on to say he'd just come over the bridge, and how the creek was rushing!

Clarence asked eagerly, Would there be an overflow?

No, of course there wouldn't be an overflow—not when the snow went by degrees, as it was doing this year. That was when it all melted too fast.

"Why, do you *want* an overflow?"

Clarence nodded his head. The others laughed. But he remembered, and it all seemed wonderful—the excitement, church bells and school bells ringing, men out with rowboats all over town on the other side, helping folks to get out of their houses and up on the hill before the bridge went down. All the houses on the hill were full of people that night. Mrs. Stiles had been the one to offer to take in the Groundhogs—she'd kept them several days, scrubbed up the children, made them wash their hair and clothes, and sent them home with grim rejoicing that for once they were really clean! Lillie Groundhog had come every Saturday since to see Mrs. Stiles.

"You wouldn't want an overflow," Bess said. "Maybe the parsonage would get flooded. What would happen to Delight?"

"She'd come here and live," Clarence brightly asserted.

"Well, she won't have to come here. Nobody will," his father said. "There won't be any overflow. The Creek's just where it ought to be. Ought to be high this time of year."

As soon as supper was over, Clarence went outside. He wanted to smell the fine wet mud.

He stood on the front porch sniffing in the evening air, shivering a little, but with pleasure. Snow odors and earth odors in that evening hour were mingled. There were great patches left of snow. Clarence thought of winter—of the good times—playing fox-and-geese on the vacant lot, making the first tracks in new fallen snow that lay in glittering fluff on the firm drifts underneath . . . he could feel the zigzag hurtle of his sled down the hill . . . the boys jeering at the girls all flung down to make angel patterns in the snow—how he'd run back again and helped Delight brush the snow from her kitty hood. He thought of one day that was almost a blizzard, cold that brought tears to his eyes when he'd struggled against the wind, kids coming to school with knitted fascinators tied around their faces and frozen stiff around their mouths, his feet like clumps of ice and the chilblains itching after he'd come home and toasted his feet on the oven door. A little while ago he'd still been in the midst of all this—and suddenly he was looking back upon it as "last winter." Spring was in the air, the new season, in the tingle, thin and chill, of grainy snow half melted, in the rich thick moistness of the muddy ground: the soil, piled through long ages, moist and deep, for his Uncle Andy's plow. It almost seemed to him he could catch a fresh breath from the Creek, the waters swirling darkly beneath the bridge down at the foot of the hill. He lived in that happy moment of interval.

Jamie Murdock was the first one to tell Clarence. It was one day when he and Jamie were coming home from school together.

"Did you know the minister's folks are going to move away!"

"They are not." Clarence said that loudly, disgustedly, in scorn.

"Yes, they are, honest, Clarence."

"How do *you* know?"

"My folks said so."

"Mine never did."

"Well, you ask 'em."

"They are not."

Clarence repeated that in a low voice. He couldn't think of any other retort than flat denial. Not that he believed what Jamie had just said! It couldn't possibly be true. How could Jamie's folks know about it, and not *his* folks?

He wouldn't stay and play with Jamie, however, when they reached the Murdock house. Jamie wanted him to come on in and play jackstraws. Clarence said he'd promised his mother to come right home—she wanted him for something, he guessed. What he was going home for was to repeat Jamie's story and have it denied. He could already hear Edie loudly and emphatically denying that there was anything to it. "Nonsense! The way things get around this town! Who starts 'em?"

He was mad at Jamie for saying such a thing; but troubled by the remembrance of Jamie's earnest freckled face with the bright, excited eyes. When he got near his own house, Clarence found himself slowing down.

Clarence went in the front way. Nobody seemed to be around, but voices sounded from the kitchen—those women who came for afternoon coffee. But he was reassured by hearing that same old gabble-gabble. He didn't want to go in there. Those women got hold of everything. Maybe they were repeating that same wicked story. He didn't want to ask about it in front of them. He remembered what Delight had said to him at recess, when the kids were lined up to march back into the building—she'd called out to him from the girls' line, in a loud breathy whisper, "I want to tell you something." He hadn't supposed it was much—only about something they were going to play, some kind of fun they were going to have. He thought that still. Wrath at Jamie Murdock rose again. Clarence grabbed his cap from the newel post where he'd tossed it and went out of the house and down the walk, splashing through the water at the crossing and sliding on icy slush. When he came in sight of the church and parsonage, the frame buildings faded from winter standing bare now against the sky, Clarence again felt reassured.

He went around to the back door, the way he always did, and knocked. Mrs. Greenwood opened the door.

"Oh, come in, Clarence!"

"Yes, come in, boy," Mr. Greenwood said.

Clarence stepped into the small kitchen that was warm from the cookstove. Mr. Greenwood had been reading to Mrs. Greenwood while she did the ironing—sitting comfortably with his feet on the edge of the wood box, and stopping now and then to take a bite of a large red apple; as he did now.

"Delight hasn't come home yet," Mrs. Greenwood said. "She was going to stay after school to practice her piece with Alta."

"I know it."

"Well, you just sit down then, dear, and wait for her. Will, give Clarence an apple."

"Here, Clarence, here's a big fellow. Let's see you make 'way with that."

Clarence took the apple silently, forgetting to say thanks. He held it in both hands, feeling its hard smoothness. After a while he took one cautious bite. The clock ticked on the shelf above the table. Occasionally Mrs. Greenwood went over to the stove to change irons, making as little disturbance as she could; he heard the slight hiss when she touched the iron with a wetted finger, the sizzle as she smoothed it over the wax. She smiled at Clarence, as if to bring him in on the reading—Mr. Greenwood had taken up his book and continued, while Clarence sat reserved and still.

" 'The moral element invites man to great enlargements, to find his satisfaction, not in particulars or events, but in the purpose and tendency.' "

Clarence held his apple up to his mouth and nibbled, tasting the cold, sweet, juicy flavor. He was contented. He didn't even want Delight to come back for a while. Here was the bright quiet that gave the parsonage its enchantment, with the clear, even tones of the minister's voice dominating the room. Often when Clarence came home with Delight after school, they would find the parents together, either in the study or out in the kitchen, depending upon what kind of work was going on. They helped each other —she went with him to make calls, and discussed church matters while she did some sewing, and on Mondays he helped her get the washing out of the way. Delight took all this for granted. But it was something new to Clarence; it was a relationship he had never seen before. He noted it, and puzzled over it, and kept staring at it from a little distance, never giving himself away.

With a sidelong glance, he recognized what Mrs. Greenwood was ironing. It was Delight's best apron, the one with ruffles and wide ties, that she wore to school on special days when the room held exercises. He remembered the snowy morning when he'd stopped for her on the way to school. He'd got there early, before Delight was ready; she had come running in from the bedroom to have her apron tied and her hair braided in front of the stove. "Look-it, mama! Clarence, look-it!" She had her little red comb in her hand. In that cold winter weather, her hair seemed to spring away from the comb, and long strands drifted and crackled above the light shining mass; and she had laughed out joyously, with eager eyes and wild-rose cheeks. Clarence had felt suddenly shy, and had looked away while her mother tied the strings of her starched white apron—this same apron that was on the ironing board now. She had stood then, trustful but impatient, lifting her head so that her mother could make a bow with the ribbons of her soft gray kitty hood— before they had run outdoors together, wild to get out into the snow, Delight sticking out her pink tongue to taste the delicious cold tingle of the damp snowflakes, Clarence starting to plunge into drifts; while the first bell rang out muffled behind the wintry, thick white slanting veil.

"I guess maybe I won't wait," Clarence said.

He crossed the yard, where the ground was partly squashy and partly hard, and walked on slowly in the direction of the schoolhouse, stopping when he came to the bridge. He saw the two little figures away up on the hill. They stood on the corner saying good-bye to each other—girls always took about an hour telling each other good-bye. Clarence didn't want to go to meet Delight. He stood with his hands on the cold railing and stared down at the foamy water; remembering last night, when he'd thought he could smell the Creek, and that it meant spring. She came hippity-hopping down the last stretch of boardwalk, calling out to him, "Hello, Clarence!" He wouldn't look at her. She stopped beside him.

"What you doing?"

"Nothing."

She had to tell him—if it was true. He wasn't going to ask her.

Delight asked doubtfully, "Are you mad?"

His throat hurt and he didn't answer.

"I had to stay," she assured him. "Alta and I had to practice. Teacher told us to. We have to give our piece this Friday. Clarence. Don't you know it?"

Clarence muttered finally, "I'm not mad about that."

They were both standing at the railing. Delight had put her hands on it too. Clarence glanced at her. Delight's pink lips were parted—he saw the droop of the lower lip, as she hesitated.

"Are you mad because we're going to move away?"

Clarence stared straight ahead with glassy eyes. He pretended for a moment that he hadn't heard. It seemed even to himself that he hadn't heard. But he was aware of the queerest feeling, as if a crack had opened up in solid ground, and the bridge on which they were standing had begun to drift away 'somewhere—they were both on the bridge, he and Delight, and yet they were drifting in opposite directions.

"You aren't either moving away."

"We are too."

She had said that. Delight! When Clarence turned to her in horrified disbelief, he saw how her eyes were shining. They didn't see him, standing right beside her. Like her father's blue eyes, they were looking into distance.

"My papa's had a call," she said.

Clarence stared. He didn't know just what the word meant, but there was a largeness in the sound that seemed to reverberate in the damp fresh air. He felt as if he were still listening to those awesome reverberations at a further and further distance, when Delight turned and began to talk to him eagerly.

The call was from away off in Oregon, from a great big town—"Oh, lots bigger than this one!" Just think, they were going away out there two thousand miles! At first her papa wasn't going to accept the call, but her mama said he couldn't refuse. He'd walked and walked, all over town, all by himself, trying to make his decision. And now it was made. The conviction was slowly growing in Clarence's mind, while she was telling him all this, that Delight was glad.

He wanted to run. But his feet felt heavy, and didn't seem to belong to him. He had taken hold of the railing again and looked stubbornly down at the water. He wouldn't answer Delight. After a long while he heard her say doubtfully:

"I'm going home then."

Clarence let her go. The reverberations from that awesome word had died away, and everything seemed silent.

After another long while he took his cold hands from the railing, and started trudging up the hill toward home. He walked along just the same as he always did, stooping once to pick up an icy lump of dirt and throw it at a hitching post—proving that he didn't care, and nothing had happened anyway. But it was like that time he'd fallen out of the swing and had known he was hurt but not just how, until a big bruise on his shoulder had started aching. The brightness was gone from the snow patches, from the streams of water coursing down the muddy road; and that mud smell, which last night had held all the good, rich promise of springtime, was only dirty and dismal.

The roof of the barn had been reshingled. The ladder was still leaning against the side of the building. The children had climbed up and now they were on top of the barn! They could look out all over the yard, and down upon the little birch tree, and the place where the sweet peas would be planted later on.

"You must play with Delight all you can. You won't have her much longer."

The folks had kept telling Clarence that. But the two children had been together less, these last few weeks, instead of more. The coming separation had raised a barrier between them; and ever since that time on the bridge, when Delight had told Clarence about her father's call, they had been oddly shy with each other.

Clarence hadn't got over his astonishment at his family's attitude. He had gone home that day confidently expecting that everybody would feel just the way he did—for the Greenwoods to leave New Hope would be the worst calamity the town could know, and when the folks heard about it they would not allow it to happen!

But the folks had heard about it, he'd discovered; and far from refusing to let the minister go, seemed to have taken it for granted that the call would be accepted. It conferred honor upon the whole church, was what Aunt Belle said, and particularly upon those who had been responsible for bringing Mr. Greenwood to New Hope. "Shows we know a good thing when we see it!" Dave agreed. Clarence knew his father was boasting downtown about how their preacher had been called to a fine big church in a growing western city at a thousand dollars increase in salary! His mother was nodding her head and saying, ja, she'd known how it would be. Bess seemed excited, almost elated over the news—and Irene said snippily anybody would leave this dinky burg who got the chance! Edie didn't say anything like that. She burst into tears one moment, declaring she'd never forgive the Vances, she hated Mrs. Vance's brother, wished he'd never heard their minister preach!—and then she exulted, almost as loudly as her father, because when the West Coast wanted somebody good they had to come back here!

Everybody chimed in; everybody seemed to be repeating more or less what Clarence heard his own family say. Cass Story's editorial first extolled the minister "and his loyal helpmate," and then went on to boast, much in Edie's vein: as it was New Hope that had earlier given the West one of its great business leaders, now again it was to "our little city" that the West was looking for a leader in spiritual things. Mrs. Stiles told people resolutely, this had to come, so let's rejoice. When these rich men found something they liked they had to get it for themselves!—she added with grim humor. Folks all fell over themselves when Aubrey Broadwater came back here a millionaire, or something close to it—so now let them accept the consequences! But she was sad; she showed that at times. Mr. Stiles meantime had his sly triumph over Mrs. Stiles. The West, he said, was where the good folks went, and she'd have to admit it now. *You* came away from there, she sharply retorted. "Well," he drawled slowly, a twinkle in his one good eye, "that proves your opinion of me, Lecty, proves what an ornery critter I am!" Mrs. Stiles tossed her head and turned away in a huff.

Clarence was shaken and confused; but secretly resentful. He didn't go over to the parsonage for some time, although he didn't let the folks know it. But that Saturday morning, Delight had come over to *his* house, to play with him; and after hanging around, pretending he didn't want to leave what he was doing, he had finally gone out into the yard with her. The weather was so fine that he couldn't stay mad.

He sat astride the peak of the roof. The new rough shingles were bright and woody-smelling under the April sun. It was so warm that the children had left their jackets down below. The great blue spring time sky promised time without end—until Clarence leaned down over the gable peak and found he was looking into the sunflower patch. It was where he had hidden that very first day before he'd gone down to the station to meet Delight. He remembered that time—his excitement as he'd lain hidden beneath the great sunflowers, and how afterwards the world had taken on magic brightness.

"What you looking at, Clarence?"

Delight hitched herself along toward him, with her skirts pulled up above her knees, showing her garters.

"Nothing," he said.

He felt the pain of keeping secrets from her. But he couldn't acknowledge to her, or even to himself, that he didn't want her to go away. It meant more than he could take in at that moment. And nobody else felt that way about it.

Clarence scrambled around until he sat facing Delight.

One of her braids had loosened at the end into wavy raveled strands. Clarence didn't want to think about her long hair, and his pride because his girl had the longest hair of any girl in the whole school building.

"Oh, isn't it nice and beautiful up here!" she cried.

Clarence stared off toward the sky line. It seemed to him, at that moment, as if he somehow could make time last.

"Clarence, when I get out on the West-coast"—she always said it that way, one word—"I'm going up in a lighthouse. Oh, just think how far out I can see then! Over *every*thing."

The deep bruise started aching again. "I can see the schoolhouse from here," he said. "I can see the cupola."

"Just think!" she repeated. "Up in a lighthouse! I can look across the whole Pacific Ocean."

"That's just water," Clarence said distantly.

"I know it. The ocean *is* water."

Delight was braiding her hair; biting her pink lower lip and slightly frowning. She looked up again with a shining far gaze.

"I'll be just like Star," she said, "in *Captain January*."

"You won't live in the lighthouse, though."

"I don't want to live in it."

"It won't be like *Captain January* then. I don't like that story."

"I do."

"It's just a little girl's story," Clarence taunted.

"I am a little girl."

Delight said that with such self-satisfaction that it made Clarence mad. He hated girls. He wished he'd gone over to Jamie's. He thought obliquely of the tough boys' gang—Delight didn't know about that. But she didn't seem to notice, and promised him graciously:

"I'll take *you* up, Clarence, when you come to visit

us. Clarence, won't it be fun if there's an old lighthouse keeper maybe, and he lets us stay up where the big light is, and have our playhouse and look out over the ocean?"

Clarence wouldn't answer. But he was comforted by her saying that he should visit out there; she seemed to be counting on it and taking it for granted that he'd come, and they'd have their playhouse just the same.

That might come true! Clarence hadn't believed it at first, but now he almost did. Delight's father had said so. He'd said, "The first thing you know, Clarence, you'll be out to pay us a visit." Clarence's mother had looked scared and said, "Who knows." But his father had retorted, "Well, who *does* know?" Edie was furious at the way the Vances kept writing folks back here about the roses and the ocean. Clarence had felt the same jealousy toward those marvels that Edie did. If the Vances wanted to stay out there, Edie said, let them, but they didn't have to try to get everybody out of New Hope after them! But it seemed different to Clarence if he were to share those distant wonders with Delight. He wanted to go up in a lighthouse more than almost anything. He felt excited, and remembered how Mr. Greenwood had said he must look forward to coming out there instead of thinking how he would miss Delight here at home. Now he would have more ahead of him.

Delight tossed her braid over her shoulder. She looked straight at Clarence now with her eager, shining eyes.

"When you come out there, just think, Clarence, we can go and see Chinamen. Chinamen live on the West-coast, Japanese people do too. Don't you hope maybe we can play with a little Chinese boy and a little Jap girl? Oh, wouldn't that be fun! Mr. Aubrey Broadwater has a Chinaman that cooks his meals. Mrs. Vance said so. Isn't that *fun*ny? Maybe we can eat our meals with chopsticks. Mr. Aubrey Broadwater has a boat, too. We can sail out on the ocean."

"Vincent Harper has a boat at the Lakes," Clarence said.

"The Lakes aren't nearly as big as the ocean. Even Okoboji. Those boats aren't like ocean boats."

"They are too," Clarence muttered—but mechanically, without conviction.

"You can sleep on ocean boats."

He was silent. Everything would be bigger out there on the West Coast. The Greenwoods were going to live in a beautiful new eight-room parsonage with a wonderful bathroom and electric lights. He hadn't yet got over his astonishment that there could be any town more up-and-coming than New Hope! Chicago was bigger. So was Horton. Fox Center was about the same size. But the other towns wouldn't be bigger always. Clarence believed that implicitly. He'd always taken it for granted without the slightest doubt that New Hope was the best town in the world. People came here from other places. Nobody moved *away*. Then for his own father to talk about "city advantages"—Mr. Greenwood couldn't give up so many "new advantages"! New Hope and "advantages" and "opportunities" went together! Clarence hadn't been able to understand. There would be the ocean out there. But he didn't think of the ocean as an "advantage." Oceans were strange and foreign and belonged in storybooks and geographies.

But Delight was talking in that breathless voice in which she used to tell him fairy tales; and as he listened, sitting up on top of the barn, Clarence reluctantly felt the strange places taking on reality, like the fairy-tale scenes, and Grandma Pettibone's back yard and Judge Lewis's house in Ballard. He wanted to go to the West Coast. He wanted to see things faraway. He didn't want to lose the ocean, and the Festival of Roses, the ships going to China, the lighthouse, the forests . . . although it hurt him to suppose that any forest could be more wonderful than Rundle's

Woods where he and Delight had picked bluebells. That was something he didn't believe.

"When you grow up, Clarence, maybe you can be a forester man and wear a green suit. Like Robin Hood maybe, only you won't be a robber. Then we could have a little hut in the forest, and live on the wonderful apples, and the wonderful all kinds of fruit that grow out in Oregon. The trees would be so tall we couldn't see the tops, could we? Like those Mr. Stiles told us about. And we'd have deer, but we'd tame the deer, we wouldn't shoot them. I don't like Mr. Stiles so much any more. I'm going to have a little speckled fawn that eats apples out of my hand, Clarence—you can have a roebuck."

Clarence listened in a mixture of credulity and incredulity, of resentment, elation. They would be together again, this didn't mean they'd really have to be separated. It seemed as if right at that moment he was looking over the great shining ocean, the Pacific, bigger than the Atlantic, and more shining—the biggest Big-Sea Water. The actual scene below him—his own yard, the sunflower patch, the fenced-in chicken yard, even the cupola of the school building farther on up the hill—shrank, and grew small. Something had given way, some limit, some reluctance. Clarence realized with wonder that he would no longer want to keep the Greenwoods from going away. The future had shifted to out there. And yet he didn't believe it, either.

Delight's little face was right in front of him. Clarence looked at her wistfully, to make out if all she was telling him could really come true. That head so confidently lifted—the face that kept changing so he could never be sure what it looked like—the eyes . . . he looked straight at the eyes, but he couldn't see into their light, shining, changeable color. She had that fleeting air. It seemed as if she was already faraway, and he would have to follow. He had made the start already.

The girls had got the house cleaned the day before, so that they could spend all their time on preparations for the reception. Nobody was allowed to go in and muss up the front rooms. The folding doors were locked between the parlor and hall and the dining room and sitting room, so that everybody who entered the house would have to go straight on out to the kitchen. Otherwise, Edie said, folks would be tracking up the whole place. When Irene and Ella Murdock went into the front rooms to arrange the flowers, they unlocked the doors with much secrecy and giggling, and locked them immediately. The girls' voices, their movements in the shut-off rooms, sounded hushed and mysterious from behind the tall, blank, varnished doors.

Excitement began with the early morning. Soon after breakfast the ladies started sending over baskets with extra dishes and silverware. It was going to be a job to keep all those things straight! The house was full of helpers; and those who didn't come to the house to work had offered to help in other ways. Some of the ladies were baking cakes in their own kitchens. Dora Palmer had promised to bring over a basketful of her mother's wonderful Swedish cookies. Some of the boys had come over to make themselves useful, as they said—useful as well as ornamental. Merrill and Franklin were out in the back yard turning the big ice-cream freezer; every little while coming to the house and demanding that the girls come out to lend advice. Dave Miller said he wasn't going downtown. He had Mollie hitched up and tied outside—he and the rig would be at the womenfolks' disposal.

"Clarence, you stay around here too. We may need you for errands."

"Papa's got Mollie."

"Well, we don't want to use the buggy every time. We need you too."

Clarence didn't actually mind; he had no intention of

going away from the place when there was so much going on there. Jamie Murdock came over with his mother's basket, and then there were two of them to run errands. In between times, they hung around the ice-cream freezer, picking up lumps of salty ice to suck, and always on hand for a taste when the freezer was opened. Once when they were crossing the bridge on their way downtown, they had met Willie Schnitts; and Willie had begun nastily chanting, "Clar'nce's girl is going a-way-ay! His girl is going a-way-hay!"—dancing and prancing ahead of them, but always just out of reach. Jamie was almost as mad as Clarence was. "Shut your big mouth," he said fiercely. Clarence felt the consolation of having Jamie back him up—Jamie liked Delight too—if she hadn't been Clarence's girl, she would have been Jamie's.

By six o'clock, the Miller house was ready for the reception. The family had been invited to Aunt Belle's for supper, "to avoid setting the table." Edie at the last minute refused to go. She didn't care to eat, she said. Edie had been in a funny state all the day before, when the girls were cleaning. At first she'd announced that she didn't feel well and they needn't count on her to help—and then a few minutes later, there she was downstairs, with her hair on curlers and her head tied up in an old green veil, looking, as Bess said, like the wrath of God. Even her lips were spotted from crying. She would work like all possessed—then suddenly she would throw down her cleaning cloth and rush upstairs to bang her door and go on bawling.

"We shouldn't leave her there," her mother kept worrying, all the way over to the other house. But Irene said, they might just as well let her alone. Let her get her sulk out now, then maybe she'd be decent at the reception.

"She don't want 'em to go," Bertha mourned.

"Well," Irene said snippily, "who does? But we don't all go around bawling about it."

Clarence kept still. But he felt a sneaking sympathy for Edie. All day, underneath the lift of excitement, he was aware of a cold, small, secret trickle of reluctance and dismay.

But the excitement held. The moment they got back home, his mother and the girls hurried out to the kitchen. Clarence felt as if he were alone, for this little while, in the strange house with its fragrant, festive, waiting air. He knew a marvelous importance: their own house was to be the scene of a reception.

The folding doors were open now between the parlor and sitting room. Both rooms were decorated with plants and summer flowers. To Edie's amazement, Vincent Harper had come over, while the folks were gone, bringing two great bunches of roses! She'd asked if he was coming to the reception, and he'd told her that he was. Clarence tiptoed over and smelled the roses. Edie had put the pink ones in a tall cut glass vase on the parlor stand. Their fresh cool fragrance seemed to him more wonderful because they were cut flowers and came from a conservatory. Mrs. Harry Harper had the only conservatory in town.

Clarence wanted, and didn't want, the reception to begin. One after another, the times he'd still had to look forward to sharing with Delight had come and were over. May Day was rainy; they'd gone around with the big umbrella to deliver their baskets. On the last day of school they'd taken home all their belongings. Delight had taken hers for the last time. The class had presented her with a little gold locket. Clarence and Alta and Dosia were the committee who'd made the selection. (Clarence's sisters had giggled over his airs of importance at being chairman of a committee!) Then their birthday party had come . . . and afterwards, when all the others had gone home, Clarence and Delight had played with each other out on the lawn looking for lightning bugs in the golden-green light of early evening. There would be this night, the farewell reception; the last Sunday, when the minister would "resign"; and then Delight would go away.

The people were beginning to arrive. The invitation had been general, not limited to the minister's congregation, and folks from all over town seemed to be taking advantage of it. The ladies thanked their stars they'd prepared what had seemed more than enough refreshments. Every one of the cakes would have to be cut! The Groundhogs, Lizzie Murdock whispered to Belle Miller—with a sly nod toward Mrs. Stiles—needn't count on any feast for themselves to-morrow on the leavings. There'd be no basket to take over!

"I guess *this* shows whether our minister is appreciated," Edie asserted. Her eyes sparkled; the size of the gathering seemed highly to console her. "I'd like to see the whole town turn out like this if 'twas either of the other preachers leaving!"

Bess winked at Irene, and Irene replied by a bored lift of one shoulder.

Many of the countrypeople had driven in on that beautiful evening. Teams were fastened at all the hitching posts outside on both sides of the block. Clarence ran out to greet his Uncle Andy and Aunt Mary. That was the first time they'd ever brought the new baby to any gathering; the first time Aunt Mary had been in town since Thanksgiving Day. The girls cooed and exclaimed over the dear little fellow, as Edie unwrapped his blanket, and Bess untied the strings of his tiny bonnet. The parents smiled proudly, but didn't have much to say. Mary seemed more shy and quiet than ever, Bess said later; she'd sat back in a corner all evening. Folks didn't see much of Emmett and Trixie, either, these days; their farm was eight miles out, and it was hard for them to get away. That night they were warmly welcomed. There were the Blaisdell family, from the south road; the Parkinsons who had the farm beyond; and Clarence stared to see his father heartily greeting and ushering in the whole Hans Gunderson family from the farm near Rundle's Pond, where he and Delight had gone that May Day—three small tow-headed boys stomped along behind their father, and the mother carried still another one. It was *his* duty, Clarence was informed, to see that the Gunderson boys had a good time.

The rooms were filling up fast. Grandma Story had come early, because she might want to leave before the reception was over. She was getting more feeble; she'd worn her bonnet tonight and her cape with jet trimmings, just as though it hadn't been summer. She sat smiling in the best rocking chair, and everybody who entered went up to shake hands with her. When Lute Fairbrother, immensely tall and uncomfortable in his best black suit, looking (Mr. Stiles said) like a scarecrow in mourning, stood beside her, Grandma patted his arm approvingly. In her eyes, her son's printer was just a motherless youth who had no woman to keep his clothes in order or see that he got the right things to eat; she took a pitying interest in him. Lute Fairbrother, Wes Bibbs, and Tom Burchard had come together: "the three jolly bachelors," Willis Vance had once slily called them, tickled because the name so obviously didn't fit.

There was another bachelor, far more impressive than any of these three—Vincent Harper!—slight but elegant, with a rosebud in his buttonhole, and wearing beautiful white flannel pants. Clarence and Jamie stared at him open-mouthed, while they edged away, not sure whether to despise or admire him. Vincent Harper showed an uneasiness under his air of vaguely bored politeness.

Both the other ministers were present with their wives. Nobody had really expected the Baptist man to come! He'd even preached a sermon striking at Mr. Greenwood's lack of gospel—oh, not by name, but everybody knew whom he meant!

Lizzie Murdock dashed back to the kitchen to report, every single soul in the countryside seemed to be coming!—except, thank heaven, the Groundhogs. Mrs. Ira said she wasn't to thank heaven too soon! They always showed up where refreshments were free.

The Greenwoods themselves were almost the last to arrive. Clarence had been impatient, waiting for them. Every few minutes he'd gone out to the porch to see if they weren't coming. But when he finally caught sight of them, still some distance down the boardwalk—Mr. Greenwood walking between the other two with Mrs. Greenwood on his arm and Delight holding his other hand as she skipped along—they seemed suddenly strangers. Clarence sneaked back into the house and hid in the dining room. He stood there with blank face and wary eyes, until he was sure that the greetings were over, and he could slip back into the front room unnoticed.

The gathering was stiff, at first; and the children were glad enough to go outdoors to play. They didn't need any second invitation.

But when they got outside, they felt stiff and awkward even there. They all had on their best clothes. Bonita Button had on her new pink china silk dress. The Gunderson boys had clumped solemnly out after Clarence. They stood in a silent row, all different sizes, but with shocks of tow hair combed down and plastered alike. Clarence didn't know what to do with them. One of the Groundhogs *had* come—the Groundhog girl, for whom Clarence and Delight had left the May basket. She would have been in their room at school if she had started in time. Mrs. Stiles had been sharply on the lookout for any of the Groundhog contingent, and had grabbed the little girl the moment she appeared and taken her out to the kitchen sink for a good scrubbing up and to get her hair decently combed out and braided. Now the youngster was clean—at least where she had any skin showing!—and Mrs. Stiles had brought her out to play with the other children. Her "right name," Mrs. Stiles warned them, was Lillie: it was a nice name, very pretty, and they were to call her by it. Mind now. She would expect Dosia Murdock, Mrs. Stiles stated firmly, to take Lillie in charge. Dosia set her little mouth, but didn't dare answer back.

The children stood around on the porch and on the lawn, and nobody seemed able to think of anything else to do. They were waiting for Delight. She hadn't come out yet; she was still in the house with the grown people.

But when she did come, they stood away in awed respect. She looked just as she did every Sunday at Sunday school, in the same white dotted swiss dress with puffed sleeves and lace insertion, and her hair crimped and hanging down her back. But she didn't seem the same. She was going to move away. She didn't belong with them any more. Clarence turned away his head. He couldn't bear to see her eager face and shining hair.

"Aren't you playing anything?"

They were waiting for her, they said. They wanted her to choose. Delight cried eagerly:

"We'll play drop-the-handkerchief! I like Statuary better. But we don't want to get grass stains on our nice clothes. Come on."

"Come on!" the others shouted. "Let's play!"

They ran out on the lawn. The circle began forming immediately. Alta grabbed one of Delight's hands, and Jamie was about to take the other when Walter Shafer pushed in between. Clarence admired Walter's boldness, although it made him mad that any other boy should stand beside Delight. Dosia had dropped the Groundhog girl's hand the moment she was away from Mrs. Stiles's sharp eyes. The Groundhog girl didn't know what to do, until Delight called

out to her "Come on, Lillie, and play," and imperiously made
a place for her in the circle. Delight was the queen that evening. She could do whatever she pleased and the others would
follow. But Clarence couldn't get rid of *his* charges so easily.
He kept urging, "Come on, don't you want to come on?"
He couldn't get any response out of their wooden silence.
"I'm going to play," he said finally. He kept lingering and
looking back to see if any of them were coming. The oldest
one did. He followed Clarence in silence, and stood outside
the circle until the little queen noticed him too, and said
with gracious authority, "That boy wants to join." The other
two still were standing on the porch in petrified bashfulness.
Whenever Clarence glanced back he could see them. Bonita
had offered him her hand, smiling coyly, and Clarence had
taken it in a limp clasp. The minute he had the chance, he
was going to get near Delight.

Some of the girls had been counting out, and Jamie was
It. The hands tightened, as the circle spread out and grew
tense. They heard Jamie's footsteps, stealthy at first, on the
thick wet grass—then he dropped the handkerchief to
Bonita, who was smiling brightly at him, and both of them
were running. Now Jamie was back in place, and Bonita was
walking around the circle. She switched her pink silk skirt
and walked with short little steps in her shiny best slippers.
She'd meant to drop the handkerchief to Walter—but he
looked suddenly around, and she gave a shriek, and tossed it
down behind Delight instead. "Ha-ha, she gave it to a girl!"
the kids were yelling. Bonita said, "I don't care." Clarence
saw that she was squeezing Walter's hand just the way she
had squeezed his—she needn't think she would be his girl
when Delight was gone! That was what some of the kids
were telling: that Bonita had said she was going to be Clarence's girl. Nobody was going to be his girl. Nobody else.

Delight had the handkerchief now. The clasp of hands
grew tight and warm. The children could smell the wet

grass and the flowers. She was coming around the circle, walking lightly, not looking at anybody. She might throw the handkerchief down behind the Gunderson boy—she might do that to be nice. But Clarence knew. It was almost as though he could see and feel the handerchief dropped softly behind him. He turned around, and picked it up and ran, his shoe soles slipping on the wet grass—he followed her white dress, and her long shining hair, he knew he was going to catch her . . . He held her, with his arms around her, in front of all of them, both breathing fast. The kids all shouted, and then took up their chanting:

> "Delight is Clar'nce's gur-rull,
> Delight is Clar'nce's gur-rull."

He let her go. But he could still feel the tense slenderness of her little body in the flimsy, stiff, dotted swiss that crushed under his hands like gauze. His heart beat fast and exultantly, and he was glad he'd shown all of them. For a moment he'd caught and kept hold of her, even if she was going away. He didn't care how much the other kids yelled and chanted. He wasn't teased. She *was* his girl and he wanted the others to know it—Bonita, and Walter, and everybody.

But it got too dark to play; and time came for the program. The children were called into the house. The rooms were so crowded that they had to sit on the floor in front of the grown people's chairs. They were still panting and hot from running. It was hard for them to settle down and keep quiet, especially during the early part of the program, Dora Palmer's piano selection, the song by the quartet, and the farewell on behalf of the other churches given by the Methodist minister, ending in prayer and a loudly abrupt "Amen!"—hardest of all for Clarence, because he knew what was coming next, and Delight didn't. She sat next to him, and he was almost bursting with his secrets.

A hush fell. The time was at hand; the secrets would soon be out. Clarence looked at Delight to see whether she had any suspicion. Her eyes were round and brightly solemn, and her face was innocent. Her mother and father didn't know, either.

There had been considerable debate as to who should make the presentation. Willis Vance had always been counted upon for such things; no one could quite take his place. H. C., of course, was no talker. A. D. was even worse. For once, Dave Miller didn't want to take the leading part—and certainly it couldn't be Ira! Some had thought of Mr. Stiles, but Mrs. Stiles herself was against that: she said James Stiles couldn't be trusted, not if he saw any chance to make a joke. Cass Story had been settled upon as the final choice. In his long frockcoat, with his black string tie, and his thick hair brushed back on his "leonine head"—his wife's proud expression—he had a senatorial, governmental air. Jim Stiles had slily drawled, when told that the editor was to make the chief remarks of the evening: Well, Friend Cass could always be counted upon to carry his audience—to carry 'em on and on and on! But now even Jim Stiles sat looking preternaturally solemn; with Mrs. Stiles beside him, severely upright, and frowning.

The editor cleared his throat, and then came the mellow rumble of his voice. He began with the history of the church, its humble start and small beginnings, ". . . the man who has built it into the flourishing institution which we have today . . . impossible to believe he has been with us but two brief years—but these two years the brightest of our short but illustrious history—and, my friends, no one among us will deny that this has been largely due to his magnificent efforts, seconded and supported by his wife and ever-faithful helpmate whom let us not forget . . . the state, the nation

. . . could not let him go, but that we realize with pride in all our hearts that he is going forth from us called to a larger field and spreading further and ever further the glorious message it has been our privilege to receive . . . carrying the spirit of our small but splendid little city out into the great world beyond . . ." The room was quiet while he spoke. People scarcely dared glance at the Greenwoods—but they could see that Mrs. Greenwood was looking down, with her hands tightly clasped, and that the minister's face was set. Grandma Story rocked and beamingly nodded her head in time to her rocking. Mrs. Story was almost dissolved in blissful pride. Edie kept her handkerchief to her mouth and tried to swallow the sobs that rose like hiccoughs. Clarence was the most impressed listener of all. He had heard his father praise Cass Story's wonderful command of language; and Clarence devoutly believed him to be—next to Mr. Greenwood—the greatest orator in the United States. Clarence was sure this was the greatest speech he had ever heard.

But there was something still more wonderful to follow. Dave Miller had tiptoed out of the room in heavy caution; and he now stood ready. He laid the big package down on the piano stool. The high moment of the evening was at hand. Clarence sat frozen. His eyes were staring and he could hardly breathe. This was the mighty secret—the farewell gift of the church to the Greenwood family. His own father was making the presentation. Clarence's heart beat heavily as he listened to the words: brief—Dave said afterwards he couldn't trust himself. The present was then unwrapped— Franklin Story cut the cords, and the minister's wife herself undid the many wrappings. The silver coffee service—coffee pot, cream pitcher and sugar bowl with tongs; for which Mr. Elderkin the jeweler had sent away—was revealed. Edie could hold in no longer; her sobs burst loudly forth and she left the room.

The minister's face was youthfully flushed and his clear,

blue eyes suffused, as he rose to make his reply. But his few words were exactly the right ones—they were always the right ones—and broke the tension. He said the grandeur of the present would dwarf any speech! Besides, his friend the editor of the *Citizen* had set a standard too lofty. He told them he was going away so he could find harder work! He had just one complaint about the people of New Hope: they made a minister's work too easy. But neither he nor his wife would find better friends, since there weren't any better, anywhere! "Isn't that so, Alice?" he asked. Mrs. Greenwood nodded. Mr. Greenwood waved his hand, and said, "That's all!"

Then came a general hubbub of relief. Mr. Stiles had gone after Edie and now he made her come back into the room. He put his arm around her, and with a great display of gallantry, flourished an enormous handkerchief, and then wiped her eyes. People all laughed and said, "Trust Jim Stiles!" Mrs. Stiles threw up her hands. Clarence had solemnly assured Delight that the presents were solid sterling silver guaranteed. Now she went dancing all about the room telling people, "Come and see our solid sterling silver presents!" Folks all crowded around the piano stool. A few were too bashful to leave their seats, and Bess carried the coffee service around the room. The Gundersons looked at it in silence. The little boys all drew back. "Lift the coffee pot and see how heavy it is," Bess urged; but Mrs. Gunderson couldn't be prevailed upon to touch it. "Call this heavy?" Mr. Stiles said. "No solid sterling silver in this!" He winked at Delight. He swung the coffee pot above his head and held it aloft while the women shrieked. Then giving it back to Bess, he caught up Delight and swung her aloft! Her long fair hair spread out like a shining veil, and she shrieked too, but with joy.

Franklin Story came up to his grandmother and petted her wrinkled cheek. "Time for this little girl to go home now," he said. Mrs. Story proudly smiled: Franklin was so good to his grandmother! It showed how good he would be to a wife, she had once significantly remarked to Bess. The old lady herself received the pat with beaming complacency. But she said, "No, Frankie, I must show the folks my rag bag first. I'm not a-going till they've seen my rag bag." Franklin good-naturedly waited, while Clarence was sent on a search. The rag bag was found under a pile of wraps on the hall tree. This, Grandma said, proudly opening the bag, and nodding at the minister's wife, was *her* present. 'Twan't so grand as the other one, but 'twould maybe be just as useful. 'Twould help the folkses to keep warm on those cold nights "out there by the ocean," and be a keepsake from friends back home, besides. People gathered around as Grandma spread out on her lap the bright-colored pieces of silk and velvet: all cut from the womenfolks' best dresses, she said, and from the menfolks' neckties—ties were all the menfolks had to contribute! When she'd got the pieces all collected, she would put them together with featherstitching and make up a spread. Grandma was noted for her featherstitching. "Us? Can we have pieces in it too?" the children were all pleading. Grandma told them, yes, everybody would contribute pieces, little ones as well as big. Clarence determined that he would put in his Roman-striped windsor tie. The folks would have to let him. Grandma Story was stuffing the pieces back into her bag, and saying with satisfaction, she thought 'twould make up a right nice covering. She stood up, to let her grandson fasten her long black cape with its sparkling jetty fringe, while Bess tied her bonnet strings in a coquettish bow. Then she wished everybody a good night.

"Good night, Grandma!" they answered in chorus.

"Good night, folkses."

Coffee—real coffee—had been brewing for some time. Mrs. Zissler had been out in the kitchen all evening—had just slipped into the front room for a moment when the farewell gift was presented. Now everybody could smell the delicious fragrance as the kitchen door was opened and the girls started bringing plates of refreshments into the front rooms. Merrill had brought over the big coffee pot that belonged to the church and was used for church suppers. The old tin pot might not be so swell as this new silver one, Dave Miller said exuberantly, but it seemed to make pretty good coffee! "But think of the coffee maker," Jim Stiles said. The minister's folks would have the silver service, but New Hope would keep the coffee maker! Somebody proposed giving Mrs. Zissler a silver coffee pot, too! Folks all began shouting that Mrs. Zissler must come in and take a bow. "You young fellows go after her," Jim Stiles roared. "You're the ones!" Lute Fairbrother wanted to know if he and Wes Bibbs were the young fellows! Everybody laughed and clapped. Meanwhile, Franklin and Merrill had gone out to the kitchen and now came leading Mrs. Zissler, flushed and embarrassed, still wearing her big kitchen apron, into the front room to take a bow. Jim Stiles got up to lead three rousing cheers, and Mrs. Zissler made her escape.

The girls passed the sandwiches and cake, followed and aided by a retinue of young men. Vincent Harper had stuck right with Irene the whole evening. "Look who *she's* got in tow!" Lizzie Murdock said to Mrs. Story in a hissing whisper. Vincent followed close behind Irene carrying a whole trayful of sloppy frappé cups. Getting *him* to work! Could you beat that? But Irene was just as nonchalant as ever, and cool as a flower in her thin white summer dress. Far from showing any consciousness of having attracted a special prize, she ordered Vincent about just as she pleased—and Vincent Harper seemed to like it. He was actually perspiring! Mrs. Stiles's black eyes snapped with pleasure as she observed the couple. She told Lizzie Murdock, emphatically nodding, "*She'll* lead him a chase. It'll be good for him. He needs a

taking-down." Mrs. Stiles had gone herself, to ask Harry
Harper and his wife to attend the reception. She'd thought
they might show *that* much courtesy before the minister
left! But no!—oh no, they didn't believe they'd be able to
come. Mrs. Stiles gave a disgusted smirk when she told some
of the other women about it. Electa Stiles wasn't accustomed
to receiving rebuffs nor did she take kindly to it! Those silly
people! They never would get over making fools of themselves.

The people were all going home. Those who had to drive
out to the country left the moment their refreshments were
eaten. The girls had gone upstairs to get the babies—there
were three others besides Aunt Mary's and Uncle Andy's on
the bed in the east room. The little things had slept through
most of the evening, but when they were brought down into
the light they set up a great to-do about it; or so Mr. Stiles
said. "To-do!" Mrs. Stiles echoed indignantly. "You'd to-do
yourself if you were waked up and brought downstairs!"
"Not if these young ladies were to bring me," Mr. Stiles
answered gallantly, with a naughty wink of his good eye.
Mrs. Stiles said, "Oh, you! Get on home," and gave him a
push.

The young people remained to help with the work.
There was a big clatter of gathering up dishes; exclamations
about the frappé that had been spilled. "Those kids!" Edie
was spluttering. "We should have made them take theirs outside. They've just spilled it all over this house." The boys
grabbed pieces of cake that were left. Their cheeks stuck out
like squirrels'! Didn't they ever get filled up? the girls demanded. Ray Putnam answered solemnly, No, never! The
girls shrieked when he went out to the kitchen carrying a
tottering pile of plates. Irene had daringly tied her little
dotted swiss apron—trimmed with rosettes of blue baby
ribbon—around Vincent Harper's elegant waist. Then she

put him to wiping dishes. "Oh, I say!" he protested. He was actually blushing. But he took it! The others looked on amazed. "The little devil," Mil Anderson whispered admiringly to Bess. "Look how she enjoys it. She's just putting him through his paces." Irene never turned a hair.

Clarence had stayed outside until most of the people had gone. His father drove Delight and Mrs. Greenwood back to the parsonage; but the minister preferred to walk. Poor old Mollie! Bertha sighed that *Mollie* would be glad when this night was over. She'd been standing hitched up since early morning. Bertha said, "Ja, I bet her poor old legs ache—just like mine." Clarence watched the buggy drive off down the hill; and then he went into the house.

He stuck around with the big crowd, admiring and wistful, watching everything they did. Most of the time they paid no attention to him; but when they all sat down to the kitchen table for a midnight lunch of fresh coffee and the leftovers of the cake, he managed to wiggle in on it. Irene said idly, that kid would have a stomach-ache tomorrow; but she was too much engrossed in her deft and delicate game with Vincent Harper to care much what her kid brother did. Afterwards, Clarence went back to the front room for a last look, a last smell of the plants and flowers. Now that the great evening was over, he felt a kind of excited emptiness. He could still hear the mellow, rolling tones of Cass Story. He felt as if his eyes were still blinded by the white dazzle of the flashlight when Mr. LeValley had taken a photograph of the assembled company. The pink roses from the conservatory bloomed in the cut glass vase.

But the great proud secret was a secret no longer. The solid sterling silver coffee service had been presented. One more occasion was over. There were only a few days left. He didn't believe that; couldn't feel what it meant. But as he went through the front hall and breathed the evening fragrance from the open door, it seemed to him that the circle was still formed outside on the trampled lawn, he was still following the little flying figure, in her thin white dress, with her long hair streaming; his feet were slipping on the wet green grass.

The last days went fast. The minister made his final calls on members. He went downtown to settle his accounts and to say good-bye to some of the merchants; stopping in at the print shop for a talk with Lute Fairbrother, and to say a few words to Ollie Jenks at the marble works. Ollie wanted to bring out a bottle of whisky for a farewell drink. It wouldn't matter now, the minister was going off so far they couldn't catch him, Ollie slily urged, with an ambiguous sparkle of his deep-set little eyes. The minister laughed, and declined.

Everywhere people said to him, "Well, I guess it's a fine country out there where you're going!" He nodded briskly in assent. There seemed to be no doubt in his mind. Only one person knew he had ever felt doubts; he had confided them to only one person, who could well be trusted to keep whatever he told her to herself—not his wife, since she was so determined upon the move, but Electa Stiles.

It was the day following the reception. The minister had stopped in to see Mrs. Stiles, and to ask her to play for him once more. The minister was the one person for whom Mrs. Stiles liked to play. No one knew anything about that visit until years later; when Mrs. Stiles told a few people about it.

She had played, and then they had sat for a while talking in the parlor that was dim and cool with the blinds partly closed. The minister had told her then about his reluctance to accept the call; in spite of the fact that Alice was resolved upon it. Alice said he lacked ambition—she had to have ambition for him. He said he'd had a strange experience last night. For a moment, with the blinding from the

camera bulb when Mr. LeValley was taking the group
photograph, he'd seen all those people in a new and different
way—as individual human beings separately picked out and
illuminated. All their lives had for that instant been outlined
with a blinding clarity. It was the kind of experience at
which he had always scoffed. He'd tried many times to talk
Alice out of all those things she "divined," as she said, or
"knew through intuition"!

Afterwards he'd walked home alone. Human ties were
heavy upon him as he went down the long boardwalk
through the summer darkness. He had stopped when he came
to the bridge, and rested his arms upon the iron railing; hearing the whisper of the Creek beneath where he stood. Its
faint music was intimate at that hour of midnight. The idea,
the principle behind the thing—that had always occupied his
thought. But then concreteness held him rather than abstract
principle. The town had seemed to close around him, warm
and familiar, in the midst of the rolling land. He felt that
he was standing in the interior of the mighty continent.

Far up the hill, beyond him, still glowed the lights of
the noisy, warm-hearted household where he had spent his
first days in the town. It was a very short time, only two
years, that he had lived in New Hope; and yet he felt that
he would never know any other town so well. He was leaving the town in the brightness of the morning when only a
few first shadows had fallen; the promise of the name was
still a promise—so it seemed to him.

He had been turning with eagerness to the thought of
"union." He was to preach in a "union church." But old divisions even in the fresh young town lay beneath the surface,
unhealed. The Donohue household . . . that worried him
more than any other. Regarded separately, each of the members was a good enough individual. Each admitted that about
the others. Then why not let matters stand in a spirit of
charity? The parents did center on Winifred, as the minis-

ter's wife had hoped; but the little girl seemed to be a cause of dissension rather than of harmony. She would come running home from school, red-cheeked—she had Alicia's bright complexion, Trixie's soft brown hair—and would bang the old warped kitchen door. Happy at first to get home, the child soon felt oppressed by the heavy stillness. She went to stand near her mother, for comfort—whispering, when Mrs. Donohue lifted the hem of her apron to wipe her eyes, "Mama, don't!" Friends had seen this and described it. Then came supper, unlike the old hearty, noisy meals before the division was made final. Angry at her father when she saw her mother's tears, Winifred was bewildered now—she went to stand beside *him*, to show that she cared for both. The shadow of the black sheep brother still hung over the family. The minister thought, he and his wife had seen the beginning of all this! Would a new man understand, or care in the same way? The minister wouldn't admit that the situation was hopeless; not unless the people themselves were foolish enough to make it so. Then there was Bess Miller—he had told Bess to follow her heart. According to his own best conviction, he could have said nothing else. But might his advice be helping to disrupt the household of his own most loyal friends? Alice feared so—although that had been her advice as well as his.

The minister thought of all the people who had come, at one time or another, to his small study with windows that looked out upon the vacant lots: young people and old. Someone else would perform the marriage services for these young people; would baptize their children; say the last words for the aged ones.

The frame structure of the church was barely visible in the night. The minister had felt an impulse to go into the church alone. He had let himself in with his own key at his own side door; and then groped his way in darkness to his pulpit. He looked forward with eagerness to the new prospect. But in that hour he could see the possibility of another way: it would have meant staying throughout the years, helping to make early vision into some kind of concrete actuality, slowly, painstakingly, in this one small place. He did not know whether he was being untrue to that way—or which would be the better choice: going on "called to a larger field" in the words of Cass Story, or standing firm and building from this small center outward. He had laid his hand upon his pulpit with affection for the actual grain of the wood.

Yet if he had chosen to stay, and not make the new attempt, he would never have been satisfied. So Mrs. Stiles told him—and he knew it was true.

"My papa's going to resign!" All through those last days Delight had been saying that, repeating it over and over. Her voice took on a sound of breathless importance. Her eyes gleamed. "You must be in church next Sunday and hear my papa give his resignation!" Clarence heard that with a strange mixture of excitement and dismay. When he was alone, he whispered to himself, "Resignation." The word seemed to echo with solemn mystery. Clarence pictured the minister making some grand final gesture.

Sunday had come; a Sunday morning in July, hot and cloudless like that other morning, that lay now in the past— far, it seemed, in the past. Mr. Greenwood had begun his pastorate in New Hope upon that other day. People gathered now to hear him preach his last sermon.

The church was filled long before the hour. It had been decided not to hold Sunday school. The Methodist minister was to dismiss his congregation immediately after the opening prayer, so that all who wished could be present at this last service. Several rows of pews were reserved for the visiting Methodists. Merrill Miller and Ray Putnam had come over before breakfast to get the folding chairs set up in the

primary room. That room was filled too. But the service
would not start until the Methodists had arrived. They entered in a hush, and took their seats in the creaking pews. The
last bell rang after they all were seated. There was another
short interval of waiting.

Visitors had come besides the Methodist people; some
who had never entered the church before. That queer little
Ollie Jenks had slipped in early and was sitting almost out
of sight in a far corner of the primary room. The Groundhogs! They were actually coming to attend this service, after
all the time and effort vainly spent to persuade them to enter
the church! Dean Robinson, with solemn countenance,
ushered them all to a pew, the parent Groundhogs followed
by a straggle of little ones. They were washed and quite
decent; although Mrs. Groundhog wore a sunbonnet. The
other children hung their heads, but Lillie held hers up pertly
and proudly. Lillie Groundhog had on the blue dimity dress
that had been Dosia Murdock's best dress two summers ago.
Her hair was braided in tight little hammocks, the way Mrs.
Stiles had taught her. Mrs. Stiles nodded her head in approval.

The members of the church were present in force.
Scarcely one was missing; except those few who had been
lost either by death or removal. The Widow Budd, shriveled
and small, occupied her old place; while near her sat the
Livermores, coldly silent. Folks could just see the tremulous
nodding of Grandma Story's bonnet; and they remembered
how old Mr. Broadwater used to sit beside her, there on the
front row directly beneath the pulpit, and how he would
gallantly assist her to rise when the service was over. Willis
and Nellie Vance would never return; people all said that.
But the church had gathered in many more members than
it had lost those two years. Mrs. Stiles sat, as always, austerely
upright, with her lips compressed. Jim Stiles's glass eye had a
bright, empty glare, giving him too a look of unconscious
sternness. Mrs. Donohue, wearing black as though in mourn-

ing, sat with Trixie and Emmett; they had got up before daylight so they could get their work done and drive in to church. Trixie held her mother's hand in frowning defiance. Mrs. Donohue kept crying all through the service. The Dave Millers occupied their accustomed pew. For once they had been among the earliest arrivals! Dave and Edie both didn't want anybody else to get their seat. Dave sat with arms folded on his chest, while he glanced sharply around to see who all were present. On his ruddy face was a look of sober exaltation. Andy and Mary had driven in; Andy was holding the baby, while Mary kept anxiously lifting a corner of the blanket to see whether the little fellow was still asleep. The Ira Millers were up near the front. Ira stared glumly; but Belle was blandly complacent, as she nodded to this person and that. She had reason to look smug!—Edie later remarked very tartly. Aunt Belle had already begun "making inquiries." She was already looking forward to picking a new minister! She couldn't even wait for Mr. Greenwood to step down from the pulpit. "I suppose that's being 'forward looking,' that she's always talking about," Edie said with irony.

The platform was brilliant with summer flowers. The red roses beside the pulpit came from Harry Harper's garden. Irene can be thanked for those!—Edie leaned across Clarence to whisper to her mother. Irene had kept Vincent Harper in attendance all the day before when the Young Ladies had decorated the church. He'd never worked so hard in all his life. To see him up on a stepladder, Mill Anderson told everybody, was a beautiful sight! Well, whoever was responsible, the church looked wonderful that day. The minister, when he rose to preach, would stand in a bower of flowers.

The service began. Dora Palmer played "Hark! Hark! the Lark" for her prelude: the piece she had played on that other Sunday. That was at the minister's request. He liked joyous music; never the minor note. The chorus choir would sing that morning, since there would be no evening service.

The young people filled the loft. The girls had to take off
their wide-brimmed, flower-laden hats. A few had married,
a few dropped out; but the big crowd made a fine showing.
The minister, youthfully fresh in his Sunday black-and-
white, came upon the platform, and—briskly parting his
coattails—sat down in the pulpit chair; glancing out over
the audience just as they had often seen him do. The music
of the first hymn, brightly soaring, beat down the solemn
uneasiness of the congregation.

"Joy to the world, the Lord is come!"

It was a Christmas hymn, but the minister's favorite; so they
were singing it that day.

The first part of the service seemed to pass in a dream.
It came time for the sermon. The minister stepped forward;
and in the hush that greeted him, as he paused a moment before starting to speak, people saw the bright, clear sanity
of his ordinary expression heightened by the lofty impersonality of a faraway gaze. He glanced down at the large
open Bible. Then, resting his hand lightly on the pulpit edge,
he gave out the text from memory. (Clarence looked for that
verse long afterward—looked all through the pages, thin
and tissuey, and stained at the margins, of the old Bible he
used to take to Sunday school. He found the verse at last and
read it over, with new understanding, deepened by the memory of an early emotion.)

" 'If ye continue in the faith grounded and settled, and
be not moved away from the hope of the gospel, which ye
have heard, and which was preached to every creature which
is under heaven. . . .' "

The minister's voice sounded as always: clear, vigorous,
direct. Mr. Barbour on his last Sunday had wept and prayed
at sonorous length! But if there was drama today, it would
be contained in the situation itself. The minister would not

exploit it. Nothing could be further from his mind! For his last sermon, he would give the best of which he was capable. People might accept is as they would. Dave Miller found, in the forceful accents, his own robust sense of change, growth, expansion. Electa Stiles drew from its strict organization and clear expression that noble simplicity in which she exulted. She would never forget that last sermon, she said long afterwards; like the music of Bach, it built up, in clear tones, out of close actualities, a shining, invisible structure that remained. Grandma Story leaned forward, with her head tilted, her best ear turned toward the pulpit, not to miss a single word. Lute Fairbrother stared straight ahead, his bony hands folded on his knee. Clarence, squeezed in between his mother and Edie, could scarcely be seen. His face was pale and his lips parted. While the minister was speaking, from the moment he gave out his text, Clarence had that same feeling as on Christmas Eve: the feeling of brightness spreading and opening outward—out toward the shining ocean where stood the lighthouse, white and tall, from which he and Delight would someday look out together upon the world that stretched beyond their own shores.

But now came a pause. Now the minister would "resign." The actual moment was at hand. Clarence felt his heart beating heavily in expectation.

An uneasy movement passed through the audience. People glanced toward the minister's wife. She looked down at her clasped hands, her face very pale. Delight's little head was eagerly lifted. Clarence could feel the shining intentness of her eyes.

Clarence had a wild impulse to run—to go and hide himself down in the secret stillness of the shadow underneath the bridge. He had been almost as eager as Delight to hear the "resignation." But he didn't want to hear it now. He would have escaped if he could. He realized that this was the last time he would ever sit listening, here in this place, to the clear, strong voice which he admired with such stainless confidence; accepting every word spoken by that voice as true beyond question.

The voice was speaking now; so firmly that there seemed no possibility for doubt. There was no sign that the minister himself could ever have doubted. He had made up his mind and had accepted the call. There would be no turning back. His few words of farewell were spoken straight to his audience. He told them that he laid down his work in the faith expressed in the text, knowing that the outcome did not depend upon one man but upon the members themselves; upon their own congregation. When he turned aside to leave the pulpit, the line of his profile was keenly cut— as though the face itself were the face in a portrait, meant always to be seen in relief against a far background. The blue of his eyes—"the eyes of an innocent eagle"—was the blue of distance. The minister had "resigned"; and the great western coastland to which he was going had suddenly become the horizon of the inland prairie town.

But another pause followed before the congregation stood up to sing the final hymn. The great moment was past. The resignation was accepted. When that service had come to a close, the church would be empty. Clarence could feel already the blank pulsation of the emptiness.

CHAPTER XII

Exodus

THE JULY MORNING again dawned hot. The day would be a scorcher. The whole great cloudless sky shone with a burning blue. The trees stood motionless and the leaves seemed faded. The leaves of the little birch tree were limp. The long boardwalk leading down the hill glittered with a blinding light. The hitching posts were too hot to touch.

Excitement intensified the heat. There was a sense of waiting, all over town: on the roads that were cloudy with dust, on the bridge above the dry, burning Creek bed. Everybody must feel that, from the moment of waking; as Clarence did. The Greenwoods were leaving today. They were starting for Oregon. They were going out to the West Coast.

The Miller house was once more a scene of commotion. The train was not due until eleven thirty-five; but the Miller kitchen was headquarters for the packing of the two great boxes of lunch that the women of the church had prepared for the minister's family—enough food to last them all the way to Oregon! Folks kept coming with donations all through the morning. All that stuff wouldn't keep! Edie was sputtering. What was the use of putting up so much? They'd have to go to the diner anyway before the journey was over.

Oh well, they could pass things around, her father said generously, to other folks in the train. There'd be folks glad enough to get some New Hope cooking.

Clarence wandered about. He was in the house and then out of the house. It was too hot to stay inside, and then it was too hot to stay outside. He could find comfort nowhere —not among the burning sunflowers, nor in the thick, still heat of the barn where the sunlight showed through blazing cracks and the hay smelled dusty. The wooden stairway, with its worn, shiny steps, led up to the empty playroom. Delight had chosen the things that she wanted to take with her: "precious stones" they had gathered down by the Creek, Queen Isabella's jewels, the pure white feather Clarence had found at the farm. He wished she'd taken everything. That was Delight's last morning in New Hope. But Clarence didn't want to be with her. He was glad she hadn't stayed at his house last night. He didn't want to see her until they met at the station . . . he was only living for train time.

At last his father had come out to hitch up Mollie. Clarence went into the back yard. But he kept wandering around again, not able to stand still. Sun blazed on the buggy top, and on the hydrant at the side of the house. The new shingles on the barn roof gave off a blinding glitter. Grass was already getting brown and dry; the hard, brown earth showed through in patches. The dust in the road was thick, soft, and burning. But over this vision, so immediate and acute, another was strangely imposed—like two kodak pictures taken on one film: of that other day, when he was waiting to go down to the train. He saw the grass a fresh, bright green and the petunias blooming in radiant colors. Then, as now, he had waited in a fearful expectancy. But then his dread was edged with bright happiness.

"Come on now!" his father was shouting. "Come on, you womenfolks, if you want to get down to the train! Where's Clarence?"

"I'm here," Clarence said.

He climbed into the buggy and waited; so hot, eager, excited, miserable, that he was glad to be starting. He couldn't bear to wait any longer.

They reached the station considerably before train time. Dave Miller had never started so early before! But a crowd was already assembled on the platform. The Miller carriage was greeted with shouts of welcome.

"Come on. Hurry up!" Cass Story cried. "Join the mighty throng!"

The railroad would think they were putting on an excursion! It seemed at first glance that everybody must be down at the station: the two Murdock families, of course, and the Wrights, the Staleys, the Ira Millers, the Buttons, the Shafers, the Storys; even the Methodist minister and his wife. Mr. Stiles had come, but not Mrs. Stiles—she'd said her good-byes, and didn't intend to say 'em over again; but it looked as if she were the only one lacking. Little Mrs. Zissler was there in her blue percale kitchen dress. She'd been helping at the Story's, and they'd made her come along, just as she was; would wait only while she took off her apron. People were glad to see that Barney Donohue had come down to the train. Jim Stiles cried, "Come on, Barney. Get in here. Don't be bashful." But he wouldn't do that; he'd just wanted to shake hands with the folks for good-bye. Lute Fairbrother towered above the others; while Tom Burchard stood beside him, silent and downcast. Most of the young people kept together. Franklin Story had gone over to Bess the moment she got out of the buggy. He wouldn't let her get a step away. Vincent Harper had stopped at the Miller house for Irene and driven her to the station in his red-wheeled trap. They stood apart from the crowd in elegant isolation. There was a whole herd of children.

The minister's family stood in the center of the gathering. They had stayed at the Story house the night before, after closing up the parsonage; and had eaten breakfast with the Storys that morning. The minister's face was eager under his shiny new straw hat. The bright impersonality was in his eyes. Mrs. Greenwood's delicate face was flushed with heat and excitement. Her face showed tear stains; but her lips were resolute. The Dave Millers had been asked over to the Storys' the night before. They had spent the evening with the Greenwoods. But now Mr. and Mrs. Greenwood seemed changed. They were going away.

Edie ran forward at once and fiercely caught hold of Mrs. Greenwood's hand. Dora Palmer took the other. Dave laughed at them. That was just the way little girls did with their teacher! he said. But Edie didn't care. Mrs. Greenwood smiled, and bit her lip. She acknowledged that it was hard to leave her friends, but she felt that her husband was going on to great things; she would not look back.

Delight was with the other children. Clarence saw her from a distance, and felt bashful again. She stood, composed and demure, in the unapproachable superiority of a traveler. She wore a new blue-and-white sailor dress and a round sailor hat. Her long braids, tied in neat shining loops, gave her an air of conscious primness. But her eyes still made her seem "unusual." The others all felt humble. They stood solemnly staring.

Clarence's mother gave him a push. "Go on," she urged. But at first he hung back.

Delight sweetly promised to write.

"Will you write to me?"

"Will you to me too?"

"Yes, I will to you too. I'll write to everybody."

Clarence felt a sharp thrust of jealousy. It seemed as if she liked the others just the same as she did him; and he couldn't bear that. Last night, at the supper table, Clarence and Delight had sat next to each other, just the way they always did, and had fun all through the meal; and later, sitting together on the steps of the back porch, they'd made a solemn promise, cross their hearts, to meet each other someday in the lighthouse. No matter what she said to anybody else, she was his girl. She wore the little gold heart, set with a tiny garnet, on her gold chain bracelet. Clarence had given her that. His father had let him go to the jewelry store and pick it out himself. Now she lifted her wrist, and the little garnet caught the light. Clarence glanced, and glanced away. He felt a deeply secret satisfaction; and he knew she felt it too.

Everything was dreamlike. The scene was real and unreal. When Clarence looked at Delight, he remembered their promises, repeated over and over "in unison" to make them more sacred: that they would go up in the lighthouse together, and they would go to college together. They would go to college in a wonderful school on the West Coast—Clarence saw great buildings with pillars standing white and dreamlike in an ethereal atmosphere, beside the blue ocean. They had kissed each other for the first time since that winter night when the choir had practiced at the Miller house—in the hot, close darkness, beside the wild cucumber vines, a kiss both timid and confident; and then looking up at the great night sky, they had solemnly wished on the brightest star. The promise had stayed with Clarence all night, marvelous and sustaining; and always somewhere at the edge of his dreams the lighthouse stood looking out upon the shine and wash of ocean water.

But now, for moments, the excitement that had hung over these last days would lift. There would stand the depot harshly actual in the sunshine that had blistered the yellow paint. The steely blaze on the railroad tracks seared his eyes. Over those tracks the train would come—it would soon be coming.

The children caught the excitement and keyed-up feeling of the older people. The determined jesting made Clarence think again that it must be wonderful that the Greenwoods were going away.

The men were joking about the lunch that the women had packed. The folks must eat every bit of it, every scrap —Mr. Stiles said solemnly—before 'twas spoiled by the heat. Then, if they got good and filled up, they could hold out for the rest of the journey.

"We're going to the diner," Delight told him, with pride.

Why, Mr. Stiles teased her, there wouldn't be New Hope cooking in the diner! Didn't she know there wasn't any good cooking except here in New Hope? She stared up at him with bright, doubtful eyes. Oh well, Mr. Stiles consoled her, when she got hungry and peaked out there, the folks would send her back to visit and to have a good meal. They might even come back themselves.

Oh yes, they must come back! Everybody said that; everybody joined. If they didn't promise—Edie cried, hugging Mrs. Greenwood—she wouldn't let them get on the train! Think of all these young folks, Mr. Stiles put in slily. Some of them might be calling for a preacher's services pretty soon. That right, Franklin? That was right!—Franklin proudly admitted. He smiled at Bess and openly took her hand. They wouldn't need *him* for such services, the minister tried to protest. Any minister would do. But the others wouldn't have that. Lute Fairbrother said drily he guessed these young folks thought nobody else's knot would hold. Clarence looked from one to the other, eagerly. He thought maybe now the minister would decide not to go.

But it was too late for that. The minister was displaying the long green tickets. Why should the tickets be so long?— Dosia Murdock naïvely asked; and Mr. Story told her it was because these folks were going so faraway. Oh, she faintly answered. All the children crowded around to stare.

"But you folks must come out there!" the minister's wife was saying.

A wave of interest seemed to pass through the group. Some shared it, others held back. But everybody could feel it—like a wind of change and movement that brought a new breath of far distance and shifted the air.

Who could say?—Mrs. H. C. Murdock smartly answered. It wouldn't be too surprising if some of them did turn up out there! "Will we go too, mama?" Jamie cried—while Clarence held his breath to listen. But Mrs. A. D. shook her head with silent stubbornness. "Well, *I'm* going," Mrs. H. C. said again. "Whether H. C. says we can or not. I'm going to see the world. I'm not going to stick in one spot all my born days." Some of the other folks applauded. How about that, H. C.? they inquired. He refused to commit himself; but he didn't seem averse. 'Twas the finest place on earth, Jim Stiles said. There was no place like the West. He'd go himself if he could pry out Lecty. But she said she'd torn up roots once and wouldn't do it again.

"Why, you'll all come," the minister cried. "We'll have a new New Hope out there!"

Everything had begun moving out that way! The Vances were already there. They were as good as settled and sure that others would follow.

The people were all stirred—all were listening eagerly; children as well as grownups. The young people especially felt as if they were wild to move out West. The vacant lots around them seemed dry and empty, and the town was drab, in this light of new interest. Clarence looked at his parents. His mother shook her head and hung back. But his father was half persuaded. Clarence felt the pull—he was crazy to have his father say they would go; and yet, like his mother, he resisted. But he felt, with eagerness and reluctance, that shift of air and sense of a different season; although there wasn't much chance to understand it now.

All the while, the time was inexorably passing. Ira Miller kept pulling out his watch—Iry would sit up in his coffin at his own funeral if 'twan't running exactly on time, Mrs. Stiles had once said! "Oh, put that watch back," Ira's wife begged him. He told her drily, he couldn't help what the watch said.

But now that departure was so close, all were feverishly ready for the train to come. Even Clarence was ready, while Delight's little voice took an edge of shrillness. There was a sense of elation that everybody seemed to share. People no longer wanted to keep the Greenwoods. By their going, new regions were opened up; and once again possibilities seemed boundless.

But there was one last moment, just before the train came, when they saw the minister in the light of departure. Clarence did—and it seemed to him, so must everybody else. That keen individuality represented something that could not be replaced. But for the minister to stay now would be anticlimax.

The far-off whistle sounded. There was movement throughout the crowd. Dave Miller and Franklin Story picked up the suitcases. The Greenwoods were to go as far as Omaha on the day coach and there change to the sleeper —the children all thought it wonderful that Delight was going to ride in the sleeper.

"Here she comes!"

Merrill shouted that, in a tone of jubilance. All the faces were eager; lighted up and joyful, as if everybody was glad that the time had come. But Clarence had never expected it to come! He realized that now. He had always believed that his father, Edie, Mrs. Stiles, *someone*—would not allow the departure to come to pass. He knew that he was not pre-pared; and that more was contained in that moment than he could grasp.

The train was slowing down, and folks were all moving toward it.

Delight's eager face changed. Her bright color wavered. She had been standing between Alta and Dosia; they didn't want to let her go. She jerked her hand out of Alta's sweaty little clasp, and looked all around. Her face was set in a grimace of woeful astonishment.

"No," she screamed. "NO!"

Her eyes shone with outraged tears. She held out piteous hands to Clarence, as she was borne along toward the train. Through the commotion of departure, with the grown people exchanging promises and farewells, the two children managed to reach each other and for an instant clung together. But Delight's father, alert, impatient, was crying "Come on, come on!" The children were torn apart. "Say good-bye," somebody was telling them. The voice sounded hard and bright. Somebody else lifted Delight onto the platform of the train. Faces were staring out from the train windows—curious, sympathetic, blank; the faces of strangers. . . .

Merrill and Franklin Story had gone into the train to find seats for the Greenwoods. Clarence wanted to go too, but his mother held him back. He struggled in his mother's hands. People were moving forward trying to locate the travelers. Aunt Belle, with brisk kindness, pushed Clarence along.

"There she is. There's Delight. At the window there. Now Clarence, you must wave."

Clarence let himself be pushed forward. He had no motion of his own; no consciousness outside events themselves. His eyes searched wildly for his little playmate. There he saw her—saw her own little face! . . . but still set in that outraged astonishment, its brightness drowned in tears. Her eyes were seeking him too, as he went along close to the train, so close he could almost feel the iron wheels; his Aunt

Belle propelling him—he couldn't have moved of himself.
He was making futile motions to her. Now she caught sight
of him. For an instant, Clarence looked straight into the
great deep pupils of her frightened eyes. They belonged together, and didn't want to part. They were here together
now—at this moment—but with the glass of the train window shutting her off from him. They were only children,
helpless under the force of events; and whatever the moment
might mean to them, they could not keep it, or hold it back
as it slipped away from them, or alter by their own desires
and needs the impersonal inexorability of time and change.
Movement had seized upon their small world, that seemed so
stable and sufficient. They didn't know where the movement
came from, or where it was leading, or why it should be;
but it was sweeping them apart, as once it had brought them
together.

The train had begun pulling out. Merrill leaped off just
in time. Clarence ran a short futile distance along the
wooden platform. He was living still in the moment of
parting, still saw Delight's face looking out at him, her
shining eyes open . . . but all the while she was being carried farther and farther away. The train windows flashed
more and more rapidly. Then came the last swaying coach.
The rails were left humming in the summer heat. The water
tank showed in stark structure at a short distance down the
tracks. People were still in the attitude of waving good-bye;
until now they realized that the train was gone.

Even in that moment, with his childhood sweetheart's
face still vivid before him, it seemed he had halfway known
—that they would not see each other again. The early love
was gone and could never be brought back, even if they were
to meet again some day—but they would not. Even then,
he had come to believe, the little boy had somehow sensed
that this marked the end of a time. The morning world

where the two children had lived together, encircled by communal closeness, seemed already to have retreated; had become a vision that lived long ago.

When Clarence turned away with the others at last, the town itself seemed different. Most of the morning was gone, the grown people said. They must get back. There was plenty waiting to be done.

Clarence had pulled himself away, and started mechanically on the long walk home. He saw nothing at first, it seemed, only felt the sun and the still, dry air. Then the familiar streets had come into his vision, as if all too familiar, all known, and with the full hot glare of the sunlight upon them.

Against that look into the strange distance, which for a moment he had seen, New Hope was empty and tame. A light had gone from it—Clarence could almost see the magical light shining even now ahead of the train, rushing on into the unexplored distance. He had felt a revulsion from the town—his town—with the first fresh morning glow gone from it, and in its place now this ordinary daylight.

But the glaring sidewalks were real, as more and more he became conscious of walking home through the hot, late morning. The town itself was real—the frame and sandstone buildings, the box elder trees, the wide streets with their outlook upon the rolling fields, just lifting to the horizon. Then he had known, in his deepest heart—stopping on the bridge, his old haunt—that he was not going away. The thin bright trickle of the Creek flowed under the bridge and along through sandy flats. This was his town, where he was born. He had not come here from somewhere else, seeing what the place might be. He had started from here, was himself a product, an inheritor, of the morning promise.

The town had seemed desolate and bereft, as Clarence stood there by himself, looking down at the Creek, not daring to glance up at the house with the empty stare of windows no longer veiled by the enchantment of the sheer white curtains, or at the church on the rough swell of ground.

Still, it was not like the earliest time, dark and vaguely troubled in his memory, before the minister's family had come to New Hope. It seemed to Clarence now as if that were before he was awake—almost before he was born. He had begun to live on the summer morning when he had gone down with his father to meet the train, when the little girl had come—had been awakened to that bright early hour of time, with the freshness of beginnings upon it.

It could not last. It was not here any more. Those who could see only by that unstained morning light must push beyond and look for it elsewhere; keep on looking for it elsewhere, always elsewhere. The glow was transitory.

Yet it had been; it existed; and here, in his town of New Hope—exuberantly named, yet not without meaning —were the elements that could support fulfillment. That particular brief fulfillment belonged to the morning. But the elements had not vanished—they continued into the day. The individual who had experienced the combining of those elements, though in childhood and briefly, in the seeming magic of completeness, could not be satisfied merely to recapture that early time as in a dream—not unless, in later time, he were to count himself a failure. He had come to feel the force of that experience, the need born of a fortunate start: to renew the sequence and finish out the early promises in fuller light and mature form. He faced the austere, enlarged demand to place completion far ahead, if necessary, beyond his own time; beyond any time he could see or realize; but to find his individual fulfillment in acting in accordance with its realization.

OTHER BUR OAK BOOKS OF INTEREST